KRISTIN

a Bargain of BLOOD and GOLD

CITY OWL
PRESS

A BARGAIN OF BLOOD AND GOLD
Midnight Guardians, Book 1

CITY OWL PRESS
www.cityowlpress.com

Cover Design by MiblArt. All stock photos licensed appropriately.

Edited by Charissa Weaks.

For information on subsidiary rights, please contact the publisher at info@cityowlpress.com.

Print Edition ISBN: 978-1-64898-060-2

Digital Edition ISBN: 978-1-64898-059-6

Printed in the United States of America

To my mother, your ghost has been my stalwart companion since this journey began.

To Tim, for your patience and your love, through all my hard moments.

PRAISE FOR THE WORKS OF KRISTIN JACQUES

"Jacques has a talent for pacing that feels effortless, and moves the story along with snappy dialogue, adorable flirting, and winning found-family relationships. This delightful romp, *A Bargain of Blood and Gold*, is sure to appeal to fans of Cat Sebastian and Gail Carriger."
– *Publisher's Weekly*

"Jacques does a wondrous job crafting a world rich with creatures lurking among the shadows... If you love vampires, detective work, mysterious creatures, and a little romance this book, *A Bargain of Blood and Gold*, is for you! I can't wait for the next one!"
– *Jessica Julien, YA Fantasy Author*

"In a moment when words are greatly needed, I am at a loss to properly articulate the captivating read, *Marrow Charm*, was for me. The author writes fluently and effortlessly bringing scenes and characters to life in your mind."
– *Permanently Booked*

"I fell in love with the characters within the first few pages of *Ragnarok Unwound,* and the story had me hooked by the end of chapter one. This is one of those books where I didn't want to finish it because I didn't want it to be over."
– *The Paper Valley*

"*Zombies vs Aliens* is a fabulous mix of rollicking romp through zombie-land, action, and adventure that is pure entertainment."
– *Leigh W. Stuart, Contemporary Romance Author*

CHAPTER ONE

THERE WAS A VAMPIRE IN CRESS HAVEN, AND IT WAS JOHNATHAN'S duty to snuff it out.

"Are you quite certain of this location?" Johnathan peered at his traveling companion as the coach rolled through the unkempt dirt roads. Wilderness surrounded them, the relentless forests of backcountry Maine muffling the rattle and buck of the wheels that spat up a cloud of dust in their wake.

Dr. Evans raised an imperious brow, thick white mustache twitching over his mouth. "You have my assurances, Prospective Newman," said the doctor. "The legitimacy of the reports are thoroughly verified before we assign a man on the case. There is a fiend here, squatting among the populace. Multiple victims have gone missing. The fiend appears to have a preference for young ladies. Your task is identification and elimination."

"Shouldn't be too difficult." Johnathan eyed the roll of handwritten instructions, neat pen scratches detailing all the requisite information he needed for a successful hunt. "The town's population was barely a thousand souls all told at last census. It's somewhat baffling why a vampire would settle here. One would think a fiend's peculiarities would quickly pinpoint its identity among humans."

"Careful, Johnathan," said Dr. Evans, catching his attention. The good doctor only used Johnathan's first name when he was worried. "A fiend, alone and secluded, possesses a great deal of cunning and trickery compared to the nests we cleansed in Boston and New York. Be on your guard and vigilant."

Johnathan blinked. His gaze strayed to the custom-made crossbows lying on the seat beside Dr. Evans. Most Hunters preferred melee weapons to pin their fast-moving prey, but his mentor enjoyed the challenge. He could wield the weapon like no other, a master marksman in archery, skilled at the art of ambushing fiends despite their extraordinary senses. Johnathan always felt safe with the doctor, unless what he feared was the doctor himself.

That was a circumstance in which he'd found himself a time or two or twelve. Dr. Evans was a mentor, a leader. He was also a killer, and he wouldn't go easy on Johnathan, no matter how fond he was of his students.

This assignment couldn't be *that* dangerous, or the society wouldn't have sent someone like Johnathan out here. *Would they?* The more he thought about it, the more certain he was that Dr. Evans was about to toss him into a pit of vipers. Trial by fire was the truest method of ascertaining if one was suited for the life.

"Sir?" The thick wool of Johnathan's trousers wicked the sweat from his palms.

Dr. Evans' expression softened. "You're at the top of your class, dear boy. I have complete faith you'll turn in a more than adequate performance." There was a twinkle of sentiment in the older man's eyes. He clapped Johnathan on the shoulder. "We shall return in a month to retrieve you."

"A *month?*" Johnathan sputtered. "What if I require extraction before then? Or I encounter more than a lone fiend?"

Affability drained out of the doctor's gaze. "Adapt. Enlist local aid. Consider this your graduation ceremony. But if you should find the situation beyond your capability, send word through post. Our agents will be here within a fortnight."

There was no need for the doctor to clarify further. A call for aid would be considered failure.

Johnathan swallowed hard, the rumble of the coach accentuating the sensation of the world sinking out from under him. There was nothing outside except trees surrounded by more trees, but the coach was slowing. The conveyance rolled to a stop in the thick of the forest, the setting sun swallowed up by the coniferous treetops, brushing the sky like serrated teeth.

"The society has provided you with a generous stipend to cover your expenses," said the doctor, "though we suggest you practice frugality. There is a reputable boarding house at the edge of town for the seasonal woodsmen that should accommodate you." The coach wobbled to a standstill. Dr. Evans opened the coach door, gesturing with middling patience for Johnathan to disembark.

The young man hesitated. "It's almost dark, sir."

"Oh, tosh." The doctor's expression darkened. He seized Johnathan's arm with surprising strength for a man his size and stature, before tossing him bodily from the coach. Johnathan's battered traveling case followed a moment later, bouncing resignedly to a stop on top of his boots. "The town is two miles down the coach road," said the doctor. "I suggest you start walking, lad, before true nightfall."

Without further fanfare, the coachman steered the horses in a wide circle around Johnathan, kicking off at a fast trot back in the direction they came.

Dr. Evans could have at least left him with a suitable weapon. Even a vial of dead man's blood, which slowed a fiend's ability to heal, wouldn't be remiss. But part of his trial was to find weapons of opportunity in a foreign environment, no matter how sparse that environment.

Johnathan tensed, seized with the acute urge to chase down the coach and cling to the back all the way to Boston. This wouldn't do. For one, Dr. Evans would be terribly disappointed in him. For another, it was likely they'd toss him right back out here, this time tied at the ankles.

He watched the coach until it rumbled out of sight through the trees before he finally turned toward Cress Haven. It was alarming how much darker the forest seemed in those spare moments. Shadows slithered out from between the trees, casting the coach road in intermittent patches of deep darkness. The sun had firmly given up the sky to dusk, the light rapidly fading with each passing second. He needed to get moving rather than stand in the middle of the road like a slab of beef fallen off the butcher's wagon.

Johnathan scooped up his valise. The leather case banged against his thigh in time to his steps, a comforting thump as he picked his way over the pitted dirt road. Stones skittered out from under his boots. It would be just his luck to twist an ankle in the dark and fall prey to the local wildlife.

This was to be his final exam? He doubted the assignment would occupy him more than a fortnight. What would he do for the remaining half of the month? Take up logging, he supposed. Maybe catch a spot of fishing. He'd heard the fishing in Maine was quite excellent.

That settled it. Hell, in a settlement this small, he would locate the fiend outside of a week. Yes, this would be his final test, and a vacation to boot.

Caught up in plotting his leisure time, the first howl took him off guard.

Johnathan froze, eyeing the dense forest with unease. He reached for his boot knife as a second howl split the falling night, an eerie, unnatural sound. Chills rippled under his skin.

What on earth was that? He'd heard the baying of hounds and wolves enough to compare the two, but this sound matched neither, possessing a quality that spoke to his deep instinct to flee the hungry dark.

A third howl rose, much closer this time. Something crashed and crackled in the woods a moment before movement made him jump. Johnathan yelped, covering his head as several creatures fled the woods right in his path. He didn't recognize them at first, not until a fox collided with his legs, panic-blind and snapping at Johnathan's trousers.

He jumped aside, wide-eyed, as a herd of deer, several foxes, skunks, and a badger fled past him into the woods on the other side of the coach road. He heard a whisper of sound overhead and glanced up to find the flight extended to winged creatures as well, an assortment of daytime birds, startled from their roosts, mixed with the hunters of night.

An owl flapped frantically overhead. That worried him.

Owls were not so easily spooked.

Johnathan shifted his stance, knife out and ready as he scanned the trees. A prickling sensation crawled along his skin. He had the distinct impression of being watched. By what? Had the vampire come to meet him? Unlikely. Vampires didn't scare wild animals. The undead were beneath their notice. Only cats reacted to fiends, and it wasn't with fear.

Silence swallowed him up, falling thick and heavy, so that his own breath roared in his ears. Johnathan stared hard through the trees, trying to pinpoint the source of the disturbance.

A harsh chuffing came from his left, close enough to stir the hair at his collar. Startled, he whipped around, fear squeezing his lungs. There was nothing there. Panting, he spun in a full circle, squeezing the hilt of his knife so tight his fingers went numb.

His frantic gaze connected with a glowing set of eyes within the trees. The snarl made his bladder clench. It was a small miracle he didn't void his waters as the unseen creature suddenly bounded away. It made no noise as it took off through the bracken, but Johnathan knew it was gone as the weighted silence dissipated.

It was still several long minutes before the sounds of wildlife filtered back into the night, now fully fallen, and several minutes more before Johnathan's footsteps resumed, albeit at a much faster pace. He didn't dare return the knife to his boot until his steps carried him past the first houses of Cress Haven.

CHAPTER TWO

JOHNATHAN FINALLY LIMPED INTO CRESS HAVEN AND BEHELD THE lumber town in the faint light of its meager streetlamps. He paused to shake out the sharp stones that had collected in his boots, attempting to gain a proper bearing of his destination.

Calling Cress Haven a town seemed too generous, though he supposed its clustered population was too dense to be a village. The main street buildings were drab and rough-hewn, a community that had sprung up from necessity over style. The seasonal lumber-mill boarding house at the far end of the lane appeared decent, but even in the dim light, Johnathan could see that the building desperately needed a fresh coat of paint.

Attached to the boarding house was another rough-hewn building, warm light and laughter spilling into the deepening night. A recognizable and welcome combination. After his odd encounter on the road, Johnathan could do with a pint and respite to ease his nerves, the company of others a welcome idea for once.

He winced and tucked his weary feet back into his boots, a particularly sharp pebble still stuck in the sole stabbed into the soft tissue of his arch. Johnathan grumbled as he picked his way along the lane. He'd had his fill of fun this evening and prayed the vampire was occupied elsewhere.

Johnathan paused at the hinged door, taking a moment to straighten himself into a somewhat presentable gentleman. There was nothing to be done about his sweaty appearance, but at least his shirt was straight, buttons done up neat. Tucking his valise under one arm, he pushed his way inside.

The heat of the room washed over him, the breath of a great animal. He hesitated, tempted to return to the cool evening air outside, but he needed to secure lodging. Now that he'd stopped moving, the rumble of his stomach made itself known, aggravated by the scent of stew blending with smoke and ale. The patrons of the bar were a mix of well-dressed country gentlemen and grime-ridden workmen, though the contrast seemed to bother neither party as they mingled in clusters around polished tables.

As Johnathan stood in the vise of indecision, another patron stumbled into him, a grizzled man so bedraggled he could've been anywhere from thirty to sixty years in age. The unfortunate man mumbled what may have been an apology as he pressed his filthy hands against Johnathan's chest, leaving questionable smudges of muck on his dark wool coat.

Johnathan cringed. "No trouble. Really." He eased a step back from the fellow, who ambled onward and outward into the dark. Johnathan watched him go, contemplating whether to follow him in hopes of the vampire going after such an easy mark. What a coup that would be, to land his target on the first night! The society would be impressed, possibly promote him. But his stomach gave another troublesome grumble, demanding sustenance, and Johnathan suddenly couldn't remember his last meal. With a bereaved sigh, he headed to the bar, observing the woman behind it.

With a flushed face, she snatched a towel and began swabbing out a glass mug while conversing with a row of grizzled men nursing their ale. The sleeves of her non-nonsense work dress were rolled past her elbows, revealing forearms nearly twice the size of his own.

Johnathan set his bag on the end, politely waiting for the woman's attention. At least he *attempted* to politely wait for her attention. But as the minutes dragged and his hunger grew, his good manners frayed.

"Excuse me, madame, might you be the proprietor of this establishment?"

She turned to him then, an appraising glance as she looked over his tailored coat and buffed travel valise. Johnathan was not a wealthy man, but he took fine care of his things, which gave the needed illusion of wealth, one that often eased his interactions with strangers.

"That'd be me," she answered. "What can I do for a fine gentleman as yourself?"

The hard emphasis on *"fine"* made him vaguely uncomfortable, as if she sized him up like a prime cut of roast, but Johnathan was damn near ravenous now. A long day of travel and his flight along the coach road left him wanting nothing more than a bowl of hot food and a cot to sleep on.

"Are you also in charge of the boarding house next door?" he asked.

One thick, dark eyebrow rose at the question. Her gaze turned mercenary. "You come to work in the mills, boy?"

From fine gentleman to boy? He bristled at the shift. He'd turned twenty last winter, at least he thought so. He hadn't lived the kind of life that celebrated such occasions, nor was he certain of his age when the Society took him in. Even still, while he shaved as a requirement of the Society, he felt his features weren't that youthful. Were they? Johnathan fidgeted with his valise.

He cleared his throat, deepening his voice a notch. "I would like to rent a room, possibly for the month." He reached into his coat for his allotted funds. "I can pay—"

His fingers met nothing.

Johnathan spun around and scanned the crowded room, panic lancing through him as he came to the unpleasant realization he'd been robbed. "Son of a bitch," he muttered under his breath.

"What was that you were saying about pay?"

He flinched and turned to find the matron leaning over the bar, so close he had to bite down on the desire to jump back.

"I'm afraid I seem to have misplaced my wallet."

She squinted into his face with a critical eye. "Why, you really are no more than a lad," she murmured.

His shoulders hunched up at her words. "Madame, you presume falsely."

"Do I, now?" She straightened, giving him space to breathe. She folded her arms, her gaze still far too intense for his liking. The matron sucked loudly on a front tooth with a sharp "tch" sound. "Rooms are three dollars for the week, twelve dollars for the month. Tack on an extra five dollars for two meals a day. You can pay me after you collect your wages."

"But I didn't intend, that is, I wasn't set up for the mill—"

"Did you come here to work or not, boy? We have no rooms for dandy prats up from the city."

Johnathan grit his teeth. Working the mills was the furthest thing from his agenda, and the work would take him away from his mission. "Is there other work I could do, round the bar perhaps?"

The woman pursed her lips, clearly at the end of her patience. She looked to ream into him when a gentleman's stiff, black top hat landed on the bar, followed by a pair of dove gray gloves.

"I'll pay for his board, Mrs. Meech," said a light voice. "Would you be so kind as to bring us both a pint? Oh, and a bowl of that divine stew for the boy."

Johnathan felt the muscles of his jaw creak as he turned to the stranger. "Thank you, sir, that isn't necessary. I had this situation well in hand—"

The young man flapped a careless hand at him. "Don't be daft. She was about to lay you flat. Now shut your mouth and eat before you pass out on me."

Baffled and unable to think of a decent comeback, Johnathan sat and studied his well-timed savior.

The stranger had to be the most fine-boned man he'd ever seen. He was clearly one of the wealthy mercantile lot that snapped up country estates and emulated the gentry class of the old world. He was also a man of contradictions, like the intermingled patrons of the bar. Despite their location at the rough final strip of the American north, the man wore an impeccably tailored suit. The make and cloth spoke volumes of his wealth. Yet his slicked-back auburn hair, tied in a queue at the nape of his neck, was unfashionably long, making his features more effeminate and highlighting the smooth rounded line of his jaw. That delicate mien was further exacerbated by his elegant hands, which took the pints from Mrs. Meech and placed one in front of Johnathan.

"You're staring," said the stranger, meeting his gaze with large gray eyes.

"Why help me?" Johnathan colored, feeling a right fool. Didn't Dr. Evans impress upon him the importance of befriending and securing the aid of the locals? "My apologies. I am out of sorts."

The stranger snorted. "I'm an absolute bear when I'm famished," he said, winking at Johnathan.

The gesture heated the back of Johnathan's neck. He felt peculiar, sitting next to the beautiful young man.

He cleared his throat. "Thank you for the offer, but I must decline—"

"Now, now, don't let your mouth run away with you again. Stay, have a bowl of stew, converse with me. You're new here, yes? Where do you hail from?" The stranger punctuated his questions by sliding a bowl of stew before Johnathan.

The scent invaded his nostrils, crippling his reservations of the odd situation. For a solid minute, he shoveled food into his mouth before he remembered himself, choking down a mouthful at the stranger's surprised expression.

"I was hungry," Johnathan said, cheeks burning after that spectacularly ineloquent explanation.

"So it appears," said the stranger, flagging down Mrs. Meech. "Another bowl if you please, love."

"Oh no, you don't have to—"

"I insist," he said, winking at the older woman, who actually giggled. The beautiful man winked a lot. Perhaps he had a twitch of the eye.

Johnathan took a moment to collect himself and dab bits of stew from around his mouth. He held out a hand to the stranger to properly introduce himself. "Thank you for your hospitality. I'm Johnathan Newman."

The stranger took his hand, his skin surprisingly hot, almost feverish, though Johnathan dismissed the thought. He was faintly surprised by the callouses that brushed against his own, reassessing his judgment of the man with every new minute.

"Victor, though most round here just call me Vic."

Johnathan noted the lack of surname, a gesture that was borderline rude, but with a meal in his belly, he was feeling rather benevolent on the subject of country manners. Another bowl of steaming stew slid in front of him. Good manners be damned. He remembered Vic's other question.

"I'm up by way of Boston," he said, spooning stew down his gullet.

Vic tapped the side of his mug, still full, as he watched Johnathan eat. "No wonder you don't want to work in the mills. City lad like you wouldn't last a day in the woods."

Johnathan snorted around a chunk of potato. "I've worked on the docks, offloading cargo. I think I can handle hauling a few trees."

"Then why don't you?"

Johnathan paused, stew dripping off his spoon. There, he'd talked himself into a corner with so very little effort.

Vic took pity on him and clapped him on the shoulder, his grip stronger than Johnathan expected. "If you're looking to escape the chaos of the city, there are better locations, John. But if you insist on staying, what employment do you expect to find?"

"I—I don't know." Johnathan scowled into the dregs of his stew. So far, he was performing marvelously on his mission, managing to lose his funds and find himself on the outs with room and board. How was he supposed to hunt down the bloody vampire if he was scuttling about the forest, hacking down trees? Not to mention that encounter on the road...

A chill flushed over his skin as he remembered that eerie moment of stillness, the sensation of something unseen hunting him. His spoonful of stew plopped into the bowl with a small splatter.

"You alright, lad?" Vic's fingers squeezed his shoulder hard enough for the muscle to protest.

"It's nothing. It's just that..." Johnathan glanced up as Vic peered at him with those intense gray eyes. Johnathan's gaze shifted, taking in the rest of the bar. None of the patrons would listen to him rave about the encounter on the road, but something about Vic put him at ease. If he was going to befriend the locals, might as well start with the friendliest of them. This was an opportunity to see how aware of the lurking evil the townsfolk were.

"There was something on the road," said Johnathan carefully, studying Vic's reaction, though the man must have been a champion card sharp. His expression gave away nothing, leaving Johnathan hanging off a figurative cliff.

Vic shook himself, as if realizing the predicament he'd created, and rose to fill his role. "Something? Were you robbed on the road?"

Johnathan couldn't pinpoint what it was—a slight hitch in the man's voice, a flicker of calculated disinterest—but he felt Vic hung on his every word, waiting for the reveal. People, as a rule, left him uneasy, but he had an uncanny knack, Dr. Evans would say, for catching those subtle gestures and cues.

Johnathan inhaled a breath, catching a faint scent of something floral and fairly musty beneath the stink of smoke and ale. He set his spoon down and turned to fully face Vic. "You know what I saw on the road, don't you?"

"This is a small settlement, and people talk after enough ale, but no, I don't." Vic's fingers rapped along the top of the bar, a hard staccato drumming as the man took his measure. "Do *you* know what you saw on the road?"

Johnathan caught a reprieve from answering as a raspy scream broke through the chatter of the bar. A hush fell over the room. The two of them shared a brief wide-eyed glance. Johnathan surged to his feet, Vic on his heels as a cluster of patrons followed the sound, the mass moving with the safety of numbers.

Outside, a heavy darkness blanketed the town, broken by sparsely dotted streetlamps. Johnathan scanned the empty avenue, trying to find the source of the brutal cry, when Vic's hand landed on his shoulder once more.

"This way," said Vic, his expression grim.

Johnathan didn't argue, following the man's sure steps toward a pitch-black alley roughly half a dozen yards from the boarding house. His eyes failed to adjust before he tripped over the quivering lump of a man between the buildings. Vic caught Johnathan at the elbow, helping him regain his footing. Johnathan's eyes slowly caught up to the appallingly faint lighting. He quickly wished they hadn't as he saw the small shape lying crumpled deeper within.

It registered in flashes at first, a dainty shoe off to the side, scattered bits of lace, the long dark curls fanned out and plastered to the ground in a liquid mess. Johnathan focused on the hand outstretched towards him, pale and smooth, slim fingers curled up to reveal buffed nails. He followed the arm down, catching her face, so young, not a woman grown. Her vacant eyes stared up at him, dark stains marring her complexion. Johnathan couldn't meet those vacant eyes for long, tearing his gaze away to look at the rest of her. The stew soured in his gut.

The girl was torn in half.

CHAPTER THREE

THIS WAS NOT THE WORK OF A VAMPIRE.

Johnathan wasn't sure why he was so certain, but the idea sat there, rattling around his skull, unwilling to settle down. The sour-sick feeling in his stomach left the bitter taste of bile in his mouth, but he refused to vomit. Who knew the next time a free meal would come his way? And, Dr. Evans had drilled all the lads to never sully the scene with sick.

Apparently, the other patrons did not adhere to such rules.

The few men from the bar who had followed Johnathan and Vic now stood in the shadows, retching at their own feet. Most were pale and sweaty, calling for a man named Stebbins, who likely operated in capacity of sheriff. More townsfolk arrived, milling about the scene, muttering and plodding around, a constant babbling murmur of distress. Their heat and noise felt stark against the dark death sprawled across the alley ground.

The sounds washed over him, a verbal tide in time to the pounding of his pulse in his ears. The nausea ebbed as the facet of Johnathan's personality forged in the streets of his childhood slipped its leash. That cool, clinical, calculating half rose to the fore as Johnathan crouched next to the body.

A stillness settled between his shoulders as his other side—the side even the hard-edged veterans of the Society didn't understand—slowly took in the scene. He focused, until the only sound he heard was the steady beat of his heart. The details of the victim sharpened. Her face was intact, resignation clinging to her lifeless visage.

This killer had no care if her identity was discovered. Odd, when Johnathan factored in the small population of Cress Haven. Fiends were so rare in small towns because they lacked the anonymity of the city. It was why the Society considered this assignment a test run. But the state of her...

As his vision finished adjusting to the light of the sputtering streetlamps, he could see what appeared to be dirt beneath her nails and scrapes on her fingertips. She tried to drag her ruined body out of the alley, which meant she was alive for a time after the attack. Not a quick death but a violent one. Her stomach was torn open; the stink of viscera stung his nostrils, but he ignored it. His gaze shifted, studying the dark wet mass, attempting to discern what the shredded remains could be and what was missing.

Her attacker ripped something from her while she was alive and left her to the cruelty of a slow death. Johnathan's jaw clenched. It was an inhuman kill. That is what bothered him the most. The Society liked to believe all vampire kills were brutal and violent, but there were many vampires who remembered they had once been human. The bodies they left behind hinted at guilt and mercy.

This monster had no memory of humanity.

Johnathan's gaze wandered, searching, until he found what he was looking for. He plucked it from the pool of blood at the girl's savaged stomach. With an exaggerated flap, Johnathan drew out his handkerchief and covered his mouth. He gave a coughing retch, transferring the object into the cloth, before carefully tucking his prize into his pocket.

He looked up to find Vic staring right at him.

Johnathan tensed, waiting for a reaction, but the moment broke with the arrival of "Stebbins". The patrons parted for a burly little man, his beer-rounded belly leading the way. He'd rolled up to the scene in a rickety open cart pulled by a sad-looking nag.

"My, my. What a mess." He crossed himself and spat. The gesture seemed off for a lawman, but the tape measure in the man's hand truly confused Johnathan. The portly little fellow knelt in a pool of blood, mindless as it soaked his trousers, while he measured the body.

Johnathan glanced at the others. Surely this wasn't expected behavior for a lawman, even in the country, where professions blended into one another? Was he the town's coroner? Aside from the careless cross gesture, Stebbins appeared completely unaffected by the state of the body, though the gruesome manner of death and the age of the victim couldn't be a commonplace occurrence out here. Vic met his gaze, a single haughty eyebrow raised. Johnathan quickly looked away; the muscles of his jaw clenched. There was nothing for it. He had to ask, even if it drew unwanted attention to himself.

"Pardon me, sir, why are you measuring the body?"

Stebbins startled, as if Johnathan had shouted in his ear. His knee slid further into the gore. Wasn't he aware of Johnathan's presence? How could he not be? Did this man realize how badly he'd compromised the scene? Johnathan itched to intervene before further evidence was lost to Stebbins' clumsy actions.

The portly man blinked at him. "Why? It's my job, boy," he said, flustered. He frowned and glanced down, finally noticing his knee as it inched toward a knot of intestines. "Oh bother, my best trousers!"

Johnathan gaped. Stebbins remained unaware of the attention, muttering on about his ruined pants and the inconvenience of collecting bodies in the dark. This man was not a coroner or any other officer of the law. He was a glorified grave keeper, here to measure the girl's remains for a pine box.

"But what about an investigation?" he said. "To determine the cause of death?"

Stebbins made a face. "Might be due to her guts hanging out, I'd say."

A muscle twitched behind Johnathan's left eye. Where was the law in this town? Cress Haven was at the edge of the wilderness, but it had to have some sort of office, if only to resolve disputes and keep matters civil. If there was no lawman, who'd reported the presence of a vampire here to the Society? How were any of these gawking rubes aware of the Society to send word?

A hand settled on his shoulder, slender fingers that curled to his collarbone. He'd failed to notice Vic move up behind him, a terrible misstep, preoccupied as he was by Cress Haven's apparent lawless state.

"Once the undertaker removes the body, the townsfolk will elect someone to investigate," Vic explained in a low voice.

Johnathan glanced at the gathered crowd, who clearly didn't have the common sense to seek safety. They gaped and gasped but clearly wanted nothing to do with eradicating such violence. He'd seen this sort of reaction in Boston, perverse spectators drawn like flies to a body, willing to flit and buzz but altogether useless. There was something almost comical in their disaffection and unexpected in what he thought would be such a close-knit population.

"Fat lot of good *that* will do," said Johnathan.

"Oh, don't be so disparaging. You'd be surprised what a simple country gentleman can accomplish with the right motivation," said Vic.

Johnathan glanced up at the man, surprised by the solemn set of his smooth jaw. A fire smoldered in Vic's gaze. Whatever else the others thought of this matter, it clearly upset him.

"What do you think did this, sir?" Johnathan asked him. His mind wandered back to his encounter on the road, the unseen presence lurking in the woods that sent the wild animals fleeing from their nests and dens. Could that...*thing*...be the culprit?

Vic focused on him, his expression unreadable. "Don't you mean *who* did this?"

Johnathan flushed, too aware of the crowd around them to voice his honest thoughts on the matter, even if he thought—*hoped*—Vic would listen. "Right you are, sir."

"I say, what a pretty young lady, though she is a ghastly ruin now," remarked Stebbins with all the sensitivity of a gossiping matron. "Do we know who she was?"

The gathered patrons went silent and shuffled in place around the girl's remains, a few of whom produced lanterns to better see the body.

A man stepped forward, his face mostly concealed by a massive shaggy beard, the tops of his cheeks ruddy as he rubbed the back of his neck. "It might be Alyse Shaw."

"Pastor Shaw's daughter?" one of the others sputtered. "What was she doing out this time of night?"

Vic's slender fingers balled into fists, pressed hard against his thighs. Johnathan would have missed the reaction if he hadn't been eye level to the crowd's waistlines. A subtle gesture, one not meant to be seen, that hinted at a possible connection, though Vic's expression remained closed.

Johnathan's thoughts began to turn, reaching for connections, for reasons the young woman would be out in the dark. A beautiful girl beginning to bloom with womanhood, roaming the streets to meet up with a lover? Perhaps a tryst wasn't out of the question. Johnathan knew plenty a pastor's daughter who felt a little too caged by the rules of the house. Except...the theory didn't sit right with him.

Johnathan looked down at the young woman's face, barely out of girlhood. He doubted she'd reached courting age, though she was a lovely one, once he could see past the details of her death. She looked like...*bait*.

A crackle of ice ran through his veins. He shook himself as buried memories stirred, determined to derail that train of thought before it left the station. There were miles and years between Johnathan and that chapter of his life, and besides, he reminded himself, this was not the work of a vampire.

Mrs. Meech's voice cut through the murmuring crowd, the distress clear on her face. "That's it. I'm closing up early."

Johnathan abruptly stood, his prospects for a room rapidly slipping through his fingers. "Excuse me, ma'am? Uh, ma'am?"

The crowd turned in tandem, a solid mass of people who blocked his way until he was certain a conspiracy was afoot to keep him exposed and off balance. Johnathan wove and shoved his way through the dispersing crowd, the dead girl still heavily on his mind as he came face to face with a locked-down bar. He pounded on the door in vain hope that Mrs. Meech would open for him and allow him to barter for a room, or at least allow him to reclaim his valise. But the bar remained closed, and the streets emptied within minutes. The first streetlamps begin to flicker out, and Johnathan realized how very exposed he was.

"Dammit," he cursed under his breath. How had this evening gone so disastrously wrong?

He debated camping on the bar's stoop for the night with the ghost of Alyse Shaw and the monster that killed her for company. He reached into his pocket, tracing the shape of the object he'd plucked from the dead girl's blood, smooth and so very sharp.

"Master Newman, we meet again."

Johnathan spun around. His heart lurched in his chest. "I demand you make noise when you approach, sir." He wasn't sure whether Vic's presence filled him with relief or suspicion, though he was grateful the man carried a lantern. "Why haven't you returned to the safety of your home, sir? There's a murderer on the loose."

Vic tilted his head, long hair shifting off his shoulder. The auburn strands had fallen loose from their leather tie, the silken locks framing his face in a way that made him appear even more comely. In the play of shadow and the golden glow of his lantern, he looked absolutely angelic, which unsettled Johnathan on a soul-deep level, for reasons he could not yet surmise.

"I wanted to see if you'd found a safe haven for the night." Vic shot a disapproving look over Johnathan's head at the closed-up bar. "But as you are apparently adrift this evening, would you consider taking my guest room?"

Johnathan hesitated. His pulse quickened at the invitation. It was true he needed allies in Cress Haven, and Vic was his surest bet thus far, but he hadn't entirely dismissed the startling gentleman from the realm of suspicion either.

He peered hard through the gloom, dissecting each of Vic's features for possible tells. Although on the paler side, so was much of the populace this far north, and Vic *did* have the healthy robust complexion of a man with constant access to fresh air, not the pallor of a fiend. He was pretty enough to make Johnathan uncomfortable, but beauty was not the defining feature of the undead. That was myth. His gaze surreptitiously flickered to the man's fingernails.

The Society called it "corpse fingers," the discoloration brought on by poor circulation until it appeared like bruising beneath the nails, but Vic's were a healthy pink. At least it seemed so in the dim lantern light.

Johnathan gnawed the inside of his cheek. Did he trust his vision in near darkness?

If Vic *was* the vampire, wouldn't he have taken the opportunity to attack Johnathan by now? They were alone, and after finding a ravaged body, he doubted the townsfolk were keen on venturing out at the sound of distress. Settled, he stepped forward to accept the offer and realized his traveling valise was still inside the bar.

"I have nothing that will fit a young man your size, but I can send for your things in the morning," said Vic, clearly interpreting his distress.

"Thank you for your kindness," said Johnathan.

Vic held up a hand. "Not at all. This isn't charity."

Johnathan's brow rose in surprise. "It's not?" Once again, a brilliant response.

Vic adjusted his hold on the lantern, shoving his free hand in his pocket, out of sight of Johnathan's scrutiny. "I would like to hire you."

Johnathan blinked. "Hire me?"

Vic rolled his eyes, clearly fed up with the repetitive nature of the conversation. "I have volunteered to investigate the murder of the unfortunate Miss Shaw. I would like to hire your services in exchange for room and board."

Volunteered? When? How? With whom?

His words registered.

"My services?" Johnathan tensed, an internal alarm ringing that he'd exposed himself more than he realized.

"Oh, don't be coy, Master Newman. What do you have in your pocket?" Vic began circling him, his boots dragging through the dust of the road, his lantern light spilling across their feet. It was a slow perusal, a measuring. That much Johnathan could feel from the weight of Vic's stare. In a voice that made Johnathan shiver all while stirring his blood, Vic said, "I know you took something, which that bumbling Stebbins would have likely swept aside. Show me."

Johnathan's hesitation this time had a very different reason. Confronted in this fashion, there was no time to get a full measure of the man, and Johnathan grew increasingly off balance since his arrival in Cress Haven. The need for an ally was worth the risk, though he would have to be careful how he handled the far-too-observant Vic.

He withdrew the bloodied handkerchief from his pocket and carefully unfolded the cloth. The object sat in the middle of his palm, smooth and sharp, drinking in the shadows of the night.

It was a claw, ebony black and cold as midwinter ice.

CHAPTER FOUR

VAMPIRES DIDN'T HAVE CLAWS. JOHNATHAN KNEW, WITH INTIMATE experience, that this was a fact. Sure, in his training he'd tangled with more than one vampire with ragged torn fingernails, but nothing like the monstrous object spilling over the palm of his hand. He'd spotted it in the pool of blood, a shadow within a shadow, because he'd been looking for something, *anything*, unusual.

He certainly found the unusual, though he had no idea what, or whom, the claw belonged to. It was clear Vic shared his bafflement. He wore a stunned expression that enhanced the delicate angles of his face as he took a step forward and gently touched the tip.

He jerked his hand away with a sharp inhale.

"It's cold." Vic's wide eyes seemed to glow in the muted light. He shuddered, tugging at the lapels of his overcoat. "You'd best put that away for now, until we can examine it under proper lighting. Come, Master Newman, we have a grim task to attend to before we retire for the evening."

Johnathan tucked the claw back into his pocket, thankful the handkerchief muffled the chill it emitted. "What task would that be?"

"As I volunteered to investigate this matter, I have also been volunteered to inform Pastor Shaw of his daughter's demise." Vic continued to tug at his coat. It was a tell of discomfort, one that drew Johnathan's attention to Vic's face. He hadn't imagined his earlier assumption. The man's expression hinted at some connection, possibly a deeper emotion for the recently deceased Alyse Shaw. Rage flickered there and, in the depths of those silvery gray eyes, a promise of retribution.

Johnathan swallowed. He'd never felt that emotion for another person, but he recognized it all the same. "At such a late hour? Wouldn't it be best to wait until morning?"

Vic's jaw tightened. "Is dreadful news any less dreadful after a full night's sleep? Will their daughter be any less dead in the light of day?"

A rush of heat crawled across the back of Johnathan's neck. Road weary and exhausted were no excuse for such callousness. Perhaps it had been too long since he'd shared the company of civilians. He'd forgotten how difficult it was for him to connect.

"My apologies, I'm not...used to dealing with people," he said, revealing more to Vic than he intended in his admission, but the other man waved it off.

"Your exhaustion is clear, Master Newman," he said. "You may wait in my carriage if you wish while I deal with this unpleasant matter."

"Your carriage?" Johnathan peered down the empty street. A jolt of pain flexed through his calves, his whole posture sagging at such a hopeful prospect.

Vic's lips twitched. "Round the back of the bar, Master Newman. Though you have yet to answer my initial question."

Johnathan peered down at the man. The long day dragged on his thoughts. "What question would that be?"

"Will you work for me?"

Find allies in Cress Haven. Those were Dr. Evans' orders. But the Society couldn't have been aware of what was really happening in this secluded little town when the doctor left him here. In his limited experience as a Prospective in training, Johnathan hadn't encountered beast nor creature that fit the parameters he'd observed thus far. According to the Society's official mission statement, they sought to protect mankind from the inhuman creatures of the dark, a statement that, theoretically, covered a broad range of monsters. Vampires, who preyed explicitly on humans, were drawn to civilization and therefore the most common adversary. But *this* sort of creature was never covered in Dr. Evans' lessons.

The claw grew colder in Johnathan's pocket, burning against his thigh. It would take days to get a message to Boston. Vampire or not, innocent people were dying here. He needed all the allies he could get because one thing was for certain: He had to stop this creature before it killed again.

"Yes, sir," he answered, "but please, call me Johnathan, or even John."

Vic gave him a genuine smile that drew Johnathan's focus to his mouth. The heat along the back of his neck spread, a full flush beneath his skin. He swallowed hard and viciously reassembled his thoughts. He didn't dare consider what such a sensation meant or the last time he'd felt as such.

Johnathan cleared his throat. "You mentioned a carriage?"

The open carriage bore the same luxurious practicality as its owner, a rich exterior of dark mahogany paneling with an interior of dove gray, velvet-upholstered seats. After the hard padding of the travel coach he'd ridden in with Dr. Evans, it was akin to sitting on a cloud. The rocking motion pulled at his eyelids. It was unquestionably rude to doze off on his host, but his energy was depleted past the point of good manners.

The deceased Miss Shaw slid through his mind, alive and whole as she moved past him in a languid waltz. She paused to look over her shoulder at him, her finger crooked in a come-hither gesture. There was something terribly wrong with her hand. A trail of red ran like a ribbon, wrapped around her pale fingers. His gaze focused on her beckoning finger, to the wicked black claw that capped the tip, dripping blood.

"Come along, boy."

Johnathan jerked awake at a gentle touch on his shoulder. So startled, he'd wrapped his fingers around Vic's wrist, thumb pressed to the vulnerable grouping of bones present there.

"Easy, John," Vic murmured, his tone surprisingly soft when Johnathan was positioned to hurt him.

"My apologies, s-s-sir." Johnathan slid his fingers free, shaken by the dream. He was shocked that he'd left himself so vulnerable.

"If I am to call you John, I insist you call me Vic," said his host with an air of calm amusement as he pulled up the carriage with practiced ease. "Are you certain you wouldn't rather wait here? You're dead on your feet, lad."

Johnathan reined in a snort at being referred to as "'lad." Vic couldn't have more than a few years on him, and he was shorter than Johnathan by nearly half a foot. He took in their surroundings. It was very late indeed, the deep darkness the wide yawning mouth of the night, when the nocturnal predators were in full force, the relief of dawn still hours away. Vic brought them to a farmhouse on the outskirts of Cress Haven, a plain, neatly white-washed building that matched the chapel a stone's throw up the road, the coat fresher than any in town. In the dark, the light coating of paint appeared ghostly, a house of waiting spirits.

The thought rippled down Johnathan's spine and rose the fine hairs on the back of his neck. A sensation of being watched stole over him. Johnathan hitched his shoulders and glanced toward the trees.

For the space of a breath, he swore he saw glowing eyes peering at him from the tree line. The claw burned cold through the cloth of his pocket.

"No, I'll come along," Johnathan choked out. He descended from the coach, his legs still numb and half asleep.

Vic caught his elbow and steadied him with surprising strength as Johnathan regained his balance.

"Do try not to pass out in Pastor Shaw's parlor as I deliver the news," said Vic. "That might make a poor impression." His teasing tone didn't match the somber expression on his face.

Vic turned away and clasped his hands behind his back where Johnathan could see the fine tremor in his fists. He felt a pang of sympathy for Vic.

"I could deliver the news," Johnathan blurted. What folly. Was he still asleep? What possessed him to make such an offer other than the man's obvious pain? He didn't know these people. Cress Haven was a small community, and the pastor didn't need to learn the fate of his daughter from a callous stranger. "I'm sorry, that was—"

"Kind," said Vic. "But unnecessary." Wearing a tight smile, he squeezed Johnathan's shoulder before resuming his resolute walk to the pastor's front door.

The knock echoed through the darkened residence, swallowed up by the press of night. Johnathan held his breath in that muted lull, his ears tuned for the soft shuffle of footsteps. Vic straightened as the door opened on well-oiled hinges. Pastor Shaw stood in the doorway in his nightshirt, his features barely defined in the dark since the man bore no candle.

"Does someone require last rites, gentlemen?" The man had a voice made for sermons, a deep baritone that soothed the spirit.

Vic bowed his head. "Not as such. I'm afraid there has been another murder, Pastor Shaw."

Johnathan tried not to loom over the two men, his thoughts churning. Dr. Evans told him a vampire had preyed on the townspeople, but if the attacks were being carried out by this mysterious clawed creature, was there really a vampire here? His attention returned to Pastor Shaw as the man crossed himself and murmured a short prayer.

"Come in, Victor, come in," said the pastor. He made way for them as he went to light a candle in the small front room of his home. "Do they know who the poor soul was?"

Vic cleared his throat. "Yes, the face was intact this time."

Johnathan's muscles grew taut with each step. He latched onto Vic's statement. The face was intact *this time*? When Dr. Evans handed down this assignment, the dossier mentioned two or three victims, all young women, but it appeared the Society was terribly ill informed of the foul acts happening in Cress Haven.

A hunter's stillness settled over him, observing the older man's reactions. The flare of candle flame stung his eyes and threw the pastor's face into sharp relief. Pastor Shaw was an older gentleman, his features stone wrought and crag like, but there were laugh lines around his tired eyes that spoke of an easy nature. Despite the hour, he waited for Vic to speak with the practiced patience of a man of the cloth.

"That is why I am here, Shaw." Vic shuffled from foot to foot in an evident bid to stall the dreadful news. "You see—"

"Father, who's here at this hour? Has something happened?" A tired female voice spoke from down the hall.

Vic stiffened, his spine ramrod straight. Johnathan's unease doubled as the woman shuffled into the room, her face hauntingly familiar.

Alyse Shaw stopped beside her father, rubbing the sleep from her eyes, and very much alive.

CHAPTER FIVE

JOHNATHAN FROZE, UNCERTAIN HOW TO REACT. ALYSE SHAW BLINKED at them, her confusion clear. The sleepiness quickly evaporated from her expression. A frown creased her brow as her surprisingly sharp gaze roved over his travel-worn appearance.

"Has something happened?" She addressed the question to Vic, who rocked back on his heels.

There was a giggle from across the room. Their presence appeared to have summoned Pastor Shaw's full gaggle of children. A small cluster of boys and girls, varying in age, huddled in their night clothes around their open bedroom door.

Alyse's frown switched to the children, centering on the oldest girl. "Maddy, get them back in the room," she snapped.

The distraction gave Vic a chance to collect himself.

"I'm sorry to have disturbed you. There was another murder. We believed you were the victim." Vic blurted the words, his cool demeanor still thrown off balance. "It is clear there was a mistake."

He gave a short bow to the stunned Pastor Shaw and turned, marching out of the house without another word. Johnathan caught the glance of confusion between father and daughter, though he was at a loss if he should attempt to explain the situation or complete their awkward exit.

Alyse Shaw rescued him from the ledge of bad manners.

"Pick your jaw off the floor and go," she said. "I'll get the story from Vic later."

"You most certainly will not," snapped Paster Shaw. Johnathan took that as his cue to leave, unwilling to involve himself in a family matter.

The door closed with a muted click behind him. Johnathan looked up to find Vic leaning against the carriage, his shoulders heaving. An odd tension crackled in the air between them when Vic slammed a fist against the side of the coach, hard enough for the wood to crack.

Johnathan silently gauged the thickness of the wood against the strength of a distraught man, but he climbed past Vic into the carriage, too tired to give proper weight to any misgivings or doubts. Dr. Evans' admonishments echoed through his head as he settled into the seat. Vic clambered up beside him.

The coach traveled in pregnant silence. Johnathan was wide awake now, and after their encounter with a living, breathing Alyse Shaw, his mind spun with the image of her very deceased doppelganger. He didn't fault the assembled townsfolk or Vic for the mistaken identity. The women could have been twins.

His gaze slid to Vic who sat stone-faced, his jaw flexing as he fought to control his temper. Vic's countenance had been a pantomime of emotions when she appeared in the hall, his naked relief and shock followed by a brief yet fierce longing that seemed far too intimate for witnesses. Johnathan swore that if he and Pastor Shaw had not been present, the reunion would've been far more physical than Vic's pining stare at the sleepy, confused Alyse.

Johnathan didn't want to be the first to speak. He didn't possess the right reactions for moments like these, painfully aware what he lacked in the department of human interaction. He knew the words that weighed down his tongue would be entirely inappropriate, his mindset far and away from the intimacy of lovers. He reached into his pocket to occupy himself, his skin cold and numb from the claw. He took it out to examine it as much as to relieve the pain of the biting aura it expelled.

Silence lent fluidity to time. The sky had subtly lightened during their long drive to Vic's property, the first hint of the coming day, though dawn was still an hour or so away. There wasn't enough light to read Vic's conflicted features now, and Johnathan found he could no longer take the quiet.

"Are you angry Miss Shaw is alive?" he asked.

Vic startled at his words, but he managed not to jerk on the reins of the placid mare, who clearly followed a familiar route home. "What are you on about?"

Johnathan raised a brow. "You put a fist through your fine carriage, sir."

"Back to sir?" The apparent amusement in Vic's voice threw Johnathan. "I'm not angry she is alive, John. I'm angered at my relief. A family lost their daughter tonight, and I allowed my relief that it wasn't Alyse to take precedence. Call it shame, if you will."

He stared at the other man, surprised and cowed by his answer. In the confusion of mistaken identity, he, too, set aside the reality of the dead woman. Someone's daughter, a lost child, torn to shreds, left exposed and alone on the street.

"Who was the other girl?" he asked.

Vic's jaw flexed. "I don't know."

Johnathan fiddled with the claw, end over end between his fingers. "She looked exactly like Alyse Shaw."

"The resemblance was rather striking," Vic responded, his tone dry as dust.

"I wonder if the killer thought it was her," said Johnathan. That time, Vic *did* jerk on the reins. The poor mare drew up with an indignant grunt.

"Sorry, Bess," Vic murmured. His gray gaze lit on Johnathan with an unreadable expression. "I feel you are driving to a point, John. It's been a long night, so forgive me if I don't follow."

"Is there anyone else in Cress Haven who looks like Alyse Shaw?"

Vic's jaw flexed. "No. There isn't."

"Am I mistaken in my assumption this is a small community? Enough that you would know for certain?"

"I know every citizen who has settled in this town for the past five years I have lived here." Vic looked over the road. "You believe Alyse was the intended target, regardless of the mistaken identity."

Johnathan gnawed on the inside of his cheek, a nervous habit he'd picked up from younger days. "Were the victims all young women?" This was what the dossier stated, but he needed to be sure, and the asking helped him maintain the appearance of an inquisitive newcomer.

Vic's nostrils flared. His gaze slid to Johnathan and back to the road with a thoughtful flicker in the shadows of his face. "Three women between the ages of fifteen and twenty-one. Tonight marks the fourth."

Johnathan frowned. "Were there any discerning features between them?"

"You look young, but you speak like a Bostonian detective," said Vic. "Were you sent here?"

Vic's tone was casual, but Johnathan's cheeks burned. He'd overstepped, and he knew it. As he internally debated how much to reveal to his generous host, a sound caught his attention. A sound that wasn't a sound.

An *absence* of sound.

Johnathan turned to the woods on their left, facing away from Vic. A prickling sensation slid along his skin, like a snake slithering over his bare flesh. He was being watched. This time, he was certain.

He searched back and forth through the shadows of trees.

There. His gaze snapped to a figure crouched between the tree trunks.

A set of eyes flared like crimson flame.

Johnathan's gaze widened. His pulse pounded between his ears, a frantic hard thump that drowned out his other senses. He was an insect pinned down, his defenses stripped bare. There was a mental caress of claws, a violent promise whispered in his mind. The icy claw tore into the palm of his hand.

Johnathan yelped and clutched at his wrist as the claw landed on the carriage floor with a weighted thump. The pain was immediate, a spike of agony so intense his vision blanked. The awful roar of his heartbeat quickened to a thrumming flutter, fragile as moth wings in flight. His breath drew short at such a harsh sensation, caught off guard by its severity. He'd received bullet wounds on training missions that were less painful.

Vic swore and drew his mare up short. He yanked a silk handkerchief from his breast pocket.

"How the hell did you manage this?" Vic guided Johnathan's hand into his lap.

That touch was a momentary distraction that caused Johnathan's racing pulse to jump. He found his gaze drawn to Vic's long, elegant fingers carefully assessing the wound.

Vic frowned. "What the devil..." His words trailed off as he gently flexed Johnathan's palm.

His reaction forced Johnathan to refocus his attention to the throbbing hurt in his hand. The puncture mark was clear, the flesh ice white at the edges, but to the shock of both men, the wound didn't bleed, not a drop. The pain rapidly faded to an insistent ache. Johnathan forced more air into his lungs.

"The devil indeed," Johnathan murmured. His gaze flitted back to the tree line, but the figure was gone.

CHAPTER SIX

THE ACHE REMAINED, A LOW THROB THAT KEPT TIME TO JOHNATHAN'S pulse; it proved a catalyst for his current state of deterioration. As the miles crawled along, the sky continued to lighten with the inevitable approach of dawn. The sensation of unseen stares poured from every shadowy crevice they passed.

A fine sweat beaded on Johnathan's skin, chilled by the morning mist. His teeth chattered behind his closed lips. Tremors twitched through his legs, between his shoulders, and along the tensed muscles of his forearms. The muted clicking noise of his teeth could be heard over the plod of the mare's hooves.

What was happening to him?

The ache drew his attention to his hastily bandaged hand, a wound that didn't bleed. The edges of his vision clouded, focused on the object that lay between his feet. The claw still sat on the floor of the coach. He swore he could feel its chill radiating through his leather boots. He couldn't leave it there but couldn't bring himself to pick it up.

The back of his neck grew damp with sweat at the very idea, as if contact would summon that shadowy figure.

"We're almost there," said Vic.

Johnathan started at his voice, the other man's presence forgotten in the discourse between his mind and body. He intended to answer his host but found his tongue a thick, useless mass in a mouth gone numb.

A true thread of panic infused the tremors quivering through him. He glanced down at his palm, wrapped in Vic's handkerchief. His fingers refused to cooperate as he tried to pry the fabric off his skin. What had that claw done to him? He had to see the wound, had to know.

"Leave it alone, Johnathan." Vic's sharp tone hooked into him, pulled him free from the swirling drain of his thoughts. "That gash needs proper care," the man continued. "Besides, we're here. Welcome to my home."

Johnathan blinked, astonished to find the coach stopped in front of a large country home, the wood still raw. He made to exit the coach to find his strength had evaporated from his limbs. A hoarse cry escaped as he toppled off his seat. Vic caught him and supported him under one shoulder, something Johnathan found absurd, since his bulk eclipsed the slighter man.

"Easy now. Let's get you inside," said Vic. He half-carried, half-dragged Johnathan over the threshold into his home.

On his feet, the pulse of pain increased tenfold until all sensation in Johnathan's body seemed to drag to the puncture mark. His vision was a wobbly gray mass; he couldn't make heads or tails of Vic's home. He didn't realize how far inside they'd gone until his body twisted and collapsed onto a cushioned surface. A bed.

Johnathan felt more than saw Vic looming over him. He heard the other man's indistinct murmur before the absence of shadow and warmth.

No. No, don't go. The words, provoked by his helpless state, caught in his throat and dissipated from his thoughts into the ether.

A small whimper squeezed out as Johnathan's consciousness faded. He began the tumultuous fall toward that dark place, where his buried memories were the vile shades that haunted his dreams.

Hands caressed Johnathan's face, the fingers cool against his flushed cheeks. Icy, pallid flesh, as if the poor soul had been drowned in moonlight. An astute description for Sir Harry, drowned in moonlight, so that it saturated his skin, lent it a pearly luminescence befitting his ethereal appearance. From the corner of his eye, Johnathan could see Sir Harry's fingernails and the deep, bruised, blue-black that limned the base of each nail.

Johnathan responded to the touch, turned his face into Sir Harry's palm as the older man knelt in front of him to tug at the collar of his shirt.

"There's my pretty Johnny boy." Sir Harry's breath blew over his face like stale sea water, rife with sweet salt and the slightly putrid undertone of decay. The scent made Johnathan recoil, but he hid the reaction. That defined his relationship to Sir Harry, a push and pull like the waves that lapped the shore beneath the harbor docks.

But the sea was always connected to the shore, as Johnathan was to Sir Harry. He kept still as the older man strategically tore the worn fabric at his collar. Sir Harry swept two fingers along the ground and smudged Johnathan's cheek.

He leaned back to admire his handiwork. "There we are, a perfect little ruffian. Now, what do we say?"

"Please, help me sir, my mother, she's hurt in the alley."

"Good, good," Sir Harry murmured. "Now close your eyes, sweet boy. We must make you authentic."

Johnathan closed his eyes, his shoulders lax from a routine played out every night in memory. Wind brushed his cheek, followed by the sharp, immediate burn of torn flesh. Warmth dripped down his cheek. He let out a breath. The pain was familiar, necessary. Blood made him appear more distressed, made people uncomfortable. They wanted to fix it, to do their due diligence for the poor unfortunate waif who called to them from the shadows.

"Reel them in, Johnny boy," said Sir Harry.

Johnathan didn't have to force the stumble in his steps. It'd been two days since his last meal. Sir Harry, needing a waif, kept him lean and underfed. Johnathan didn't mind. Not for Sir Harry, but sometimes his empty belly kept him up at night. However, if he landed a mark, he'd eat his fill, an extra incentive to succeed. He edged to the alley mouth, observing the passing men and women until he saw potential.

If Sir Harry drowned in moonlight, this woman bathed in sunlight. It soaked into her gold-wrought curls and peach-kissed skin. The blue morning sky shone in her wide, innocent eyes as she took in everything around her in guileless wonder.

She was so brilliant, the sour-faced matron who shadowed her steps was easy to miss.

Johnathan took a step from the alley and froze. Push and pull. For a singular moment, the push was stronger. If he called out to her, her light would cease to be, snuffed out, engulfed in moon-borne arms, tighter than the embrace of the earth. Johnathan wavered, voice caught fast in his throat.

A pang punched through his empty stomach. His mouth watered at the prospect of eating tonight. He closed his eyes, swayed on his feet.

"M-miss," he said. Blue eyes caught him. He flexed his clammy hands. "Please, my mother, she's hurt...in the alley."

The words felt like razors in his mouth. Each sliced his tongue as they fell from his lips.

"Oh, you poor boy," said the woman. No, she was maybe a few years older than Johnathan, her curves newly formed and incomplete.

The pang flexed, sharp and unforgiving, but there was a new sensation in his empty stomach, a sour-sick feeling that coated his throat and made it hard to breathe.

"Oh, miss, don't go in there. We'll ring the constable," said the matron.

Yes, thought Johnathan. Yes, don't come in here.

The young woman worried her lip, her attention going back and forth between her chaperone and him, the little waif. Push and pull. Johnathan held his breath.

"At least let me make sure she's alright, Anne," said the girl. The matron hesitated, clearly torn by her mistress's words. "Please, look at him. Poor mite is starving, roughed up. He couldn't hurt a fly." The matron sighed, a patient, indulgent sound. His stomach bottomed out.

"Where's your mother, boy? Can you take me to her?"

"This way," Johnathan whispered. He moved backward into the shadows, each step scuffing along the cobblestones. The cut on his cheek burned where a tear tracked through it.

"It's going to be all right," said the girl. She reached for him, her golden hair dulled, enveloped by the shadows of the alley.

No, it won't. The words sat, bitter on his tongue, but he never spoke them.

His steps continued until he'd drawn both the girl and her chaperone into the alley, flies into the spider's web.

Sir Harry rose behind them. He wrapped his hands around the matron's head and twisted in a quick, clean break. Johnathan thought it a waste, but two women *meant screams, meant possible attention. One had to be silenced, and Sir Harry preferred the freshness of youth to age. The older woman's body hadn't hit the ground before he was on the girl, a hand over her mouth to catch her scream. He pulled her backward by her hair, exposing the creamy white column of her throat. Her blue eyes widened at the specter of death leering down at her with sharp, white teeth.*

She shrieked into Sir Harry's cool palm as he sank his teeth into her neck and drank, drank, drank her down. Johnathan didn't look away. He watched as Sir Harry fed, watched as the sunlight leached from her skin, and she fell from Sir Harry's arms—limp, cool, absorbed by moonlight. Her sightless blue stare bore into Johnathan, a silent accusation.

Johnathan was no longer hungry.

Sir Harry stepped over the corpse. He bit his thumb and smeared the blood across Johnathan's cheek. The tingle of knitting skin broke the spell, or set the spell anew. Johnathan was never quite certain where Sir Harry's influence began and ended. He breathed through his mouth to evade the sharp copper smell and slipped his hand into Sir Harry's cool one.

"Well done, my sweet," said Sir Harry. "You deserve a reward."

Johnathan shivered at the dark promise in Sir Harry's voice.

Push and pull.

The shiver pushed Johnathan from the caustic web of his memories. He broke through with a gasp, his head still muddled. He was freezing, his teeth chattering so hard he thought they might crack in his skull.

Johnathan rolled upright, an action he regretted. The world blurred and spun. Cold, so cold, shudders wracked his body as he fought to get his feet under him. His legs locked, tangled in a knot of fabric. A blanket, he realized, the fabric a delicate soft knit against the palm of his uninjured hand. His other hand was still numb, his fingers a little blue, while an icy sensation threaded outward from the puncture.

He tugged absently at Vic's handkerchief, needed to remove it, to see the state of the wound, but the world bore down on him in sharp bright tones, their edges muted until shapes bled together in formless masses. He breathed hard and closed his eyes, pressing the heel of his palms against his lids. His damaged hand was frigid.

A copper scent teased his nostrils. He flinched, dismissed it as a ghost of memory, but the scent came again. Johnathan always had a keen nose for blood. He studied the makeshift bandage shielding his hand, but the material was dry and free of crimson stains. Still, he smelled blood.

Vision slowly improving, Johnathan made his way on weak legs from the room. He paused just outside the door where the blood scent clouded the air. He glanced around, sniffing as he took in Vic's home. The space appeared relatively unadorned for a permanent residence, bathed in the long shadows of a day half-passed. He must have slept for hours.

Johnathan's steps were unsteady but silent, a training that kicked in without conscious thought. He moved past each room, doors flung open to flood the space with light. Movement caught in the corner of his vision, drawing his eye to one room in particular. Vic stood inside, ensconced by books and sunlight, a halo of dust motes crowning his rich auburn hair. One leg lay straddled over the arm of a chair, trousers rolled high over his thigh.

Vic's skin glowed like pearls in the sunlight, the lily white of a sheltered lordling, but the muscles flexed firm. The exposed thigh drew Johnathan's gaze like a beacon. He stared, mesmerized, as Vic pierced that luminescent skin with a filled syringe and pressed the plunger down.

Was that blood?

A tracery of red bloomed from the injection site, a peony beneath the skin, bright and flush before the bloom faded. Johnathan gasped, vision wobbling in and out of focus. His thoughts snarled and tangled, unable to decipher the implications of what he witnessed. Vic's gaze snapped up. His gray eyes once again held that unearthly glow, but his features were too blurred to read.

"This isn't what it looks like," said Vic, but the words were muffled, as if Johnathan were listening through a wall.

His legs chose that moment to buckle. With a slurred curse he fell, a fast plummet toward the floor.

Vic caught him before he hit the ground. Johnathan blinked up at him, frustrated by the lack of cooperation from his body. He hadn't felt this weak since the fever that swept through the Prospectives three winters ago, claiming six of his fellow trainees. He'd lain in bed, hallucinating then too, which was why he doubted the veracity of what he saw now. What he *thought* he saw.

"Are you sick, Victor?" he murmured, clutching at the man's arms.

"No, no. I'm fine, John," said Vic. He shuffled Johnathan's weight with apparent ease, supporting him with one arm as he smoothed Johnathan's sweat-soaked hair off his forehead. His gaze snared Johnathan, hooking into him. Vic's warm touch slid across his temple.

"Rest," said Vic. His serene voice tolled through Johnathan, the command weighing on his fatigued mind. "You won't remember any of this come morning."

Johnathan wanted to protest, but his mind drifted against his will, sinking back into that terrible dark web of memory and dream as his lucidity faded. His last grip on consciousness slipped, and his body went weightless, as if he were carried from the room.

CHAPTER SEVEN

CONSCIOUSNESS CAME AND WENT ON A PENDULUM SWING. JOHNATHAN drifted between the past and the present, chased by shadows and the constant chatter of teeth. Memories bled into dreams, a tangle of night terrors. Strung like cobwebs through his mind, they snared him until he couldn't tell up from down, truth from lie.

Sir Harry held him tight, one hand wrapped around Johnathan's slender throat as they settled in for a day's rest. "Never betray me, sweet one." It was an order and a threat. A code he lived by, and no matter how many misgivings and moments of hesitation he experienced, Johnathan never once forfeited that trust.

Never.

Memory shifted, the pendulum swung up, his face thinner, older. The knife handle was slippery in Johnathan's fingers. Slick with the blood rapidly cooling against his skin. Had he killed someone? No, he never took a human life on his own.

"You must strike the heart," instructed a voice from the shadows, chill and slippery as the blood on the icy stone beneath his feet. The man's face remained in shadow but for his spectacles, glinting orbs that floated in the dim light. He gripped a weathered wooden cross, tapping it against his thigh, looming behind Johnathan. "Strike true and leave your blade there. Or I'll be picking you out of his fangs."

Johnathan's heart thundered a furious rhythm, an off-tune beat to the soft, impatient tread behind him. He raised the blade overhead. Sir Harry opened his eyes. This hadn't happened before, no. Sir Harry's eyes had stayed closed through that terrible moment. Johnathan met the accusation in that stare, all sound scrubbed out, replaced by a high-pitched ringing in his ears, like the long drawn-out echo of a scream.

His hand throbbed. Not memory, but an intrusion of the present.

Johnathan gasped and clasped his wrist, his eyes riveted to the center of his unmarked palm. The skin blackened as he watched, festered and charred where it burned from within. Was this real? Was he awake or still dreaming?

"Hmmm, you've done it now, boy," Sir Harry murmured in his ear, that low voice piercing straight through the high-pitched ringing. Grave-tinted nails slid along his jaw until iron fingers collared him.

The pendulum swung down. The choking grip of the dream faded, and reality surged forward. Johnathan rode the momentum to consciousness, finally peeling his heavy lids open. He was in a bedroom now, surrounded by the calming earthy tones of russet and hunter green. The bed beneath him was a study of contrast, soft feather down and refined cotton, a true comfort. The previous night was a foggy murmur at the back of his thoughts. The high-pitched ringing in his ears was still there, which is why it took him so long to realize he was not alone.

Alyse Shaw sat on the edge of the bed. Her gaze was not on him, but the door, expectation in the set of her shoulders. He took the moment to study her. In the trailing afternoon light that shone through the windows, he wondered if it were a trick of the mind to draw such similarities between the murdered girl and Alyse Shaw. But the resemblance of their appearance was uncanny. It went beyond shared superficial features of dark hair and eyes. Vic thought he'd recognized her face in the dead woman as well, and Johnathan couldn't dismiss his unease in her presence. The shades of his dreams haunted him even now.

The moment passed. Alyse shifted and turned her dark gaze on him. "You're awake."

He swallowed, and heat flushed up the back of his neck. He was indeed, and the inappropriateness of the situation didn't escape him, alone with a young lady on his bed. To his great relief, he still wore clothing, although he cringed to think of his travel-filthy clothes on Vic's sheets.

Where was Vic? It struck him once more how little he knew about his host, such as the man's last name. Hard to think on that with the young lady so close.

Alyse anchored his attention. He tried not to shrink away from her innocuous presence. His experience with the fairer sex was severely limited, particularly once the Society got their hands on him, but he still knew the basics of manners. Her presence here, alone, simply wouldn't do. He sank further into the mattress. Her gaze turned puzzled.

He cleared his throat, or attempted to, caught off guard by how dry it was. It felt as if he'd gargled with cotton and sand. His eyes watered as the coughing fit took him hard.

"Got grit in your throat?" Alyse asked. "Would you like me to fetch the water pitcher?"

He rolled to his side and covered his mouth, unable to answer her. The soft rasp of a cloth bandage met his lips. He jerked his hand away and blinked through tears at the neatly wrapped dressing on his wounded palm. The wound that didn't bleed. Carefully, he eased the bandage higher, wincing as he exposed the edge of the puncture wound. There was still an unsettling lack of blood, though the skin around the hole appeared puffy, almost bruised, but numb to the touch. He dragged the bandage back in place, wondering and fearful that the strange puncture would become infected.

An infection would certainly slow him down. Johnathan's train of thought derailed when a cup was shoved between his hands. Miss Shaw knelt on the floor beside him, holding the water steady for him.

Johnathan took a long drink, the chill liquid a balm on his parched throat. The coolness spread through his system, like a soothing ripple through his veins. It cleared the fog from his head, where his mind began to simmer.

"Thank you," he rasped.

"Ah, he does speak."

Johnathan ducked his head, thoroughly discomfited by Miss Shaw's presence. "Where is Master Vic?"

Her brow rose as she settled on the bed next to him once more, clearly unaware of personal space. "*Master* Vic needed to attend to a few errands," she said. There was a note of sarcasm and amusement in her tone. "You're the man he hired." It wasn't a question.

Alyse's fingers tapped the jug of water in her hands. Johnathan couldn't quite decipher the expression in her dark eyes, but it made him feel uneasy. Her attention made him feel naked despite the reassuring texture of his roughshod clothing. He shifted beneath the covers, seized with the laughable urge to cover himself. Johnathan doubted he'd ever add enough layers not to feel exposed to that stare.

"Apologies for waking your residence so early this morning," said Johnathan. The words stumbled out his mouth, but the intensity of her silent observation was worse.

"I assure you my father was relieved for the mistake," said Miss Shaw. She finally looked away to refill his mug. He was grateful to be free of such scrutiny. "Why would Vic hire a scrapper pup like you?"

Johnathan choked on his own spit. "I beg your pardon?" he managed to gasp out.

She pursed her lips as she peered at him. "You're certainly big enough to be mistaken for a man, until you sleep. I bet you aren't a day over sixteen."

"I'm at least twenty," Johnathan shot back, and immediately regretted the admission.

She blinked at him. "At least? You don't know?"

Here he'd talked himself back against another conversational wall. He couldn't very well explain to the nosy chit why his actual age was a matter of contention. He could be anywhere between eighteen or two and twenty, though he suspected he was somewhere between. Instead, Johnathan curled his limbs away from her, flustered by the entirely improper Miss Shaw.

"How old are you, then?" he asked. "Shouldn't you have a chaperone?"

Miss Shaw's incredulous expression broke into a grin. "Look at you blushing. I'm three and twenty, practically a spinster, and I don't think a chaperone could keep up with me."

"Truer words than scripture." Vic's voice announced his arrival before he entered the room. Johnathan felt an invisible weight lift off his shoulders, relieved to have an ally against the insufferable woman. That feeling dissipated slightly as Vic's cool gaze slid over him. There was a hard question in his stare that Johnathan didn't understand and possibly imagined, gone from one second to the next as the corners of his eyes creased with good-natured crow's feet. The appearance of those lines surprised him, placing Vic's age higher than Johnathan first surmised, or hinted at a harder life than he'd imagined.

"I think you've tortured my guest enough for one evening, Alyse. We have matters to attend," said Vic. The afternoon sun fell on the master of the house with a loving caress—it painted his pale skin in golden hues and offset his silvery gray eyes like sea glass. The sight banished the last vapors of tension. Something unknotted in Johnathan's chest, a final doubt laid to rest that he didn't realize he still carried.

Vampires didn't wither in the sun, but the natural light revealed too much of their inhuman nature. One would never invite such casual exposure.

A hazy memory flashed through his thoughts, of a smooth white thigh, the details frustratingly blank. Johnathan frowned, the image churned in the frothy sea of his subconscious. Was that even real? He shook himself as Alyse perked up.

"What matters?" Alyse set the jug down hard on the night table. Vic's expression turned evasive. "Oh, don't you dare clam up now!"

Vic crossed his arms, but his hands began to fidget. It was the first time Johnathan saw him as anything but cool and collected. Apparently, Miss Shaw had that effect on everyone. Vic hemmed. "We are paying Stebbins a visit—"

"I knew it." Alyse stood, braced for an argument. "I want to come."

"No!" Vic and Johnathan blurted in tandem.

"A morgue is no place for a lady," Johnathan muttered, his retort a match on kindling as Alyse spun on him.

"No place for a child either," she snapped.

He could feel his face color at Vic's puzzled expression. The other man appeared to tuck away the jab to unpack later. Gliding across the room, he set his hands on Alyse's heaving shoulders.

"I don't want you to see this. You don't realize how bad it was, worse still when I believed it was you." Vic's quiet tone squelched the fire in her. She sagged into his hands, and Johnathan suddenly felt like a voyeur.

"I'm still here, Vic, and I'm not to be coddled," said Alyse, but she didn't fight when he attempted to usher her to the door.

"Come, let's speak of this in my study and give Johnathan a chance to wash up." Vic cast a meaningful glance over Alyse's shoulder. "Johnathan, there's a wash basin on the side cabinet. If you would excuse us." Vic steered the unruly woman from the room, which left Johnathan alone to face the rising riot in his mind.

He swung his legs off the bed with care and sat with his injured hand cradled in his lap. Finally alone, he tried to process the jumble of memory that plagued his sleep. It had been months, *months* since he'd dreamed of Sir Harry, especially that particular incident. Johnathan glanced toward the ceiling, tempted to ask the higher powers why such memories made a resurgence now, here, when he needed his wits the most. His final test was quite the smashing success thus far, and he had the sinking sensation this wasn't the worst of it. His bandaged hand curled into a fist, the pads of his fingers pressed against the strangely numb center of his palm.

Johnathan didn't want another young woman to die on his watch. He had barely begun to delve into what plagued Cress Haven, but there was a sense he was already too late. He rubbed his middle finger along the bandage, a keen awareness that he'd stumbled onto something much more in the rough-hewn town of Cress Haven than what Dr. Evans led him to believe.

It would take but a moment to send a post to the Society. To hand off the whole affair to senior agents who would ensure no more torn-up girls in the streets. The temptation was there. But it wasn't curiosity or pride that drove him now. Cress Haven had become his responsibility, its citizens under his care. This mystery was his to solve, and he would solve it because that was his duty.

He would not fail.

CHAPTER EIGHT

CERTAINTY IN ONE'S COURSE OF ACTION BROUGHT A CURIOUS SENSE OF
elation. Johnathan was sharper, more focused as he washed his face and
neck with his uninjured hand. He donned a clean shirt and beat the road
dust from his coat until he was fairly presentable.

Vic's home was comfortable, the ceilings high enough for his height
without that looming architecture that marked so many wealthy
residences. Furnished for comfort over style, which appealed not only to
the wilderness around them, but Johnathan's own sensibilities. The hall
was longer than he first believed, though he'd only seen it through the
lens of fatigue and fever. He followed the sound of voices, but his steps
slowed. Alyse's words carried down the hall.

"That doesn't answer my question. Why did you bring one of them
into your home?" Her words were a hiss, like escaping steam, full of shrill
heat. "You know it's not safe to have him here when he could—"

"That's enough." Vic's words were soft but snapped like a leash pulled
taut. Alyse fell silent.

Johnathan's skin prickled. What did she mean by "one of them"? He'd
certainly fumbled along from the moment he set foot in Cress Haven,
but he never once let slip his connection to the Society, or his purpose
here. For that matter, why would it matter to Vic or Alyse?

Unease slithered through his veins, accented by a dull throb at his temples. What was she going to say before Vic cut her off? He flexed the fingers of his injured hand. For better or worse, he couldn't linger here.

Johnathan schooled his features, joining them in the study. A seated Vic looked up as he entered, his eyes chips of flint. For a moment, he thought he saw a flicker of unease in the man's expression before his features settled, a card sharp's vacuous mask. Alyse flinched when she saw him, a slight uptick of her shoulders, and turned away. Her hands crumpled her skirts.

"Good to see you on your feet again, John," said Vic, the warm tone undermining the ice in his gaze. He rose from his chair, a sinuous movement that captured Johnathan's attention.

A note of tension stole through him, one he didn't want anything to do with. He tapped his fist against his thigh as Vic spoke.

"We have an appointment with Stebbins. Shall we carry on?"

Johnathan only trusted himself to nod.

Vic turned to Alyse. "Will you continue your research about what happened to the others?"

Johnathan frowned at their exchange, uncertain what "others" Vic referred to or why he would send Miss Shaw on such a task.

"Of course, I will," Alyse retorted, stomping to the book-strewn table in the center of the room. She sat with a huff, tossing books about as she searched for a particular volume.

"There certainly are a lot of tomes on pagan lore here for a pastor's daughter," said Johnathan, glancing over the numerous piles scattered across the table.

Alyse ran the back of her hand across her brow. "My mother's people were from Ireland and Scotland. She might've married a godly man, but the old ways never left her. She held onto the family library, thankfully." Alyse threw open the first book a little too vigorously, still seething at being left behind.

She calmed as Vic placed a hand on her shoulder. "I know you'll find something useful," said Vic.

Her expression softened. "Please, be careful," she said.

Johnathan didn't imagine the brief slide of her gaze in his direction.

"I will walk on eggshells," said Vic with a slow smile that sent a flush through Alyse Shaw's face. Johnathan once again felt the voyeur. "Come along, John, daylight's waning."

He followed the other man out, and the weight of Alyse Shaw's gaze settled between his shoulder blades.

The tension didn't loosen its grip as they clambered into the open coach. Johnathan sat straight and stiff, a direct contrast to Vic's carefully relaxed posture. He waited for the hammer to fall, but Vic said nothing. Only the occasional considering glance gave a hint of the man's thoughts. Johnathan rubbed his bandaged palm, dug in hard enough to feel the twinge of protesting flesh. He couldn't let this tension reign between them. It would undermine his purpose here. He needed Vic to trust him, to an extent. He already owed the enigmatic man for the previous night.

Johnathan swallowed. "Thank you for your care. I don't know what came over me, and I confess, I don't remember much of what transpired last night, but I am grateful for the shelter. That I had someone there..." He frowned down at his hands. His words wandered off a cliff again. He sighed, and a self-deprecating chuckle slipped free. "I'm not very good at this."

"Good at what?" Vic's tone was carefully neutral.

Johnathan's shoulders fell. "Good with people." He glanced away, a sudden knot in his throat. Dr. Evans once said this was Johnathan's greatest weakness in the field. He was a skilled fighter and keen at picking up details others missed, but his ability to adapt and ingratiate himself into a strange environment, with unfamiliar people fell short compared to the rest of the Prospectives. Not that he blended in with his Society peers either.

There was a lengthy pause in which he didn't dare look at his host, but at last Vic spoke.

"There are many reasons one finds themselves unable to connect. Cress Haven is quiet, secluded, and generally populated by such individuals." There was a note of understanding in Vic's voice. The tension dispersed like morning fog.

"You seem to connect with everyone," said Johnathan, surprised by the wistful tone in his own words.

"You can thank Alyse for that. I had a devil of a time integrating before her friendship. It was her acceptance that helped me forge a place here."

"She's a bit terrifying, to be honest," said Johnathan.

Vic snorted and clutched the reins before he erupted into a rich laugh. "Aye, she is at that. One couldn't ask for a fiercer friend."

Johnathan was curious over Vic's description of Alyse as a friend. Human connection was an issue, but he was observant. He wondered why Vic hadn't offered for the headstrong woman. He bit back the question, certain that prying into their relationship would be a foul.

The town was heavily shadowed in twilight, the rough-cut buildings bathed in shades of gray, raw wood beaten on by the elements. There was the occasional slap-dash splash of color and chipped, faded paint where the residents put care into appearance, but the majority reflected the rough edge of the wilderness at their backs as if the woods chewed up and spat out Cress Haven.

Vic stopped the coach outside a rather trim building close to the end of the street, far from Cress Haven's main hub. The building's color had long bleached away under the sun and bore a carved sign that read Stebbins's Apothecary.

"Apothecary?" Johnathan raised a brow.

"I reckon he thought it sounded better than 'morgue,'" said Vic. "Speaking of individuals unable to connect, try not to be too unsettled by Stebbins. He's a bit odd but harmless."

Come to think of it, Johnathan recalled their first interaction, how the strange fellow tumbled about the crime scene with all the grace and regard of a curious child. "What do you mean?"

"You'll see." Vic shoved the door open, a grimace fixed on his face.

A bell slapped against the back of the door, a thud and clang to announce their arrival. Shelves lined the walls, filled with boxes of packets labeled in neat script. The room reeked of various chemicals and spoiled milk. There was an aftertaste of Epsom salt and bitter almonds on the tongue if Johnathan breathed through his mouth. The building was unnaturally cool; he could feel a chill rising up from the floorboards and knew with utter certainty, the morgue was downstairs.

The pound of footsteps announced Stebbins' arrival from below. Johnathan's first encounter in the dark didn't properly prepare him for the full picture of the man. The mortician was a rumpled figure, his coat covered in all manner of stains Johnathan didn't study too closely. There were crumbs on his lapels, and without a cap on his head, tufts of greasy gray hair stuck up every which way. Deep circles under his dark brown eyes made Stebbins look like an enormous raccoon. He approached them with a disarmingly cheerful grin, though his gaze skidded away from theirs, his attention visibly wandering before he reached them.

"Good evening, Vic, pleasure to see you here," said Stebbins. He reeled himself back in to vigorously shook Vic's hand and rounded on Johnathan. "Hello again. You're the lad I met in the alley, right? Vic said he hired the new arrival. First murder, or have you seen a few sliced up dollies in the city?"

Johnathan didn't feel this was the time or place to reveal this was far from his first body, though Stebbins wasn't fazed by his silence.

He seized Johnathan's hand with icy fingers and pumped his arm up and down. The greeting seemed to stretch on and on until he feared the limb might fall off from the man's enthusiastic greeting. Johnathan shot his companion a look of panic.

"Stebbins," Vic said, his tone a command.

Stebbins made a face akin to a surprised turtle. "Sorry, guv, I forget my manners, down in the dungeon all day."

Johnathan attempted to shake some feeling back into the limb, grateful for Vic's interference.

Stebbins clapped his hands. "You be wanting to see the body first or would you care for a spot of tea?"

"The body, if you please, Stebbins," said Vic with only a slightly aggrieved air.

"Righto, come come, and watch your head there lad, small giant that you are. Did they raise you on raw meat?"

The warning came just in time. Johnathan narrowly avoided braining himself on a low beam his companions cleared with ease. "Was always tall," he murmured. Certainly not a matter of diet. At over six feet, he was the tallest Prospective in his class.

The temperature dropped as they descended, the morgue like an icy tomb. Apt description, except for the lighting. Gas lamps hung from the ceiling and provided more than ample illumination for the handful of shrouded figures on long, narrow slabs.

"High intake this month," remarked Stebbins, gesturing toward two covered corpses.

Johnathan made a mistake and met the man's eyes, wide and shadow stained. An off-key grin stretched Stebbins' lips in an unsettling manner. Johnathan froze. The mortician suddenly leaned in, far too close, his breath fanning over Johnathan's face with the reek of spoiled milk.

"You want to see them, don't you boy?" Stebbins giggled. Johnathan took a step back, straight into Vic, who reached around him and snapped his fingers in the mortician's face.

"Focus, Stebbins," said Vic.

"Couple drunks who lost their way in the dark," Stebbins continued, as if nothing odd had transpired, leaving Johnathan more than a little unnerved. "Any number of elements could have done those poor sods in. We didn't find them for a few days, after the animals got to them. But they got nothing on our girl."

"Stebbins, the body, please," said Vic, his patience for the odd fellow seemingly unending. Vic shifted and pressed a small hand to the center of Johnathan's back. The touch grounded him, settling his nerves.

"Ah yeah, gave me quite the shock when I saw Miss Shaw making rounds this morning. A dead ringer for the victim. Course that was before."

Vic stilled. "Before?"

"Before this," said Stebbins. He whipped the sheet off from the figure on the far end with a flourish, a man who enjoyed his line of work.

"What the devil?" Vic's words were a sharp oath. They reflected Johnathan's own shock at the sight. Vic staggered forward and planted his hands on the edge of the table, careful to avoid any contact with the blackened, wilted corpse that lay there. "She—she looks—"

"Charred," said Stebbins. "As if I stored her in the stove overnight, eh?" He tsked and shook his head. "Just like the first one, though she lasted a bit longer."

Vic's patience snapped. He rounded on the undertaker, seeming to loom over the man despite their similar statures. "You never told me this happened to the other body. Any other details you care to reveal, Stebbins?"

Stebbins caught the menace in Vic's tone and flinched. He rubbed a hand along his jaw and left a smear of mystery fluid that made Johnathan shudder. "Now that you mention it, I might have made a few notes here and there."

"Do share," sneered Vic.

"Right here, guv." Stebbins spun around to a cluttered desk in the corner of the room and shuffled through various piles of chaos while Vic hovered beside him with patient irritation.

Johnathan ignored them. He approached the body, his gaze locked on the remains.

Charred, burned, the skin blackened and withered to the point it flaked from the crackled bones. Somehow, her hair was untouched, an appalling detail, her dark curls stained and matted with dried blood. Her hair clung to her blackened scalp with dogged tenacity, now the only recognizable detail of a once-vibrant young woman. Johnathan reached for a lock, the texture like feather down to the touch. He sifted it through his fingers.

What could produce such an appearance after death?

His gaze darted along her disfigured body. The ravaged stomach cavity was a puckered ruin, but he could see the shape of it now, the ragged flaps of skin where claws had raked her. Her abdomen was sunken, organs missing. But it wasn't the only entry. In the darkened alley with so much gore lying about, he'd failed to notice her cracked-open ribs.

A chill shivered through his veins. She'd been alive for that part.

The hole was a maw of black, snapped bone, like jagged rotten teeth. He peered into the space. Something flared back at him. Johnathan drew closer until the flare took shape.

"Vic?" His voice was whisper soft, but the man heard him.

"What is it?"

"Do you see that?"

Vic's eyes widened as he peered into the broken chest cavity. "The devil is that?"

"It...it almost looks like a brand," said Johnathan. The symbol, etched into the hollow flesh where her heart had once beaten, glowed like an ember in a dying fire. "Have you ever seen the like?"

"No." Vic looked thoughtful. "Stebbins! Paper, charcoal, now."

The symbol flared, a brilliant burning red. Johnathan's bandaged hand itched.

Abruptly, the corpse creaked, the internal flare glowing through cracks in the burnt husk. The blackened color lightened, the reek of burning hair clogging the air as unseen flame consumed the previously untouched curls. The process accelerated until the body went from charred to ash and the inner light snuffed itself out. The two men staggered back as the skin began to flutter away. The husk collapsed under its own weight, the bones disintegrating to dust, leaving nothing behind but a smoldering heap of fine gray ash.

Johnathan swallowed hard, a tremor rocking through him at the sight. He clutched Vic's wrist. "What could possibly cause this?" he asked, incapable of taking his eyes off the girl's...*ashes*.

Vic looked at him, nostrils flaring. "Nothing natural."

Stebbins whistled at the ruined remains. "That will be a tough one to explain to the family." He heaved a put-upon sigh. "I'll probably lose my commission for this."

Johnathan stared at the mortician. The man was absolutely cracked. He shook his head and rubbed his bandaged hand. This situation was quickly proving itself far beyond his capability as a Prospective, far beyond any Novice Hunter. There was a dark work at large in Cress Haven, not a simple fiend. He couldn't handle this on his own; he had to inform the Society. Dr. Evans wouldn't have sent someone with so little experience if he knew what was truly happening. Johnathan had never seen or heard of anything like this happening in the city.

Vic scribbled furiously on a scrap of paper while Stebbins muttered to himself over the pile of ash. They now had more questions than answers.

Johnathan's bandaged palm gave another twinge. Over the scents of preservation chemicals and faint chilled decay, he caught another scent, a pungent earthy rot that coated his mouth to the back of his throat. "I need some air," he said.

Vic flicked his fingers at him. "Go. I'll finish up here."

Johnathan couldn't get out of there fast enough. A rime of icy sweat clung to his skin. He burst from the building, gasping as if he'd run for miles, and gulped deep breaths of open air. Night had fallen while they were inside, the thick, claustrophobic press of country darkness. There were no streetlamps in this part of town where only the dead gathered.

His hand gave yet another twinge. He stared at the bandage. A streak of ash marred the pristine cloth. A dark suspicion bloomed. He had to see the wound.

His fingers fumbled with the tightly wrapped cloth. It gave way at last, in tufts of burst fibers.

Johnathan's lungs clenched at the sight. The puncture wound was now a ring of charred flesh, a disturbing echo of the girl he just watched turn to ash.

What was happening to him?

He grazed his trembling fingertips over the wound, almost too scared to touch the blackened gash. Was he damned to the same fate? To be consumed by this horrid poison, infection—whatever it was—until he crumbled to a pile of ash?

The ill tide of his thoughts had little time to linger as his training took hold. The hairs on the back of his neck stood on end.

Johnathan went still.

He was being watched.

His gaze slid up. A figure hovered at the edge of his peripheral vision. He couldn't see who—or what—it was unless he turned around, though he had a good feeling his ogler was not human. If he looked, it would *know* he looked. He weighed his options and lifted his head.

A long low growl split the silence, and molten eyes peered at him from the darkness. Johnathan couldn't see the full form, only the impression of a crouched body.

Ready to spring.

CHAPTER NINE

Johnathan's muscles went lax. He settled on the balls of his feet and slowly turned his head. His hands were deceptively loose at his sides. These were not the expected motions of prey.

The crouched figure went still. Its brilliant, fiery gaze tipped sideways as it considered him. A bitter smile curled Johnathan's mouth.

Never run from me, boy. Sir Harry's voice whispered through his thoughts. *Food runs.*

Johnathan had no weapon on his person, a factor he planned to rectify if he survived this encounter. He hunched his shoulders up and sneered, prepared to take a step forward. Blatant aggression might scare a predator off. The mark on his palm throbbed.

The figure snarled and scuttled forward, just enough for the light from Stebbins' Apothecary to catch on the shape of its maw.

"My god," Johnathan whispered. He knew by the glint of those wicked teeth that he stared at the creature who murdered those girls. There was an unmistakable lupine cast to its skull, but the shape was wrong, like a hound disassembled and haphazardly mashed back together by some vindictive, blind god. The full scope of the creature was unclear in the feeble lighting, other than a clear sense of something vicious and monstrous.

Vic slid in front of Johnathan, seeming to materialize straight from the shadows. Johnathan hadn't even heard the door open.

"When I say go, you run the other way," said Vic. The man attempted a cool and collected tone, but there was a strain to his words. Johnathan saw Vic's hands shake before he balled them into fists over his thighs.

It dawned on Johnathan that Vic hadn't cowered on the step when he saw the creature. He hadn't screamed or hidden, or any myriad of things humans do when they come face to face with the underbelly of the supernatural world.

A part of his brain wanted to analyze the actions of the man before him, but the wiser part tipped into survival mode.

"If we run, it will chase us down," said Johnathan

"Rather take your chances here?" Vic's voice rose an octave.

Johnathan cursed. He had to get both of them out of there alive. "Fine, on three we run."

"I told *you* to run," said Vic. "I'll distract it."

"You plan to play fetch with it?" Johnathan spoke far too loudly. The creature shuddered forward with a snap of teeth, a movement that revealed more of its wedge-shaped head and how ill-formed it was. It gouged the ground with massive paws tipped with familiar, stiletto-like claws.

"Blazes!" Vic gasped.

"Go, go!" Johnathan grabbed Vic by the arm and hauled him away, shocked by the non-existent weight of the shorter man. Built like a bird, but that made it easier for Johnathan to throw him forward. Vic needed no further encouragement. He flew forward, in an elegant lope that quickly outpaced Johnathan's long-legged stride.

The scrape and scrabble of the creature's pursuit kept a steady pace behind them. Johnathan didn't dare look back. That would only slow him down, a fatal mistake.

Johnathan put his head down and plowed on. They needed to get out of the open space of the street, find somewhere to hide or barricade themselves, though there were few options this far from the central point of town.

Adrenaline surged through his veins, the details of the surrounding trees and buildings blurring as his other senses sharpened. He could hear the dull crunch of the graveled road beneath his boots, the haphazard skitter of loose stones spitting out in his wake. The night air heaved through his chest and chilled the sweat that streaked along his scalp.

The closest building to the morgue was one of the town's mills, empty now but for the scent of stale sweat, grease, and sawdust. There would be plenty of nooks to conceal themselves, and more than one blade left in the building. It was as good a place as any, and Johnathan needed to make the decision. He could feel his momentum flagging

"Head for the mill!" he called to his companion, pushing through the stitch in his side. The scuff of claws through gravel spurred him to pull on his reserves.

Several paces ahead of Johnathan, Vic glanced over his shoulder and blanched. Johnathan's nerves sparked with awareness as a huff of heated breath steamed against the back of his neck. Time constricted, a drip of seconds through the physical vise of a mortal moment.

Vic spun around and launched himself back toward Johnathan. Blurred, sporadic movements, like trying to follow a hummingbird with the naked eye. *Too fast*, the thought stole into his adrenaline-saturated thoughts with the finesse of an ice pick. Vic caught Johnathan around the waist and somehow shifted their momentum sideways.

The creature's wicked claws missed Johnathan by a hair's breadth, but a spray of blood still painted the night.

Vic screamed and dropped to his knees, clutching his thigh. Blood ran over and through his fingers from a deep and vicious slash. Johnathan's mind went blank.

Something like fury blazed to life inside him, and years of brutal training took over. As the beast lunged toward them again, Johnathan grabbed Vic in a bear hug and rolled away, all while snapping his foot into the air.

His heel smashed the creature's jaw, the placement more luck than skill when his opponent was like nothing he'd ever faced before. The beast stumbled backward and tumbled over a rut in the road with a snarl. Given the second of reprieve, Johnathan lurched to his feet and plucked Vic off the ground.

"Go, or we both die," Vic hissed. He clung to Johnathan's arm, his face a mask of pain.

"Do shut up," said Johnathan, and he threw Vic over his shoulder with all the ceremony of tossing a potato sack.

He ignored the man's cussing and grunts of pain. Johnathan might not have Vic's unusual, if not downright deceptive speed, but he had stamina and a plan.

"Oh god, run!" Vic barked the order.

Johnathan launched himself toward the mill. His steps tore up the ground in clumps of dirt and sawdust. He picked up speed as he barreled for the closest entrance and leveled his free shoulder to hit the weakest spot.

The door, thankfully, splintered, but shattered his momentum. He stumbled through the entrance. Vic yelped, spilling off Johnathan's shoulder in a clumsy roll.

The muscles of Johnathan's shoulder hurt like the blazes; he suspected he'd torn them. He gritted his teeth and dragged Vic further into the mill.

Sweat stung his eyes as he maneuvered both of them behind a stack of freshly cut lumber waiting for rail transport. He placed Vic down and tore off his jacket, tying it tightly around the man's mangled thigh before he could bleed to death. He needed to stop the bleeding, but their foe was too close.

Johnathan peeked around the corner, hoping to locate the creature before it found them. He froze. The beast was right there, but it stalled at the doorway where it paced back and forth with snorts and huffs.

"It's wary," he whispered. "But of what? We're trapped unless we find weapons."

Vic sighed and craned his neck to see the beast. "We aren't trapped. There are multiple exits, if we can reach them before that bastard reaches us."

It still didn't make sense. The creature had to smell Vic's blood, had to know his prey was wounded.

Johnathan focused. His thoughts sank into the cool inner space where his Prospective training resided.

His senses ignited. He absorbed the details of their surroundings in a cursory glance, from the smears of machine oil and rotting sawdust that littered the floor, to the muted roar of the nearby river that powered the mill. The heavy scents of burnt metal, grease, and raw wood filtered through his lungs in deep, heaving breaths.

He didn't hear Vic breathing.

Johnathan turned to him. Vic was still half-twisted to look at the door. He paid no mind to his leg wound, which should have bled through his slap dash tourniquet by now with no accompanying pressure.

Johnathan reached out and peeled back the bloodied fabric of his coat.

Vic snatched at his wrist with a low hiss, but not before Johnathan saw the damning, smooth skin.

The wound was gone.

Neither of them moved. Johnathan met Vic's silver-gray gaze, the cool calculation so very reminiscent of Sir Harry.

"Shit," the vampire muttered.

"You son of a bitch," Johnathan snarled. "That monster is wary of *you.*"

Vic's grip on his wrist shifted, and Johnathan found himself airborne until he came down hard, pinned against a wood stack with Vic's hand locked around his throat. He strained upward, but Vic, the little bird, held him in place with ease.

"This is not how I wanted to do this," said Vic.

The vampire's gaze shifted from his furious companion to the doorway, attention divided, but Johnathan knew he had no advantage here.

How had he not noticed? Because the bastard did nothing to give himself away. Despite all of Johnathan's training, despite his intimate knowledge, he hadn't a clue.

"John, I need you to calm down," said Vic.

Johnathan thrashed. "*You're* the bloody vampire!"

"I'm aware of that," said Vic, with infuriating composure, "but we have more pressing matters."

As if to emphasize his statement, the beast chuffed and took a tentative step forward. Claws screeched over stone.

Vic searched Johnathan's face. "A truce until we survive this?"

Johnathan's throat worked. Vic held him firmly in place, but the grip on his neck wasn't painful. He longed to do violence, but it occurred to him that Vic could have killed him at any point during the past couple days. He could have snapped Johnathan's neck and left his body for the beast while he fled, but he hadn't, and those actions piqued Johnathan's grudging interest.

"Truce," he finally gritted through his teeth.

Vic released him and stepped back, hands lax and ready.

Johnathan stifled the fresh urge to throttle him. There was the beast to deal with, and its reluctance to enter the mill gave Johnathan an unconventional idea.

"If it's wary of you, do you think you could scare it off?"

"It's not that wary of me," snapped Vic.

"Then it won't stay hesitant forever," Johnathan retorted. "We have to do something."

The mill didn't offer much in the way of weapons. The best offerings were the heavy iron picks used to steer the logs. He seized one, unwieldy and awkward in his grip as he dragged it through the sawdust.

"What are you doing?" Vic's tone was high and tense.

"We need to go on the offense. On the count of three, I'll drive the creature back and you snap its neck or something," said Johnathan.

"That's your grand plan," Vic hissed. "We are both going to die."

Johnathan shrugged. "We'll die either way when it decides you're not a threat." He dug his heels into the floor, the vampire muttering beside him. "One—"

That was the moment the beast overcame its hesitation. It lunged forward, its slavering jaws filling Johnathan's vision. Scared out of his wits, Johnathan swung the log pick with all his strength, shoulders burning from the effort. The iron-shod end slammed against the beast's snout.

The creature yipped and fell back. Its smoldering gaze locked on Johnathan before it bowed its head with a plaintive whine that scraped his ragged nerves raw. Cracks, backlit by fire, split the soot-black flank before the beast erupted in a cloud of embers and ash.

"Blazes," muttered Vic.

Johnathan stared in shock, the log hook still clutched in his hands. He turned the hook. Oil and wood alone couldn't have done such damage, could they? What *was* that creature? Why did it react so to such an innocuous weapon? Why did it stare at him like *that?* As if he'd done something wrong. What detail was he missing? Had he actually vanquished the creature, or had it simply retreated? He feared the latter.

Johnathan dropped his arms so that the iron hook hit the floor with a dull thud. The odd wound on his palm throbbed. He had too many damn questions, and he was too damn exhausted to sort through them.

He turned to look at the stunned vampire. "We need to talk."

CHAPTER TEN

JOHNATHAN'S SHOULDERS WERE SO STIFF HE SUSPECTED SOMEONE could use him to lever open a stuck door. It was impossible to relax with Vic at his side. Their uneasy truce remained in play as they headed back for the vampire's carriage. Johnathan ground his teeth, his fingers tightened around the log hook. He refused to leave the bloody thing behind when he had no other weapon. Now he carried his makeshift club in front of him, his fluid mood swinging between exhaustion and righteous rage.

Vic flowed through the dark beside him, his features lit by pale moonlight. The revelation forced Johnathan to catalog all the little details he had to have arbitrarily dismissed once he'd decided Vic wasn't a suspect. The man did possess a near preternatural grace, the absence of regular breaths, and such stillness. Humans fidgeted constantly. Even when they attempted to be still, some part of their body twitched or rippled, a body ready for fight or flight. Vampires lacked that impulse.

Johnathan clenched his jaw hard. Except Vic had fidgeted in the presence of Alyse, and he could have sworn he even saw Vic breathe. That he didn't see those small actions now meant the fiend no longer possessed the need to pretend.

His eye twitched as irritation filled him.

"You're very good," he said to Vic. It was the first words he'd spoken since they departed the sawmill.

Vic's shoulders hunched. "I feel that is not a compliment to my character."

Johnathan stopped in the middle of the road, the log hook clasped so tight it bit into his palms. "You've been playing me this whole time—"

Vic stepped into his space. A hand reached up to silence him but Johnathan jerked back, his expression murderous.

Vic's hand stopped in midair. "Not here, damn you." He appeared apprehensive.

Johnathan scoffed. "Worried about your reputation with the gentle townsfolk?"

Anger flashed mirror-bright in Vic's eyes. He shoved at Johnathan's chest. Not a hard blow, but enough to make him stagger back a step.

"You have no idea how hard I've worked for their trust, you pig-headed, overgrown lout!"

Johnathan rubbed his chest, thoroughly confused. Vic could have laid him out with a flick of his fingers. Why hold back now? And the idea of a vampire concerned with trust issues of the ignorant citizens? He could practically hear Sir Harry cackling in his rotted grave.

"They're your food."

"They're *my people*," Vic snapped.

Johnathan's frown deepened. Nothing about Vic fit what he knew of fiends. They didn't possess a reverence for life. Humans were prey, or tools at best, a distinction Johnathan intimately understood. And yet...

He sighed. "Where then?"

Vic squinted up at him. "Will you accept a truce in my home?"

Johnathan's nostrils flared. The vampire didn't seem to have a high opinion of him either. "The truce stands until you give me a reason to break it."

Vic stepped back and straightened his long coat, effectively covering his torn, bloodied trousers. "Then we have an accord."

It was Johnathan's turn to invade Vic's space, towering over the vampire. "I fully expect you to give me a reason."

Vic had the gall to roll his eyes. "Brute." He slid around Johnathan before he could sputter a response. "Come along, you big idiot."

Johnathan vibrated from the urge to do violence. He inhaled a deep breath. He would see this truce through if for no other reason than to solve the puzzle that was Vic.

The ride back was marked by pregnant silence. Johnathan sat ramrod straight, so tense every bump in the road shot straight up his backside. Between that and the protest in his shoulder, he was one big bruise by the time they settled across from one another at Vic's dining table.

Johnathan set the log hook down with a muted clatter and traced the wood grain. His anger and confusion continued to tangle in his gut. He didn't know where to look, how to act, and no training prepared him for this situation. Vampires were to be eliminated. They were tricksters who killed without remorse or guilt and certainly were not open to negotiations.

Vic set his hands flat on the table across from Johnathan, a movement that accented his finely manicured nails. Johnathan gnawed on his inner cheek.

The hands bothered him worst of all.

"Where to begin?" Vic kept his tone light.

Johnathan finally glanced up and saw the vampire was completely at a loss. The tension didn't abate, but he felt a notch better at the knowledge Vic wasn't prepared for this situation either.

"In the mill, you said 'this isn't how I wanted to do this.'" Johnathan drummed his fingers on the table. "What, exactly, did you mean by that?"

Vic fidgeted. His hands came off the table, fingers tapping together in a tell-tale sign of nerves. Johnathan blinked at him, startled by the apparent unconscious action. A vampire who fidgeted. *This made no ruddy sense!*

"Approaching a member of the Society is a complicated task for someone like me."

Johnathan tensed. Several revelations ticked over in his mind. Vic had known who and what he was the second he stepped foot in Cress Haven.

What an utter disaster. If their situation hadn't taken such a wretched turn, the Society would never pass him for his utter failure to recognize a vampire two feet from him. Had Dr. Evans known what Johnathan was walking into? *Possibly.* He must have known Vic was here if nothing else. If Vic was the summation of his test, Johnathan spectacularly failed.

"Damn." Johnathan flopped back hard against the high-backed chair. He glared at Vic. "You set a trap."

"No." Vic looked up, his expression oddly earnest. "I sent the letter that brought you here."

Johnathan's jaw dropped. "Why would you—how could you? What was your intent?"

Vic swallowed and smoothed his hands over the table, the gesture so benignly human it distracted Johnathan until the vampire spoke. "You saw the girl. What happened to her. She's not the first. And I don't think these incidents are isolated to Cress Haven." He met Johnathan's gaze. "I don't know what to look for, how to track another predator like this. I wouldn't have spotted that claw in the gore. Or that symbol burned into her body. I would never think to look."

"You want...a Hunter's help?"

Vic huffed a self-deprecative chuckle at the incredulity in Johnathan's voice. "A measure of desperation and insanity, I assure you."

"They would never have listened to you," said Johnathan. His superiors would have killed Vic on the spot, whether they had a beast to contend with or not.

So why hadn't they?

Vic shrugged. "*You're* listening."

A pit of dread flooded Johnathan's gut. He'd hesitated to kill a vampire, *again*. The Society wouldn't stop at failing him. They would cast him out, if he was lucky. There was always the Judas Choice, a lethal concoction of poison and dead man's blood, to weaken them, in case a Prospective was in the process of transition. It was a less-than-honorable death for those the Society deemed as traitors to their cause and traitors to humanity. His anger waned in the face of such a resolution.

He rubbed his jaw. "A failing I can't seem to correct."

Vic went twitchy. Johnathan was beginning to recognize the tell. The vampire was about to say something he feared would set off Johnathan's temper.

"I thought it was because you were a rookie," said Vic. "Not what I hoped to contend with, but you showed so much promise at the scene I thought it would work."

"How did you know I was a rookie?"

Vic's features scrunched up in a very juvenile expression, like a child caught with their hand in the sweet bin. "About that." He fished something from the pocket of his coat and set it down on the table with precise movements.

Johnathan's wallet, which contained his money and identity papers. Vic tapped a finger on the leather and pushed up the coin concealed inside the inner pocket. The symbolic cast coin given to all Society Prospectives in their first year of service to identify them to other members throughout the country. Dr. Evans always pressed them to keep it on their person.

Another detail of this assignment he'd half-assed. The sinking sensation of absolute failure weighed in his gut.

Johnathan looked up at Vic. The vampire. The one responsible for this madness. The one who brought him to this godforsaken backwater town. Who dragged him into this supernatural mess of murdered girls and beasts who burst into ash. The one who'd played him from the moment he set foot into Cress Haven.

His temper erupted.

Johnathan shoved his chair back and vaulted over the table. He left the log hook where it was to contend with the vampire barehanded. His mind was a blank buzz of rage as he grabbed Vic.

It didn't matter that Vic could rip his throat out in seconds, or how outmatched in strength he was against the fiend. He was furious, stripped down to basic schoolyard instincts as he yanked the vampire from his chair into a headlock.

"You selfish bastard," Johnathan shouted.

"Really now? We were having a civilized conversation," said Vic, his words slurred through his pinched cheeks.

"Was this a bloody game to you?"

"This is just undignified."

"You've ruined my life." Johnathan's voice broke. *The second vampire to do so.*

Vic went very still. His eyes slid sideways to glance at Johnathan's face. Whatever he saw there made Vic sigh into his armpit.

"That was not my intent, John."

A throat cleared across the room, one of feminine impatience. "What exactly is going on here?"

Both men froze and looked up. Alyse Shaw glared at the pair of them, arms crossed as she tapped a foot on the floor. Each footfall made Johnathan and Vic flinch.

"Just working through a disagreement, my dear," said Vic through a mouthful of Johnathan's shirt.

My dear? Johnathan shook him. "Does she know, too?"

"Of course she does. You think I could keep something like that from her?"

Alyse gasped. "You *told* him?"

"He didn't have a choice," snarled Johnathan.

Alyse's gaze darted, noting Vic's bloodied clothes and Johnathan's less-than-presentable appearance. "What happened?"

"Perhaps we could resume our discussion?" Vic piped up from under Johnathan's arm.

Johnathan's temper dissipated, and it dawned on him that he had an impossibly patient vampire in a headlock. His mouth went dry. He released Vic, who stepped back with his hands up in a gesture of surrender.

Johnathan stared at him, baffled. "I don't understand you."

Alyse snorted. "That makes two of us." She moved beside Vic, her lips pursed as she tugged at the slash in his pants. "He saw you healing. What predicament did you two land in?"

"We had a chance encounter with our mysterious quarry," said Vic.

Alyse bounced on the balls of her feet. "You did? Did you recognize it? Was it terrible? What happened to it?"

Vic righted his chair and slumped into it. "I did. No, I didn't recognize it. It was quite dreadful. And John, here, dispatched it."

"He did?" She looked at him, eyes nearly popping out of her skull.

"Your confidence is overwhelming," sneered Johnathan. *She* didn't have to know he managed it purely by accident, or possibly not at all.

He picked up his toppled chair as he studied the pair with measured distrust. It would be daft to trust them. But what other options did he have left? He could crawl back to the Society and deal with the fallout of his failure. Why did Vic allow the headlock? Why let Johnathan live at all? Was he truly so desperate for aid?

"What did you find out?" Vic's question pulled Alyse's attention off Johnathan, a question that quenched her rabid curiosity. Her expression fell.

"You were right," she said and tapped a pile of handwritten notes on the table.

Vic closed his eyes. "I've never wanted to be more wrong."

Alyse crouched in front of him and pressed her forehead to his, their bowed heads communicating a quiet grief.

Johnathan glanced between them, caught up in their damned intimacy once again. "Right about what?"

Alyse looked to Vic first, a question in her eyes. Vic nodded.

"The latest victim wasn't from here," Alyse said, "but from Hampshire, a town fifty miles away. I don't know whether she was brought here or lured—"

The word made Johnathan's muscles go taut. The chair creaked in his grip.

"—but she was the second girl to go missing from Hampshire. There were at least nine reports all told from this region over the past year, six which took place in the last three months."

Vic stroked his upper lip, his expression distant. "Why the sudden increase?"

Johnathan scowled. The same thought occurred to him. He wanted nothing to do with this mystery, felt tricked into it, but the dead girl's face flashed through his mind. So young, so terribly young. And the distance between the murders meant there was likely more than one beast out there, running these girls down.

"How old was she?" Johnathan ignored the shared glance between Alyse and Vic.

"Not yet fifteen," said Alyse, her voice careful and slow, like she were coaxing a wounded animal. In a way, she was. "Most of the girls weren't a day over eighteen. Their features vary, this one just happened to bear a striking resemblance to, ah, me."

"What else?" Johnathan asked as a dreadful theory took root.

Alyse appeared puzzled by his question. "What do you mean?"

"Patterns, commonalities. What did these girls share?"

She pursed her lips. "Not certain about all of them, but the girls from here, and the ones in Hampshire, would be considered debutantes if they lived in the city proper."

Wealthy then, and sheltered. Country or city, the wealthy families apparently treated their daughters like delicate crystal decor.

"Virgins," said Johnathan. A blush burned the back of his neck.

Vic's gaze snapped to him. "What?"

Alyse raised a brow. "You can't possibly know that."

"No, he couldn't, though Stebbins noted as such in his autopsy notes before the bodies dissolved to ashes," said Vic. "It's likely the other girls dissolved before they were found." His sentence made her lose all color.

"They never found the other girls, none of them," she whispered.

Vic subtly leaned toward her. "What else did you find?"

Johnathan tuned them out and stared at his hands. They were not well trimmed and manicured like Vic's, or clean and kept like Alyse's. There were a fighter's hands, scarred and calloused. He turned over his injured palm, the blackened circle of flesh nearly forgotten until he held it up to the light.

He was invested in this whether he wanted to be or not. There was no simple retreat to Boston to throw himself to the mercy of the Society. He was a marked man, though for what purpose, and by what manner of creature were still unknowns. His throat felt tight. He wasn't the only one pulled into this against their will.

"What was her name?" he said.

Vic and Alyse's conversation ground to a halt.

"Mary Elizabeth," said Alyse.

We are connected, Mary Elizabeth and I, thought Johnathan. She would no longer be a nameless phantom who haunted his dreams. His fingers curled, the pad of his forefinger pressed against the black circle. Did it feel warmer than the rest of him, or was that a product of his imagination? Were the others marked beforehand? Is that how the creature found them? What on earth was it? And why this manner of death? Why did the bodies turn to ash? Why did the creature turn to ash when he struck it? The questions piled up without end.

He lowered his hands and eyed Vic. "What do you propose we do, vampire?"

Alyse glared at Johnathan, but Vic perked up, clearly surprised by his words. Johnathan was rather surprised himself. He would be an outcast back in Boston, *if* he survived Cress Haven.

"Form a partnership," said Vic. "We work together, share information and theories while solving the mystery. We protect one another." He watched Johnathan as he spoke.

"And what happens after? If we survive, that is?"

"We go our separate ways." Vic's smile was bitter. "I may have to relocate or rest with one eye open after you return to your people."

"Oh, this," Johnathan motioned between them, "will never be mentioned to the Society."

"Trust me, we won't mention you again either," said Alyse.

Johnathan's leg bounced up and down in a quick, anxious rhythm. Was he truly considering this? A partnership between nemeses? His leg went still. Could Johnathan do this on his own? Vic brought strength, speed, and preternatural healing to the fight. He was an asset Johnathan couldn't ignore against such a dangerous, unknown enemy.

Johnathan sighed. "All cards on the table. Anything else you care to share?" There was a sour note in his voice.

Alyse shifted in her seat. "Well—"

Vic's hand landed on her thigh. She went still, cheeks a brilliant red.

"Nothing of importance," said the vampire.

Johnathan clenched his jaw. Really, they were still going to keep something from him? Was the matter inconsequential enough to let it slide? If he were being honest, there were things he kept close to the vest as well. One never dealt all their cards when the partnership was so skewed, but that meant not hinting that one still withheld information. Alyse would make a terrible gambler. He would have to press the young lady another time, without Vic's guiding hand to stay her words.

He extended his unmarked hand, which Vic clasped in a firm, cool grip.

"I'm in."

CHAPTER ELEVEN

ALYSE LEFT FOR HOME SHORTLY AFTER THEY REACHED AN ACCORD, assured Johnathan wouldn't decapitate or skewer Vic without good reason. She might refer to herself as a "near spinster," but her absence from the pastor's household for any length of time was too apparent. Johnathan admittedly regretted her departure. She made him uncomfortable, but she was human.

And Vic was not.

The knowledge sat between them, unseemly, unsightly, and now, painfully obvious. Johnathan mentally berated himself for missing the blatant little signs, though he suspected he hadn't noticed them before because they weren't there. How was Vic in such control of his hunger? How did he conceal that preternatural grace so well?

A quiet tension wound through Johnathan, but he kept his face carefully blank. Would a more seasoned acolyte of the Society have picked up on the signs? His gaze strayed to Vic's fingernails, not only glossy and well-manicured, but without a hint of dead man's hands. How did the fiend hide one of the key physical signs of vampirism? The internal differences were another matter, but the discolored nails were a surefire sign, a signature of vampiric nature that kept the Society from unfortunate mistakes. A vampire might try to disguise the discoloration with dyes or ink, but that itself was a tell for further scrutinization.

No, Johnathan was certain his fellow Prospectives would take one look at Vic's hands and dismiss him as a potential vampire. That was a small comfort, but the mystery of it was a constant distraction from the true matter at hand.

Johnathan drummed an annoyed beat on the table.

Vic eased back in his chair with fluid grace, studying Johnathan in turn. His clothing was barely rumpled from their brief scuffle, the homespun linen shirt plain but well made, neatly tucked into a pair of loose dark pants that tightened around the man's thighs as he crossed his legs. The top buttons of his shirt were undone in careless contrast, a seemingly conscious choice that displayed the full breadth of Vic's pale throat. The easy elegance made Johnathan even more awkward and uncouth in comparison. His oft-hemmed and patched Society hand-me-downs were thoroughly wrinkled between outrunning beasts and wrestling vampires.

Vic's long fingers played along his jaw, drawing Johnathan's gaze. "If you were any more bottled up, I'd expect steam to come streaming out your ears. What's wrong with you?"

In for a penny, in for a pound. If they were going to be working together, there had to be a level of trust and openness between them. Johnathan would take whatever intel the vampire gave him in good faith, and it would remain in good faith unless he felt like explaining the origins of such knowledge to his superiors.

"Your hands. How did you manage to make them look so...pink?"

Still pink, since Vic bled like a stuck pig from the creature's claws, which meant he'd fed since then to replenish? With Johnathan in the house? Had he fed from Alyse? The woman didn't have the slightest weakness in her gait, hale and flush without a hint of blood loss. How was the fiend doing it?

"You mean, why don't I look like an animated corpse?" The vampire raised a brow.

Johnathan flinched. "Not in such impolite terms. But it is the most obvious sign of your condition."

"My condition?" There was a lilt of amusement in Vic's voice as he ran his splayed fingers over his full mouth. "You make it sound like a bothersome cough."

"I'm not used to discussing such matters openly." Johnathan shifted in his seat. "With one of you."

A smirk hid behind Vic's fingers. "Tit for tat. I shall answer your inquiry if you answer mine."

Johnathan went still. That was a dangerous offer, for both of them. "Maybe another time," he murmured.

Vic stared at him, taken aback. Johnathan's answer surprised him. "A man whose curiosity is tempered by what? Fear?"

"I'm not afraid," insisted Johnathan. He wasn't, not really. Truly, he wasn't. There were simply elements of his past that should stay buried. He wasn't afraid.

Vic's eyebrow rose so high it disappeared into his hairline.

"I'm not," snapped Johnathan.

The fiend leaned forward, resting his forearms on the table. There was a gleam of interest in his gray eyes. A strand of auburn hair fell from its queue, brushing along the sharp angles of his cheekbones as he tilted his head at Johnathan. "Now what would I do with your secrets, John?"

Johnathan shifted, uncomfortable with the way Vic looked at him, the tone of the fiend's voice. Far more discomfiting was the flutter in his chest. Much as he despised vampires, certainly this one, an odd warmth rose along his skin when Vic's gaze roved over him.

Johnathan swallowed hard and huffed through his nostrils, shaking off the fleeting feeling. "Fine. Three questions, three answers."

His gut churned. This was a bad idea.

Vic leaned in. "I don't take blood from the vein," he said with a conspiratorial wink.

Johnathan blinked. "Oh come now, you can't leave it at that, and I'm not going to waste three questions on how you feed."

Vic's expression couldn't be mistaken for anything but delight. "And you are clearly more than a pretty slab of muscle."

The description made him blush, but also made a muscle jump between his shoulder blades. Sir Harry used to call him pretty, one of the many descriptors he used for Johnathan. It was definitely confusing to hear the word now because, for some reason, he liked hearing the word from Vic's mouth.

"This is better explained with visuals than words." Vic rose to his feet with a flourish and flowed from the room in full predatory grace.

Johnathan's gaze locked on those familiar movements. He swallowed through the sudden painful tightness in his throat, quick to reassert a passive mask when Vic sauntered back into the room with a roll of bulky leather. However, he could not conceal his perplexed expression as the vampire unfurled the roll to reveal a collection of instruments, familiar yet not.

Johnathan picked up one of the glass tubes with care, examining the curiously fat needle. "It's hollow," he said.

A hollow needle that fed into a glass vial, a syringe, though he'd never seen one with a needle like this. The plunger served the twofold purpose of creating suction for extraction and pressure for injection.

"What is this?" A note of curious wonder tinted Johnathan's voice, and the vampire grinned.

Another oddity of the vampire clicked into place. Vic's fangs were smaller than most, fine delicate points that blended in his smile, their size seeming almost human at first glance, which is why Johnathan hadn't noticed them until he'd had cause to look for them.

"It's a syringe."

Johnathan made a face. "I meant *this* part, dolt."

"Ah, yes, of course," said Vic. "The hollow needles were developed in Europe in the last couple of years, but they aren't quite commonly used in the Americas yet. I purchased them from a fine German merchant, with a hefty commission for future stock."

Johnathan stared at the device. Summoned from the abyss of a dream, a hazy memory rose from the other night, one so convoluted it took him a moment to unravel its meaning. "You inject the blood directly to your vein, by way of your thigh."

Vic nodded. "I wondered if you'd ever remember that."

"I didn't quite remember until now," Johnathan admitted.

Vic tapped a needle against the pad of his finger. "It gives me easy access to the femoral artery. I've found this method maintains a great deal of vitality over traditional methods of consumption. Hence the lack of dead man's fingers."

"Don't you still hunger?" Johnathan blurted.

"That counts as two."

"Bugger."

A small smile played on Vic's lips. "I find myself driven by...*other* appetites."

"Other appetites. What other...*oh*." Johnathan's blush burned up through his ears.

The vampire chuckled. "How did the Society snatch up someone like you?"

Now Johnathan was truly puzzled. "I don't understand."

Vic opened his mouth and paused. He closed it with an audible click of teeth, pondering how to explain. "You're bright red at the hint of intimate relations, but you were completely unfazed by the torn-open body of a young woman. What sort of upbringing did you have before the Society brought you into the fold?"

Just the sort of question he wanted to avoid. "Not a pleasant one."

Vic snorted. "Oh, come now, you berated me for being vague."

Johnathan's jaw tightened. Dr. Evans lectured at length that the key to lies was partial truth. "My guardian was a violent, controlling brute who kept me half-starved to draw sympathy when we begged for scraps." It was truth, though incomplete in the details. "The Society saved me from a life of starvation and abuse."

"They do like to present themselves as the white hats," said Vic. "Swooping in to save the local youths from lives of petty crimes. Teach them to kill vampires without questioning orders, like a pack of well-trained dogs."

"Vampires are monsters," Johnathan said, choosing to keep the fact that his guardian had been of Vic's ilk to himself.

Vic settled into that preternatural stillness his kind were infamous for, an unreadable expression on his face, though Johnathan thought he saw a shadow of sadness there. "I am a monster to you?"

The affirmation sat bitter in his mouth. It was a simple matter to say yes, but he was in a far from simple situation. "Why did you save me?"

The vampire grinned. "A question for a question is cheating."

"Maybe I can't answer one without the other," said Johnathan. "You play human better than any vampire I've ever seen, but you exposed yourself to save me from our mystery foe."

Vic rolled his shoulders in a careless shrug. "Not necessarily. You might have explained it away as a trick of the mind. People are very good at deceiving themselves. Or perhaps I had no choice. You caught me healing."

Johnathan couldn't stop an incredulous snort. "You *let* me catch you healing."

"Your certainty in my skills of deception is heartening, but this is the truth." Vic looked away, appearing almost flustered. If he was human, he might have blushed. "I was caught off guard. You could have left me there, in the road—"

"I'm not some coward who abandons his comrades at the first sign of blood," Johnathan snapped.

"Of course not. You're the sort to risk life and limb to carry them to safety, even if they are a stranger to you. Whether you realize it or not, it is something most of your Society brethren would not do." Vic's elegant hands flexed into fists against his thighs. There was an odd lilt to his voice.

Johnathan looked at him sharply, wondering what emotion he'd heard in those words, before the vampire cleared his throat.

Their gazes met, a wariness in Vic's eyes that sent a frisson of curious shock through Johnathan's mind. Flustered as he was, he let the insult to the Society pass, though it made him wonder how many encounters Vic had with them to judge them so harshly.

"I've been assigned to root out the evil hunting this town," Johnathan offered. "It was my duty to protect you. To protect everyone." Though he was far from equipped to do so.

"It was bravery," said Vic. "Stupid bravery, but bravery."

Johnathan sighed and looked away, uncertain how he should react to such sentiment. He pulled the sheaf of Alyse's notes toward him, a welcome distraction from the odd tangle of conversation with Vic. He blindly stared at the girls' names, their descriptions, beneath the weight of Vic's studying gaze.

"You didn't answer my question. Am I a monster to you?"

Johnathan didn't look up. "You didn't really answer mine."

Vic snorted. "I would hate to be the one to interrogate you."

A reluctant smile tugged at the corner of Johnathan's mouth. "I haven't made up my mind yet. I shall inform you when I've compiled all the facts." Begrudgingly, Johnathan also found himself piqued over his shifting opinion of Vic's humanity.

"Ah well, do let me know when you decide," said Vic.

"I assure you, you will be the first to know," said Johnathan.

"I hope that revelation comes without decapitation."

"We shall see." Johnathan frowned as he read over the notes. Not one but two sets compiled by Alyse and the vampire, both far more invested than he expected. Vic kept meticulous, detailed notes in elegant script, while Alyse's looped handwriting tacked on several additions in regard to the girls outside of Cress Haven. He read the description of Mary Elizabeth and the first girl to die in Cress Haven, Lydia Fairchild, over and over, until the oddity clicked in his mind. "What happened to their parents?"

Vic shook his head. "What do you mean?"

Johnathan slid the notes across the table, squinting over them in the candlelight. "You have recorded a full account of their deaths, autopsy details, all the peculiarities of how they were found and what happened to their bodies, witness accounts of who found the bodies and where they were last seen alive, their clothing and appearance. I must commend you; I don't think half the law officials in the city would put forth so much effort." He pressed his forefinger against the paper. "But none of these witness statements include family. These are not poor, destitute women who might not be missed. These girls were found in fine dresses, carefully curled hair. Daughters of well-to-do men. Where are their families?"

A crease appeared between Vic's brows. "That is a glaring detail to miss."

"Neither you nor Alyse mention their families," said Johnathan. "This one, Lydia Fairchild, was local, but no one mentioned her when we found the other body."

Vic pursed his lips. "I believe Lydia Fairchild's status was listed as missing. There could be no body left to recover."

Indeed, there was the note in Alyse's looping cursive. If her body suffered the same fate as the girl in the morgue, there would be no reason for the villagers to think otherwise. If they'd discovered her body in the aftermath, no one would think it more than the leavings of some careless campfire. Still, the fact no one mentioned that she had gone missing was another point of contention.

Johnathan paused. "Actually, no one in town has appeared overly concerned about the murders and missing girls."

"I...I didn't notice as such," said Vic, though the vampire appeared to mull over the observation. "I don't think I've been worried about it as much as I should have either."

"Doesn't that strike you as odd?"

Vic rolled his eyes. "Well, it does now."

Johnathan hesitated. "Do you think it's people deceiving themselves, explaining away the unnatural?"

"No, this—this is something else. It's not easy to deceive the senses of a vampire." Vic rose, a thoughtful expression on his face. "There's someone we need to talk to, but it might take a couple days to pin them down."

The vague statement irritated Johnathan but he left it alone for now. There was a more pressing question to answer. "In the meantime, we need to find out why these parents aren't fighting for their girls. We need to talk to the families."

"Then we start local," said Vic. "With the first victim in Cress Haven, Lydia Fairchild."

Johnathan nodded. "Let's go."

"What? No." Vic pulled a face. "It's the middle of the night, John."

He blinked. Was it really? He'd lost track of time in the aftermath of their encounter and revelations. It felt like days passed rather than hours. The reminder allowed the events of the night to catch up to him in a punch of exhaustion. He pinched the bridge of his nose, the sharp spike of pain behind his eyes insistent. He needed rest.

"Right, right, on the morrow then."

"You, get some sleep, and that is an order." Vic made for the front door.

"Where are you off to?"

"Don't trust me?"

"Not even a little," said Johnathan.

Vic's smile was close lipped. "I told you, I need to find someone, but I have to do so alone. And I can go with far less rest than you. Good night, John."

Johnathan stayed where he was long after the door creaked shut, lost in his thoughts. It was the town's apathy that bothered him. It felt like a symptom of the creature that hunted Cress Haven, a dangerous one. If nothing else decided him before of his inadequacy to deal with their foe, it was this detail. If the vampire's mysterious contact failed to pan out, there was only one other source of information and manpower capable of rooting this monster out, one he knew they couldn't ignore. The Society taught them to hunt vampires, but Dr. Evans must have seen and dealt with many odd creatures during his tenure.

Johnathan swore as he dug for a fresh sheet of paper. He spent the better part of the night starting and stopping the letter. It was a seemingly impossible task to put his predicament into words, while also protecting the pact he'd made with the fiend. And Johnathan found he *did* want to keep his word to both Vic and Alyse, to protect them from the attentions of the Society, though he wasn't certain of his feelings on the matter.

He finally finished his carefully worded report just before dawn, managing to strip off his filthy coat and shirt before crawling to bed to the first hint of birdsong. Vic still hadn't returned. Johnathan fought the pull of sleep.

He held up his hand, studying the blackened wound. In the course events, he'd failed to mention the change to the vampire. Despite his palm's rather grisly appearance, the lack of pain led him to often forget about it, with so much else to preoccupy his mind.

He sighed, letting his arm flop back down to his side. He would have to bring it to Vic's attention sooner rather than later. As it was, he'd forfeited a solid rest to write the damned report that he dreaded sending. Johnathan hoped his exhaustion would, at least, grant him a dreamless rest.

He wasn't that lucky.

CHAPTER TWELVE

"*MISTRESS MARY, QUITE CONTRARY, HOW DOES YOUR GARDEN GROW?* *With silver bells and cockle shells, and lady bells all in a row.*" Sir Harry ran his nails through Johnathan's blond curls as he sang in a low, breathy baritone. "*See all the lady bells, Johnny, up and down the row. Which one shall we pluck tonight?*"

Johnathan shivered, the result of Sir Harry's cool, stale breath and chilled touch. The vampire rose above him, an icy shadow that eclipsed his world in a tomb-like embrace. Sir Harry clasped Johnathan to him, the possessive gesture not lost on the boy he was once, or the man he was now.

"How about that one, Johnny? I bet she tastes like candied fruit." Sir Harry chuckled when the young lady caught sight of him. She hid her blush behind a parasol, her pace quickening even though her eyes lingered. Their gazes often lingered on Sir Harry until they truly saw him. He was a beautiful monster. But once they saw the predator staring back at them, they scurried away.

They never saw a predator when they looked at Johnathan.

He shifted in Sir Harry's hold, a feeble attempt to ward off the chill, but the grip only tightened.

"Or that one, Johnny my sweet?" said Sir Harry, pointing. "She must taste like a fine claret."

An older, handsome woman crossed the street alone, lifting her skirts out of the mud, high enough to reveal her threadbare stockings. It was a detail Johnathan focused on, a sense of kinship for a woman who exuded a facade of wealth to hide the poverty of her underclothes. He understood a mask like that, the necessity of it. The longer he lived in Sir Harry's shadow, the more cracked his mask became.

"Oooh, Johnny, sweet Johnny, how does my garden grow?" A feminine voice breathed in his ear.

That wasn't Sir Harry.

Images flickered before him. The dream shifted from memory to something fresh and far more sinister. The arm that curled around him was no longer a man's arm but a lady's, pale and delicate, her skin near translucent in the light so it seemed to glow. Small breasts pressed against his back as she draped herself over him, until her glossy curls tumbled in a dark wave over his shoulder.

"With fine powder ash, and dead man's blood under the new moon," she purred into his ear.

Johnathan quaked, unable to move. His eyes focused on the face half-revealed beneath the curtain of dark hair. Mary Elizabeth curled her fingers over his chest, her fingernails impossibly sharp, like talons. He jumped as they pricked his skin. She tilted her head to look at him, her eyes matte, without a glimmer of life while her free hand stroked the side of his face.

"Why are you so scared of me, sweet boy? I'm not the monster here." She nodded her chin across the street. He didn't want to look away from her, terrified what he would see.

He couldn't stop himself. The muscles in his neck creaked from his resistance. He sucked in a breath. A creature waited for his gaze in the shadows, watched him with eyes like blistering coals, big as plums. He knew then, proportionally, something was off with this one, the creature of his nightmare far, far larger than what he'd encountered outside the morgue.

Fear closed in a fist around his heart. Those glowing eyes rose, higher, so much higher than the one he'd fought, taller than Sir Harry. A misshapen clawed foot emerged from the shadows. Johnathan's breath came in short pants. The foot slid forward, dragging the shadows with it, so that it remained half obscured. The passing pedestrians took no notice of the monstrosity, their paths curving around it, mindless of its presence.

The longer he stared, the more details Johnathan saw, but they winked in and out of his mind because he had yet to process the whole. The creature was distorted, unreal, but distinctly lupine, the echo of a misshapen wolf.

"Oh no, sweet one, a wolf answers to its pack. It needs no master," said Mary

Elizabeth in his ear, plucking the thoughts from his mind. Her fingers stroked down his neck. She left a set of burning lines in the wake of her fingers. Warm blood trickled down his neck.

A sound rolled forth from the darkness, like thunder cracking over the roar of a forest fire. Mary Elizabeth made a tutting sound.

"What—what is it?" he asked her.

She laughed, a bell-toned cackle tinged with madness. "It has your scent now."

Her hand snapped down and grabbed his wrist in a punishing grip. Johnathan yelped. The bones of his wrist ground together as she forced his arm up. In the center of his palm, a symbol blazed, a half circle crossed by a line, so that it resembled horns. The same one he saw within Mary Elizabeth's ruined ribcage. Fire licked the underside of his skin.

"Are you strong enough, sweet Johnny?" Her lips brushed his cheek.

The creature opened its maw and lunged.

Johnathan floundered in a tangle of sweat-soaked sheets until his body slid off the edge of the bed and crashed in a heap on the floor. His palms stung where they slapped the wooden boards. He lay there, gulping air, while his sweat cooled to a clammy film on his skin. Johnathan rolled onto his back. He concentrated on funneling his breath through his nose, lifting his closed fist. Clenching his jaw, he forced his fingers to unfurl.

There was no symbol on his palm. The skin was still blackened, except there was something about the discoloration that made him frown. He tentatively rubbed a forefinger over his palm. The heat was gone. The blackness came away in a fine powdery smudge.

"Soot," he murmured.

The bedroom door opened. Johnathan glanced at Vic's polished boots through the underside of the bed.

"John?"

He debated if he should bother saying anything.

"I can hear you breathing," said Vic.

Johnathan let his head fall back on the wooden floorboard with a soft thud. "Right here, fiend." If Vic wasn't going to pretend anymore, why bother at civility?

"As suitable as that term is, please refrain from using it outside of this house." Vic's boots moved around the bed with a dancer's footing, a criss-crossed pattern that made for poor balance but silent steps.

Johnathan squinted. If he ever needed to take Vic down, he'd go for the legs first.

The vampire's beautiful face leered at him from the foot of the bed. "What are you doing on the floor, John?" He made a show of perusing Johnathan's prone form. "You look like hell warmed over."

"Flatterer," Johnathan mumbled. Vic was the picture of a perfect gentleman, having exchanged his more relaxed look for a tight-fitting gray vest and dark overcoat that leant his slim frame some width and accented the brilliance of his hair.

The vampire extended a hand. "Come on, up you get."

Johnathan hesitated only a moment before accepting the offer. Vic started to haul him up. Johnathan couldn't help himself. His leg snapped out in a practiced movement while he twisted Vic's wrist. The vampire's eyes widened a fraction before he went down. The surprised whoosh of air leaving his lungs was quite satisfying.

Vic rolled to his side. Strands of auburn hair framed his expression, torn between peeved and amused. He blew the hair out of his face. "Was there a point to that exercise?"

Johnathan shrugged. "Made me feel better." He sat up, dragging the vampire with him so that they faced each other.

For a moment they paused, staring at one another, only inches apart. Vic's lips parted. This close, Johnathan could see the vampire's pupils dilate, his pulse ticking up several notches in response. He was still holding onto Vic's forearms, the muscles tense beneath his touch.

Abruptly letting go, he shook himself. "You are quiet on those tippy toes, but completely unbalanced. A toddler could flip you if they caught you off guard." His voice was too light, as if he just barely held back *something* that strained for release.

Vic laughed but caught himself, his expression turning somber. "We have serious business to attend to, John. Remember, murders, mystery beasts, and such. Are you done tossing me to the floor?"

"You done prancing around like a stage fencer?"

"My, you are surly in the morning." Vic titled his face upward. A vee creased his brow as his nostrils flared. "It smells like fire in here."

Johnathan's skin pricked.

He flexed his injured hand, debating whether to draw Vic's attention to the oddity. Ah, yes, he remembered. He needed to tell Vic about the change in the wound and about the dream. Except...

He blinked, once, twice, his thoughts dissipating like vapor.

That need curled like a wisp of smoke in the back of his mind. What had he been thinking again? Whatever it was seemed like such an insignificant thing now. In fact, the more he thought about it, the less concerned he grew, especially when there were more pressing matters at hand.

"Is Lydia Fairchild's residence within walking distance?" With the brilliant sunlight streaming through the nearby window, he craved a nice brisk walk.

Vic sniffed again and shrugged, brushing an errant smudge of soot off his sleeve. "No, it's on the opposite side of the town, out past Pastor Shaw's home. Their property borders the forest." Vic rolled to his feet with ridiculous ease. This time he didn't offer a hand, but his gaze did rove over Johnathan's bare chest. He cleared his throat. "I'll leave you to get dressed."

The vampire's gaze lingered long enough to make Johnathan blush to the roots of his hair.

He waited to rise until the vampire sauntered out of the room. Unsure how he felt about Vic ogling him, he winced through the usual crack and creak of his morning routine. Johnathan had a fighter's body, and that came with all the collective damage of one.

After a quick stretch, he went to wash, pausing at the sight of smeared soot on his palm. The ash came off with a quick scrub, revealing smooth, unmarred skin. Johnathan froze. The memory surged, ricocheted through his skull. Urgency flared to life even as a strange sense of malaise attempted to bog it down. Where was the wound? If he closed his eyes, he could still see the symbol glowing there, hear Mary Elizabeth's imagined sing-song voice and her manic laughter.

"That was a dream, just a dream," he whispered. Who did he think he was kidding? The wound was there, and now it was not. Part of him recognized he was on a collision course with the monster he'd glimpsed in his nightmares. Or didn't quite see. It was frustrating enough to make one tear their hair out, but every impulse he had to tell the vampire made his muscles lock in place. Johnathan braced his arms on either side of the wash basin, staring down at his rippling reflection, a muddied mirror of his thoughts. The internal tugging grew more insistent, a low, humming, barely heard whisper he couldn't help but focus on, desperate to hear what it said. Already he could feel the importance plucked away, until the water went still with his thoughts...

Johnathan had a job to do. He snagged the letter he'd written last night and tucked it into his vest, then made his way out of the house, pausing to add one item to his arsenal. Vic waited for him at the carriage. His ruffled hair was smoothed back and tied at the nape of his neck, clothes pressed to impress their country gentry audience, which made Johnathan's roughly spun clothing all the more obvious.

Still, Johnathan's face was washed, and his shirt was tucked in. He could have presented a worse picture. Vic handed Johnathan a cold sausage in a bun.

"Keep your strength up," said Vic. He clucked his tongue against the back of his teeth, and the placid horse pulled them into motion.

"What an absurd thing to say." Johnathan bit into the bun, a medley of soft yeasted bread and cooked pork with melty bits of fat. Dear god, it was the best thing he'd ever tasted. He finished it in three bites.

"Absurd? I don't follow?"

Johnathan swallowed his mouthful before answering. No need for Vic to find him more uncouth than he already did. "What's the point? Between you, the mystery beast, and the Society, I doubt I'll live long enough for my 'strength' to matter one way or another." Oh dear, he sounded resentful. His fitful nights were eating at him more than he could even admit to himself.

Vic was quiet for a moment. "I thought I made it clear last night. Death won't come from my corner. And I won't betray your cooperation with one of my ilk to your precious Society." His eyes were steely slits as he glanced at Johnathan. "So you only need to worry your pretty, thick head about one out of three."

Johnathan visibly flinched. The sausage bun soured in his gut. "Don't call me that."

Vic snorted. "I apologize. You aren't an idiot, but you're far too stubborn for your health."

Johnathan left it at that, unwilling to clarify which word bothered him. Vic's presence had to be the reason his memories of Sir Harry seemed to be stirring in earnest. Exhaustion and frustration were uneven scales on his shoulders, teetering and tottering for dominance. He needed to change the subject. "What do we know about the Fairchilds?"

Vic hissed softly through his teeth but answered in an even tone. "Do you remember the location of our lovely showdown last night?"

How could he forget? He'd swiped the log hook off the table, determined not to be caught out unarmed again. It now sat heavy inside his coat. Perhaps he should make a harness for it or something. It was rather cumbersome and dug into his ribs.

"Well, you might be interested to know Mr. Fairchild owned the mill until recently," Vic continued. "He sold it off shortly before his daughter went missing."

Johnathan looked at him. "Before? Not after?"

Vic nodded. "I double-checked to be sure."

Johnathan tapped the log hook through the top layer of coarse wool. To sell such a lucrative business *after* the disappearance of their child would make more sense. He wondered what drove Mr. Fairchild to part with his business, particularly in a town where a livelihood was so integral to survival and home comforts.

"Were there any notes in the sale transference papers to indicate the reason?"

Vic shook his head. "You can add it to the questions we shall ask Mr. Fairchild."

CHAPTER THIRTEEN

JOHNATHAN KEPT A WATCHFUL EYE ON THE TOWN AS THEY PASSED through. The townspeople went on about their day, with work, with errands, with gossip, and all the usual facets of town life. He caught snippets of conversation, mentions of the latest wares to arrive by coach delivery, who was sleeping with who, who committed some gaffe or another, but not a single mention of the dead girl found in the middle of their streets. Not a whisper of missing girls or a call for action. There was something fundamentally wrong with the lack of conversation on the matter. Johnathan knew how small-town news functioned. A matter like this should have consumed the gossipmongers. The names of the dead girls should be on the lips of every housewife and ale house patron. That it was not proved how deeply rooted the problem was in Cress Haven.

Johnathan called for Vic to stop outside the boarding house tavern. The building served another purpose as Cress Haven's post office. He passed along a hefty tip to Mrs. Meech for his letter to be sent with the afternoon coach. Rejoining Vic, he pushed the letter from his mind. It was a precautionary measure, something he would be foolish not to take. Johnathan was certain his unease had nothing to do with his tenuous agreement with the vampire, nothing at all.

The coach continued through the town proper, following a road that took them past the church and the Shaw household. The venerable pastor himself was outside the church, tending the grounds with meticulous care, surrounded by two boys and a girl who were Alyse's younger siblings. Pastor Shaw nodded to Vic's coach as they passed, a neutral expression on his heavily lined face. Johnathan waited until they were long out of ear shot before he spoke.

"Does that man have any notion of your relationship with his daughter?" Johnathan frowned at himself. What did it matter if Alyse placed herself in an untoward position with the vampire? It wasn't like she was coerced or had no grasp over her faculties. He doubted Alyse could be forced into any sort of relationship, be it with a vampire or the Devil himself. The question was, why did he feel the need to broach the subject with Vic?

"Why, John, do you believe I am compromising the innocent Miss Shaw?" The smallest hint of sarcasm resonated in the vampire's voice.

"It is not my business to question the nature of your relationship with Miss Shaw," Johnathan said through his teeth. "I inquire to the level of your restraint. It would be a shame for the good pastor to be caught unaware at the sudden loss of his child."

Vic paused, his voice touched with ice when he spoke. "I don't know what I find to be the greater insult, that you thought I lied about the handling of my appetites, or that you consider me so careless with a bed partner that I would break them in a moment of passion."

Johnathan couldn't help but notice that Vic didn't confirm whether Alyse was his bed partner or not. Unwilling to back down from the argument, Johnathan said, "You have a predator's nature. That is not so easily stymied despite honorable intentions." Even as the words left his mouth, he knew how they sounded.

Vic ground his teeth together and tightened his hands on the reins until the leather whined. "This might be difficult for you, Johnathan, but attempt to stifle your tendency to be an absolute prick in the presence of the Fairchilds."

Johnathan knew he should have left well enough alone, especially with Vic watching his back in this matter. The ghost of Sir Harry lingered in his thoughts, laughing at his failed dealings with the vampire.

Vic was not Sir Harry, and Johnathan needed to separate the two in his mind.

The coach drew to a stop outside of the town proper, at a painted Dutch colonial. At first glance, the structure of the house and the surrounding grounds spoke of wealth in a league above the majority of residents in Cress Haven, but the grounds bore evidence of inattention, overgrown and choked with weeds.

The house itself was a silent sentinel to their arrival, not a hint of movement within from any household staff or the Fairchilds themselves. Vic appeared undeterred by the lack of reception. He smoothly dismounted from the coach.

Johnathan hesitated, his eyes on the multitude of windows that faced the road, the windowpanes broader and more open than he was used to seeing in a house of that structure. A lot of glass for a country house, specially this far north, on the fringe of the wilderness. The Fairchilds must have brought wealth with them before acquiring the lumber mill, perhaps inherited wealth, though that didn't account for Mr. Fairchild's change of heart regarding his business property.

Johnathan slid from the coach and sped up to match the vampire's pace. Nobody in the house stirred to greet them. Peculiar, a house this size usually boasted a small staff, someone to intercept visitors before they reached the door.

Johnathan didn't like it. The grounds felt stale and still.

"I'm sorry. I shouldn't have lashed out at you." Johnathan spoke softly; the atmosphere called for silence.

Vic's pace remained steady, but he peered at Johnathan from the corner of his eye. "How did you sleep last night, John?"

Johnathan scowled. Couldn't the fiend just accept an apology for what it was? "Poorly," he bit out, "through no fault of the furnishings, I assure you."

Vic stopped halfway up the path to the door, halting Johnathan's steps with a light touch on his wrist. "I know. I heard you. You talk in your sleep." There was no judgement in Vic's gaze, only concern, which threw Johnathan into a riot of confusion. Concern was the last emotion he expected or wanted from the vampire.

He shrugged off Vic's touch. "This is neither the time nor the place for this discussion, Vic." He didn't snap, too unbalanced by the shift in Vic's demeanor to put any real irritation into his words. He glanced at the silent house. "Are you certain the Fairchilds are present?"

"I can hear their heartbeats," said Vic. That didn't bode well, considering how dead the house seemed. Vic patted Johnathan's shoulder. "Let me lead here?"

Johnathan snorted. "Whatever for?"

"You have the charm of a bulldog." Vic shifted around Johnathan to the Fairchild's front door.

He used the hanging knocker, the sound echoing through the domicile. Johnathan ceased grumbling as the two waited for movement inside. It was possible the Fairchilds would leave their visitors in the lurch. Everything about the premise suggested a family in the depths of mourning, so it was to Johnathan's great surprise when the front door opened.

A woman stood there, her face pale and wan. Bitter lines bracketed her pinched mouth, and shadows haunted her watery blue eyes. Grief telegraphed itself through the lines of her body as she stepped forward and half closed the door behind her.

"Good day, gentlemen," said the woman. "What can I do for you?"

It wasn't an outright dismissal. The woman appeared to have far too much good breeding for that, but her irritation over their visitation was evident in the tension that held her there, a wilted butterfly pinned on display to the weather-worn front door.

Vic bowed his head in a somber gesture, the picture of the charming country gentlemen paying his respects to a neighbor. "Greetings, Mrs. Fairchild. My associate and I understand this is a delicate time for your family, but we were hoping Mr. Fairchild and yourself would be willing to cooperate with information regarding the matter of your daughter?"

Johnathan shuffled a step, the oddity of the situation deepening. This was the lady of the house? Why had she come to greet them herself?

Mrs. Fairchild stared at Vic as if he'd grown a second head. She blinked, a vacant expression settling over her features in a perfected mask. "I'm sorry, I don't know what you mean."

Johnathan frowned. She didn't send them away, but her wording was strange. She knew what Vic spoke of, he could see that in the way her hands clenched the fabric of her skirts, but her eyes bore into Vic, daring him to say the actual words.

Vic cleared his throat. "Pardon us, Mrs. Fairchild. We have been tasked with investigating the missing girls, and your daughter was the first to vanish from Cress Haven."

"But not the first to die," whispered Mrs. Fairchild.

Vic went still. Johnathan glanced from the haggard woman to the vampire, sensing the predatory agitation that surrounded Vic.

"Is that so, Mrs. Fairchild?" Johnathan took a step forward and stopped when she cringed like a mouse caught in the open. "Please, Mrs. Fairchild, we want to find what—" He paused, correcting himself. "Who. We want to find *who* did this to your daughter," he said gently. "We want to stop this from happening to anyone else."

She swallowed. "You can't—can't come in," she stuttered. "Mr. Fairchild isn't home."

Vic sent Johnathan a weighted glance. Johnathan didn't need the obvious gesture. He could hear the lie in her voice. Time to press her for a real reaction.

"Mrs. Fairchild, why did your husband sell the lumber mill before Lydia went missing?" he asked.

The woman staggered, her expression appalled, as if he'd said something obscene. "He...he didn't, he..."

Vic took the opening. He gathered the woman's hands, a touch that drew her attention to him. "Please, Mrs. Fairchild. We only want to see Lydia's room." That wasn't the long and the short of it, but if Vic could charm them inside, it might be enough.

Mrs. Fairchild stared down at their hands, her eyes glassy. A lone tear spilled down her cheek. She seemed to age ten years in seconds as her gaze drifted up to Vic's. "I didn't want this."

Another curious statement, one that hinted Mrs. Fairchild possibly knew far more of the strange events plaguing Cress Haven than either Johnathan or Vic, and that she felt at least a partial responsibility for the fate of her daughter.

She pulled her hands away and opened the door to usher them inside. "Her room faced the woods," said Mrs. Fairchild. "She loved the birdsong and the sight of grazing deer at dawn."

Her tired voice dragged them into the house's suffocating gloom. The air was choked with dust, the windows long shuttered and latched, stale and slightly sour. It gave the impression of a tomb, a mausoleum where Mr. and Mrs. Fairchild continued to reside. There was a creak of floorboards from another section of the house that sent a tick through Mrs. Fairchild's shoulders. She kept moving until they reached Lydia's room, where Mrs. Fairchild unlocked the door.

Why lock it at all?

A cloth had been draped over the mirror, but otherwise the room remained untouched, a shrine to the deceased. Johnathan entered the room first, Vic on his heels.

The vampire leaned in close. "Do you smell it?" he said under his breath.

Mrs. Fairchild hovered at the door, her hands clasped in front of her so tight, the bones of her fingers pressed against the skin. Johnathan caught the scent the moment Vic mentioned it, strong enough even for his human nose. A faint whiff of rotten eggs and ash that teased his senses, a scent that still lingered months after Lydia's disappearance, closed up in her tomb of a room. He nodded.

"I'm going to see what I can pry out of our reluctant hostess," said Vic. "I'll leave you to it, Prospective Newman." He gave Johnathan a mock salute and slid back to Mrs. Fairchild before Johnathan could get his hands on him. "Tell me, what interests did the young Miss Fairchild possess?" The vampire smoothly guided the woman away, which gave Johnathan complete, unobserved access to the room.

The desire to strangle Vic warred with admiration that he'd managed to give Johnathan exactly what he wanted. He refused to give the prat any praise.

Johnathan slowly circled the premise in a methodical perusal of each item, each piece of furniture and article of clothing. The contents created the picture of normality, the Lydia Fairchild who stood on the cusp of womanhood. A collection of creased, oft-read ladies' journals lay in a careless stack on her vanity, articles of note marked by carefully folded napkins and dried flowers. A lovely, carefully arranged porcelain doll occupied the center of her bed, propped up against the pillows in a place of honor. A remnant of her childhood that she clung to, evidence to her innocence. One of her pretty dresses hung from a hook on the back of a changing divider, prepped for an event never attended.

Why was this girl singled out to die?

Johnathan padded across the dust-laden rug, searching for something, any sort of clue to her disappearance. He could hear the murmur of voices from another portion of the house, Mrs. Fairchild's tone reedy and thin compared to the vampire's velvet intonation. Vic couldn't keep the woman occupied forever though. It was only a matter of time before Mr. Fairchild emerged to contend with the visitors his wife failed to dismiss.

"Come on," Johnathan muttered. "Come on, where are you?"

His gaze slid back to the covered mirror. It was an old tradition to keep demons and restless spirits away from a family in mourning. Johnathan never put much stock in such practice. If evil creatures were determined enough, no flimsy cloth would keep them at bay.

He plucked the drape free, greeted by the sight of his own reflection. He looked worn enough to fit right in with the Fairchild household. Behind him was a clear view of Lydia's bedroom window, the woods beyond visible through the glass. He caught something in the corner of his gaze as he turned away, frustrated. It might have been a smudge, but that didn't fit the image of the dusty but well-kept room.

Johnathan approached the window. There was something scored in the wood, partially hidden beneath the closed sill. He unlatched it and lifted the sash to reveal the rest.

There it was, the symbol, the same damn symbol he saw burned into Mary Elizabeth's bones, a half circle split by a straight line, reminiscent of horns.

"Behold, a clue," he said. Little bits and pieces of the puzzle were clicking into place, and Johnathan had a very sobering theory: both of Lydia Fairchild's parents knew a great deal about her disappearance. What bothered him more was why they would hide their knowledge. Or were they hiding their shame? The thought set his teeth on edge.

Raised voices carried through the house, dominated by the unfamiliar boom of an angry male voice. Mr. Fairchild had emerged.

Johnathan sighed through his nose. It was time to inquire why this symbol had been carved into their dead daughter's windowsill. Vic might have the tact to get them into the house, but this revelation called for Johnathan's "bulldog charm" to shake loose the information they needed. He wanted to know how involved these two were with their daughter's death. No, needed to know. The need flared in his chest, hot and sharp.

It wasn't the sound of movement, but the sense of something watching him that made the hair on his arms rise. Johnathan looked up.

The beast stood in the yard, outside Lydia's window, bare to the full light of day.

CHAPTER FOURTEEN

SUNLIGHT SOAKED THE BACKYARD IN WARM, BUTTERY POOLS, LIT THE brilliant green blades of grass, and filtered through the branches at the edge of the woods in a tangle of shadows like a Gordian knot. There were no shadows hiding the beast. It stood in the barest shade of the house, its hindquarters struck by the sun. The light shone off a glossy black coat of fur.

It had the rough shape of a hound, but that was where the comparison ended. The body was wrong, the musculature too bulky for such a whippet-thin build, the muscles bunched in thick slabs across its shoulders and hind legs, built for speed and power. The legs were too long, bent at an odd angle that suggested the creature wasn't a quadruped by natural design, and tipped in curved talons reminiscent of a hawk or owl rather than a canine. That disproportionate build carried through the wide set of its chest to the skull, the jaw too large, too long, the hinge of the mandible much too high, evident even though its head dipped down to watch Johnathan with two forward facing eyes that glowed within its dark face.

Johnathan registered the details rapidly, committing a mental picture to memory. He shoved the sash higher before backing up a couple steps;

he needed space. The creature maintained eye contact, watching him, waiting. For what? Johnathan dropped low and tensed.

"Vic, it's here!" he roared as he surged forward and dove out the window.

He hit the ground in a roll that should have put him face to face with the beast. Instead, he came up with the log hook in his hands and swore at the sight of the creature racing for the cover of the woods.

"It's going for the woods!" Johnathan lurched into a run. The vampire could bloody well catch up.

He tore across the lawn and smashed into the tree line. Branches slapped and stung the exposed skin of his neck and face. Pine sap clung to his hair. He could see the beast, following its flight as it wove and ducked through the tree trunks, but the only footsteps he heard were his own as he ran headlong, a pursuit without stealth or restraint.

The beast made no sound at all, no yips or snarls or warning howls while it led him deeper into the woods. Johnathan stumbled, so caught up in the mindless chase that he didn't catch the tactic for several moments.

He was being led.

His grip on the log hook tightened. He should stop. But if he stopped now he would lose the beast. If he followed it, it would likely lead him to a trap.

With a snarl of frustration, Johnathan skidded to a halt over a carpet of slippery yellow pine needles while the beast vanished between the trees. The run caught up to him, pinching his lungs. His pulse pounded between his ears.

Johnathan braced his hands on his thighs, steaming and snorting like a horse pulled up mid gallop. He could have kept that pace for another ten minutes, thanks to the Society's physical conditioning, but he would be in no shape to confront whatever waited at the end of the run. Time to get his bearings while he waited for the vampire.

Where *was* the vampire?

"Vic?"

The forest swallowed his voice. Johnathan straightened. The surrounding trees weren't densely packed together. There were wide gaps between the trunks, old pines that were green and feathery at the top while the lower branches were bare, jutting from the trunks like broken bones.

Johnathan tilted his head as he looked at those skeletal midriffs, trying to pinpoint what was wrong with the picture. Pine, so much pine surrounding him. Pine was a soft wood, an ideal wood for mass construction, but this stretch of trees was untouched by the bite of axes. A plum spot of lumber, unscathed, behind the home of a former mill owner. Johnathan took a step over the spongy layer of dead pine needles at least an inch deep. The scent of pine was cloyingly thick, but he could still catch a whiff of rot, of moss, and other growing and decaying things.

"Vic?" he called again.

Silence, complete silence. The forest soaked up his voice the second it left his lips. The quiet was absolute, no birds, no squirrels, not a hint of life among those bone-riddled trees. The only sound Johnathan heard were ones of his own making.

He spun with a sharp inhale, trying to gauge how far he'd chased the beast. The trees surrounded him without end. Tension threaded through his spine, a feeling of claustrophobia. Johnathan knew a box when he saw it. The question was, *what else did this one contain?*

The silence pressed around him. Again, the sensation of being watched clawed at his nerves. Johnathan pivoted, his gaze flickering amid the trees, searching. Back and forth, back and forth, where was it, where?

He stopped and stared straight ahead. What he thought were the spindly roots of a fallen tree rose from the ground. This new entity revealed itself, far larger and more imposing than the misshapen beast he'd chased here. The trap sprang around him.

Johnathan's gaze followed, up, up, until the being stood at full height, a giant construct of branch and bone and a crown of massive horns that brushed the underside of the feathery pine canopy. The horns curled up from a skull mask. He thought the skull was from an elk or stag at first, except the eye sockets faced forward, like a predator. The jaws possessed long canine teeth. It stood, tall as a house on spindle limbs in the silent stillness, some ill-summoned god of the wood, and Johnathan gawked at it like a first-year rookie.

Twin red flares lit within the skull's eye sockets, and the jaw clicked open to reveal a wet dark maw. Not a mask at all, but exposed bone fused to the tissue beneath. The creature's mouth opened wide in a soundless roar that made the tree trunks shiver.

Johnathan's breath seized. He took a step back, the desire for flight overwhelming. It was his training that held him there, rooted to the ground.

The creature tilted its head, studied him with the distant bemusement one gave an interesting insect. The log hook dropped from Johnathan's numb fingers, inane, utterly useless—it wouldn't serve him here. Nothing would save him.

The creature shambled forward, tottering on thin legs, but its torso remained poised with eerie grace, as if the two halves of its body were out of sync with each other, incomplete. A mishmash creature, discordant as the beast he'd followed here. The trees shivered with each of its steps, the ancient pines creaking and cracking. They bent away, creating room for the giant to move.

Johnathan's muscles were rigid, no longer held in place by the mettle of his training, rather pinned by the terror that ran in cold sweat down his spine.

The creature's burning red eyes skewered him, locked and shaking in place. It bore down on him, extending a hand with claws each longer than his finger, hooked at the end to tear the flesh from his bones.

His thoughts evaporated as the creature came within striking distance, terror a senseless buzz that overtook every good sense the Society had beaten into him. A small part of him latched onto the insane urge to fall to his knees in supplication, to throw himself at the being's clawed feet in an act of worship, though there was no mercy in those burning alien eyes. His knees remained locked when the creature paused, inhaling with a deep whiff that stirred Johnathan's sap-shot and sweat-drenched hair. It leaned back until that deep red gaze met his own, slitted pupils scouring his face, searching.

The movement shook loose a cord tied round the creature's neck, the metallic flash pulling at Johnathan's attention despite the instinctual fear shackling him in place. There was a coin hanging there, such an innocuous item that it broke through the buzz in his mind. His gaze followed the flash of gold until he caught sight of a symbol on the coin's face. Cold raced down his spine. The same split half circle, and now he could only think of it as horns as the creature exhaled.

The connection snapped. The creature let out a rumbling bellow, a sound that rattled birds from their nests, then staggered away into the wood.

Johnathan had been spared. And he had no idea why.

Lightheaded, Johnathan sucked in a shuddering breath, the air expanding his fear-tight chest. The creature's presence faded from the surrounding forest, as subtle as its arrival.

The trees groaned and swayed upright until the normal quiet of the woods settled around him. Fear released its chokehold on his body. He had no idea *what* he'd just encountered or why the forest creature didn't shred him, but the connection he'd felt to it still shook him.

His mind reeled. That—*thing*—was like nothing he had ever even heard of and, unsettled as he was by his choice, he was certain he'd made the right call to send off the report. Johnathan knew one thing for certain, and that was that he was far, far, over his head. Now he had to find his way out of this infernal forest and throttle a vampire for leaving him at the mercy of this primeval guardian of nature or whatever ilk it descended from.

Johnathan grit his teeth, and his shoulders drooped. Everything he'd done in the last fifteen minutes was against the Society's ingrained protocol. He'd run, without backup, chasing a creature of unknown origin, which he lost in seconds, only to encounter another entity that for some nefarious mercy hadn't killed him.

Something hot and wet slid across his palm, like the lick of an open flame. Johnathan sucked in a breath and grabbed his wrist, staring at his hand where the skin glistened, faintly red, as if scalded by the contact. The same hand he'd washed soot off this morning. The beast had licked his healed palm.

A canine whine sliced through the silence. Slowly, Johnathan turned around. The beast crouched at his feet, its limbs set with an air of uncertainty. He watched it, waited for it to attack.

The beast ducked its head, its burning eyes downcast. It whined again and crawled around him with its whip-thin tail tucked between its legs. This time Johnathan didn't follow when it disappeared into the trees, unnerved by its actions. He stood rigid, confused, but the mind-numbing terror he'd felt only moments ago was absent. There was something almost...pitiful about the beast. Or perhaps he'd exhausted his reserves of fear after his encounter with the towering creature.

Why had he been spared? That was a great question and a dangerous one. A helpless smile tugged at the corner of his mouth. Johnathan didn't believe in coincidence, not with the universe shouting in his ear. None of this bode well for him. Vic might insist he only had one of three threats to worry about, but the mysterious creatures of Cress Haven looked like the frontrunner to do him in. It was humbling, after years of brutal training, to find himself so outclassed in his first foray into the field.

Not until that moment, at the brush of the beast's tongue, did Johnathan realize how much he'd ignored the wound. The importance of it had fallen to the wayside, like the deaths of the missing girls among the townsfolk. He'd failed to bring it to Vic's attention. He'd failed to maintain his own attention.

Johnathan curled his hand into a fist, pressing it to his chest where his heart beat, far too slow and calm for what he'd just encountered. Even now, he could feel the seriousness of his situation slipping away from him, the sharp, stark details of the towering creature losing cohesion and dissolving, like silt washed away in a stream. A curious sensation, the malaise seeping through him, strong enough to banish fear and worry, but his determination to root out the source of Cress Haven's troubles remained intact. A faint sense of manipulation clung to him, settling on him like a cloak of unease he couldn't completely shake off.

Johnathan looked up. Instead of trees, he could see the Fairchild's house, when he knew it wasn't there a moment ago. Vic was still nowhere to be seen. Did this mean the vampire was still mired in the affairs of the Fairchilds while Johnathan had tossed himself into another life-threatening situation?

The idea irritated him beyond the pale. How difficult could a man and woman wrought with grief be for a vampire of Vic's skill? The fiend picked up on heartbeats through the outer walls of a house; he bloody well heard Johnathan's shout.

Grumbling, Johnathan snatched his log hook off the ground and began trudging back, his mood even darker for the confrontation ahead.

A blast of noise shredded the oppressive silence of the forest. The force of the sound punched him in the chest like a mighty fist, knocking him off his feet. Red-hot agony drove a spike through his shoulder, gasping at the ball of pain lodged there.

The copper scent of fresh blood washed over him. A wild-eyed stranger stepped through the trees, a spent pistol in one limp hand. His arm shook as he aimed a second primed gun at Johnathan's prone form.

CHAPTER FIFTEEN

JOHNATHAN'S FOCUS FUNNELED TO THE HOLLOW MUZZLE AIMED AT HIS face. Pain radiated from his shoulder. His veins throbbed, a web of fire beneath his skin. The hard knot where the bullet lay lodged in his flesh burned, not that he could do much about it while the ragged stranger held him at point-blank range.

"Unclean thing," the man spat.

A drop of spittle hit Johnathan's cheek, but he didn't move to wipe it away. The man clearly had an itchy trigger finger. The slightest twitch could send a bullet through Johnathan's teeth.

The man took a step closer. "Wretched creature. You took my daughter from me." His voice was a hoarse rasp to match the unhealthy rattle of his breath. "My sweet girl," he breathed.

Johnathan held perfectly still. "Mr. Fairchild?"

The man jolted and shook the pistol in Johnathan's face. "This wasn't the bargain we made." His hair hung flat against his skull in greasy clumps. Food and sweat stained his shirt, draped loosely on the emaciated frame of what was once a much larger man. He glared down at Johnathan with bloodshot eyes, wide and wild, the whites tinted yellow. Steeped in alcohol, a cloud of gin-soaked breath wafted from his mouth, mingling with his unwashed scent. He didn't even *see* Johnathan.

Fairchild tossed the spent pistol, wiping away the sweat dripping into his eyes. He kept his primed firearm aimed at Johnathan's face. "This isn't the bargain we made, you bastard."

The man swayed on his feet. Johnathan thought about the log hook, wondering if it had fallen nearby. Was it close enough to stop this madman? He couldn't chance it. This close, it was impossible for Fairchild to miss, though it was a matter of debate where the bullet would hit.

"You promised me...promised me..." Mr. Fairchild sobbed, the sound welling up from deep in the man's chest. "Lydia, my poor Lydia. I'm so sorry." Mr. Fairchild was a lost man, drunk and ranting, taken over by the personal demons that clouded his mind.

Johnathan grit his teeth. Pain or not, here were answers if he could simply draw them out without getting shot. "What was promised to you, Fairchild?"

The man's grip tightened on the gun. "You know," he hissed, baring his yellowed teeth.

Johnathan swallowed hard. The fire in his shoulder flared in time to his pulse. "Please, good sir, remind me of our terms," he coaxed. If the unstable man saw him as someone else, he would play the part for as long as he could hold onto consciousness.

"Wealth beyond measure," Mr. Fairchild snarled. "The bountiful wealth beneath the earth. You promised enough riches to keep my family set for generations. If only I opened..." His words trailed off, the man's unfocused gaze settling on Johnathan in a moment of bloodshot clarity. "Oh God, what have I done?" Fairchild whispered, covering his mouth with the back of his free hand.

"Please," said Johnathan, abandoning the pretense. "Tell me of your bargain."

The gun lowered a fraction. Tears spilled down the man's haggard face. "I wanted to give them everything. I wanted my family to have everything. Cernunnos promised me—" His face went slack, and the moment crumpled in on itself. The man's frayed sanity dispersed like wood smoke. He stared at something behind Johnathan, and in that fractured moment, his face contracted with fear and rage. "You! You're tainted—"

Temptation struck Johnathan, the desire to steal a glance over his shoulder, but when a snarl rolled through the air, a coarse, raw sound from an inhuman mouth, fear got the better of him, freezing him cold.

Mr. Fairchild shook violently, attempting to retrain his aim behind Johnathan. The snarl guttered into a chilling scream, a high-pitched tortured sound. A urine stain spread across the front of Mr. Fairchild's trousers.

Shock broke through the fear on the man's face, his mouth a wavering hole. The gun slipped from the man's slack fingers as the fight went out of him, a play of grief and pain etched in Mr. Fairchild's features. "This can't be. No, my darling girl, no—"

The air smelled like fire.

Curious and confused, Johnathan found his bravery. Just as he turned to face whatever lurked behind him, a long lupine form sailed overhead, knocking Mr. Fairchild to the ground. The beast's ungainly jaws clamped over the man's shoulder, its teeth ripping into soft flesh, a wound to mirror Johnathan's.

Mr. Fairchild let out a panicked shout, feebly shoving at the beast's head. His weapons had been discarded on a bed of blood-slicked pine needles. Johnathan half expected the man to reach for one of the guns—they were so close—but no. Instead, Mr. Fairchild cupped the beast's face, the gesture oddly tender, until it shook him like a rat terrier.

There was a pause, a weighted moment where the beast lifted its glowing eyes.

A frisson of awareness pulsed through Johnathan when their gazes met. His brows drew together. Johnathan needed to get up. He had to stop this. He had to help the man. It didn't matter if the bastard shot him. It was his duty to protect.

He propped himself up on his elbows. The bullet in his shoulder sank metal teeth deeper into his muscle and ate at him inside. Blood rivered down his chest, saturating his clothes.

Johnathan bit back a whimper. Black spots danced across his vision.

Mr. Fairchild groaned, hooking his fingers in the beast's muzzle in an attempt to free himself. It obliged, unhinging its jaw. Fairchild choked and reached a shaking hand towards the beast's head, the expression on his pain-creased face full of terrible, aching hope.

Black lips curled in a bloodied snarl before the beast snapped forward and tore out Mr. Fairchild's throat. The man's blood-soaked body fell into a lifeless heap, his eyes open with resignation, staring straight at Johnathan.

The beast stood a few strides away, hovering over its kill, its ears flat against its skull.

It whined at Johnathan but still didn't attack.

Johnathan focused on the pain, using it like a lever to rise to his knees. Mr. Fairchild's guns lay nearby, a bullet in at least one of the chambers, but the beast would never let him get that close.

A thought flashed through his mind. He ran his hands through the bracken around him, searching. It couldn't have gone that far. Finally, his fingers closed on the cool metal length of the log hook. Doubtful that he had the strength to swing it, but it was better than nothing.

Mrs. Fairchild burst through the trees. Her pinched features drew into a mask of shock as she took in the scene.

"Nathaniel!" she shrieked. She dropped to her knees in a billow of skirts, hands reaching for her fallen husband. It seemed she cared not that a monster stood a foot away.

The beast lowered into a threatened stance and let out a low growl. Mrs. Fairchild looked up, her wide eyes locked on the beast's bloodstained muzzle.

Johnathan raised the log hook, ignoring the burst of fiery pain from his wound. Where was that damn vampire? But then he caught the glint in Mrs. Fairchild's eyes, the note of recognition.

"Lydia," Mrs. Fairchild said, her words drenched in anger and sadness and a legion of other heart-rending emotions. "How could you? How *could* you?"

Johnathan startled when the beast cowered like a scolded child. His gaze snapped between the crouching beast and the woman.

Blazes. It couldn't be.

"Lydia." Mrs. Fairchild's voice went soft with a motherly tone Johnathan had never known. She sank to all fours and crawled toward the beast. Blood seeped into the fabric of her skirts, a bright red bloom that rose from her knees. Her lost expression anchored Johnathan in place. His thoughts churned, rapid-fire, as the pieces slid together. He thought of the reports he'd read last night. Lydia Fairchild... Missing...

He would have never imagined this outcome.

He stared at the growling creature, unable to reconcile the monster with the missing girl. Mrs. Fairchild continued to inch forward. Tears streaming down her cheeks, she lifted her hands toward the misshapen creature.

It loosened a high-pitched whine, flesh rippling beneath its soot-black fur, when the beast appeared to collapse in on itself. Mrs. Fairchild gasped.

Johnathan stared in horror as the beast's fur withered away, revealing smooth pink skin. A girl crouched on the ground, lifting her face to peer at Johnathan with feral eyes. Her human lips curled in a snarl.

Vic appeared in a rush of air, the front of his shirt soaked in blood, a fire poker in his hands. He bared his teeth at the beast-turned-girl, launching the poker like a spear.

Mrs. Fairchild screamed, but the girl vanished in a burst of smoke and ash, leaving Vic's weapon to do no more than pierce the empty ground.

"My daughter! My little girl!" Mrs. Fairchild collapsed, weeping, beside the torn corpse of her husband.

"That was no girl." Vic's shoulders heaved. His gaze snapped with fury. It was the closest to unhinged Johnathan had ever seen the vampire.

"You're late," Johnathan wheezed. Holding his shoulder, he sank back on his heels, exhausted and lightheaded.

Mrs. Fairchild rose with a shriek, her husband's missing gun in hand.

Capable of little more, Johnathan sighed in disgust. Of course she found one, though it could be the empty one or the primed one for all he knew. She pressed the gun to her temple.

"Stop her!" Johnathan shouted.

He needn't have bothered. Vic was next to her in a blink. He snatched the pistol from her hand and snapped the barrel in half with a look of disdain.

Crestfallen, Mrs. Fairchild sagged like a broken doll, her eyes on her husband's torn-out throat. Vic crouched next to her, tucking two fingers under her chin. His grip was almost gentle as he made her look at him.

Awareness was a fair-weather companion to Mrs. Fairchild. Her eyes slowly focused on Vic's face.

"I stabbed you through the heart," she murmured.

She'd stabbed him? Why?

What the hell had gone on in that house after he left?

Johnathan blinked through the haze slowly overtaking him and looked the vampire over. Vic was a great deal paler. A bright red stain covered much of his back, where he must have lain in a pool of his own blood. There was a faint bluish tinge at the base of his fingernails. Johnathan shifted his grip on the log hook. The vampire lost an awful lot of blood, very quickly, and now they were in the forest, one man's corpse draining crimson into the earth while another's life leaked from his shoulder. And if that weren't enough, Vic held a human woman at his fingertips, a woman who wanted to die.

This was *not* the situation Johnathan wanted to find himself in when the limits of Vic's control came into question.

"You missed," Vic said to Mrs. Fairchild, a strange lilt to his voice.

The woman jerked her chin, but he didn't let go of her. "I pushed to the hilt. You should be dead."

"Let's agree to disagree," said Vic amiably.

Johnathan studied him. The vampire didn't look ready to tear into Mrs. Fairchild, though she admitted to stabbing him. Frankly, Johnathan couldn't do much to stop Vic if he did attack the woman, and that helpless feeling gave him enough rage to shuffle closer on his knees, using the hook to drag himself forward.

Vic's gaze shifted, a sidelong glance that gave Johnathan pause. The vampire gave a slight shake of his head, a subtle warning, before he turned back to Lydia's mother.

"Tell me about the bargain your husband made, Mrs. Fairchild." Vic kept a hold on her chin. A suggestive tone spiraled within his voice, betraying a hint of his age as he nudged her secrets forth. But the woman's gaze slid away to her husband's body, her mind too cracked even for a fiend's compulsion. Her throat worked. She looked ready to crumble, her very foundations ruined, so overwhelmed by the situation. Vic pressed the pad of his thumb into her chin. "Your husband brought this on your family, on your daughter. Tell us what happened."

"He didn't tell me everything." Mrs. Fairchild's voice was a hoarse whisper. Johnathan strained to hear her, listening for the waver of a lie. "He said not to worry, that we would have everything we ever dreamed of. That Lydia would be taken care of for the rest of her life." She wobbled. Her hands curled into her bloodstained skirts. "He said a stranger told him how to strike a bargain with the spirits of the wood."

Vic's brow rose. "Your husband believed a stranger?"

Mrs. Fairchild grimaced. "Nathaniel was a man of faith, but he was raised on the old stories. He believed enough to try."

"And he succeeded," said Vic. He released his hold on Mrs. Fairchild. "Does he know *what* he made a bargain with?"

She shook her head. "He said it was a spirit of the wood, that if we didn't harm the woods here, we would be fine." She looked up at them, her expression shattered. "It was a lie."

"Ask her if she ever saw the stranger," Johnathan wheezed.

The vampire nodded, but whether his compulsion was still in effect or Mrs. Fairchild saw no point to withholding information in a pool of her husband's blood, she answered without prompting.

"It was a man. Tall, older. He wore a uniform of sorts and spectacles. I remember his cross, old and wooden. Stained by... It didn't suit him." She shuddered. "That man was no priest."

Johnathan frowned. Her description held a note of familiarity. He shook the thought from his mind, too absurd to entertain.

Vic stood up, his jaw set. "What happened to your daughter?"

Mrs. Fairchild swayed. "Nathaniel opened a door that must not be opened."

There was a sing-song quality to her voice that made Johnathan's skin prickle. Too reminiscent of the phantom Mary Elizabeth from his nightmare.

A manic smile lit Mrs. Fairchild's face, one that made him question what sort of spell this spirit of the wood had cast upon her mind, and now that he considered it, perhaps all the minds of the citizens of Cress Haven, including his own.

"He bargained for wealth, for material possessions. Our coffers filled, and the price was our child. We paid for our greed with our future." Her hand moved behind her. "My child is gone. My husband gone. I have nothing left." The second pistol appeared in her hand.

Vic didn't move to stop her this time. Johnathan tried, shoving to his feet, but his body gave out immediately. Vic caught him before he hit the ground. Blessedly, the pistol clicked over, already spent. Mrs. Fairchild, defeated, dropped the weapon and let out a thin wail of despair.

"Looks like you'll have to live with yourself," said Vic. His attention turned to Johnathan. "Good grief, man, did she manage to stab you, too?"

"Shot," Johnathan said through gritted teeth. "By Mr. Fairchild." Black spots ate at his vision. He refused to pass out, bleeding, in a vampire's grip no less.

Vic frowned and tore away the layers of fabric over the wound. The vampire frowned. "You say he shot you?"

Johnathan managed a halfhearted sneer. "No Vic, I simply tripped and fell on the bullet."

He swung his head to peer at the wound and paused. Mrs. Fairchild was looking at him. She held his gaze, an expression full of secrets and vicious delight. Her head dropped back as she laughed. Rising, she staggered on unsteady legs deeper into the woods, away from her now-empty house.

"You shouldn't let her wander off," Johnathan rasped.

"That woman wants to die, John," said Vic. "And you require medical aid."

Johnathan wanted to protest. He should insist Vic retrieve her. She could only wander so far before she found the death she was looking for.

Vic slid his arms under Johnathan's larger frame and lifted him off the ground as if he were a small child rather than a six-foot man. Ridiculous as it was, the movement was too much. Johnathan's head swam, the world around him spinning.

He was about to pass out. Again.

"I feel like some mythic hero, rescuing the fair maiden from the heart of a cursed wood," Vic said. "Are you always so taken to keeling over?"

A sarcastic and lengthy retort balanced on Johnathan's tongue, but staring into the beautiful face above him, he could only manage, "Blood-sucking scoundrel."

Vic's laugh echoed through the wood. Johnathan's attention turned behind them. Through the trees, beyond the blood-spattered shift of Mrs. Fairchild's skirts, Johnathan thought he saw the shape of a horned skull watching, waiting, before the blackness of unconsciousness dragged him down.

CHAPTER SIXTEEN

D AMMIT, HE'D PASSED OUT, BLEEDING, IN THE VAMPIRE'S ARMS. Johnathan had been well and truly coldcocked.

He came to awareness in increments, anchored by the ache in his shoulder. There was a new dressing of clean, stiff cloth wrapped around his bare chest. The fiery pain was gone, thank goodness, but the soreness was enough to keep him floating in a half-state of waking. He tried to gauge his surroundings without opening his eyes. There was a firm mattress under him, and the mellow heat of sunshine bathed down the side of his face and neck.

"Is he still out?" a voice said.

Johnathan stilled, listening for Alyse. Was he in Vic's house? The mattress felt different, and the homely scent of fresh linen and sage surrounded him. He was suddenly keenly aware that he'd been stripped to his drawers.

"He'll wake up soon." There was a strain of exhaustion in the vampire's tone. Just how long was Johnathan out for?

"You've been here all night," pleaded Alyse. "Please, let me help you."

The vampire watched over him all night? Johnathan wasn't sure how he felt about that. What did Alyse mean to help with?

Curiosity burned off the lingering fog clouding Johnathan's thoughts. The previous day rushed to the fore with violent clarity. Time to open his eyes and get some answers.

"Have you spoken to your father about my offer?" Vic asked.

Johnathan kept his eyes shut tight. He heard Alyse sigh, her light footsteps treading the floor. He could almost see her shadow pacing against the back of his eyelids.

"You know what he'll say."

"Did you bother to ask?"

There was a weighted pause, punctuated by the strained creak of wood and the soft swish of skirts. "I can't leave my sisters, Vic. I just can't. They're too young. Maddy's not yet fifteen." Alyse sobbed, and Johnathan's fingers curled into a fist beneath the blanket. A woman like Alyse didn't seem like the sort to cry for anything. "That's too close in age to the other victims."

"I saw that symbol Alyse, it was carved on *your* sill, " said Vic quietly. Johnathan went completely still. This *was not* the direction he expected from their conversation.

"We share a bedroom, dolt. My father is a pastor, not some country gentleman. He certainly didn't make any deals with strange beings in the woods," Alyse retorted, the usual surliness reasserting itself.

"We don't know if that's the commonality," Vic said. "The Fairchilds might have let it in, but who knows what rules it operates under now."

"Mercy, it almost seems like you should take a moment to search through those carefully notated files for connections," said Alyse, sniffling. "You know, the ones I made for you, at your house."

"Alyse, the last victim looked just like you! It must have wanted you! It marked *your* house, for devil's sake."

That muted thud had to be Alyse stomping her foot. "A similar appearance is a coincidence, not a portent, Vic. We don't know which one it wants. What if this creature decides it wants to take a boy? I have young brothers. I'm not leaving my siblings vulnerable to satisfy your overprotective sentiments. Make a better offer!" Her steps rapped across the floorboards, but the door shut with a soft click behind her.

Mad as she was, Alyse wouldn't slam the door in a sick room to make a point. Johnathan grudgingly realized he might have to reevaluate the nature of her relationship with Vic. Lord help him, but the vampire genuinely appeared to care for her.

Wood whined. The vampire sighed. "You can stop pretending. I know you're awake."

Johnathan flinched, cracking one eye to peer at Vic. "I didn't want to interrupt."

He glanced around. This had to be the Shaw household. Everything was remarkably clean, with sparse decor.

Vic snorted. "I'm sure you found a fiend being told off by a chit of a girl highly entertaining."

Johnathan opened both eyes and stared at the vampire lounging by his bedside. Vic looked terrible. His skin was paper white and had the translucent quality of long illness, the delicate tracery of his veins visible in faint blue lines. His eyes were sunken with half-moon shadows pouched beneath them, but the most telling detail was still the fingernails. Vic now had dead man's fingers, the nails discolored and bruised at the base of the nail.

Vic's brows drew together at Johnathan's apparent appraisal. "You look like hell," said the vampire.

Johnathan's chuckle was more of a painful cough. "Pot meet kettle."

"Gracious, was that a joke? Don't tell me you're going soft on me, Prospective," said Vic.

Johnathan winced as he sat up. The twinge in his shoulder was a dull roar, bearing much semblance to previous wounds he'd suffered. He'd been stabbed a dozen times by a surly senior Prospective who Johnathan outscored for blade accuracy. Sharp, searing cuts, but the boy never hit anything vital. Not from lack of trying; he truly couldn't aim for shit.

During his first hunt, Johnathan had been shot by a newborn vampire who still preferred guns to teeth. That bullet took him in the thigh and broke his femur. Incredible as the pain was then, it was nothing to the pain of this wound. Akin to being pierced by a hot iron rod that continued to sear away at his flesh. The memory of that unbearable agony was fresh in his mind. As were the circumstances he lost consciousness in.

"I've made up my mind," he told Vic.

Vic's face betrayed only a hint of confusion. "Oh?"

"You're not a monster." Johnathan looked up, his gaze connecting with Vic's stare when he belatedly realized he was, once again, shirtless.

Vic had changed out of his blood-soaked clothing, the fresh shirt a tighter fit on his slim form, accenting his lean muscles. Johnathan's face grew warm from noticing such a detail.

Vic leaned back in his chair, drawing a finger across his lush lips. "Flattered as I am by your answer, what led you to such a conclusion?" His gaze dipped, perusing Johnathan's exposed abdomen.

Johnathan blushed and looked away, clenching his teeth at the sharp twinge in his shoulder. The vampire managed to leave him so discomfited with merely a look. "Aside from the great deal of charity and delicacy in your treatment of Mrs. Fairchild," he answered, "you also showed remarkable restraint as I bled out on the ground."

There was also his "sentiment" for Alyse, though Johnathan would rather slam his wounded shoulder into the wall than bring that into the conversation. Simply, he knew he didn't care for the idea of Vic with Alyse—not in a romantic way.

Vic's eyes gleamed with a mix of heat and amusement that made Johnathan's face burn even hotter. "How certain are you that I didn't take a sip while you were under? You do have a rather intoxicating aroma."

Johnathan's gaze snapped up, meeting Vic's head on. There was an odd tension pulling taut between them that made his muscles go tight. "I would know if I had been tasted. And you think I don't recognize a starving vampire? I see it all over you."

Vic smiled, revealing much more prominent fangs, yet the alluring curve of his mouth promised something far more dangerous than an *attack*.

"And I told you John, I have my own methods of dealing with bloodlust." He leaned forward, elbows resting on his knees. "I have more than one insatiable appetite."

A flush of heat rushed down through Johnathan's chest, its destination unmistakable. If this continued, he was certain his hair would catch fire from the heat of his blush.

He swallowed with difficulty. Their relationship had been far simpler when Johnathan had been certain that Vic was a vicious fiend who would eventually turn on him. This version of Vic, though...

Johnathan didn't rise to the bait. He couldn't reconcile himself to the stirrings of emotion the vampire roused in him, a confusing, complicated mix he was in no shape to untangle now. Or ever.

He cleared his throat. "Why is it that I find myself waking up in Pastor Shaw's house? I know Alyse is aware of your condition but what of her father and siblings?"

Vic pursed his lips. "Nice subject change. You are the epitome of subtleness, John. In answer to your question, it was either bring you to Alyse or Alyse to you, and I wasn't sure you would last for the latter." He smirked at the question in Johnathan's expression. "Shaw wasn't always a pastor. He was a trained surgeon before he settled here and taught Alyse more than a few techniques. I certainly trust them more than what passes for a doctor in this town."

"But the pastor—" John's words were interrupted by the passing of the pastor's brood, the younger children trampling past the sick room louder than a pack of banshees, with Alyse in their wake, commanding their silence. The pastor's baritone rose once in a quick short command that brought the noise to an abrupt halt.

A small smile played on Vic's mouth as he listened to the familial chaos. "The pastor does not approve of my...friendship with Alyse, but he is a man of faith, and a good one. He wouldn't turn away an injured man or ask too many questions."

Johnathan struggled to give himself more leverage on the bed. His shoulder would be a sore mess for several days, but he didn't have time to wait for recovery. "Who found the symbol on Alyse's windowsill?"

Vic leaned back and folded his hands together over his chest. "Alyse's little sister found the mark. It showed up last night while you slept. She didn't know what it was."

"I need to see if it's the same as the others," said Johnathan. He swung his bare legs over the bed.

Vic was there in a blink, chair and all, sitting before him. His cool hand rested on Johnathan's good shoulder, pinning him in place.

He set his jaw to keep from shouting at a hungry, irritable vampire. "What do you think you're doing?"

"You think I didn't check Miss Fairchild's room after you went through the damn window chasing the beast? I recognized the symbol, John." He released Johnathan and ran a hand through his hair, auburn strands falling from the queue at his nape. "It's the same bloody symbol as the rest." He released a long, very human breath.

Johnathan followed the vampire's telling motions. "What happened to you after I gave chase?"

"Thought you were still conscious for that part. The lovely Mrs. Fairchild stabbed me." Vic tapped his chest. "Silly twit drove the blade right through my breastbone."

Johnathan recalled Mrs. Fairchild's words. The act of stabbing someone in the chest to kill them was no easy feat, and attempting to go through the breastbone was an obvious amateur move. Even with some real force behind it, Mrs. Fairchild shouldn't have achieved much more than scraping against bone.

"I was awake. Up to the hilt?'

Vic sneered and held his fingers a couple inches apart. "It was a damn paring knife."

Johnathan raised a brow. "Awful lot of blood for such a small blade."

"Ah, that would be the fire poker her husband put through my back before he went hunting for you." Vic made a face, reaching to rub a spot on his lower back. "He was drunk and incensed by questions he felt I had no business asking."

No wonder the vampire took so long to reach Johnathan.

"Mrs. Fairchild neglected to mention that," Johnathan said lightly. He looked down at his legs, wondering who'd divested him of his trousers. "Did you leave her in the woods?"

Vic was silent for so long, Johnathan had to glance up to see if he was still there, half expecting to see the vampire ogling his bare legs. "I did," Vic said. "I had more pressing concerns. When I peeled back your shirt, the wound was a pulsing mass of blackened skin, oozing brownish black liquid. I thought you'd been poisoned."

Johnathan gaped at him, his hand flying to cup his shoulder. "What? What the hell did he shoot me with?"

Vic retrieved an object from his pocket and held it out to him. The bullet sat in the palm of the vampire's hand, far more warped than he expected of a plain lead ball, but on closer inspection, the metal had a peculiar color. "It's silver. The moment we managed to pry it from your flesh, your blood ran red again."

There was a detail here, significant and terribly important, they were missing.

Johnathan clutched his sore shoulder, mentally piecing together an incomplete picture. "What does it mean?"

"I don't know." Vic leaned forward and rolled the ball between his fingers. It was a telling display of his agitation, the small movements a hint of his deep distraction. Vampires were normally still, and Vic was hungry and anxious, his predatory instincts running high. Not a good combination in a household full of children.

"You should feed," said Johnathan. He looked at the ceiling, wondering if it were possible to winch his lips shut before he made a bigger fool of himself.

Vic tilted his head, biting his lower lip. "Are you offering, John?"

His fingers danced up Johnathan's bare calf.

The back of Johnathan's neck heated, and though every instinct told him not to be a fool, to get as far away from this fiend as possible, he soldiered forth in his foolishness anyway. "If Alyse can't or won't, then yes. I'm offering."

Better him than Pastor Shaw's children. This was what he told himself, anyway.

Vic's smirk vanished, and his brows knitted together. "You're actually serious." He sighed. Looking put upon, he slid out of the chair and settled his weight onto the bed.

Before Johnathan could properly react, Vic began to crawl over him, causing him to shrink back, resting on the elbow of his good arm, wide eyed as the vampire hovered over him, fangs bright.

"You're certain you're ready for this?" Vic breathed. His auburn hair dangled in Johnathan's face, tickling his cheek.

Johnathan flinched, his body held in a supremely awkward position while his mind rioted. *What should he do? Where should he put his hands? Would it hurt?*

He shifted slightly, trying to ease the tension in his bad shoulder, and promptly slid off the bed. Vic caught him midway to the floor, but jostling his shoulder sent a fresh stab of pain through his chest.

"Ow," Johnathan groaned. Vic, with that abnormal vampiric strength of his, gently set him back to rights on the bed and returned to his chair.

"Consider this a teaching moment. Do you have any idea how much blood you lost, you idiot?" Vic said in disgust. "I think you lost more than I did, by half. And I told you I would not be the one to kill you. Feeding on you in this state would be certain death." Vic's expression turned troubled. "What exactly happened out there, John?"

"I saw something." Johnathan's gaze turned inward, unfocused as he recalled the horned skull and long spindle limbs.

"How utterly vague. Care to elaborate for the late arrivals?"

Johnathan glared at him. "My apologies. My recall is a bit slow thanks to the bullet wound I sustained to the shoulder."

Vic held up his hands in mock surrender. "Sarcasm is the defense of a man lacking imagination."

"I've changed my mind. You *are* a monster."

Vic ducked his head, a smile tilted at the corner of his mouth. "Do you remember?"

"I do." He hesitated, trying to summon the memory. At first his mind wouldn't cooperate, but the determined Prospective who refused to be deterred rose to the fore. Johnathan described the creature with halting but accurate, if not perfect, recall. The little details gave him trouble, such as the number of branches present in the horns, a number far greater than he'd seen in any actual buck or elk. He even managed a fairly accurate estimate of the creature's height and length of its limbs, though such minutiae were difficult to gauge from a considerable distance. What his description did lack was the mind-blanking terror he felt, and something else, an important detail that lingered just out of his grasp.

Vic nodded, his brow raised. "Well done, Prospective Newman," he murmured.

There was something about Vic's soft words that made him feel defensive, though there was no real bite to them.

"I'm a trained Society investigator. I must take note of as many details as I can," said Johnathan. For a heartbeat, he wondered if Vic attempted to compel him, but when he reached for the details of his memory, they came readily enough. Perhaps he'd broken through whatever influence sapped their importance away, except...he didn't believe he'd escaped it entirely.

He frowned, unable to dismiss that niggling sense that he was forgetting something, when Vic's sinuous movements derailed his thoughts.

The vampire stood and began to pace the short length of the floor, flowing with grace in the midst of frustration. "What you're describing, in theory, *almost* sounds like a spirit of the wood." He paused, tugging on his lip. "Or something that could be mistaken for one."

"Mistaken for one?" Johnathan carefully rubbed his sore shoulder. "Before I came here, I didn't think much more than vampires existed."

Vic frowned. "I thought the Society gave you an extensive education."

There it was again, the desire to defend, to snap back, though Vic's tone was far from accusatory. Johnathan hunched over, puzzled by the mercurial shift of his temper. "It *is* extensive, where it concerns *real* threats. This isn't the typical fare." He scrubbed a hand through his hair, not believing what he was about to say. "We're out here chasing creatures that feel as though they belong in a fairy tale. These are unknown entities."

A knowing look flashed across Vic's face. "There are a great deal of entities out there who don't wish to be known, John." He looked troubled. "When I brought you into this, I believed the Society possessed a greater understanding of the world's mysteries." He glanced at the silver ball he'd pulled from Johnathan's shoulder. "It seems I was mistaken."

"The Society must have encountered something like this before," insisted Johnathan, disliking the sense of ignorance that rose as Vic spoke. "Their Hunters have traveled throughout the world. They—"

Vic rolled his eyes. "If they have encountered such beings, why haven't they informed their Prospectives about them?"

"I don't know," said Johnathan, hating the note of uncertainty in his voice. Vic paused, staring at him with a look that brought a very different heat to the back of Johnathan's neck.

The vampire shook himself. "Well, shortly before we left yesterday, I did track down the contact I was looking for." His expression turned closed. "I might be able to acquire some clarity to our mystery, but you're staying here. It's too much of a risk to bring you," said Vic, a hint of regret in his voice before his face tightened.

"You're leaving? Who are you meeting?" Johnathan heaved himself off the bed. The room spun beneath his feet. He ignored the sensation and snatched the bullet from Vic's hand. "I am not a bloody hindrance."

"You would never be a hindrance," Vic murmured, lifting his hands to catch Johnathan if pitched over. A frown knotted between his delicate brows. "I said risk, as in I'm not willing to risk further harm to you. Please, John, rest. You won't be of much help to us if you don't heal."

Johnathan ignored that too. He was getting awfully skilled at ignoring good advice, though he knew he remained standing through sheer stubbornness. Despite this, he refused to let the vampire dictate what he did now.

"Just tell me," Johnathan demanded.

Vic straightened. His mood was difficult to decipher as he rolled his shoulders and released a slow breath. Johnathan thought he almost looked...afraid? "Who I should have sought out in the first place, rather than entreating the Society to send me a green Hunter." His nostrils flared. "Though the price for their knowledge will be high."

Johnathan scowled. "How astonishingly clear. Care to specify who *they* are?"

"No," said Vic. "In this case, it is better to keep your ignorance." The sincerity of his words gave Johnathan pause. The vampire's gaze glinted. "Don't follow me, John. If I don't return, I need you to keep Alyse and her family safe."

The vampire looked like he wanted to say something else, his expression so torn that Johnathan found himself reaching for him, though he wasn't sure what he would do if he caught hold of Vic.

His fingers brushed the vampire's sleeve, but Vic slid away like a breeze, leaving Johnathan grasping air. The door slammed shut a second behind the fleeing vampire.

A tangle of feelings wrestled in Johnathan's chest. *If I don't return...*

He staggered a step forward, bracing himself on the wall. Panic and outrage vied for dominance. Outrage won.

"Don't you dare think you can leave me behind, you bloody stupid vampire!"

CHAPTER SEVENTEEN

OUTRAGE GAVE HIM THE SURGE OF ENERGY HE NEEDED TO BURST FROM the room with all the delicacy of a raging bull. Johnathan's chest heaved, each breath filled with hot irrational anger. Using both walls of the hall to shove himself forward, he caught up to the vampire in the foyer, toppling a chair in his clumsy charge across the small room. Vic froze at the sight of him, wide-eyed at the anger on Johnathan's face.

Johnathan tried to rein himself in so he could hold a rational conversation. He would not let Vic dictate this situation, and especially wouldn't let the idiot go alone to a meeting *he might not come back from.*

"Like hell are you leaving me here."

Vic's mouth set in a grim line. "John, you can barely stand. Go back to bed."

Johnathan shook his head. "I won't be a liability.

The vampire's brows snapped together, his own patience fraying in the face of Johnathan's mulish attitude. "Dammit man, did you not hear me? You can't handle this."

Too ignorant, too weak. Johnathan snarled and shoved him, a childish reaction. And like a child shoving an adult, Vic didn't move an inch. "Don't you dare assume what I can and can't handle." The heat inside him intensified. He fisted the fabric of Vic's shirt. A flash of pity came and went across the vampire's face stoking Johnathan's anger further.

"Big, bad Hunter that you are," said Vic, his voice dangerously soft as he wrapped a hand around Johnathan's wrist. He suddenly loomed in hard and fast, with a snap of teeth that forced Johnathan back a step. "You can't even handle me."

The snap of teeth echoed through Johnathan's mind. Heat exploded inside him. The pain in his shoulder vanished as Johnathan picked Vic up and slammed him against the wall beside the front door, hard enough to crack the plaster. Johnathan pinned him there, feet dangling several inches off the ground, breath steaming in his lungs. "Don't you ever snap your teeth at me again."

"Christ, I did not see that coming," the vampire wheezed. He gently squeezed Johnathan's wrists. "John, I'm sorry. I didn't mean it. Please put me down."

Johnathan didn't respond. His eyes were focused on Vic's mouth, where the edges of sharp teeth were visible through parted lips. A tremor ran through his limbs. The coppery tang of blood bloomed in the air. Vic inhaled and flinched. His grip on Johnathan's wrists tightened.

"You need to put me down, John." There was a desperate, panicked note in that voice.

Johnathan looked into the vampire's eyes. Vic's pupils had dilated until the silvery blue of his irises were a thin band around a well of black.

"Put me down." Vic's jaw quivered.

A soft, muffled gasp sounded through the room. Vic's eyes darted over Johnathan's shoulder, and Johnathan knew by the contorted look of shame on the vampire's face that Alyse was behind them.

Johnathan dropped him and rocked back while Vic practically shoved himself through the front door, shutting it with a determined snap.

Alyse didn't go after him, nor did she offer John help when he turned and flopped against the wall, sliding down to brace his knees. Johnathan ignored her in the hopes she would follow her lover and dropped his head in his hands. He felt like a right bastard. He knew exactly what Vic was doing with that little stunt—saving Johnathan from his own stubbornness—but his body simply reacted, driven by old fears. In a snap of teeth, he was ten years old again, Sir Harry at his throat. The worst part was Vic *let* Johnathan toss him around. There was no way he could have lifted the vampire off the ground in his current state, no matter how angry he was. Was there?

He frowned down at his hands. The burn of anger had finally cooled in his gut, leaving him achy and hollow.

Alyse rounded on him. "You're lucky my father took the children out to work in the garden, so they didn't witness that little show," she said, her tone fringing on anger. "Why on earth did you do that?"

Of course she was still here. Of course she couldn't leave it well enough alone. Though Johnathan was embarrassed he'd forgotten his manners so quickly in her home.

"Alyse, it's not appropriate for you to be in the same room with a half-naked man."

"You're the one who left your room dressed down to the skin, dolt." A pair of trousers slapped him in the face. He clenched his teeth and struggled into his pants while Alyse seethed with her back to him. "*Now* you worry about propriety."

"He snapped his teeth at me—"

"Oh, the big bad vampire hunter got scared." Alyse's words echoed Vic's, but this time Johnathan flinched in shame. "Vic watched over you the whole damn night. I've never seen him so rattled, not once in the five years of our association, not even when that first lot from the Society came sniffing around here."

Johnathan half turned to look at her. His mind stumbled over which detail of that loaded sentence to tackle first, but the one that hooked him, that rattled him in turn, were the last words to leave her mouth. "The Society has sent Hunters here before?"

Alyse blinked at him. "A little over a year ago. There were three of them. Didn't they tell you when they sent you here?"

They should have. Why didn't they? Johnathan didn't know what to think or how to respond.

Alyse softened at the lost look on his face. "You didn't know," she murmured, biting her lip. "You're ah, bleeding again from your shoulder. Would you let me redress your wound? I worked awfully hard on those stitches."

Despite the blood loss, a blush readily heated the back of his neck.

Alyse continued to unsettle him, but he couldn't afford to turn away her aid. He nodded, not trusting his voice to hold back a waver. Alyse steered him to a chair and fetched a fresh cloth. He kept his gaze downcast while she carefully unwrapped the soiled linen with a sympathetic hiss.

"You might have torn your stitches," she scolded him. Her touch was feather light and cool against his fevered skin.

"A fresh dressing will have to do," said Johnathan. He had the sinking feeling Vic wouldn't return for him. He would have to go after the vampire on his own—the stupid, starving, over-protective vampire who tried to scare him away rather than risk his safety with whatever windmill that foolish fiend chased like some puffed up Don Quixote. "How do you reconcile with what he is?"

Alyse's hands stilled. He held his breath as he looked up at her. Her gaze was sharp and serious, miles away from the prevalent convention of the demure country lady. She reminded him of the other women he knew from the city, who lived by their wit and their will, though Johnathan suspected the "demure country lady" was a greater myth than old gods and spirits of the forest.

"That wasn't the question I expected from you," she said.

"What question were you expecting of me?"

Alyse shrugged and resumed tying his bandages. "How I met Vic? Why I trust him so much? Why I still live in my father's house rather than take up with a vampire? Take your pick."

The very tips of Johnathan's ears burned, the cursed blush revealing the depth of his inexperience. "Good Heavens, why would I ask any of those?"

Alyse snorted. "The impiety of youth?"

He shifted, uncomfortable beyond belief with this line of conversation. "I have no right to ask such questions, Alyse, though you must have heard them before."

A small smile lit Alyse's face. "Careful, Johnathan, you sound like you almost care about my reputation."

Johnathan scowled at her. She coughed to cover a laugh, the humor muted by her sigh. "Vic is Vic," she said. "I don't think about the snap of teeth, or that he will still be here long after I turn to dust. There is only the now, and as much time as I can have with him while he's here." She smiled, tinged with such sadness that Johnathan caught his breath. "What he is means nothing to me. Only *who* he is." She pressed a fist over her heart.

"I didn't need a confession of your undying affection for him, Alyse," said Johnathan, trying to ignore the unusual pang of envy that hit his chest. "Pun intended."

She rolled her eyes. "It's a miracle I haven't strangled you yet. You're too much like my younger brothers." She had the nerve to ruffle his hair. "Are you going after him?" There was a hint of encouragement and hope in her gaze. "You should. I think you want to."

Johnathan swallowed at the sudden tightness in his throat. He did want to. For more reasons than he could bring himself to acknowledge.

"Do you know where he went?" he asked.

She frowned. "What did he say before you scared him off?"

"I did not scare him off," Johnathan snapped. "He said he should have asked *them* first, whoever *they* are."

Alyse's face drained of color. "Oh."

"*Oh?* Oh *what?* Why does everyone know more about *this mysterious them* than I do?" Johnathan inhaled. That sounded awfully close to whining.

"Maybe he was right to keep you here," she said, her voice small.

"I'm going, whether you help me or not." His tone was sharper than he intended.

Alyse's hands twisted the fabric of her skirts. "You'll find him in the woods. He probably took the road out of town."

"Why out of town? There are plenty of woods around here."

Her head gave a sharp shake. "They don't like the town. They won't come too close."

He blinked in surprise. The prospect of trailing the vampire with those creatures roaming in broad daylight was enough to give Johnathan pause. Much as he denied being a hindrance, he knew he was far from fighting fit. "Alyse, what exactly am I walking into here?"

She held her breath for a long moment before she let it out in a gasp. "I can't tell you, Johnathan. I dare not mention their name. I am my mother's daughter as much as my father's. Just keep your wits and listen to everything Vic tells you."

"Does your father own a pistol?"

Another head shake, more vigorous than the last. "Pistol won't do you much good," she said.

He frowned, intent to ask her more when she held up a hand. "Listen to Vic, and don't...don't trust all your senses."

Picking up her skirts, Alyse rushed from the room before Johnathan could question her further. Damn. Now he had to locate his boots and hope Vic wasn't too far ahead of him. He frowned at his unclothed torso. A shirt wouldn't be amiss either. He looked down at his bare feet. The silver ball Vic pulled from his shoulder rested between his big toes. He plucked it off the ground and tucked it into his trousers' pocket.

Alyse reappeared with a bundle of fabric, his boots, and a familiar length of metal in one hand. "I would take this with you. Just in case."

Johnathan looked at her. "It's a log hook. Not exactly a trusty saber."

"No," said Alyse, dropping his boots at his feet. "But it's iron, isn't it? It's your best defense against them."

Johnathan's brows rose in a silent question. Alyse kept her silence, white-faced though she gripped the log hook like a talisman to ward off the threat she refused to name. He mulled over her and Vic's reactions, shrugging his wounded shoulder into the shirt she'd brought him. When he was fully dressed, she solemnly offered the log hook.

"Watch his back, John," said Alyse.

Johnathan didn't know what humbled him more, her obvious worry that the vampire couldn't take care of himself, or that she trusted Johnathan to bring him home.

———

The mysterious *they* be damned. Johnathan left the house irritated enough to ignore the knot of pain in his shoulder, the log hook tucked inside the coat that belonged to Pastor Shaw. It was far too tight for him in the shoulders and short at the waist, since he had a couple inches on the man, but it covered him from the fair-weather chill. Summer pitched a losing battle to fall. The morning was brisk, but Johnathan broke a sweat before he made it through the town proper.

He breathed through his teeth as he walked. There was a fleeting thought of getting a horse but that thought died a quick death. The bounce and jolt of footsteps was bad enough. The plod of a horse would merely amplify the sensation of his shoulder trying to unwind within itself. He considered the poor wisdom in his plan for the umpteenth time, wincing at the sharp pebbles that poked through the soles of his boots. How well he remembered this experience.

The constant beat of the sun should have left him boiling, and while a film of sweat coated his face, it was a feverish one, chilled by the cooler air. His fresh dressing grew promptly drenched, his shirt plastered to his back, and the combination of chilly air and exertion so soon after his injury caused his teeth to chatter. Unpleasant as it was, he spent more time watching the placement of his feet to avoid those sharp stones rather than where he was going until familiar scuffed boots entered his field of vision.

Vic stood in the middle of the road, his gaze fixed on the woods beyond. Johnathan glanced back. He thought he couldn't have been more than a mile or two from town, but Cress Haven was long out of sight. The woods stood tall on either side of the solitary road, where they cast long shadows that swallowed the sunlight in a constant state of gloom.

The vampire didn't acknowledge him until Johnathan was nearly close enough to reach out and touch him. Vic's hand shot out, pressing his fingertips against Johnathan's chest. There was restrained anger in the gesture, but angry as the vampire was, Johnathan realized Vic wouldn't hurt him.

From beneath thick black lashes, his gaze pierced through Johnathan. Vic hissed at him. "What are you doing here? I told you not to come." The vampire was far too pale. He still hadn't fed. Johnathan wanted to strangle him. One of them should be at fighting strength.

"And I ignored you," said Johnathan. He thought that was a perfectly valid argument. The muscles of Vic's face twitched. He worried the vampire was about to have apoplexy. "Why didn't you feed or inject yourself?"

Vic scowled at him. "I did, dolt. It's not a miraculous rejuvenation. The process takes time."

Johnathan leaned back to study him with a critical eye.

Vic stiffened. "What?"

"I'm trying to decide if you're lying or not," said Johnathan.

Vic grimaced. "You will turn around right now and march back to Pastor Shaw's house." There was a familiar glimmer in the vampire's eye, but this was something the Society had well prepared him for. He held his breath, focusing on the air trapped in his lungs rather than the mental tug at the back of his mind.

Johnathan made a show of glancing back the way he came. "You'd send me back on my own? I barely made it here. How would you feel if I passed out on the road, alone and defenseless, to be picked off by those murderous beasts while you're off gallivanting in the woods with the mysterious *they*?"

A muscle ticked in Vic's cheek. He covered his mouth, muffling a frustrated scream with his hand. Johnathan politely waited for the vampire to get ahold of himself.

"Of course, I can't compel you when you're in charge of your faculties. That would make this so much easier," Vic breathed out. "I can't make up my mind if you're brave or an idiot."

Johnathan shrugged and threw Vic's former words back at him. "You'll let me know when you make up your mind? Preferably before you abandon me as fodder for whatever is chasing us?"

Vic pinched the bridge of his nose, annoyance etched in his countenance. "You'll be the first to know," he sighed. He glanced up at Johnathan, his irritation muted. "John, you shouldn't come." There was a flicker of desperation in Vic's eyes that hinted to his faltering resolve.

Anxiety tinged the air around Vic, sending a shock through Johnathan's system. "You're not going in there alone."

The vampire's lips parted, a quicksilver flash of wonder there and gone in a blink, but Johnathan saw it.

Vic straightened. "So, beyond bloodsucking fiends, did the Society train you to counter *anything* else?"

Johnathan shifted on his feet. He wasn't divulging covert secrets here. Vic knew exactly what the Society was and its purpose, but Johnathan felt, not for the first time, that his Society training was inadequate against the strange happenings in Cress Haven.

He grimaced, adjusting his wounded shoulder. "Vampires, ghouls, the usual fare."

Vic pursed his lips. Johnathan looked away.

"Right." Vic stepped off the road in silent foot falls, a style Johnathan attempted to emulate until his foot came down in a crackle of bracken. Vic's shoulders hunched. He glanced back at Johnathan in exasperation, who held up his hands in mock outrage. The vampire huffed in disgust and gave up the pretense of stealth. "They know we're here anyway," he muttered.

Johnathan fought to keep pace. "Mind enlightening me who we are meeting out here?"

"What? Don't appreciate the air of mystery?"

Johnathan didn't have the extra breath to fire off the retort that comment deserved.

"You can stop glaring at me John," said Vic. He held Johnathan steady as they clambered over a fallen tree. "Before the Europeans came here in droves, there was another great migration."

"Oh?" Johnathan wasn't sure where the vampire was leading with this conversation.

"The Americas were one of the last bastions of untouched wilderness," Vic pressed on. "Now humans are slowly spoiling that with the advancement of industry and progress." There was a surprisingly bitter sentiment in that statement. "It's only a matter of time before they pull back from this realm entirely, but for now, the Fair Folk still linger at the edges."

Johnathan stumbled and caught himself on a sturdy sapling. He stared at Vic. "The Fair Folk?"

Vic stopped when he realized Johnathan still stood there, clutching the sapling, a stunned look on his face.

"They were here when humans were stumbling babes," Vic said. "And they still see humans as little more than children. It's as you said, John. Like creatures out of a fairy tale. Only I assure you they are far worse than the subjects of their stories." He turned and came closer, until the two men stood boot to boot. "You must be especially careful because they will tempt you. They will make you offers of food that you must not eat. They will offer you a dance that you must not refuse but will carry you away if you let it. If they really like you, and they will John, because you are young and beautiful and damaged, they will offer to bring you to their realm." Vic clutched the lapels of Johnathan's coat. "You must say no on your own. If you accept, I can't interfere. They will take you through, and they will pamper and adore you for what will feel like hours, before they tire of you. And when they bring you back, everyone you know will be dead."

Johnathan gaped at him. Vic inhaled and glanced at the dense forest around them. "I shouldn't have let you come," he said. "It is selfish and careless of me." He worried his lip, a gesture oddly reminiscent of Alyse. "They don't like my kind, you see, and they are very cruel." Vic released a shuddering breath. "And I'm a coward."

The forest closed them in with fingers of coarse bark and velvety smooth leaves. The deep gloom breathed around them, an ancient entity that watched the two of them with cool disinterest. The awareness of its attention skittered along their skin, fine as spider webs. Vic tensed, uneasy under the scrutiny of unseen beings.

"We're out here chasing goddamn fairies?" Johnathan blurted.

CHAPTER EIGHTEEN

VIC SLAPPED A HAND OVER JOHNATHAN'S MOUTH. HE LOOKED AROUND with jerky, nervous movements. Johnathan pried him off, unsettled by the feeling of cool flesh, squeezing the vampire's wrist so tight that Vic's attention pulled back to him.

Vic frowned. "What's wrong with you?"

"What's wrong—you dragged us out on a wild chase for bleeding fairies," Johnathan snapped. His chest heaved, too angered and unbalanced to deal with this nonsense. Vampires, ghouls, even the strange beasts here were tangible threats. But fairies?

"It's not—" Vic paused to look around. "It's not nonsense, John." He scowled. "That aside, you insisted on coming, my dear idiot."

Johnathan wasn't listening because through the trees he saw the sight of antlers, dipping and weaving amid the branches. "Please be a stag."

"What?" Vic turned to follow his gaze. "Shit."

"Is now a good time to admit my poor fighting condition?"

Vic's hand shot out, crushing the wooden buttons of Pastor Shaw's coat in his bid to keep Johnathan from moving. "If you try to fight one of them, we'll be in worse than poor condition."

Johnathan rolled his eyes. "If that is your clever way of saying the fairies will kill us—"

"They won't kill us," said Vic.

Johnathan looked at him. "You're serious."

"Are you sure you don't want to stay here? They might need a pet."

Johnathan clenched his jaw. "Don't accept any food. Acquiesce to a dance, but don't dance too long. Refuse further invitation through my own will."

"You listened," Vic said softly.

"Ridiculous as I find this whole exercise, it is never wise to ignore instruction."

"I guess Society training has its merits."

"Do shut up," said Johnathan. He peered back through the trees, but the hint of antlers was gone. "It might have only been a deer."

"Doubtful," Vic muttered.

"Pastor Shaw will be put out by the destruction of his buttons," remarked Johnathan. He frowned. "It's the middle of the day."

"Last time I looked."

"Don't fairies wait until the light of the blue moon or some other such nonsense before they reveal themselves to mortals?"

"Those are stories, John. This is the real thing, and they follow their own rules." Vic inhaled deep for patience. "You're from Boston, yes? Lots of Irishmen there. And you've obviously heard a tale or two."

Johnathan thought of Dr. Evans. He was the son of an Irish immigrant, and sometimes, after too many drinks, he rambled off stories from his father's homeland.

"What makes you think their legends aren't as real as vampires?" Vic went on. "Every land has its lore, Johnathan, but understand that the inhabitants of such places aren't bound by map lines. Just as fairies are accessible in the cairns of Ireland, they're also accessible here, in a creepy woodland in Maine."

Vic released his hold on the pastor's much-abused coat and followed an unseen path, straight and true. Johnathan followed in his footsteps, wary and more than a little skeptical of the forest around them. Flashes of movement flicked through the corners of his vision, flights of brightly colored feathers, darting shapes with strange edges, but when he jerked his head around to look, nothing was there.

The first trickle of true unease slid through him. Johnathan's steps quickened to catch up to Vic. "When you said you had a lead to track down the other day, was this who you were referring to?"

"They are difficult to find," said Vic, "but you can if you know how to look."

"Did you find them?" The woods filled with muted sounds, baseless words and whispers that blended with the wind rustling through the leaves.

There was a snort from the vampire beside him. "No. I know they are here, but they're being difficult."

The wind teased Johnathan's senses, laden with sweet, fragrant scents —fresh blooming lilacs, honeysuckle, moss after rain—cut with the clean cold scent of new-fallen snow and something else, raw and sharp, that left a taste of metal on the tongue, both repellent and tantalizing. He lifted his face, trying to fill his lungs with the scent, turning to follow it.

"I fully intended to spend days out here...if necessary," said Vic. "I will find them one way or another."

The tension seeped out of Johnathan's muscles, so relaxed, the pain in his shoulder faded to a dull ache. Was that singing?

"The problem is..." said Vic, his voice whisper soft.

Johnathan was only half listening. He'd turned away from Vic as he searched for that distant music. If he listened hard, he could make out the tune, a half-remembered lullaby from a mother whose face he couldn't remember. His lids dropped, his body swaying to the long-forgotten song.

"They like to play hard to get. I'll run them to ground eventually," Vic continued. "If I were human, it would be a bit easier but—" The vampire sucked in a breath. "Johnathan, stop!"

Johnathan staggered. The song choked and died, replaced by a roar in his head. Irritation simmered at a low boil as he looked up at the vampire. "Did you use me as bait? Again?"

Vic took a step back, a bewildered look of alarm on his face. "No! I didn't expect them to show up this fast." He frowned. "Normally they would lead us in circles for hours yet."

Johnathan's brows lifted. "Does that make this a trap or an invitation?"

Vic made a face, clearly unsettled. "Neither option is good. They wouldn't freely invite someone like me into their midst. I'd have to pry my way in."

Johnathan's brows drew together. "Because of what you are?"

Vic looked away, the faintest flush tinging his cheeks. "I told you. They don't like my kind. I'm not vulnerable to their glamour, therefore I'm boring, but eventually they would come for me, make a game of it. For you, they've left the door open." He gestured with a small flourish to Johnathan's left.

Johnathan looked. The trees were crooked, bent into a semicircle that formed a small clearing. Sunlight streamed down on a ring of wild mushrooms. Toadstools, their broad flat heads still glistening with morning dew. Parents would warn their children in playful rhymes not to dance in a fairy ring lest the fairies steal them away. Nothing more than a bedtime story or a cautionary tale to keep their little ones from wandering too far into the woods, but as Johnathan stood there, a physical hum vibrated against his skin, making the fine hairs on his arms stand on end.

The song led him here.

"I found this," he whispered.

"Yes. And now, you should go back," said Vic. "I don't like this. They're too eager with you here."

That warning again. He turned to tell Vic to knock it off and stopped. The vampire looked terrified. He hid it well, but Johnathan and fear were old friends. He saw that fear in the very lines of Vic's body. He saw it where tension flared in blanched white spots over tightly curled knuckles and pressed lips. There was a dangerous vulnerability there that made Vic look even younger, the delicate angles of his face softer.

Johnathan looked away, disconcerted by the mix of emotions such a sight stirred within him.

"We go together," he said. "Watch out for each other." He looked up. Vic stared at him as if he'd never seen him before.

"John," he said, a hesitant note thick in his voice. "What you see in here, they're cruel, and they smell secrets. They'll say things, about you, about me. I should tell you that my past—"

"You take too long," a sibilant voice hissed. It shivered through the leaves in a wave of frost-kissed darkness. Johnathan didn't see the hands that grabbed him, gasping as they wrapped around his waist and yanked him through the shimmering air. The portal immediately coalesced in his wake like a closing door. They meant to separate him from the vampire.

"Vic!" Johnathan cried out.

He extended both arms, reaching blind. Panic siphoned his pain. A wide-eyed Vic hurtled through the opening, and slammed into Johnathan, snarling at whatever creature had hold of him. A fearsome predatory reaction, but the unseen creature answered with a simpering high-pitched giggle that made the hair on the back of Johnathan's neck rise.

The air solidified behind Vic, and realization sank deep. They were trapped, and now Johnathan could see the arms around him.

He made a sound in the back of his throat at the sight of slick, silvery scales, like fish skin covering thin arms. Rawboned fingers pressed into his belly tipped in long claws that came to fine black points. The arms pulled him flush against another body, cold, far colder than the vampire. One claw-tipped hand released his middle to stroke his cheek.

"What a wonderful toy you've brought us, little liar," purred the creature, a hissing lisp that made the words skitter like dried leaves over frozen water. One claw dragged along Johnathan's throat in a thin burning line that scented the air with his blood. "I wonder how he tastes." A touch of ice flitted against the cut.

Vic's hand shot out over Johnathan's shoulder. "I didn't bring him here to share," he said through his teeth.

The thing chuckled, releasing Johnathan. He practically fell on Vic, who caught him with grace and spun him around to see. He dearly wished Vic hadn't bothered. Vaguely, he pondered the stories he'd heard of fairies being beautiful. Though he supposed there was a sort of terrible beauty to the fairy, the same way a river snake was beautiful as its serpentine body moved through the water. Once his vision adjusted to such a sight, he noticed the others standing around in a rough assembly, a waiting audience of nightmarish features and finery, fixated on their *guests*. The gathered assembly was all there was to this place, this pocket of another world, with no exit in sight.

CHAPTER NINETEEN

Johnathan's muscles went rigid.

"You must calm," Vic whispered in his ear.

The fairies tittered at Vic's words, sharp edges to their gleaming smiles. Johnathan looked away, trying to gain his bearings in their new surroundings. A mistake. Beyond the spit of lush green grass and a dancing floor of polished black and white stone, the world fell away, a stomach-turning mash of angles and color. Smears of what could almost be tree trunks lumped together with rock, shot through with glittering veins that pulsed a dozen colors in the seconds he watched, so fast the sight would break his equilibrium if he stared a moment longer. The realm of the fairies felt unfinished, as if they couldn't be bothered to create the details of their realm beyond what they desired in the moment.

He tore his gaze away from the scenery, focusing on the beings that brought them to this incomplete place. The weight of the log hook was gone, these creatures being unlikely to allow any weapon that would hurt them into their realm. Its absence deepened his trepidation.

The closest creature, a being of brazen color like living fire, smiled at Johnathan. They all possessed that otherworldly quality about them, stalking around Johnathan and Vic in an elegant swish of skirts made from impossible material, cobweb trains, and jewel-toned flower petals sewn like sequins. Their limbs all held the same brittle quality of spun glass. A strong breeze could break them. Johnathan couldn't think of a greater lie. Ethereal and airy, he saw flashes of massive dragonfly wings, like paper-thin stained glass, folded neatly along the backs of several creatures. Others bore scales, short fur, or stomach-churning combinations of both. They were a collection of glamorous nightmares, and Johnathan found his gaze riveted to each of them. A flash of feverish sweat beaded his brow as he shivered.

"Has the little liar returned?" This voice was discordant, echoing within itself. A new being stepped into view, the gathered fairies parting for her like an arriving debutante.

Johnathan's breath left him in a rush. Her face was child-sweet, a deceptive facade to a body constructed of soft lush curves. She peered at them with liquid-dark eyes, like a curious doe, her head tilted while her weaving steps created a purposeful hypnotic dance. The dress that clung to her body was light lavender that seeped into deeper shades of red and violet, like a deep sweet bruise. A promise of violence flowed in liquid waves down her body and pooled on the ground at her feet. Her movements shimmered in Johnathan's vision until she swam into focus in front of him, where she lifted a hand so her nails could trace the curve of his face.

"I like this one," she said. Her quiet voice reverberated in the space around him until he imagined she spoke two different sentences at once.

Johnathan could almost understand the other voice if he listened harder.

He leaned in closer to her, brought up short by Vic's arm around his chest. Johnathan frowned and tried to push forward. A smile curled her lips as she watched him struggle. It sent a spike of fear down his spine. He stiffened in Vic's hold.

"Stop it," he whispered to the strange female.

Vic hissed behind him.

The fairy threw back her head and laughed, the high and mocking call of a crow, her bow-shaped lips parted to reveal a mouth of sharp, black- stained teeth. The sight of those teeth wavered in his vision until the smile she gave him was white, pure as fresh snow. The hand she extended was fine boned, but normal.

Johnathan's mind swam in the thick scent of lilacs and something else, something he couldn't name but stung his senses and pricked behind his eyes.

"Come, dance with me," she said, the echo of her voice melting into a humming song that pounded through his skull, carrying a beat too primal to ignore.

Vic released a long breath behind him and the arm around his chest went slack.

Johnathan took her hand. She led him through the cluster of watching faces and dazzling finery, the grass beneath their feet shifting seamlessly to polished stone. The rhythm throbbed in his bones.

He tugged the woman's hand until she glanced back, puzzled. Johnathan spun her inward, his body flowing in a sinuous dance he'd learned from a childhood of bonfire nights, when bodies danced around an altar of flames that lapped at their shadows. She laughed in clear delight when Johnathan took the lead in a high energy dance of spins and dips. The music went on without end, the pulse of it demanding, and Johnathan might have heeded the call until he dropped from exhaustion. Pain pierced through the fog choking his mind. He stopped, panting; the surrounding fairies wavered out of focus. The fairy leaned back in his arms, laughing high and wild with her black-stained teeth, her hands clutching him.

She straightened, a cruel smile playing on her lips. "You smell of death and sweet nectar." Her breath washed over him, trying to drown him in the thick, sickly floral scent, entwined with that pungent, eye-watering underlay. "Care for another dance, my sweet Johnny boy?"

In a vise of pain and anger, the illusion snapped, and Johnathan beheld a nightmare in his arms. Her flawless skin withered and sloughed away in seconds to unveil a creature of rot and ruin. Those liquid black eyes melted away to squirming pits of maggots, and the scent of decay punched through the floral perfume.

"Come," said Death with a black rot smile. "Dance with me."

Johnathan froze, his mind unable to process the vision. In a blink, the horror was gone, but the truth rang through his senses.

A fist squeezed his lungs. Vic's warning clamored in his skull. He jolted back from her, unable to draw a breath. Clarity bloomed, the pain of his injuries breaking through the fairy's influence on his mind.

"No, thank you," said Johnathan. Pain was the answer, a secret weapon against their devious tactics. He took another step away from the fairy. The blind retreat might have led him into more waiting claws, but Vic appeared beside him, sliding his hand into Johnathan's, braiding their fingers together. The pressure eased enough for Johnathan to breathe. The female pouted, and for a bare breath Johnathan glimpsed the shadow of that rotted visage once more.

He shivered and looked up into Vic's silvered gaze. "What?"

Vic's gaze darted, a question on his lips, but they were surrounded by too many keen ears. Instead, the vampire squared his shoulders and faced the fairies. "Will you answer our questions?"

The one who danced with Johnathan stepped forward, tapping a nail against her lips. "Will your answers be worth the price? Will your pretty companion give—"

"*I* ask the questions," said Vic. The pressure of his hand drew Johnathan's focus back to the vampire. Vic trembled where he stood, nostrils flaring. He licked his lips. "Are you murdering the girls of Cress Haven and Hampshire?"

Johnathan frowned. Why risk their wrath with a borderline accusation? But the fairy woman laughed, echoed by the ghastly gathered lot.

"Oh, little liar, what use would we have with such distasteful business?" She circled them, the dual tone of her voice a low lull. Her fingers danced along the back of Vic's shoulders. "Now why would a fiend involve themselves in such matters?"

Vic's smile was a baring of teeth. "You haven't answered my question."

The fairy woman's smile twisted into a sneer. "How should we know the fate of every hapless mortal that wanders these woods? Humans are such fragile things." Her gaze flickered to Johnathan, a predatory hunger in its black depths.

"That's still not an answer," said Vic.

The fairy woman snarled. Her rotted visage flickered through as she snapped her teeth in Vic's face. The vampire held completely still.

"Such a wicked little boy," the fairy cooed.

Johnathan frowned. Her words made his ears buzz. His gaze slipped to the tight expression on Vic's face, following the graceful curve of his jaw and admiring the smooth skin. Vic was a beautiful man, though Johnathan never allowed himself to look for too long, afraid he would never stop looking. He'd never really...not really...let his gaze linger, not when the prejudice he carried from boyhood colored their every interaction. Johnathan could see the faint lines of age around Vic's eyes, faded like scars by the transition from human to vampire.

Why call him boy, though?

Beneath the hunger in their faces, the moment gained weight in a dreadful creep of awareness. Vic told him they demanded secrets, and it was clear now that Johnathan's presence provided them with another significant entertainment factor.

It dawned on Johnathan that the fairy was not speaking of Vic at all. He glanced at the fairy from the corner of his eye, her ravenous gaze riveted to him even as she wove around Vic.

Dread burned the back of his neck. Johnathan quickly donned the same stone-faced facade he used as Sir Harry's pawn.

Vic turned to face the fairy woman, jaw so tight the vampire spoke through clenched teeth. "I told you, I am the one asking the questions. If you attempt to exact payment from my companion, I shall invoke the old rites."

Dark delight bloomed on the fairy woman's face. "No, I did not kill the girls."

Johnathan saw a muscle twitch in the vampire's face, and he saw how the question went sideways. A very careful answer, a very specific answer, that told them absolutely nothing except that this one creature was not responsible.

The fairy woman danced her fingers down Vic's chest, the only warning before the silken coat and cloth layers beneath turned brittle and began to peel away like dried onion skins. Vic hissed and wrenched free of Johnathan's grip, trying and failing to catch the rotted cloth as it fell. Nearly exposed, the vampire held the remaining scraps in place.

Vic's body was a handsome and lithe specimen, but for the prominent scars that marred his arms and back, a deep pale pink like blush roses. For all his confidence, it was clear being stripped bare this way was a blow to Vic, a secret shame Johnathan didn't quite understand, though he could see it in the tense lines of the vampire's body and the tight expression on his face. The fairies giggled at his nudity, as if the slight were a great party trick.

The buzz grew worse in Johnathan's head. It trickled through his veins until his entire body hummed with it. He stepped in front of the vampire, allowing Vic to recover what he could of his clothing. His thoughts coalesced to a single focus. Johnathan refused to let the fairies keep degrading Vic. He would do the asking. The wording had to be precise, so these slick-tongued creatures couldn't twist it to their advantage.

He rapidly tossed away one question after the other the moment they nestled in his mouth. He had to make the sting worth the bite. He ignored Vic's intake of breath as he faced off the monstrous gathering. The visage of the group winked in and out in time to the throbbing ache in his shoulder. He focused on that monstrous side, the terrible truth of the fairies, and tried not to think what they would do to him.

Johnathan clenched his hands hard against his thighs. The fairy woman's image wavered in time to his pulse. Pain stilted the power of their allurement.

Anchored within, he faced off with the fairy woman. "What killed the girls of Cress Haven?"

Was it the right inquiry? He could have asked any number of questions that could be twisted and evaded by the fairy woman's artful tongue, but they had to find the root, the vital piece Vic was clearly missing.

The fairy woman focused on him, her expression curious.

Vic tugged at the back of his jacket. "John, no."

Johnathan ignored him, forced to stillness as the fairy loomed closer.

Her fetid breath stung his nose as she traced along the pulse point in his neck with a single crooked nail. "Do you agree to the price, pretty one?"

His nostrils flared. "Would I ask if I possessed no currency?"

A smirk curved her lips. "You mince words as well as you dance,

Prospective Newman."

His skin tingled at the use of the title. He didn't question how the fairy woman knew. These creatures were far too adept at scraping pieces of information from his mind.

Vic's fingers dug into the back of Johnathan's jacket. "No—"

"The question has been asked, little liar," said the fairy woman. She spun away in a swirl of skirts. The others swayed, their voices inaudible murmurs that tugged at Johnathan's focus.

"Do you think we were the only ones to wander this world when humans were blind, weak beasts in the dark?" The fairy woman sang to him, spinning in a blur. "Do you think we are the only ones who venture forth, to snatch, and steal, and play?"

Another damn evasion. Johnathan bit back a swear. The urge was strong to snatch the fairy by her shoulders and shake the answer from her. Would she keep slipping him snips and scraps without real truth while the fairies laid his secrets bare? Vic warned him of their cruelty and their love for games, and still, he charged in, confident he could outwit these creatures if only he were clever enough. Johnathan was a fool. His fingers twitched when she drew near, anger and pain twining together. Heat flared behind his eyes.

"Do you think we are the only ones to twist words? The only ones to bargain for more than we give?" She bowed to him as she passed with an exaggerated wink.

Johnathan's irritation boiled over. His hand snapped out and snagged the fairy woman's spider silk skirts so fast she stumbled. "I won't pay for nothing."

Her fury was swift and violent. A strip of tattered fabric tore free in his grip when she came at him. Somehow taller and greater than before, she loomed in, her true, terrible face revealed.

"You think I fear your anger, child of Adam? You think I won't tear you to pieces for your insolence?" She spat and growled at him. Her maggot-stuffed eye sockets eclipsed his field of vision and his stomach roiled.

Vic grabbed at him from behind, trying to pull him away from the fairy, but Johnathan pressed back. Through the horror of her true face, his mind caught the wordplay. The fairy's threats, frightening as her visage, were posed as questions, and had all the substance of shadows. It was another trick, another evasion. Vic told him they wouldn't kill him. Could they kill him, even if they wanted to?

"I think, tricky and terrifying as you are, you follow certain rules." He wasn't ashamed of the waver in his voice. His knowledge was based around half-remembered rhymes and songs from a childhood with little time for such merry pursuits. Vic's body pressed hard against his back. Johnathan was grateful for his physical presence but confused by it. He merely hoped he had the chance to process that thought if they survived this night. His words must have hit a mark, for the fairy woman's horrid face twisted with deep, ugly rage, but something brought her up short.

A humming song rolled through the clearing. The fairy woman's features crumpled in panic. She fell back from Johnathan to drop in a low cower. The inaudible murmur was laced with incredulity, a single word rising clear as a bell as the other fairies slunk to the edges of the clearing, a lone figure left standing in their wake.

Morrigan. The name shot into his mind, as if the realm branded the knowledge into him.

The newcomer was female, though her appearance didn't confirm it. Her face and body were draped in gauzy veils that concealed all but the barest hint of her shape. Her presence was tangible, primal, ancient, and alien where it brushed against Johnathan's mind. She evoked something beyond terror in him, pinning him in place surer than a mouse frozen beneath the gaze of a snake. A crown of branching antlers rose from her skull, swathed in clumps of spiderwebs like bunched silk. The veils that covered her were equally organic—webs, moss—held down by the weighted counterpoints of tangled teeth and bone so that her clothing clicked with each step.

Her attention was a boulder around his neck; it crushed the air from his lungs.

The rotted fairy was a child's bogey compared to her, the Morrigan. Johnathan couldn't look up as she drew closer. Instead, he stared at the shadow that trailed her, one that stretched longer and longer like a bridal train. That shadow sucked at his mind, filled his thoughts with roughshod screams and broken pleas.

His gaze snapped back to her veiled face.

"Brave boy, beautiful boy, why did you come?" Her voice was the worst of all, for the deception it presented. A soft and sleepy voice, like a tired mother comforting her babe from a night terror, when the Morrigan was the source, the deepest terror in the darkest night.

It made his instincts scream. He didn't need Vic's fingers digging into his sides to sense the danger there, and he knew better than to lie.

"I had to," said Johnathan. Her focus flitted to Vic behind him, but she paid little attention to the vampire. When she reached for Johnathan with bone-white hands, he couldn't quite swallow the whimper in his throat, but the Morrigan simply cupped his cheek.

"The taint of death marks you, but your innocence tastes like honeyed wine." She sighed and released him, looking back at the cowering ranks of fairies.

Released from the weight of her attention, Johnathan would have pitched forward if Vic hadn't hauled him to his feet.

The Morrigan tilted her head at the other fairies, speaking in that smooth voice of lullabies. "We cannot lie. We gild our tongues in silver and spin a net of half-truths. Beings of the Other, the Benign, and the Nether, do not possess the gift of deceit." The gathered fairies flinched at her words.

"But you glamour," said Johnathan. "Illusion is a lie." He could feel Vic shaking his shoulders, but the words left his mouth before he could stop them.

The Morrigan merely chuckled. "I suppose you are right, brave boy. It is our defense against the iron and flame of Adam's ilk." Her pale hands reached up and lifted the veils from her face.

Johnathan stopped breathing. It wasn't the nightmare of the rotted fairy woman, but a face of hard sharp features, the First Mother, a half-forgotten memory that faded from his mind even as he stared at her. If he closed his eyes right then, he could not recall her face to save his life, but knew it would haunt his dreams until he died.

"I also cannot lie, but I follow the old rites, and I cannot give an answer without a question."

Johnathan's leg muscles trembled as he struggled to keep his feet under him. He knew she didn't include the vampire in her statement. The Morrigan came for him, and that terrified him.

"What is killing the girls of Cress Haven?" he asked again.

The Morrigan clicked her tongue against her teeth. "Question asked, answer given. The ones who die do not have the strength for living."

"What?" Johnathan stared at her, a riot of confusion knocked around in his skull. The Morrigan struck him as an ancient terror, and he foolishly believed she wouldn't play the same word games.

"Oh, brave boy," said the Morrigan, her expression a mockery of pity. "The abandoned boy, left to the mercy of the streets and death's cool embrace." Her words were stones hitting his skin, but it was not his worst secret. She suddenly gripped his chin, pinched in the clamp of merciless white fingers. "You must ask the right questions."

Johnathan swallowed. Would this go on forever? It could. He had no doubt the Morrigan could answer every question in a similarly vague manner, an empty bargaining that would see his secrets completely unraveled like rind from fruit. He began to feel like she might work him until everything he'd ever buried in the dark depths of his soul had been brought to bright and humiliating light.

Vic clutched his shoulder. "John, let me do this—"

"You have no more secrets for me, vampire," said the Morrigan. "I have no time or patience for sad little boys who don't have the good grace to stay dead."

Johnathan shut them out, trying to think. He hadn't much time to accumulate many secrets, but the ones he did have drained the color from his face until he nearly matched the Morrigan's complexion. He wanted to ask what was happening to the girls, what the Morrigan meant from her cryptic answer, but he could see one question after another peeling away his secrets until he had nothing left to bargain. Instead, he thought of the woods outside the Fairchild home. He thought of the horned creature he encountered when he chased after the beastly form of Lydia Fairchild, so similar and yet so different from the creature before him. He thought of Nathaniel Fairchild.

This wasn't the bargain we made.

"Who did Nathaniel Fairchild bargain with?" Please be the right question.

A small smile played on the Morrigan's lips. Johnathan did not know if that bode well or ill for him.

"We often make merry with the children of Eve," she said.

Johnathan inwardly groaned, certain he'd failed again.

"We tease and cajole," she went on. "We make fine offers but never promises. Our words are binding."

The other fairies hissed and fidgeted at the Morrigan's words, as if she handed Johnathan their great weakness. Maybe she had.

She tapped her chin. "Those from the Nether, however, do love their bargains."

Vic flinched against Johnathan's back and swore in a torrent of curses that made the Morrigan's smile widen. Bewildered as he was by her answer, it appeared that a few pieces of this puzzle had clicked into place for the vampire at least. Wonderful, since Johnathan would pay for the information.

He braced himself when the Morrigan dipped forward and spoke in a hushed voice, acting like there wasn't a pack of vicious fairies hanging on her every word. "There is your answer, pretty Johnny boy, now grown but once a dead man's toy."

She ran her fingers through his hair as she sang the words. He heard Vic's intake of breath behind him but didn't dare take his eyes off the Morrigan. She watched him, an expectant air in her expression. What was she waiting for?

Vic cleared his throat. "John, I need you to ask one more question." The vampire's voice was thick with regret. "We need to know how the victims are chosen."

Didn't they already? Or did they? Johnathan wanted to deny it, but he knew, deep in his gut, that Vic wouldn't ask this of him if it wasn't important.

The Morrigan waited. He had to ask the question himself.

"How are the girls chosen?"

The faintest crease of worry formed around the Morrigan's eyes. What did that mean?

"Marked in ash, by fire and soot, branded to stone, and flesh, and root." Her bottomless gaze held him, searching for something. He couldn't shake the feeling he'd failed to find the correct wording for this one.

"Dammit," Vic muttered. Johnathan shook himself, grateful for the distraction to break from that powerful stare. The Morrigan's expression was unreadable. A mutinous side thought to try again, but Johnathan feared what she would exact from him in return. Already, he was anxious for what came next.

"Take your payment," Johnathan rasped. His throat was so dry the words caught and scraped his tongue raw.

"Brave boy," said the Morrigan. "What is your darkest secret? That you were Sir Harry's lure, or that you enjoyed it?"

He shuddered at her words. He understood now. She wouldn't pull the secret from him. He had to offer it freely. "My darkest secret is that... I loved him," Johnathan whispered.

The Morrigan's smile softened. She reached out and took Johnathan's hands. Her thumbs brushed over his palms and stopped. The Morrigan stiffened, her thumb pressing into his once-injured palm. Her mouth opened as if she were about to say something else. Heat sparked beneath his skin at her touch. The healed-over wound itched. Johnathan fought the urge to yank his hand from her grip.

The rotted fairy appeared at her side, full of fear and fury. She seized the Morrigan's wrist. "You can't give them knowledge without payment offered," the fairy woman hissed. "Even you cannot disavow the old rites."

The Morrigan turned that terrible gaze on her. Quaking, the rotted fairy held her ground. The Morrigan released Johnathan and stepped away.

Questions rose in his mouth, sour and sharp, but the weight of exhaustion hit him all at once. Johnathan was drained beyond measure, the pain in his shoulder a constant dull roar like a relentless surf pounding the shore. He slumped in Vic's grip, his limbs heavy and limp. He found he could barely keep his eyes open.

Vic took a shuddering breath. "We have to go. It'll be dawn soon."

Dawn? But it wasn't yet midday when they arrived.

The Morrigan looked up at them. "Would you rather stay with us, brave boy? Stay here, with us, safe and warm. We will feed you sweet cakes and ripe fruits and dance until morn."

Her words seeped into him like the warmth of a hearth fire. A beckoning warmth, away from blood and fear and from the sharp teeth that waited in the woods.

Johnathan glanced up and locked gazes with the Morrigan. Her attention would be as wonderful and terrible as the sun. Nourishing. Painful. Addictive. He could love a creature like the Morrigan as surely as he'd loved Sir Harry. The temptation rose, lending strength to his weary limbs.

Vic shifted Johnathan's weight further onto his shoulder. Johnathan looked down at Vic's pale, pinched face. The vampire watched the Morrigan with bitter resignation. Johnathan had questions for him, dammit. It was *his* turn for answers.

"I must politely decline," said Johnathan.

Vic's shocked gaze flashed up at him.

The Morrigan sighed. "Then go." She flicked her fingers. The air heated behind them. The shimmering portal was open for them once more.

Vic released a shuddering breath and turned both of them toward it.

"Little liar, ask me," the Morrigan called after them.

Vic paused. "You said it yourself. I have nothing left to give you." The vampire dragged them both another step forward and stopped. He grit his teeth though, and stomped the ground before glancing over his shoulder. "Ask you what?"

There was another pause. Vic winced at the absurdity of his question. Johnathan wondered what the Morrigan would do with the slip, but knew if he turned around, the fairies would ensnare him again.

"They have to be tainted," the Morrigan said, followed by, "They have to be pure."

Johnathan caught Vic's frown. The whole exchange was odd, as if the Morrigan gave Vic a pass for his wasted question by giving him another nonsense answer.

Vic cursed and, with Johnathan hanging on his arm, headed out of the wood. "Don't look back," said Vic. "No matter what."

It took every ounce of willpower Johnathan had left to keep his gaze forward, but this time, he obeyed.

CHAPTER TWENTY

THE WEIGHT OF THE HEAVENS SLAMMED DOWN ONTO JOHNATHAN. The sensation was beyond exhaustion, and he fought to keep his eyes from rolling up into his skull. Vic kept him upright when he sagged, resettling Johnathan's good arm around his shoulders as he half dragged him away from the now normal patch of air.

"Here we are again," said Vic, his voice light, but there was a note of weariness in his voice he couldn't hide. "Me rescuing my damsel in distress."

Johnathan couldn't find the energy to retort, fighting the strong desire to lie down on the ground and sleep for a year. He wanted to be as far away as possible from the fairies, but his body was at its limits. *Beyond* its limits. If not for Vic's immense strength, he wouldn't have made it this far. Those cool hands on his were a strange comfort after his encounter with the fairies, one that brought his tangled emotions brimming to the surface.

"I don't think my dignity can survive you carrying me right now," said Johnathan. A small lie to hide the truth of his sudden awkwardness. His voice was a rasp of parchment over stone, the words like dust in his mouth.

"Good, because I don't think I could carry you further if I tried," said Vic.

There was notable strain in the vampire's voice, but he set Johnathan down gently against the soft moss of a fallen log, collapsing beside him with legs splayed. The salvaged shreds of his trousers hung around his lower body in a ragged apron that covered little, the fabric held fast by the remains of his leather belt. That they were both spent was worrisome. They were deep in the forest, the morning light still worming down from the treetops. The two of them sat braced against the trunk.

"How long were we gone?" said Johnathan.

"A day at most." Vic's brows pinched with a hint of uncertainty.

Unease settled in. Johnathan couldn't help but recall Vic's warning before the fairies yanked them through the portal about the rapid passage of time. What if seasons had passed, the world speeding along while they swam through the mire of the fairy realm? The pain of his ignored shoulder wound compounded into a sour note of agony. Johnathan dreaded what festered beneath his bandages.

He pushed the fear down. There wasn't time, not nearly enough time, and Johnathan knew they were on a clock even now, though they didn't understand how the passage of it was measured. The fairies spoke in evasive riddles, but he knew they didn't lie. The beasts would attack again. Not that he could rise and fight if he wanted to.

The revelations of the fairy realm nipped at his thoughts. He rolled his head to study his companion. The scrap of fabric Vic recovered from his trousers was enough to provide him a modicum of modesty but left his pale, perfect chest and long lean legs bare. His gaze wandered down the strong planes of muscle, admiring their definition, more akin to a laborer's build than the lithe dancer he so often attributed to Vic. Through all the time they'd spent together, it wasn't until now Johnathan allowed himself the curiosity of Vic's past. What sort of man was he before he turned? Johnathan burned to know, but his weary mind couldn't find a way to broach the subject.

Johnathan realized he was still staring at the man's chest. He cleared his throat, clenching his teeth to keep from yelping as he struggled out of his coat and offered it.

Vic stiffened, his expression openly surprised by the gesture, before he gingerly plucked it from Johnathan's fingers and turned away to put it on. His expression was set as he turned around. "Let me look at that shoulder."

"It's fine," said Johnathan. He'd much rather close his eyes for a few moments.

A sound of frustration escaped the vampire. "I can smell the blood, John. Please, let me see it."

If he had an ounce of energy to spare, Johnathan might have tensed as those cool fingers gently tugged and peeled the saturated cloth away. Instead, Johnathan watched Vic's face, expressionless but for the small movement of his throat as he swallowed. "That bad, huh?"

Vic's gaze flashed with worry. "It's inflamed, likely infected. We need to drain the wound."

Johnathan closed his eyes. "How would you recommend we do so? Sponge it with moss and tree bark?"

"Pain makes you surly," said Vic. He carefully redressed the wound with dirty bandages. The only bandages they had. "I shouldn't have let you come."

Johnathan smiled. "You couldn't stop me."

"Yes, I could have," Vic snapped, his words punctuated by knotting the bandage with enough force to make Johnathan wince. He sighed. "Sorry."

Johnathan leaned back against the log. The state of his wound was worrisome, but there was not much he could do about it now. That it hadn't healed like the puncture in his hand was worth noting, though he couldn't seem to summon much alarm about the strange wound. Rather, the thought filled him with a sliver of hope that the magical nature of the puncture was why it vanished. A weak theory, but he clung to it, unable to deduce why he'd kept the puncture's miraculous healing from Vic. Why couldn't he tell him now? Even as he worked up the gumption to do so, the will drained from him. Why couldn't he hold onto that sense of dread? Disgusted with himself, Johnathan could not stand the unnatural quiet in his own head.

"So. What are beings from the Nether?"

Vic's head snapped up, his face incredulous. "*That's* what you want to talk about?"

Johnathan's brows creased. "Seems fairly relevant to our situation."

Vic sat back, bare legs bent so that his arms rested loosely on his knees, fingers knitting and unknitting together in a study of nervous energy. Johnathan wondered what he had to be nervous about, but clearly his exposure in the fairy realm left Vic more unsettled than Johnathan realized.

"Aren't you dying to ask me about," he gestured to his now covered arms and back, "this?"

"What does that have to do with the price of peas in Portugal?"

"What?" Vic almost sounded outraged by Johnathan's unflappable manner. He stared at him. "Do you want to talk about...any of it?"

Johnathan blinked, mildly alarmed by the heaviness of his eyelids. "Do you care that I was a lure?" He didn't mention the other secret, the one that still burned on his tongue.

"I don't," said Vic without a beat of hesitation.

"You don't have to tell me about the marks," said Johnathan. What did he care about scars? He had more than his share from training at the Society. The life of a Prospective was a rough one. The Society cared little for one's past or the scars they carried from before. They only cared about their resolve. The kind of resolve it took for a boy to drive a blade through the heart of the one he loved.

He watched Vic shift in the overlarge coat, unsettled and depleted from their encounter with the fairies. Johnathan hadn't forgotten how Vic kept tugging at his back, how the vampire tried to take his place over and over. How Vic kept him standing and dragged him away from that hellish illusion.

"Tell me what we're up against."

Vic's fingers knit together and held in a tight knot. "The Nether is full of demons."

Johnathan wanted to slam his head against the tree trunk. "Of course. First fairies, now demons. Are all our childhood tales true?"

Vic shrugged. "Your guess is as good as mine. I've walked this earth for a few centuries now, and I've only ever seen *one*." His knuckles cracked. "One was more than enough."

"Centuries? Really?" said Johnathan.

Just how old *was* Vic? Why had he never asked the vampire more about himself? He flinched inwardly at his own question. Johnathan knew why he hadn't asked. Part of him had clung to the idea that at some point he might have to end the vampire.

"The Morrigan said—"

"Try not to say her name out loud," said Vic.

"The big scary fairy said the ones who died weren't strong enough to survive," said Johnathan. He winced at a twinge in his shoulder and pressed a hand to the wound. It was hot to touch despite the layers of cloth, a sign of infection. "I don't think this creature, demon, whatever it may be, is actually out to kill."

"I think it's collecting them," said Vic.

"What do you mean? For what purpose?"

"I'm not quite certain yet."

"So, we are dealing with a demon, an actual demon." Johnathan released a shaky breath. "We know it found a way into our world through a bargain with the late Mr. Fairchild, whose own child was one of the victims. The beast that attacked us was Lydia Fairchild. Does that mean the demons change the girls into those...things?"

"Yes. If they establish a foothold in our realm, demons have more power over humans than fairies. They can use their mark to taint and change humans. I believe the girls, if they survive the process, become servants. Demons, like the creature that made them," Vic explained, his voice hesitant at points, as if he was uncertain about the veracity of his information.

Johnathan swallowed with a grunt. His mouth was beyond parched, an effect, no doubt, of the fairy realm to further tempt him. "But how are they selecting their victims? What does 'they have to be tainted but pure' mean? Damn fairies and their riddles."

Vic's throat worked. "They are famous for their wordplay. It should be an obvious answer, but it's never straightforward with them. Could be purity of soul. Could be purity of body. If I knew more about the processes of demons, I might be able to answer it."

Johnathan paused to mull it over. "Virgins," he mumbled.

He'd suspected before that the victims had maintained their virginity, though he wondered how chaste Vic's relationship with Alyse could possibly be, and wasn't she a mark?

His head lolled towards Vic. "You think they are coming for Miss Shaw? Or have you corrupted her beyond their desires?"

He wanted to drag the words back inside him the moment they left his lips. Yet part of him wanted, needed to know the answer, and that need was a hard lump in his chest.

Vic gave a weak smile, the cat too tired to play with the mouse, thank the stars. "The nature of my relationship with Miss Shaw may meet the criteria for purity, but she is no virgin, I assure you. Her sister fit what I knew of the original parameters, but now I wonder how accurate our information was." Vic looked truly worried, tugging on the battered buttons of the coat. "I feel like I'm missing something important, but I am certain the Shaw household will be hit next."

Johnathan didn't say anything, a thought niggling at the back of his mind. There was an important detail just out of reach. Dammit, he was too drained to organize his thoughts, bruised inside his skin. Those half-forgotten memories nipped at the ragged edges of his self-control.

"We need to get back," Johnathan said without inflection.

"Yes," Vic answered, his tone equally void of emotion.

Neither of them moved. Johnathan finally noticed Vic leaned against him, shoulder to shoulder. The vampire's arm dropped to the ground, only a few inches from his own, a reminder of the way Vic had slid his hand into Johnathan's earlier. Without letting himself overthink, Johnathan closed the distance between them, the sides of their hands touching. Vic hooked two fingers around his, the touch as grounding now as it had been in the fairy realm.

Johnathan sniffed, shocked to realize there were tears gathering in the corner of his eyes. He hadn't shed a tear since that day so long ago, when Sir Harry's blood was on his hands.

"Don't you dare start crying," said Vic. "Because if you start, then I'll start, and my dignity has already taken a fair knock today. Yesterday? Blast."

Johnathan chuckled and obligingly wiped his eyes. "Wouldn't want that now, would we." Silence settled between them, not awkward or comfortable but brimming with unspoken questions. "You know, I am a tad curious about your life," he said, glancing at the sliver of Vic's skin bared to him from beneath the collar of Alyse's father's coat. "But if you tell me to ask you a question first, I will tell you to stuff it."

"Likewise," said Vic, a spark of humor in his gray eyes. "To the curiosity and the stuffing."

"Just so we understand each other," said Johnathan. The log dug into his sore back, but he closed his eyes. The devil of the Nether could take him now for all he cared, so long as it let him sleep.

"I was a monk," said Vic.

Johnathan's brows rose, but his eyes remained shut. Though, he had a feeling Vic would continue to speak whether he reacted or not.

"My father said he had too many sons, and I needed to better my relationship with God. That might have had something to do with my friendship with the local lord's daughter...and son."

A smile tugged at the corner of Johnathan's mouth.

"I didn't mind the life. It was austere but simple, and more than one man in the monastery was sent there for similar affections."

"You had lovers in a monastery?"

"I thought we agreed on no questions," Vic teased. "It's not as difficult as you would believe, lovers. There are many hours in the day, and you can only pray to the stone around you for so long."

There was another question, but Johnathan would not speak it. Vic paused for so long, Johnathan's exhausted mind thought him done and began to drift.

"The plague hit my second year there. We were brothers under God, and it was our duty to give God's mercy where we could. There was so much suffering, so much death, and holy vows gave no protection against the disease. It took everyone, young and old, rich and poor, the lowest criminal to the most pious saint." There was a dull cadence to his words, as if time and distance subdued the pain of the moment.

Johnathan knew the technique well, and he was tired enough for his defenses to slip. Least, that is what he told himself as he slid his hand further over Vic's, twining their fingers together in a hold both comforting and intimate.

Vic's muscles tensed and released. "It didn't spare me either. I flogged myself for weeks with the rest of my brothers to purify our bodies. Not that it mattered. The whole monastery took sick."

That explained the scars on his body, wounds that had time to heal before he transitioned.

Vic sucked in a breath and held it. "One night, a vampire slipped in. He fed on the dying in their beds. I woke to their cries, their pleas for mercy as they choked on their own blood."

He swallowed more than once. A vampire's memory was long. It didn't fade and wane like a human one, but remained sharp, a living script of their history, especially their regrets.

"I didn't try to save them. I panicked. I wanted to run, but my legs were too weak to support me. I knew my body was failing, but I was desperate. I crawled across the floor. The stone scraped my stomach raw. That is how he found me."

Vic turned their twined hands over, tracing the veins on the back of Johnathan's hand. The gesture would have lulled him to sleep if he wasn't so invested in the vampire's story.

"I don't know why he turned me. I wasn't the most handsome or the most passionate. I was closer to death than some, further than others."

"I know why," Johnathan murmured, his gaze riveted to the dance of Vic's fingers down his wrist. "Because when the others called for God to save them, for mercy, you crawled."

"Why would that matter?"

Memory knocked on Johnathan's exhausted core until he sank into the murky depths of his past. A flash of silver in the dark, tears running down his face, cool against his feverish flesh. The knife handle slid in his blood-drenched hands, limbs shaking with fear and hesitation. He didn't want to do this thing. *"Press the blade deeper, boy. We don't have all day."*

Unseen by Vic, the fingers of Johnathan's free hand curled under until the knuckles of his fist burned a waxy white. "His name was Sir Harry. He was a vampire, and he caught me stealing bread."

Vic was silent for a moment, then, "The man you loved?"

Johnathan nodded, a burning sickness swelling in his gut, the truth wanting out. "My mother died of consumption that winter, my father long lost to drink and cards. I was another scrawny street kid in a pack of them, scrounging and stealing to survive."

Johnathan remembered that hunger. Sir Harry kept him lean to suit his purposes, but never again did he experience that all-consuming hunger of that winter. An empty belly kept him sharp and desperate, until food became the only thing he could think of, and his focus narrowed to that singular focal point.

"The baker was a mean son of a bitch. One time, he tossed his rolling pin at the children picking through his garbage for scraps. It caught one of the boys in the side of the head; he didn't get up the next morning."

There was a tightness in his chest at the memory. That was the world Johnathan lived in.

"I was so hungry. Possible death was worth the risk, and I was brazen enough to go right for the baker's front display. So focused on filling my belly, I didn't even hear the bastard coming until he seized me by the collar."

Worse than rats. You know what we do with rats round here? Johnathan knew.

"He was ready to club me over the head with that rolling pin, so I shoved the bread in my mouth. Might as well die with a full stomach."

Vic chuckled. "Defiant to the end. That sounds about right."

Johnathan didn't think of it as particularly brave, merely desperate. He remembered bracing himself. But the blow never came.

"Sir Harry saved me from a beating. Said I was too much of a spitfire to waste." Johnathan's throat closed, choked by the memory, the first caress of those cool fingers, the baker's look of shock and fear. The other children melted into the shadows like morning vapor before the sun, but Sir Harry was a solid pillar behind him, permeating the air with the sharp tang of danger and the illusive promise of something more.

"He felt safe," whispered Johnathan.

It was something he'd never told anyone before. He could picture the disgust on Dr. Evans' face over such a confession, but Vic's fingers gave the barest squeeze, a silent acknowledgement to those complicated feelings. "He took me in, fed me, protected me, told me stories. He was mother and father and more."

Johnathan finally swallowed the tight mass in his throat, letting his head fall back to look up at the sky. It stretched above the trees, that endless ceiling of the heavens that made man and beast alike so very small in the great wide world. Under the vault of the sky, Johnathan's secrets felt insignificant. *He* felt insignificant in the company of a being who—how did Alyse put it?—would roam the Earth long after he was dust, as Sir Harry would have if Johnathan had just kept walking that last day.

"I knew what I was doing," Johnathan went on. "Knew what it meant. Part of me hated it, hated myself. He was what he was, but what was I? A traitor to my own species, leading innocents to their deaths."

Vic stilled. "He didn't have to kill," he whispered.

"He didn't know another way," said Johnathan. "He didn't *want* to know another way."

The specter of death dogged his every step as a boy, fear that warred with love, a toxic combination that fell prey to the whispers from the Society recruiter.

"I was so afraid of the day I wouldn't be of use to him anymore, that I led the hunt that killed him."

He didn't tell Vic the full truth, that his hand held the weapon that pierced Sir Harry's chest. Tears ran down his face.

"You went from the keep of a murderous vampire to the iron grip of the Society," murmured Vic. "Oh John, no wonder you have no sense of humor."

Johnathan snorted. The action made the gruesome wound of his shoulder protest. "The Society purports all vampires are evil fiends. They battered that doctrine into my bones, into every vein through fist and blade. Yet here I am. With you."

Vic sighed. "Still despise me for existing?"

"I don't," he said. "That's the problem, I fear."

He didn't dare look at Vic, for the pity he might see and the bleak sense of his future. He couldn't examine the nature of the bond that existed between them, but he had to acknowledge it existed, new and fragile as it was. It would damn him in the Society's eyes. Did Dr. Evans know the nature of the vampire that resided in this isolated corner of the world? Perhaps Johnathan's final test wasn't his skill, but his resolve to the mission from the beginning.

"I'm a failure as a Hunter," he murmured, his head so easily resting on Vic's solid shoulder. He teetered on the brink of unconsciousness.

"Rest, John." Vic touched his face, so softly. "The hunt isn't over yet."

CHAPTER TWENTY-ONE

J OHNATHAN WOKE UNDER A PLASTER SKY. H E RECOGNIZED THE CRACKS in Pastor Shaw's ceiling, the sight now too familiar for his comfort. Though he couldn't recall how he managed the journey from the woods to the pastor's residence, he was immeasurably relieved that he needn't have summoned the energy to move his carcass.

Urgency bloomed up from the pit of his stomach. The previous night's events rushed to the fore. Alyse! Her family! Their house was marked! They had a demon to contend with!

Johnathan swore and sat up. Immediate regret set in as the limits of his body caught him up in a vise. His stomach rolled. Every inch of him ached. The fluid rush of his pulse drowned out everything until cool hands gently forced him back down.

"Good god, man, you're going to undo all of Alyse's work," said Vic.

"He's going to tear his stitches. Again." Alyse tutted from somewhere to his left.

Johnathan attempted to reassure her that her exemplary stitch work would hold just fine, though his wound might be a touch infected from cavorting with sadistic fairies, but his tongue sat thick and useless in his mouth.

"Could you hand me that cup of water, love?" Vic asked.

"He'll drain this. I'll fill the jug."

The sound of Alyse's retreating footsteps rolled through his head in a booming echo. Johnathan squeezed his eyes shut through the assault and collapsed back against the wooden headboard, angered by the failings of his body. Icy liquid pressed against his lips and he parted them, grateful for the water that soothed his muddled senses. Grit scraped beneath his eyelids as he looked up at Vic's concerned face.

"How long have I been out?" Johnathan rasped, but he could feel the strength slowly returning to his limbs, revitalized by the water like he'd swallowed a magic elixir.

"Not long, half a day at most since," said Vic.

Johnathan appraised the vampire. Long enough for a change of clothes and a feeding, he thought, the vampire's appearance nearly as slick as when he'd first seen him, the mask of a civilized country gentleman firmly back in place.

The door opened and Vic turned, his expression minutely shifting when Alyse entered in such a way that Johnathan went still. Something akin to jealousy flared through him, one that made him long for their quiet confessions beneath the open sky instead of the hot knot of emotion that buzzed in his thoughts. Until Vic's hand sought his, threading their fingers together on the other side of Johnathan's legs, out of Alyse's sight.

"Alyse arrived on horseback roughly an hour after you blacked out. You didn't rouse, so we tossed you across a saddle blanket and brought you here."

"You used a blanket? How thoughtful."

Alyse made a small choking noise that sounded suspiciously like a laugh. She sniffed. "I patched you up again while Vic tended to his own...needs."

Johnathan glanced at her, a little paler than he'd last seen her, but she wore the same stubborn expression. "You don't have to be coy about his needs—"

Vic's hand slid over Johnathan's mouth, and his lips touched Johnathan's temple. "Shhh. Remember, you aren't the only listening ears in this house."

Alyse's eyes widened. Her appraising glance went between the two of them, though Johnathan wasn't sure what she saw. "What else happened in those wretched woods?" she mused.

A haunted expression flickered through the vampire's eyes. "Too much."

"Obviously. You were gone for nearly a week," said Alyse.

Johnathan jerked. "What?"

Vic winced. "I was working up to that."

"You said we weren't in there more than a day," said Johnathan, fighting to sit up. The ache of fever bloomed beneath the surface of his skin, the angry red heat of it beat beneath his wounded shoulder.

"Easy," said Alyse, taking the chair by the bed. She smoothed her plain woolen skirts so that not a crease was out of place. The prim and proper picture of a pastor's daughter, Johnathan realized her appearance was as much a facade as Vic's, though he didn't know the woman beneath as well as the vampire did. "Your wound *was* infected. We lanced it, but your body needs to heal."

Healing be damned. They'd been gone for a week! Yet there was no urgency in Miss Shaw's demeanor. "How are you so calm?" Johnathan asked. "Your house was marked. What happened while we were gone?"

One of those glances passed between Vic and Alyse, the sort that made Johnathan feel every inch the outsider, as if the secrets he shared with Vic never happened. Irritation flared. It shouldn't matter if they shut him out, but now, it did. Johnathan stifled the urge to snap at her until Vic gently squeezed his hand.

"It's been quiet," Alyse admitted. Worry bracketed her mouth. "No more disappearances, no creatures, nothing except—" She bit her lip and looked to Vic as though for permission.

"A group of gentlemen arrived from Boston yesterday morn." Vic's long fingers tapped along his thigh, his expression carefully blank. "Would you know anything about that, Johnathan?"

Johnathan flinched, remembering the moment he'd slid a letter to Mrs. Meech. They were earlier than he expected. "Let me handle them."

The lines of Alyse's face deepened. "You sent for them," she seethed.

He sat up, stiffly. "Look, I came here to hunt a single vampire, not woodland monsters, not ruddy fairies, and certainly not a pack of demons. I am but one man, and I fear we need an army."

Alyse didn't bat a lash at the statement, which meant Vic already filled her in, of course. Did the vampire share Johnathan's intimate secrets with her as well?

His jaw clenched. "I am ill equipped and inexperienced, even with such allies as yourselves." His gaze flickered to Vic, but he pressed on. "I knew that if we couldn't contain the threat, the townspeople would have been left unprotected."

"You bastard," Alyse snarled.

"He's right," said Vic.

Johnathan and Alyse stared at him.

Vic shrugged. "We still don't know the extent of what we are dealing with. If we fail to stop these creatures, they could consume the town."

Alyse gripped his hand, the tendons taut to expose her fear. "If they find you, they'll kill you," she said.

There it was again, that unguarded expression in Vic's eyes.

Johnathan's throat went tight. "They won't," he said. "Vic fooled me. He'll fool them."

A sneer tugged at Alyse's mouth. "Fooling a pile of fresh meat straight out of the Society grinder doesn't inspire much confidence."

Johnathan bit back a retort and turned to Vic. "You know that I won't tell them about you, but I need to report in. Preferably before they come looking for me."

"You can barely stand," Alyse snorted. "My little sister could knock you off your feet with one finger."

He didn't doubt that. His muscles were weak and wobbly as a newborn fawn, but he didn't have the luxury of rest. "I'll manage."

Alyse threw up her hands in a huff and paced the room. The lack of activity bothered him. What were the demons waiting for? They had an apparent target in the Shaw household but failed to act. The other Society members hadn't arrived until yesterday, which left several days of opportunity. Johnathan couldn't believe the damn fairies held them for nearly seven whole days. A week of his life stolen for a few scraps of information.

The fairies seemed to fear the creatures from the Nether, but by holding Vic and Johnathan there, they allowed the demons to continue their dark deeds unhindered. And yet, no harm had been done.

What was he missing?

Pieces dangled out of reach, taunting him with his own ignorance. He needed to speak to the Society men, not just for backup, but for knowledge. They must have encountered something like this before, even if it wasn't taught to Prospectives.

Vic sighed, releasing Johnathan's hand to stand. His sinuous grace drew Johnathan's gaze more so than before. "I'll take him into town."

"Like hell you will." Alyse whirled on her friend. "Does your life mean so little that you'd walk into a nest of vipers?"

"Alyse," Vic said quietly, his gray eyes wreathed in weighted shadows as he stepped toward the distraught woman.

"No." Alyse held up a hand to fend off Vic's calming influence. "I won't let you risk yourself. I can take him."

Johnathan didn't like this plan any more than Vic appeared to, but it was difficult to argue with Miss Shaw's logic. She didn't have to pretend at humanity, and her presence would also help Johnathan convince whoever the Society sent that he had indeed made allies of the locals.

That portion of their plan decided, Alyse left the room so Johnathan could dress...with Vic's help.

The vampire held out a shirt. "Come on. Let's get you dressed."

Johnathan deadpanned. "You must be joking."

A self-deprecating smirk tugged at Vic's lips. "Would you care for me to turn around instead while you struggle with your one good arm?"

Johnathan's jaw worked while he silently took stock of his watery muscles. This did not bode well for convincing the Society to act as their back up. Could he even hold a pistol right now?

He flexed the arm below his injured shoulder, curling each finger. There was a fine, bone-deep ache from the action, but he managed. Putting on a fresh shirt and coat was another matter. He cursed softly. "I suppose I could use your help."

Vic helped him shift to the edge of the bed and moved behind him. The vampire's grip remained gentle as he guided Johnathan's wounded shoulder into respectable dress. Johnathan hated that he couldn't see Vic's expression while he ran his hands down Johnathan's back, smoothing the creases of the shirt as much as the awkward bandaging would allow. The action made him draw a breath, pinched by shame.

Johnathan almost wished Vic would yell at him for bringing the Society to Cress Haven.

He caught Vic's wrist when the vampire began to move away. Vic turned back, a soft expression on that breathtaking face.

"I won't tell them about you," swore Johnathan. "I won't."

It was one thing to say it in front of Alyse, another to promise Vic himself.

Vic's skin was warmer than Johnathan had expected, a result of feeding, but Johnathan thought of it as an attribute of Vic himself. Somewhere between following him into the wood and their encounter with the fairies, he'd stopped thinking of Vic as simply "the vampire," and he knew that personal revelation would make the coming encounter all the more difficult.

"You're not a fiend," said Johnathan.

Vic looked down at him, gaze somber as he took Johnathan's face in his hands. "Some of us are, John. Some of us are predators to our bones." He leaned down and brushed his mouth against Johnathan's ear.

Johnathan swallowed hard; his heart pounded at the contact. His hands twitched at the strange desire to pull Vic even closer.

"I would never take from you like that." Vic's hand trailed down Johnathan's neck. "Not without explicit permission, but you make me crave other things than your blood."

Johnathan couldn't breathe. He couldn't look away from that silver gaze, too entranced to pull away from the moment, but too inexperienced and uncertain to express his thoughts and wants. A turn of the head would brush his lips across Vic's.

This was dangerous territory.

Johnathan finally pulled back from Vic's grasp, the moment shattered with his retreat.

He sucked in a ragged breath, trying to dismiss the flush that burned up from his neck, across his face. "Yes, well, there are other issues at hand. Help me to the door so I can go make a fool of myself before my superiors."

Vic shook his head, a dark and knowing smile stretching across his mouth. "Business as usual, then?"

Johnathan could offer no more. Not yet.

"As our lives and the lives of townsfolk depend on it," he said, "yes."

But after? That was another matter.

Vic bowed his head graciously, acquiescing, and gestured to the door. "Lead the way then, good sir."

CHAPTER TWENTY-TWO

AFTER THE FIRST FEW MINUTES OF BONE-JARRING AGONY, Johnathan's injured side went blessedly numb, and he rather enjoyed the fresh air on his face as the flat-bed cart ambled into the center of town. He hoped to enjoy those spare moments of peace until Miss Shaw pulled to the side of the road, still a fair walk from town. Her knuckles were hard knobs inside her leather driving gloves, and she gripped the reins so tightly the hide squeaked.

"I don't protest your presence to be difficult," she said, and Johnathan roused himself to attention. "I do care about the town and the people. And I care about Vic. It's just..." Her voice faltered. She stared down at her hands, unable to find the words she needed to explain herself.

Johnathan understood that all too well. In his time with Miss Shaw and Vic, the former remained aloof. She held herself away from Johnathan, and while he theorized why, that theory changed as his knowledge of Vic changed. Through that altered lens, though their circumstances were vastly different, Alyse reminded Johnathan a great deal of himself, or more accurately, what he could have been.

"You're very brave, Miss Shaw, and I don't say that to tease." Johnathan eased himself around to properly face her and gently pried the reins from her hands. "It's not fair to be asked to risk the one you love over the people you tolerate." His lips twitched at what likely described her view of him. "Even when it is what is right. And you do what is right, Miss Shaw. You will leave me at the drinking house and return to Vic so they can't look too closely at the connection between us."

"You idiot, of course I'm not leaving you here," said Alyse. "You're still kitten-weak, and I want to see these monsters."

His brows raised. "The Society aren't—"

A shadow loomed in his thoughts, forcing a young boy to shove a blade through the heart of the one he loved. *That will do.*

Alyse leaned into him, her pose outwardly intimate as her lips brushed his ear. "Look around you, John. Don't you feel it?"

Johnathan licked his lips, letting his attention broadened. He'd missed them entering the main street, too preoccupied with other thoughts, but he saw it now, a shade of itself. The townsfolk scurried about in fast half-steps, faces drawn in tense caricatures. Their eyes avoided the Society men stationed along the street who stood in a scattershot pattern, meant to give a full visual range of the area. Two men were already staring at Shaw's cart, their gazes expectant. Did they think Johnathan would make the worst rookie error by acknowledging them? The others radiated an air of menace, their eyes tinged with the quiet bloodlust of predators on the hunt. It was the exact opposite of Johnathan's assignment, a complete lack of subterfuge.

What the hell were they doing?

"Miss Shaw, who are they answering to?" He didn't insult her by asking if she investigated the newcomers. This was Alyse.

"An older gentleman," she said, "more white in his hair than my grandfather, but I don't think he's half as old. Hard to get a read on him through those damn spectacles." Her gaze searched his face. "Johnathan, he was one of the Society Hunters that showed up before."

A small thrill surged in his gut. Johnathan's jaw flexed. The revelation was one he wasn't sure how to process now, or how it connected to what was happening in Cress Haven as a whole, but he couldn't shake the sense he'd been thoroughly deceived. As for the depth of that deception and what it entailed, he would only know by confronting the man he once called mentor.

He attempted to dismount the wagon, overestimating the strength of his legs, despite Alyse's warning, but she was already there, a living crutch with his arm slung over her shoulders.

"Come on," she whispered, but Johnathan hesitated, a real sliver of fear worming through him.

"Miss Shaw, I might have to be stupidly gallant and insist you stay here."

She reared back, her mouth twisted to argue, when she caught sight of his expression. "We're not doing this."

He forced his watery legs to hold him, and he staggered off her. "I have to go in. He already knows I'm coming."

Her gaze flickered between him and the entrance of the drinking house. "No, we should leave now. I have a bad feeling."

There was an ominous air to the benign building now, the door a waiting mouth to snap him up should he be so foolish to wander inside.

"He won't kill me," said Johnathan. He knew what he sounded like. He stumbled into a fast trot before she could catch him and didn't dare look back. Alyse would follow him if he did, she would anyway, but the others would stop her. The effort of that short distance caused the edges of his vision to gray, but he pushed on.

The drinking house appeared abandoned. A town like this would have a handful of day drinkers, but they were likely scared off with the rest by the unfettered hostility of the Society. His brethren were waltzing about the town like a group of thugs set to take over. Johnathan had never seen their ruthlessness on such display before, even found it unnerving.

Two familiar faces greeted him at the entrance. Sykes and Dodd emanated their own air of lazy menace, dressed in the road-worn dark clothing the Society used for hunts. Sykes' flinty gaze appraised Johnathan as he approached, burly arms crossed over his wide chest. The man was a brawler, born and bred, and he used his rough bearing to his advantage. Next to him, Dodd was a smaller man but no less intimidating, casually picking his fingernails with an oft-used and well-kept blade.

Dodd leered at Johnathan who slowed to a stop between them. "Get yourself a bit roughed up there, Johnny?"

Johnathan ignored him. He was never a fan of Dodd. Both he and

Sykes enjoyed the violent side of their missions a little too much. Evans often sent them to do some of the Society's dirtiest tasks, and their being here was not good. He nodded to Sykes, usually the more levelheaded of the two.

The big man sucked on a tooth. "He's waiting for you, Prospective Newman."

Neither of the men moved, forcing Johnathan to push through them to enter the building.

There was no sign of Mrs. Meech's ruddy face behind the bar. One lone figure occupied the room, their back to the door. The table before them was strewn with papers and a single empty glass. A still-smoking cigarette burned down in a nearby ashtray. The position was intentional. A power play.

Dr. Evans didn't turn when the door opened. He continued to read from a document. The only movement he made was to lift the cigarette for a quick, efficient drag. Dr. Evans was the epitome of quick, efficient movements.

"Come, sit," said the doctor. He didn't spare Johnathan a glance.

Johnathan fought the urge to tense, his injury a burning lump, emanating down through the nerves of his legs, one that gave him a lilting, cautious gait as he settled into a seat across from Dr. Evans.

He stared at the man who'd once helped guide a blade into Sir Harry's chest.

Dr. Evans set the paper down and peered at Johnathan through a curl of smoke. Through the lens of his glasses, his eyes were a dark brown, almost black, and burned with an inner light Johnathan attributed to zealous ambition. The deceptive calm was one of his best techniques. Evans was a man who let others dig their own graves, but Johnathan was one of his own students.

Johnathan eased into the hardback chair, careful not to draw any more attention to his wounded shoulder, and waited for the doctor to speak first. The silence stretched into long minutes. Johnathan could hear Alyse's outrage beyond the door, held up by Evans' men. Johnathan's brethren.

Evans nodded, a small smile on his lips. "Fiery, that one."

Johnathan didn't acknowledge her; Evans didn't expect him to. That would be acknowledging a potential weakness. Instead, the man shifted back in his seat and rapped a slow methodical rhythm with his knuckles on the scarred wooden tabletop.

"Your letter stressed a note of urgency, Prospective Newman. Yet, when we arrived, you were nowhere to be found. On inquiry, you hadn't been seen in days."

Tread carefully now.

Johnathan's hand flexed open and closed where it rested on his thigh. Dr. Evans asked no questions of him, only stated what he knew. It was a matter of word play, something Johnathan never quite mastered, though his experience with the fairies gave him a couple new tricks.

He couldn't tell the truth. The second he started rambling on about fairies and alliances with fiends, Evans would scuttle him in a coach bound for Boston and, most likely, lockup. They wouldn't need a trial to declare him unfit for duty; he'd be labeled insane and promptly cast from the Society, straight to the asylum. He wouldn't be the first Prospective shunted there, who cracked under the conditions of their service.

"I was on reconnaissance in the surrounding wood," said Johnathan. "During that time, there was an altercation. I was injured and eventually found by my allies among the locals." A full answer, brusque, but there was enough detail to hint at an embarrassing situation. Better Evans think him an incompetent twit than reveal the barest hint of his relationship with Vic. Though that begged the question of how to convince Evans of a demonic threat.

"You encountered the local fiend," said Evans.

Johnathan stopped fidgeting, replaying the words in his head. That wasn't a question.

Careful, tread careful.

"The danger here is not fiend related," said Johnathan. "There is an entity in the woods, creatures of otherworldly origins—"

Evans slapped an open palm down on the table. "Your assignment was to rid the town of its resident fiend."

A throbbing note rang in Johnathan's ears. He stared at Dr. Evans, the man's face the picture of calm despite the outburst. "There is no fiend." He meant it. He no longer saw Vic as a fiend, and that conviction is what Evans read in his expression. "There is a demon in the wood," he went on. "Killing the locals."

The doctor rapped his knuckles again. Each hollow thump rang like a judge's gavel. Johnathan held his breath. He didn't dare blink.

Evans tilted his head; his gaze slid to the door where Alyse continued to berate his men, unseen. "Tell me about this otherworldly threat, Prospective Newman."

"One of the local entrepreneurs made a pact with a creature, a demon, currently sheltering in the woods," said Johnathan. "Whatever deal he made gave it a foothold here."

"You claim this *creature* is responsible for the reported disappearances in this area."

"Yes, sir." He couldn't very well tell Dr. Evans those reports were sourced by the "nonexistent" fiend. "It's not just killing. It's making more of its kind."

"Your claim is absurd. Your failure to eliminate the fiend shall be noted, and you will return to headquarters. It is obvious you are not ready for field work. Agent Morrow will take over your assignment here—"

"I saw them, sir!" Cold panic squeezed the words out of him, though he knew what interruption would cost him. Nothing he could say would get Dr. Evans to change his mind, and by interrupting, he invited immediate punishment.

Dr. Evans rose and circled the table. Johnathan braced himself a second before the blow, a flare of fresh pain across his cheekbone. He still nearly lost his seat and would have if not for the doctor's iron grip on his uninjured shoulder. Motion drew his gaze to the weathered wooden cross hanging from the man's belt. How many times had he seen that cross, though he never once thought of Dr. Evans as remotely religious?

The memory rose, unbidden, of Mrs. Fairchild's drawn pale face. *He wore some sort of uniform and spectacles. I remember the cross. He was no man of God.* Johnathan quickly buried his thoughts, as a matter of survival.

Instead, he gave himself over to pain, fresh and new, attempting to leverage both against Evans' hold. The effort filled his mouth with the taste of hot copper. The skin of his healed-over palm twinged, fingers flexing at the useless anger spiraling through him.

"Tell me what you saw, Prospective." Evans leaned over him, the filtered daylight catching on the lens of his glasses, obscuring his eyes from view.

The command confused him as it chilled his blood. Johnathan's sentence had been given, so why would Evans ask again? The man's grip on his shoulder dug in, a sharp reminder of Evans' limited patience. In that moment, the jovial mentor who accompanied him to Cress Haven was long gone. This was the man who led him through his first kill, who put a blade in the hands of a boy.

"Demons, sir," he gasped out. "I saw demons."

"Did you, now. Pray tell, how did you conclude they were demons? How did you survive an encounter with a supposed demonic entity?"

Johnathan saw the trap as it snapped around him. Evans neatly maneuvered him into a corner to admit to Vic's involvement. Evans' grip on his shoulder wasn't for a show of control. The man's fingertips rested on a pulse point in Johnathan's shoulder, ready to catch the lie. He tried to think through the pain and the pressure. He made a promise, dammit.

Both encounters with the beasts played through his mind, the oddities rising to the fore. So caught up in other events, there were details he'd stored to examine later, when he had a moment to mull them over proper, but that moment never came. He couldn't explicitly tell Dr. Evans about his first encounter with the beast. Vic was too close to the situation to work around. But his second encounter...*that* he was alone for.

"It—it didn't attack me," Johnathan said.

There was the subtlest shift in Dr. Evans' grip. "Why not?"

"I—I don't know." The confusion in Johnathan's voice was genuine, though he wished he could examine the encounter again anywhere but in Evans' presence.

The doctor's hand slid off his shoulder, the release of pressure making Johnathan lightheaded. Evans resumed his seat at the table, his attention back on the papers before him, but Johnathan knew he wasn't in the clear. Alyse's voice went quiet outside.

Evans let the silence deepen until Johnathan's posture grew rigid from anxiety, before he finally spoke. "What course of action will you pursue against this threat?"

Johnathan swallowed. "I have allied myself with some of the locals to deal with this entity at a targeted domicile."

"You will have backup," Evans said without looking up.

"With all due respect sir, I believe more men will dissuade the creature. It may seek out another innocent."

Evans' gaze flickered upward, cut through by the silver rim of his spectacles. "Interesting theory, Prospective Newman. I didn't realize your experience with demonic entities was so in-depth that you could predict their behavior."

Johnathan didn't look away. "Perhaps if an agent is posted at other potential marks, we could reduce the chances of the creature seeking alternate victims."

"A sound proposal, Prospective Newman. I will take it into consideration." Evans finally broke eye contact with a shuffle of paper. "Why don't you return to that charming young lady outside. I will expect your report tomorrow morning."

"Sir?"

"You are dismissed."

Johnathan stared for a solid minute, but the dismissal was clear. Evans didn't so much as look at him as he struggled to his feet and shuffled to the door. It wasn't until Johnathan had a hand against the rough wood that the doctor's voice stopped him.

"I will keep my men back, Prospective Newman, due to your sound advisement, but you will be under observation." There was a pause, punctuated by the soft crimp of paper in hand. "The Shaw household holds a particular note of interest."

Johnathan kept his eyes on the raw-hewn door, his jaw clenched tight. Bitter words burnt the back of his throat, but he kept them at bay as he pushed his way out through the gauntlet of Sykes and Dodd, certain they heard every word of his exchange with Dr. Evans. There was a cruel smirk on Dodd's face, but Sykes remained stoic.

"See you in the morning, Prospective Newman," called Sykes. "Try to keep your head."

Alyse waited by her cart, her expression mulish until she saw him. He knew he was a sight when her lips parted in a quiet gasp. She helped Johnathan onto the flat bed, where a pile of burlap sacks cushioned his weight, her voice quiet as her gaze shifted to the lodge house. "Are we safe?"

We never were.

"He agreed to keep his men back," was Johnathan's terse reply. Alyse was clearly dissatisfied with his answer but kept it to herself through the bumps and pitches of their return journey.

Johnathan replayed his encounter with Dr. Evans over and over in his mind. A dozen dark theories played through his thoughts, each more unsettling than the last, but each time he wondered at the depth of his mentor's involvement in the unfolding events, the more frustrated and puzzled he grew.

Dr. Evans had been here before. He knew Vic was here, but didn't expunge the vampire himself. Why? Was it even remotely possible Evans was the stranger Mrs. Fairchild spoke of? Dropping hints of ensnaring forest spirits to a rich country mill owner? But why? To what purpose?

Johnathan's long-time mentor knew exactly what was happening in Cress Haven, but Johnathan didn't have the faintest idea *why* he knew. Or what he intended to do with the knowledge. Dr. Evans always, *always*, had a plan.

CHAPTER TWENTY-THREE

"THEY APPEARED WHILE YOU WERE AWAY," SAID VIC, VISIBLY SHAKEN. He stood between Johnathan and Alyse, the three of them staring at the horned symbol burned into the windowsill. This one was not in the bedroom but the front living room. It wasn't the only one.

"*Every* windowsill? You're sure?" An undercurrent of panic laced Alyse's voice. Not that Johnathan could blame her. "Why *every* sill? What does that mean? Are they coming for my whole family?"

"I don't know," said Vic, his frustration clear.

Johnathan caught his eye. "Is there someone in town your siblings can stay with?"

Alyse's nostrils flared with outrage. "Where we can't protect them? Are you daft?"

Johnathan countered. "The Society agents will be posted throughout town. The beast will face a gauntlet of trained operatives before it reaches sniffing distance of your family."

"Oh," said Alyse.

Vic exhaled. "I don't suppose you would stay in town with them, love?"

"No." Alyse glared at her friend. "And don't ask again. Besides, don't you need bait?"

Johnathan listened to their exchange with half an ear, his concentration on the symbol carved by flame. How had the beast managed to mark the house in broad daylight under Vic's very nose? Why mark the house again, now that they had returned?

Alyse paced, her plain skirts flapping about her legs like the impatient wings of a bird. Sequestered in the other room, her siblings whispered, the older ones comforting the little ones while their father read verses from their family Bible out loud. Alyse's family were as spooked by the sudden appearance of the symbols as Vic, though they did not share the same knowledge of their meaning. It had been a point of contention between them how much Vic should share with her family of their predicament, but Alyse firmly steered him away from revealing too much. Pastor Shaw *was* a religious man, and that meant he could react very badly. However, the man wasn't a fool, either, and surmised his family had been targeted by the violence plaguing their town.

It was enough of an incentive that when Alyse gathered up her father and siblings to bring them to safety, the pastor didn't protest. Alyse intended to take them to a family friend's residence in the center of town, well away from the central point of danger and out of direct scrutiny of the Society. Though her father immediately began to argue when his eldest daughter made it clear she wouldn't be staying with them.

Alyse left in mid-quarrel, with a promise and a rebuke that she would return by nightfall.

Vic stood next to Johnathan, watching the afternoon sun waning through the Shaw's front windows. The easy silence they shared before was absent in light of tonight's impending confrontation. Johnathan's gaze was inevitably drawn to the symbol, charred into the wood.

"You truly sensed nothing?" he asked aloud.

"Nothing at all," said Vic. "Fair troubling, isn't it?"

"What are we missing, Vic?"

"Motive. Why target the Shaws now? Why hold off an attack until now?"

Similar questions to his own. Johnathan pursed his lips, reaching for the mark. He debated how much to share with Vic of what he suspected about Dr. Evans. "It's still warm."

"What?" Vic prodded the area. "Scratch troubling, I am downright flustered."

Johnathan's palm suddenly itched. He ignored it, the mild discomfort laughable compared to his shoulder. "I need you to redress my wound. Tight as you can make it."

"You should have gone to town with the little ones," Vic grumbled.

"If I'm not here, Dr. Evans will be suspicious." Not to mention, he dare not leave Vic alone with the Society Hunters so close.

Vic cleared his throat. "Did he give you that bloom on your cheek?"

Amid all the little aches, Johnathan barely noticed the bruise on his face, punishment for interruption, a training standard. "It's nothing."

"At least let me put a cool cloth on it," said Vic. His fingers feathered over Johnathan's cheek, a soothing touch that roused a corresponding flutter in his chest. Johnathan caught his hand, leaning into Vic's palm, his trepidation of the incoming night momentarily forgotten.

"It's nothing." His lips brushed Vic's thumb. Johnathan was somewhat bemused by Vic's concern for his well-being. There was a part of him that wanted to stretch this moment, to let it unwind in whatever direction it took him, but the sun was too low in the sky and the monsters would soon be at the door. Johnathan sighed. "Please, help me change this dressing."

Vic nodded, as if he didn't trust himself to speak, but there was a sadness in his expression. He led Johnathan to a chair and helped him work free of his shirt and bandages.

Johnathan held onto his resolve to keep the exchange businesslike, but it was difficult to concentrate with Vic's fingers smoothing down his back, the gentle caress numbing the ache in his shoulder. A responding warmth simmered in his chest. The contrast of cooling air and Vic's touch against his heated skin was almost too much sensation for him to bear, and Johnathan honestly didn't know what to do with this new awareness. A life of desperation and hard training had left him with little time for romantic endeavors, or to even explore his sexuality. He found himself so flustered by his growing feelings for Vic because he hadn't expected them, and he was far too virginal—

Johnathan's sensual thoughts stuttered. He *was* a virgin.

Frowning, he held up his palm, the puncture long gone, though he swore the healed-over skin itched beneath his scrutiny. No, this demon had a clear preference for young women. Every victim thus far was a young woman. He didn't fit the pattern, not really...

"The wound looks better," Vic said. "But nowhere near fit for fight."

Vic's words confused him, until Johnathan realized he referred to his shoulder. That's right, Vic had forgotten the wound as easily as he had, and Johnathan didn't bother to draw attention to it now. He shook himself. "I'll be fine."

"Will you," said Vic, "because Alyse said you looked pale as death when you staggered from the lodge house. What happened in there?"

"We can assume the target is Alyse," said Johnathan. He ignored Vic's noise of disgust over his avoidance. There was nothing Johnathan could tell him that wouldn't put Vic and Alyse in greater danger. "I will hold a perimeter and call to you when the beast approaches. You stay inside so that you may deal with the beast when—"

"That is absurd. It will tear you apart, John!"

"You can't be seen." Johnathan caught Vic's hand when he pulled back. "Evans has eyes on the house. He knows more than he's letting on, and he's willing to put others in danger for his plan. Don't give him this."

"How do you know? Maybe he's just an ignorant ass."

If only it were that simple.

"He's my mentor."

Vic's jaw worked for a moment before he spoke. "He was there when..."

"Yes. He was the one who recruited me."

Johnathan couldn't look at Vic just then. Shame at his connection to the Society was a newer emotion, especially when he still considered himself to be a part of that Society. He still believed the Society was there to protect the people of Cress Haven, but there were other doubts, about his future, about Vic's fate, that left him unsettled.

Vic ran his thumb over the top of Johnathan's knuckles. "You were a boy. You were scared and trying to survive."

"I regret it," Johnathan whispered.

Vic inhaled a sharp breath. "Don't do this now. This isn't a deathbed confession, John."

It might as well be. Dr. Evans set him on this course, but Johnathan had begun to suspect his former mentor still had a larger part to play. That bothered him more than anything else about this situation. How well did he really know the man? Before he came here and met Vic and Alyse, before everything that happened since he arrived, he would have never suspected anything ill of his mentor.

"You're right. It will be night soon. We need to prepare." Johnathan moved out of the shelter of Vic's presence and eased into his clothes. There was a stiffness in his fingers that could prove difficult for gripping a gun. Long as he could pull a trigger, he'd manage.

Vic stopped him at the door, sliding a hand around his waist, a far more forward move than he expected. His breath caught as he stared into Vic's concerned gaze. "John, be careful tonight. Don't draw attention to yourself."

Johnathan braced a hand on the vampire's chest, not exactly pushing the man away, but a firm barrier. "Of course. Do I look capable of heroics?"

"You never did, and yet here we are," said Vic. There was a hint of disappointment in the vampire's gaze, disappointment that Johnathan kept him at bay.

Johnathan wondered himself why he'd staved off Vic, though the way his pulse throbbed, he knew if he let Vic carry through with his intentions, they wouldn't stop. Johnathan couldn't afford to be derailed, not with so much on the line.

Damn Vic and his terrible timing.

"If you don't stop flattering me, we'll be absolutely caught off guard." Johnathan kept his tone teasing to cover the tremor in his fingers as he pulled away.

The reply lifted a corner of Vic's mouth, and Johnathan put on a good show until he was well out of sight.

The late afternoon sun soaked into his weary bones. He perched himself against the outer wall of the Shaw household, noting when Alyse returned to the household, alone, before dark. He wasn't surprised, though he did wonder how she convinced her father to let her go.

Still, Johnathan was grateful to have fewer variables in play. Waiting for the hammer to fall, as it were, gave him time to ruminate over the twisting situation. It did seem to keep spiraling in a new direction on him. Between fairies and demons, he hadn't expected Dr. Evans to present such a kink in their endeavors. Johnathan still couldn't puzzle out where the doctor fit into it all. Nor could he figure out why the symbols had reappeared in such sudden abundance.

The warmth and light of the long afternoon lulled him. He knew he'd dozed off when Alyse gently shook him awake, the sun long sunk below the horizon. Dusk leached the light from the sky.

"I'm sorry," he muttered.

Alyse waved off the apology. "You needed it. If you weren't so stubborn, Vic would have dragged you inside to rest, but it seemed safe enough in the daylight."

"Did he stay inside?"

Alyse nodded. She lingered, pinching the fabric of her skirts, unspoken words in the shuffle of her feet. "About earlier, I'm sorry, John. I—"

"Don't," he said. "It doesn't suit you."

Alyse bit her lip, clearly caught between an insult and a laugh.

"Get inside, will you?" he said. "Unless you plan to use me as a temporary shield."

She scowled. "The second you catch a hint of one of those demon beasts, you better hobble inside."

She stalked away from him but shut the door to the house with tedious care. The quiet set in, a confirmation something was coming in the absence of noise—no birds, no rustle of brush and bracken. The silence was weighted, the hush before the swing of the executioner's ax.

Supposedly, Dr. Evans' men watched the household. Did they sense it too?

The fine hairs on Johnathan's arms rose, but not a creature stirred. Gray twilight faded into true night, an inky darkness so thick he could barely see his hand if he held it in front of his face. Johnathan wasn't worried.

He would see the beasts by their eyes.

Instead, Johnathan settled on a tree stump close to the pastor's house and let his mind turn to puzzles surrounding Cress Haven. There were many. They knew the beasts were servants of the demon, but what was their purpose in marking a house other than to build their ranks? Why did the demon feel the need to keep making others of its ilk? The number of disappearances and deaths had increased dramatically in the past few months, which hinted that the demon was rushing to build up his horde of servants. There was also the outlier of the Shaw household. It didn't quite fit any of their known criteria, and the fact the demon hadn't taken advantage of Vic and Johnathan's absence whilst they were trapped in the fairy realm was another piece that didn't fit. Why choose Alyse and her family at all?

"They have to be tainted, they have to be pure," he murmured. He was close enough to one of the windows to see the mark. How did the demons evade Vic's enhanced senses? "None of this makes bloody sense." He stared at the mark, the same one they found etched in the rib cage of Mary Elizabeth, the same symbol that haunted his dreams. "Why can't I remember?"

Bidden, the memory stirred, of his encounter in the forest with the antlered creature, the horned symbol engraved in a gold coin around its neck. Sweat slicked the small of his back. How did he not remember that until now?

The palm of his hand gave a twinge. A hint of something rotten and burnt teased his senses. He recognized the whiff of sulfur. Johnathan frowned and ventured closer, kneeling on the ground below the window. Despite the dark, he swore he could make out the faint shape of paw prints on the ground, the dirt blistered and blackened.

His palm gave a twinge again, the pain so sudden and sharp it cut through the fierce ache of his shoulder. "The hell?"

The faint drag of cloth over the ground caught his attention. His fatigue faded at the flood of adrenaline in his system when Mrs. Fairchild padded barefoot from the womb of the night.

His breath caught at the sight of her, pale and ethereal, a fallen angel, her hair in tattered wisps that clung to her scalp. Her dress was reduced to frayed streamers that hung from her thinned frame. The bones of her face stood stark against her waxen skin, further exaggerated by the whimsical smile she wore, her head tilted as if she listened to a faraway song. She stopped a few steps from him, her eyes lit by an unholy gleam.

"They have to be tainted; they have to be pure," she whispered, her voice a shattered husk of sound. "Did the old fairy whisper her useless warnings? Did she drip pretty promises into your ear?"

Johnathan jumped up from the ground, the rough wood of the house siding at his back. "Mrs. Fairchild? We thought you were dead." He tried not to show how unnerved her words left him.

"Aren't I? I was certain I was." She spun in a half circle, and the moisture dried up in Johnathan's mouth. The back of her skull was simply gone, cleaved away to reveal an oozing mass of gristle and jagged bone.

He couldn't breathe; he couldn't move. His palm burned. "What does it mean? They have to be tainted; they have to be pure." His voice was a whisper.

She turned back to him, her smile ghoulish now as she circled him. He needed to call for Vic, for the Society agents hovering in the dark. The words remained stuck to the back of his throat. She bore down on him, until the sweet bitter scent of rot pressed on his senses and her dead fingers brushed his cheek.

"Don't you know? Haven't you suspected?"

The pain in his hand intensified, demanding his attention, though he couldn't look away from her. Sweat popped on his brow as the burn sank into the nerves of his arm. He *had to* look away.

The symbol burned up through the skin of his palm, the cherry red of live coals. The surrounding flesh blistered and puckered black, right where the claw pierced him that first night.

A mental dam burst and left him reeling. The secrets of his nightmares, his stifled urgency, and the need to tell Vic poured into him. Too late, far too late, in a searing instant, Johnathan saw the influence of the demon. It had been on him since it marked him, keeping his will subdued, leaching away his urge to act, to see the clues until it was ready to strike.

"We waited so long for you," Mrs. Fairchild whispered against his ear.

A low snarl sounded close, too close. The dead woman laughed and spun away from him. Johnathan looked up as the beast launched at him, silently sailing through the dark. There was an impression of teeth—sharp, wet, and white—and a lick of flame at his throat before the beast tore into his flesh.

The world was full of teeth and flame.

Johnathan choked on his own blood. The beast hovered above him, muzzle stained bright crimson, the color so very vivid that it blazed. How could something be so bright in the dark?

The wedge-shaped head dipped down. A hot wet nose pressed against the fresh bruise on his cheek with an inquisitive whine that echoed in his ear. The beast licked the wound at his neck, the scent of burnt meat wicked the air.

Johnathan's muscles spasmed as his veins ignited. He tried to gulp air through a torn-out throat, his breath a wet wheeze, his lungs drowning in boiling liquid.

Fire inside. He was going to burn to a pile of ashes.

He jerked at the heat rippling through his chest, soaking each organ in molten fire. The scream finally bubbled up through the blood and torn flesh, a horrible, twisted shriek that shredded the inside of his mouth. Time stretched; the final seconds of life distilled as Johnathan boiled alive inside his skin.

A burst of motion shifted above him. Vic tackled the beast, their fight beyond his awareness. A pantomime of fury and rage, snarls and snapping teeth he vaguely registered through the frayed edges of his consciousness, until Alyse's horrified face loomed above him.

"No, no, no, no," she murmured. Pressure against his throat, distant and cool, the brush of her skirts where she tried to staunch the flow of blood from his wound. The cloth smoked and caught fire. "Vic!" Alyse screamed, her tear-streaked face white with terror. "Vic, help me!"

Vic dropped beside her. Ribbons of skin dangled from his cheek. "Oh god. We have to stop the blood. We have to—"

"Don't touch the blood!" Alyse shrieked.

Johnathan's head lolled. He couldn't take a breath. His limbs jerked and twitched. He was aware of it all. He tried to catch Vic's eye, to beg him for death. Anything to stop the fire.

Vic stared at him, his expression lost. The skin on his cheek began to knit together while Johnathan watched. His awareness faded.

Idiot, he wanted to yell at Vic. *Evans' men are watching!*

They had to have seen the attack.

Through the agony, bitterness clawed at his throat. Dr. Evans' dismissive tones echoed in his ears. His mentor never changed his mind so easily. If Johnathan had allowed himself to pull his theories together, allowed himself to fully see the monster that was his mentor, he would have known that by sending him here, Evans never meant for him to survive the night.

That will do, boy.

Johnathan sank into the fire.

CHAPTER TWENTY-FOUR

PAIN AND MEMORY WERE CLOSE COMPANIONS IN JOHNATHAN'S LIFE.
Now, as pain ate at him, the two bled into one another, mirages wavering
around him, until he couldn't tell past from present.

*Johnathan didn't want to go home. Sir Harry's temper was high last night. His
touch rough, the press of his teeth edged in pain. He took too much. Left Johnathan
lightheaded and weak. There was a flicker of regret in the older man's eyes.*

*"I'm sorry, Johnny sweet. I'm not myself tonight." He'd held Johnathan to his
chest long after, whispered apologies long after the sun rose, but the damage was
done.*

*Johnathan crouched on the broken brick wall, long legs dangling past the cuff
of his pants. Growing sure as weeds, Sir Harry would say. His neck ached, the bite
still raw. How could he? He promised he would never bite Johnathan in anger.
Promised he'd never take too much. Except it was harder and harder for
Johnathan to lure the pretty maids and concerned matrons, his frame too long and
lean to pass for an unfortunate youth. How long before he was no longer useful to
Sir Harry? What would he do then? How long until Sir Harry took and took,
until he took it all?*

*He hugged his knees tight. He didn't want to go home. In the shadows of the
building, a man watched him, a faint glint shone off the spectacles on his face.
"Hello, boy. What happened to your neck?"*

The brick beside him crumbled to dust. Long fingers painted in soot curled over the top of the wall. Johnathan didn't remember this part.

"Don't look." Mary Elizabeth grasped his chin and turned his face to her. Lovely dead girl, what was she doing here? She looked so sad. "Are you strong enough, sweet Johnny?"

The scene crackled at the edges. He could smell burning. "What's happening?" he whispered.

"You're dying," said Mary Elizabeth.

The world wobbled at the edges.

"Don't you dare die on me, John!"

"God, Vic, he's burning up."

"Vic?" Johnathan looked up, seeking the vampire's face, but the sky was full of fire. The flames licked and dripped from the belly of the horizon, a silent storm of flame that roiled above him, eclipsing his vision. He shivered. Why was he so cold?

A shadow fell over him, blocking the flames. "Tell me, boy, what would you do to be free of this fiend?" Johnathan's attention snapped to the figure before him, not the sweet dead girl but another, a shadow of memory. Dr. Evans stood before him, a sentinel in tweed and leather, his head wreathed in cigarette smoke so that only his glasses could be seen, round orbs glinting from the fire above. The wooden cross swung at Dr. Evans' waist, even though he stood still. That flaming glass gaze pierced Johnathan through to the scared little boy who cowered day in and day out in a monster's lair.

No, he loved Sir Harry. The man was his father, his brother, his friend. How long until Sir Harry drank him down?

He wouldn't!

The bitter memory of the bite ate away his resistance. He just wanted to be safe. He wanted to live.

"You were only a boy," said Mary Elizabeth at his side. Her words echoed as she slipped her hand into his, her fingers icy. Because she was dead. A ghost companion through the dark pantomime of his memories and an anchor to the present. "A scared little boy and a monster who took advantage of your fear."

"He's not a monster," said Johnathan.

But the words felt confused. He wasn't sure who he defended.

Dr. Evans kept a hand on the back of his neck during that long walk. Johnathan once thought it comfort. Iron fingers circled his throat, a living collar to contain a street dog or a human scrap. It was a lead, to control. Dr. Evans' steps never faltered. He knew where Sir Harry slept. He must have watched Johnathan for days before he approached, waited for a boy's moment of weakness.

"He's a predator," said Mary Elizabeth.

"He's my mentor," said Johnathan, again caught by the sense that he didn't know who he defended or to which side he belonged.

They were in the moment, the worst moment of Johnathan's life. Evans pressed the knife into his hand. "First lesson, you must aim for the heart. You can't jab straight on; you'll just scrape bone and get your throat torn out. Best to stab up through the stomach, twist the blade to inflict as much damage as possible."

"I—I couldn't possibly—"

"Don't lose your nerve now boy. Do you want to die?"

"He's my family," whispered Johnathan.

Dr. Evans shoved him forward by the scruff of his neck, so hard his teeth chattered in his skull. Sir Harry lay before him. It didn't occur to him then how unnaturally still Sir Harry was. Vampires were not dead to the world when they slept. To catch them unaware required stealth and care, yet Sir Harry did not wake while Dr. Evans bellowed and berated Johnathan. He didn't move when Johnathan pressed the blade to the soft, vulnerable flesh beneath his ribs. The blade began to slide into his flesh, chill blood oozing down the length of metal, coating Johnathan's fingers.

Why didn't he move?

"Do it, boy!"

Johnathan froze. His body shivered with sobs, but he couldn't, wouldn't, shove the blade further. Sir Harry didn't so much as flinch in his sleep.

"I can't. I can't do this," he sobbed.

Blackened fingers curled around his. The memory fractured, wavered. He could hear the crackle of fire in Dr. Evans' voice. "Do it now!"

"It wasn't your fault," said Mary Elizabeth. She stood on the other side of Sir Harry's coffin; a twin spill of tears painted her mournful face. But her ghost couldn't erase what happened next, or excuse it.

Johnathan looked up into Dr. Evans' face, pleaded for him to stop. His vision flickered. Dr. Evans morphed into the skull-masked creature of the wood, though the cold black eyes remained the same, glowering down at him, full of hunger.

"You will do this." Evans' voice echoed with shadows. He bore down, his *breath tinged with sulfur. The vision snapped back as Dr. Evans wrapped his hands around Johnathan's and shoved the blade up through Sir Harry's rib cage.*

Johnathan cried out at the gush of fluid, shocked by the sensation of the blade piercing through tissue and muscle. Sir Harry never opened his eyes. Johnathan never saw that last look of betrayal, though he imagined it a thousand times.

"He was already dead, sweet Johnny," said Mary Elizabeth.

The truth of her words rang through him, far too late for the guilt and shame he'd carried deep in his heart for so many years.

"That will do, boy," said Dr. Evans.

The blade slid from his blood-coated fingers. Johnathan stared as his hands, unable to take a breath. Dr. Evans' hand collared the nape of his neck once again. "Welcome to the Society, Prospective Newman."

The man's fingers were sharp, like teeth as they dug into Johnathan's bruised neck.

The fire crackled overhead, a lick of heat, the breath of an expectant, waiting beast. It spilled down onto him, wrapped him in a blanket of blazing agony. It singed his veins. There was a furnace in his chest, his breath a bellows that fanned the intensity with each drag of his lungs, hot coals stuffed inside his skin. He looked down, watched the flesh of his chest blister and crack. The glow of fire blazed through the seams.

"I'm dying," he said.

"Don't." Mary Elizabeth grasped his hands. "Don't give in."

Her cold hands were a relief against his fevered flesh, a balm to the raging heat. Her smile so sad until she crumbled to ash at his feet, but the cold pressure of her grip remained.

"I don't know if you can hear me." Vic's voice.

Johnathan wanted to turn to it, longed to clasp the man to him and follow through on all the little gestures that had budded between them.

The flames roared all around him, but he clung to Vic's voice, their bond an intangible line as the fire consumed him.

"You owe me nothing, John, but please, please live. This isn't fair." Vic's voice broke. "We aren't finished, you and I."

Johnathan's blood boiled and steamed into a crimson haze. His nerves crisped and dissolved, nothing more than black soot.

"This is my fault. I didn't see—I didn't realize until it was too late.

They warned me, and I couldn't piece it together in time." Vic's words tethered Johnathan, but the fire continued to eat him alive.

His flesh peeled away from bone, charred flakes swept up in the rush of the inferno.

"Come on, come on. Don't succumb, John. Come on!" That beautiful voice was so insistent.

The flames coalesced, funneled into a torrent that poured into his chest, soaked into the struggling muscle of his heart. His pulse fluttered, battered by the heat. It sputtered and skipped, the fire wrapping around his bones, melting the marrow. Heat seeped into every pore. His heart stopped.

The pressure shifted, blanketed him, a cool darkness, but it did little to smother the fire.

"LIVE, DAMN YOU!"

Vic's shout pierced him, drove through the burnt remains of his being until they chained him to the physical plane. Each syllable rippled through him, an anchor he clutched in desperation, a scared boy who only wanted to survive.

His heart shuddered. The fire bloomed up from his bones, through the sizzling construction of muscles and tendons. New nerves and blood vessels crackled and snapped into place, bled up through his skin, baked from within. Johnathan exhaled a breath full of sparks and steam.

The flames receded at last, drawn back to the furnace inside his chest. The fire was still there but contained. His vision swam.

Vic's face appeared in sharp relief above him. His hands still gripped Johnathan's shoulders. He drew in a breath of surprise. "John?"

A haze of smoke wreathed the lens of his gaze. Through it he saw Mary Elizabeth, a hovering specter on the other side of a room, both familiar and strange in the diminishing grip of flame. *"You survived,"* she whispered. *"I'm so sorry."* She shimmered and vanished, where she had never been.

Johnathan bolted upright, his body curiously light. Without a second thought, he pulled the vampire into his lap.

CHAPTER TWENTY-FIVE

THEY STARED AT ONE ANOTHER IN ARRESTED ASTONISHMENT. VIC'S gaze flitted from Johnathan's face to his torso, over and over. Johnathan could only imagine what sort of hell-spat survivor he presented, but there was an odd absence of pain. His bones were weightless, muscles loose and wobbly, though his skin was stretched, too small for his frame. His throat was dry roasted from the inside out. Bodily discomforts he dismissed. There were other issues at large. He was, for want of a better word, inexplicably alive.

Vic sat in his lap, not only alive but unshackled, which meant Dr. Evans' men hadn't intervened. Where was Alyse? What happened to the creature that bit him? Where were the Society Hunters?

He needed to know how the others fared but couldn't staunch his utter relief at seeing Vic alive and whole, smoothing a shaky hand down the vampire's chest. "What happened?"

His voice was a rusted croak. A miracle he could talk when the last thing he remembered was the snap of teeth on his throat. He blinked, the rush of air in his lungs hot and tight as he reached for his neck. Vic caught his hand, his expression shattered. He shook his head when Johnathan looked at him.

A weighted silence floated between them and a crackling awareness that Vic sat astride him. The press of his weight, the coolness of his hand, his proximity, all fired against Johnathan's senses. He swore he could smell Vic, an intoxicating blend of spice and snow, a hint of old blood, and something floral that felt like an afterthought.

Johnathan inhaled again, teasing out the scent of water lilies and clean linens, not Vic's scent, but somehow familiar. The scents were so sharp, so clean. He leaned forward, pressing his nose into the man's neck where he drank his fill of that luscious scent.

"Oh," Vic breathed, a slight tremor in his limbs that drew a smile from Johnathan before a wave of dizziness rolled over him, dampening his amorous mood.

Johnathan drew away and shook his head; the disorientation failed to abate. The world spun out of focus. He gulped air in an attempt to steady himself, shocked by the sense of heat that rose in his lungs. He pressed a hand against his sternum, his breath coming in shorter, frantic pants, each lungful a scrape of sand to the parched wasteland of his throat.

The pressure of Vic's body disappeared. Johnathan gripped the mattress under him for purchase, certain if he didn't hold onto something he would fall off the edge of the world. He flinched at the touch of cold metal to his lips.

"Drink," Vic commanded.

There was no hesitation. Johnathan lost himself to the blessed relief of water. In seconds, he drained the cup Vic held to his mouth, barely conscious when he switched in another cup and another until Johnathan clasped the carafe in his hands and drank the contents down. It still wasn't enough, but the horrid, dry emptiness inside eased.

Johnathan recognized his surroundings now, ensconced in the relative safety of Vic's house. He collapsed back against the headboard, aware that Vic watched him, his gaze wary, clutching the empty carafe in his hands.

"How do you feel?"

"What sort of question is that?" Johnathan frowned. His voice was... off. Rougher. Deeper. He reached for his throat. This time, Vic didn't stop him.

He expected to meet another blood-stiff bandage, unnerved by the touch of unbroken skin. His eyes widened with alarm. "Why am I—"

Vic grabbed his hands, rubbing deep circles with his thumbs in an attempt to soothe Johnathan's mounting panic. "Stop. Breathe."

The expression on that angelic face could almost be called fear.

Johnathan's stomach clenched. The water he'd guzzled soured until he wondered if it would all come back up. He was caught up in the moment, distracted, which is why it took him so long to notice the lack of pain from his previously infected shoulder. There were no bandages across his filthy, bare chest.

A thread of dread suffused his system. "Tell me what happened?"

The question snapped out from between his teeth.

"You need to calm down first. I—," Vic's earnest voice was interrupted by a crash within the house. Tension whipped through his slim body as he rolled to the floor. "Stay here. Don't make a sound." He rushed from the room in a blur, or what would have been a blur. Johnathan caught his breath, tracking Vic with ease, every individual shift of his limbs visible as he ran from the room.

That crushing sense of suffocation returned with a vengeance. There was something terribly amiss.

Despite Vic's warning, he rose from the bed, surprised that his limbs held him without protest, but his head swayed enough that he needed to grip the vanity table to anchor himself.

The vanity mirror wobbled on its fastenings, and his reflection rippled for a moment before the glass settled. A hell-spat survivor indeed, his blond hair in willy-nilly tufts, his unshaven cheeks stained with dried blood. In fact, his neck and the upper portion of his chest were still filthy, coated in the Lord-knew-what fluids. How could that be when...

Johnathan brushed his fingers over his throat. Teeth flashed through his memory, a visceral reminder of what he'd thought were his final moments, the hot breath of the beast like fire against his skin. He swallowed, transfixed by the movement of his unmarred throat.

Not a hint of a scar marked his flesh.

Not good. Not good at all.

His pulse ticked up a notch. His eyes strayed further, to his shoulder.

The wood of the vanity whined under his grip. The bullet wound was gone, as if it had never been.

It was impossible to heal that fast, unless he didn't, and that curious lighter-than-air sensation that plagued his muscles was the result of one gray-eyed idiot's interference.

"Oh God, he wouldn't." Johnathan stumbled back a step and stared at his fingers. His hands shook, but his fingernails were a healthy, ruddy pink, without a hint of dead man's tinge. "But...how?"

The sound of shattering wood broke through his panic. Johnathan seized his tattered shirt from the end of the bed, his senses reeling in fresh dismay. His sense of propriety warred with a gut reaction to the stiff, blood-saturated fabric. It was either this or enter the fray half naked.

The door slammed open with enough force to destroy the hinges. Startled, he dropped the shirt.

A familiar face, a face Johnathan did not want to see, stalked into the room, a pistol levered over his forearm. Sykes was a man Evans sent in to tie up loose ends. For a bare second, Johnathan thought there was surprise on the agent's face to see him on his feet, though it only confirmed what he knew. Dr. Evans held back the others because he believed Johnathan about the demon. That he waited until after the encounter meant he thought Johnathan wouldn't survive or would be too injured to interfere when his agents mopped up the aftermath.

Evans meant for him to die. One way or another.

The surprise vanished, offering Johnathan a neutral mask. "Good to see you alive, Prospective Newman." The man's voice was level despite the blood that poured from his nose, clearly broken.

A beat of fear ticked inside Johnathan's chest. Where was Vic?

It suddenly didn't matter that Vic was a faster, stronger creature. Society agents were cunning, nasty fighters. Sir Harry's still form flickered in his memory.

"I'm afraid I don't return the sentiment, Sykes." Johnathan dropped into a crouch. A flicker of heat sparked in the pit of his stomach. "Where's Vic—" He bit off the question with a curse. Idiot!

An unpleasant smile curled Sykes's thin lips. "You always were keen on them bloodsuckers, eh, Newman? Odd little poof this one, all buttoned up in fine clothes, neat as you please. Tough too, though he still bleeds just fine. Now, why don't you come quietly and maybe Dodd will end the dandy nice and quick."

Johnathan's pulse echoed in his ears, a rushing crash that drowned out the panicked circle of his thoughts until the realization finally dawned on him. It wasn't his pulse that thundered in his ears. It was Sykes'.

The heat in his stomach went molten.

Johnathan surged forward. He seized Sykes' wrist and pulled the man forward. The gun went off, the brief graze of pain along his side quickly forgotten as he rammed Sykes like an incensed wild boar.

Sykes had fifty solid pounds of muscle over Johnathan and several more years of experience and training, but Johnathan's rage took the man off his feet. The advantage didn't last long when Sykes rolled him over and neatly pinned him face down on the floor.

The man had Johnathan's arms locked behind him in seconds, dislocating the shoulder joint to emphasize his point. The noise that poured out of Johnathan's mouth was closer to a feral snarl. He fought stupid and reckless; Sykes took full advantage.

"There we go, boyo, easy, easy," Sykes murmured.

Johnathan heard the rustle of leather and the muted clink of glass. Dread flushed through his system. He realized Sykes' aim as the needle pierced his neck.

Johnathan was a loose end, too dangerous to be left alive. That meant the Judas Choice, a dose of poison and dead man's blood to ensure it killed him if he was human or in transition to something other.

"No, no, no!" The silken chill of liquid poison flooded into his veins from the point of puncture. Johnathan cried out, his senses balking while the dose went to work.

His vision wavered. He'd failed. Even now, Vic was likely dead. The Society wouldn't spare Alyse either. They wouldn't give her the Judas Choice they gave him, not that she would go down lightly. He knew she wouldn't. The only consolation this gambit brought him was at least the Society would stop the demon and its servants.

Johnathan's stomach rolled. He curled inward beneath Sykes' hold.

The fire in his gut didn't subside. It burned hotter and hotter. He whimpered as it pushed into his veins.

"What the bleeding hell?" Sykes' grip loosened a fraction. The fog of the drug evaporated.

A pop vibrated through his body, and his shoulder neatly sank back into the joint on its own. Johnathan straightened in a rush and shoved Sykes off balance. He spun on his knees and caught Sykes mid-scramble to his feet. Johnathan knew a grapple was futile with the larger man, but desperation spurned him onward.

The man outclassed him, but dumb luck was on Johnathan's side when Sykes slid on his own gun, a second's falter that allowed Johnathan to lock him in a choke hold.

"Come on, come on, go down, you big bastard," Johnathan shouted. Sykes lifted him right off the ground. There were plenty of walls to slam him into; Sykes would have him off in a second. "Dammit!" He squeezed with everything he had.

The crack was deafening. Sykes dropped, a limp sack of meat, so fast he pinned Johnathan, who was too shocked to move, underneath him.

"Oh, God." He unwrapped his arm from Sykes' neck, unnerved by the crackle of bone beneath the skin. "Oh, God."

A gunshot roared through the house. Johnathan struggled to heave the dead man off him. Dead man, dead weight, like a sack of bricks.

"Johnathan!"

He sucked air into his lungs, torn between relief and fear at the sound of Alyse's worried voice. "Here! I'm in here!"

She appeared a moment later, strands of hair framed her white face, a hunting rifle still clutched in her hands. Despite her disheveled state, grim determination bracketed the sides of her mouth. She set the gun down on the floor and grabbed Johnathan by the shoulders. Between the two of them, they managed to free his legs. Alyse snatched up her gun.

"Come quick," she snapped. "Vic's hurt." She rushed from the room without a backward glance.

Johnathan climbed to his feet, itching to rush to the vampire's side. Fear sat thick and heavy in his limbs. Did Alyse manage to kill Dodd? Sykes said the vampire bled just fine...

He braced himself as he emerged from the room.

The parlor looked like a brawl pit straight out of the dockyards, the floor littered with blood spatter and the shattered remnants of furniture and decor. He found Dodd first. It wasn't difficult.

"Crazy bitch. Come back here! I'll wear your guts for suspenders!" Dodd lay slumped against the wall. His legs bent at such an angle that Johnathan suspected he didn't feel them anymore. The man sneered and jeered, clutching a gaping wound in his stomach. A gut shot, a nasty one, though he didn't feel a flicker of guilt or remorse for the man's fate.

"I think you should concern yourself with your own guts, Dodd," said Johnathan. That sneer turned on him.

"You kill Sykes then, you bleeding cur?" He bared his bloodied teeth.

Johnathan blinked. This was his second time seeing blood, and he didn't feel the slightest pull to it. His thoughts turned over. He turned away from Dodd, suddenly frantic to find Vic.

"They'll come for you, Newman. They'll kill them all, you murdering bastard!"

Johnathan ignored him. Dodd would spit in the face of the Devil soon enough. Instead, he followed the blood and bit his tongue hard when he found Vic.

It didn't look right to see Vic cower. He lay barely conscious on the floor behind the remains of the settee, openly bleeding from a dozen wounds that showed no signs of healing. They must have stuck him with a dose of Judas Choice to weaken him.

Vic flinched away, one bloody hand extended to fend Johnathan off, his eyes glassy and unfocused.

"Vic? It's me," he said. "It's Johnathan."

Vic's breath was far too ragged. Blood seeped through his fingers, pressed hard against his side. His fingernails were a dark blue-black. Could a vampire die like this? Johnathan was ashamed to realize he wasn't sure. The Society possessed so many methods of dispatching the undead, but they always took the head to be certain.

"I've got it," said Alyse. She hustled into the room, a physician's satchel under one arm. "John, bring him here." Alyse pointed to the settee.

Vic shook his head with a whimper. "Stay back. S'dangerous."

"Dangerous as a cornered kitten." Johnathan gently brushed Vic's hand aside and scooped him up. Vic cried out at the contact, the injuries on his back bled into Johnathan's palms. Fury burned inside him, his lungs a bellows as he carried Vic, carefully as he could, and set him down where Alyse waited. "What do we do?"

"He needs blood." Alyse laid out tools, her manner brisk.

Johnathan picked up a length of hollow tubing with a skeptical eye. It was no syringe. "This will get him blood?"

"A transfusion." She snatched the tubing from his hands. "He taught me how to do it. Just in case." She broke off. Her throat worked, struggling for control. Her nostrils flared. She tore her sleeve at the shoulder seam, halfway to tying a silk cord around her upper arm before Johnathan grabbed her.

"What do you think you're doing?"

"Are you truly that dense?" Alyse snarled. She attempted to shove past him and slapped at his face when he held her fast.

"Stop, Alyse, stop! He needs more blood than you can give." She was a bird, beating herself against the bars of her cage. Her pulse thundered at their point of contact, his hands at her wrists. Her fear and desperation bruised the air.

"Then I'll give it all!" Alyse yelled in his face. "He's family."

"Don't you dare," Vic gasped. Tears spilled down his battered face.

A shock of realization jolted through Johnathan, finally understanding the nature of Alyse and Vic's relationship. He pulled Alyse into him, handling her like crystal, the memory of Sykes' broken neck still raw as he held her in his arms.

"Listen to me. There will be more Hunters coming. Don't sacrifice yourself like this."

"Do you volunteer, then?" Alyse sobbed, her voice bitter and strained.

"I can do it," he said, and he meant it. Alyse went quiet in his hold, trying to pull back to get a look at his face, shocked by his sincerity. But the tactical side of Johnathan's mind quietly kicked in. If he let Vic drain him, he would merely die in the next fight or the one after that. The Society would keep sending its agents, however long it took, until all targets were dispatched. Next time, they would likely come with more men to ensure success.

Johnathan stared at the sputtering Dodd. His jaw clenched. "We do have another option."

Alyse stiffened, only for a moment, before her gaze followed his. "He's your man," she said, her voice rife with disbelief.

"He's a dead man, either way. Make use of him," said Johnathan. "Get him set up. I'll bring Vic over. And don't put anything sharp where Dodd can grab it."

Alyse glanced back at him, her expression one he'd never seen on her before. "You're serious—"

"Go!" John snapped. He waited for her back to turn before he brought his mouth to Vic's ear.

Vic shivered with a soft groan, likely lashed by a dozen impulses only his weakened state kept him from acting on.

"Where did they stick you?" Johnathan prayed for somewhere moderately accessible.

"Thigh," he gasped out.

"Damn," Johnathan muttered. He glanced at Vic's trousers. There wasn't time to namby-pamby about.

Vic's pants had enough tears for him to seize a gap and tear it open, exposing the violated thigh from groin to knee. He hissed through his teeth in sympathy at the sight, the veins blackened around the injection site like a poisonous lightning strike. There was a fast, if unpleasant, method of removing the poison, just as one would remove the venom from a snakebite.

"What are you doing?" Vic wheezed.

"Shut up before I lose my nerve."

Johnathan closed his mouth on the wound. He ignored Vic's tiny sound of surprise, prayed Alyse kept busy, and filled his mouth with poison so potent it burned like acid on his tongue.

He lifted his head long enough to spit on the floor. Johnathan would know the moment he hit clean blood. If the poison was bad, vampire blood was ten times worse, like sliding a razor blade down your throat, too potent for human senses to adapt to. That was what he expected, which is why a taste he hadn't expected made him break off.

Quickly, he spat out the mouthful, his thoughts a tangled mess while the wound on Vic's thigh sealed. Vic heaved a breath. His other wounds were already closing as well. He still needed blood, badly, but when he clutched Johnathan's wrist, his grip was iron.

"You—you—" he sputtered. "How did you know to do that?"

With his free hand, Johnathan wiped at his mouth. "Extensive training." He stopped, a moment of clarity born from his twisting fever dream.

This was how they killed Sir Harry.

How they kept him so still to force a scared boy to end his keeper. He shook the pall of bitterness off. Sir Harry was now, firmly, his past, and he would not let that guilt weigh him any longer.

"Allow me to whisk you away, my dear damsel." Johnathan lifted Vic off the settee and carried him across the room. Dodd was blessedly unconscious when they got there, though Johnathan suspected that had to do with the table leg in Alyse's lap.

"The mouth on this one," she muttered as Johnathan set Vic down. "Oh good, you prepped him for me." She held an alarmingly large needle in one hand, ready to plunge it into Vic's now-healed thigh. Alyse blinked at Vic. "You look remarkably better. Blood will fix you right up."

Broken necks, gut shots, poisonous wounds, and it was the sight of that ridiculously large needle plunged into Vic's thigh that made Johnathan's head swim. He sat down on the floor hard enough to bruise his tailbone.

"Damn." He squeezed his eyes shut when the attached tube filled with blood from the unfortunate Dodd.

"John."

He held his breath, risking a peek at Vic. Alyse cradled her friend's head in her lap, the embrace more motherly than intimate. There was no intimacy in her gestures, her hands stroking Vic's hair, her expression one of pure concern and worry. Johnathan stared, wondering when he'd internalized the fact Alyse was an ally and not competition for the affection of the man between them.

Vic grabbed for his hand, his grip still terribly weak. "Thank you."

"This is my fault," said Johnathan. "I sent for them."

"No," said Alyse. She inhaled a shaky breath. Vic wrapped his other hand around her wrist, connecting the three of them. "You did what you thought was right."

"Some good it did me," said Johnathan.

Johnathan bowed his head, lifting Vic's hand to brush a kiss over his fingers. Relief was a palpable drug, elation blooming as Johnathan watched the slow rise of color in Vic's face. He caught the small smile of approval on Alyse's face before his mood darkened. Yes, they had survived, but he'd led more danger to them. He'd failed to act on his theories and instincts until it was too late, unable to grasp the clues to his condition thanks to the demonic influence that hung over Cress Haven like an executioner's blade.

Vic caught his gaze. "I didn't realize you were the target until it was too late."

"Neither did I. I think that was the demon's intent. But Evans…I think he knew," Johnathan replied, more certain than ever that his mentor had a heavy hand in the matter, though the pieces still didn't quite connect. The core of the mystery plagued him. Why was Evans involved? Why was any of this happening? What part did his mentor ultimately play?

"How?" Alyse clutched Vic closer to her. "How could he know? I thought this demon only targeted women. Why would it go after you, John? And why didn't this Society bully stop it?"

"I don't know." Johnathan truly couldn't answer those questions. He found himself torn between the need for answers and the pain they would bring. "What happened to the beast?"

"It was a bit of a cluster when you went down," said Vic, his voice strengthening slightly as he shook off the final traces of poison. "But I think a couple of the Society agents peeled off in pursuit. I took you and ran. I knew they were coming. You were dying, and I refused to let them take you."

"But I didn't die," said Johnathan.

Alyse looked at him, the mark of exhaustion smudged beneath her wary eyes. "Are you sure of that?"

He swallowed. He couldn't truly answer that either. "What happened?"

Vic pulled the needle from his thigh and sat up. Johnathan failed to look away, pressing a hand to his mouth to keep from retching.

"I've never seen a fever like that," said Vic, his skin still too pale. "I thought I would watch you burst into flames, but you stubbornly clung to life." He paused. His fingers flexed. "Until you didn't. Your body started to give out. Your skin started to crack and blacken. Your heart stopped beating. You were losing."

"But I—I came back." An impossibility.

Vic shook his head and looked away. "I don't know how. I was certain you would burn to ash, same as poor Mary Elizabeth, but it stopped."

There was a beat of silence. "That can't be good." Johnathan held up his hands. They were covered in dried blood and dirt but appeared whole and healthy. "It seems I didn't wake up a demon's servant either, like Lydia Fairchild. What does that mean?"

"Your guess is as good as mine," said Vic.

"Dammit, more questions." John looked at the ruin of Vic's home. His gaze skirted Dodd's quiet form. "We can't stay here. Evans will send more men. They will go on the hunt as well, especially after they find their dead brethren."

Alyse bit her lip. "Where the hell are we going to go?"

"There is no *we*. *You're* going to go to your family and make sure they're safe," said Vic.

"They'll be perfectly safe." Alyse stuck out her chin. "Don't you dare try to keep me out of this, Vic. I'm not some wilting fair maiden in need of rescue."

Vic took her hands. "I know you're not, and that's why you need to do the most dangerous job." She drew herself up at Vic's words. "I need you to watch Evans and his men."

"But don't interact," Johnathan interjected. It was a sound task to keep Alyse out of immediate danger.

"They don't care about me," she said.

"Actually, they do," said Johnathan. "A fiend's companions are considered traitors to their species. If they believe they can reap answers from you, they will go after you."

Vic shot Johnathan a horrified look. "On second thought," said Vic, "come with us."

Alyse punched him in the shoulder. "I knew you were trying to keep me out of danger."

"We *do* need eyes on them. We need to know when they mobilize."

Johnathan avoided the venom in Vic's glare. Alyse had beyond proved herself able. "It will be dangerous, and if they see you, they might kill you or use you as bait."

"I don't agree to this," Vic snapped.

Alyse ignored him. A grin lit her face. "Where shall I report in, sir?"

Johnathan's mouth set in a hard line. "Do you remember where you found us in the wood?"

"Oh, bother." Vic scrubbed his pretty little forehead.

"And I'll need a fresh shirt, please." Johnathan glanced down at his bare chest.

"You'll have to borrow one of mine," said Vic, his mouth a pinched line, belying his displeasure.

Johnathan frowned when Vic stalked from the room. "I didn't expect him to be so upset."

"He'll get over it." Alyse snorted. "He can't protect me forever, which is why I am leaving before he comes back." He turned back to her, meeting her solemn gaze. "Try not to be too reckless, Johnathan."

It wasn't until Alyse left to play spy that Johnathan turned to the agent watching him. Surprised the vile man had remained quiet, it was possible Dodd was too weak to spit his usual bile.

"Would you like last rights?"

Dodd wasn't a religious man, most of the Society agents weren't, but every man deserved a final send off if they wished.

Dodd coughed weakly, the fire in his eyes smoldering with unspent rage. Between the bullet and the impromptu transfusion, the man was only alive through sheer stubbornness. "Filthy traitor."

"Well, I'm sure Evans will put a bullet through my skull when he catches up to me." Johnathan knew it was coming. He wasn't supposed to survive last night or this attack. He hoped to save Cress Haven before his borrowed time came due.

Dodd choked out a laugh in a gush of too-dark blood. "Oh no, boyo, the doc has some grand plans for you."

Johnathan's blood chilled, which was saying a lot at the moment. "What the hell does that mean?"

But Dodd was already gone, the leer on his face slowly going lax in the fade of death.

CHAPTER TWENTY-SIX

"WHAT MAKES YOU THINK THE FAIRIES WILL TALK TO US A SECOND time, John?"

"Call it a hunch?" Johnathan didn't have a clue what he was doing. He sure as hell didn't know if he could find the shimmering portal again, but the fairies knew about demons, and he would get answers, dammit, if he had to nail their slippery tongues to the nearest tree stump.

"Even if we do find them," said Vic, who kept pace without a single hitch in his breath, "their clues are about as clear as mud. Maybe, and do let me finish, if we got your Dr. Evans alone—"

"Absolutely not."

"I say, let me finish," said Vic. "We get him alone, we might be able to convince him to focus on the true threat—"

Johnathan slid to a stop, his borrowed shirt so tight it nearly tore at the seams. "If they were fighting a horde of demons here, Evans would still stop mid-battle to remove your head from your shoulders. You can't coax him or bribe him or use your compulsion, Vic, because he doesn't see you as anything but a monster to be dispatched, even if you had valuable information to offer him."

Vic threw up his hands. "You sent for the bastards, John, which I supported until they proved so bloody unreasonable."

Johnathan's head dropped. "I didn't expect Evans to come himself. There are a dozen field agents that should have been sent in his place, any of them far more flexible to an unusual situation."

Vic frowned. "Didn't you say he brought you here?"

The thought made Johnathan stop walking, overwhelmed by the dreaded crawl of implication. Johnathan didn't think it unusual at the time. Evans was his mentor. He personally chose Johnathan's solo assignment from a pool of several recent incidents. That was before Alyse told him that Evans had been to Cress Haven over a year ago. Before Mrs. Fairchild described the stranger who set her husband on the path to his doom, the recognizable details Johnathan scoffed at, unwilling to connect the pieces because he couldn't bring himself to think of Dr. Evans as a villain. What purpose did Evans have to bring him here?

He'd avoided the question because he didn't understand it. But to Johnathan, it wasn't the most troubling aspect of his situation. There was that moment, removing the poison from Vic's system, when Vic's blood hit his tongue—

"John."

He startled at Vic's voice. "What is it?"

"We're here. You led us right to it." Vic looked at him, his expression difficult to discern.

Johnathan glanced at the surrounding trees. The area was vaguely familiar, but there was no shimmering portal in the air. "How can you tell? There's nothing here."

"Exactly my point. This is a fool's errand. Neither of us have any secrets left to barter. We're not interesting enough to tempt them again."

"Maybe we should have brought Alyse," Johnathan mumbled.

Vic shoved him right off his feet. He landed in a flurry of dead leaves and bracken as Vic got in his face, features rigid with anger. "Don't you think you've put her in enough danger?"

Johnathan slapped the ground, struggling to stand. The movement was too much for the strained seams at his shoulders, which promptly ripped under both his armpits.

Vic's mouth pinched. "And you owe me a new shirt," he hissed.

Johnathan sighed and stayed on the ground. Might as well enjoy the fresh breeze through the torn seams. He was sweating like the Devil breathed down his neck. It was apparent his brush with death took more of his stamina than he realized.

"She's more capable than you give her credit for."

Vic drew back. His anger burst like a deflated air bladder. "Because of the company she keeps? She has no training or supernatural ability to bolster her, John."

Johnathan glared at him. "You know, it's actually not all about you. Alyse has good instincts and a strong will."

"She's *human*. She shouldn't be tangled up in demonic murders and vampire hunters—"

"She lives here, Vic. Do you think this entity is creating demon beasts out of young women for a lark? There is something building here, and Mr. Fairchild would have made his bargain whether you were here or not."

Vic stared at him, incredulous. "I—I didn't think of that."

"I don't believe you were meant to." Johnathan ran a hand through his sweat-laden hair. "This demon's influence over this town, this malaise that's kept the townsfolk complaisant, it's affected us too. You felt it. I felt it. Even as we followed the trail, neither of us were able to summon the urgency we should have. I couldn't summon the urgency I needed."

The vampire drew in a breath at Johnathan's words, but it was no wonder. A vampire being controlled, compelled even, to remain docile was a rare thing.

"Your presence does make a difference, however," said Johnathan. "You were able to break through that influence enough to recognize these murders were preternatural. You risked everything to save this town, to save Alyse."

Vic looked away, a flicker of shame on his face. "I meant to be far from here by now. I knew what I was inviting when I sent that letter to the Society." His throat worked. "I didn't want to ever put her in danger. But when you rolled into town, fresh off the wagon, and so amateur that the town drunk fleeced you, I couldn't leave."

"Yes, you could have," Johnathan said quietly.

"Only a monster would have," said Vic.

"And you're not a monster," said Johnathan. He waited for the rebuke, but Vic kept his head down.

"I had plenty of evidence you were competent enough. Alyse would never forgive me, but I could have left."

"Of course, she would forgive you," Johnathan scoffed. "She shot a man for you. That sort of devotion is rare and to be treasured."

Vic scratched at the upturned corner of his mouth, but he couldn't quite hide the smile. He knelt down in the bracken beside Johnathan. "Believe me, I do treasure Alyse. But she wasn't why I failed to leave. The longer I stayed, the more I realized I couldn't leave, and it wasn't Alyse who held me here."

"Oh." Johnathan breathed deeply.

Their gazes locked. Vic leaned in, and Johnathan froze, snared again by inexperience. Their reason for venturing out here was forgotten, his focus narrowing on the beckoning shape of Vic's soft lips.

Heat billowed up through his chest, but there was a new edge to it, an instinctual hunger that snapped Johnathan out of his awkward uncertainty. He surged up, hands seizing Vic's face as he brought their mouths crashing together, swallowing the other man's surprised grunt.

Vic enthusiastically returned the embrace, threading his fingers through Johnathan's hair, his tongue seeking out the corner of his mouth, tasting Johnathan as he tasted Vic in turn.

Vic tasted like honeyed wine. The heat intensified, wracking Johnathan with urges he didn't know how to follow through, but it was Vic who broke off the kiss, his expression one of gasping delight that left Johnathan supremely satisfied. Lack of experience or not, he'd left the centuries-old Vic breathless.

Vic framed his face, his fingers tracing Johnathan's jaw and trailing down his neck. Those gray eyes shone silver in the light, yearning evident in their depths. "Have you any notion what you do to me, John?"

Johnathan swallowed hard. He absolutely knew because Vic did the same to him. As if lightning sizzled through his veins at Vic's nearness, but that kiss... That kiss had stirred him in a way that left him aching with a need only ever met by his own hand. He wanted Vic, wanted him here and now, hard and soft, cruel and gentle. He just...*wanted.*

But, damn it all, this was the worst time for such a desperate revelation.

Johnathan pressed his forehead against Vic's and sighed. "I would love for you to show me what I do to you, but we should probably wait. At least until we're anywhere else but this forsaken forest filled with fucking fairies."

A laugh tripped off Vic's beautiful mouth, and he reluctantly pulled away. "Yes, I'm sure you're right. As wonderful and long-wanted as that kiss was, we need to focus."

Yes, focus. Reluctantly, Johnathan pried himself out of their embrace, settling to wait on the damp ground to see if the fairies would grant them an audience. The silence was thick, the visceral memory of Vic's lips still fresh on Johnathan's skin when Vic's uncertain voice invaded his thoughts.

"There's something I've been meaning to ask you, but we haven't had the time," he said. "I saw the agent in the bedroom. How did he break his neck? What happened there?"

The memory was ice water on his arousal. Johnathan shook himself, forcing himself to examine his brief, disastrous scuffle with Sykes. "We were fighting. He had the upper hand. He..."

He forgot, the sensation of the needle in his neck.

Vic wasn't the only one they poisoned.

Johnathan's hand went to his neck. So caught up in the adrenaline and fury of the moment, he hadn't processed how he'd survived the Judas Choice. It should have killed him. Sykes injected him, and the agent had been shocked when it didn't work.

Sweat dripped down Johnathan's spine.

Vic touched his chin. "John, what is it?"

"He's beginning to see," said a horribly familiar voice.

Vic shoved himself in front of Johnathan, nearly toppling both of them off balance from their hunched positions. "Mother Mary and Joseph."

"How amusing to hear such words from your mouth, little liar." The Morrigan emerged from between the shimmering shadows of the trees. Her steps were silent through the bracken but for the muted rustle of her gauzy skirts over the dead leaves.

There was no breeze to tease the airy garment, but it clung to her frame in such a way that the veil pressed against her face, throwing one side of her countenance into sharp relief. There was a peculiar little smile there, not quite amusement. She didn't stop until she stood directly in front of Johnathan.

Her crown of antlers tilted as she looked down at him. "You could have stayed with us, beautiful boy."

Johnathan swallowed. "You're not speaking in riddles now?"

The Morrigan crouched down, running a finger along the curve of his jaw, the gesture an echo of Vic's but far from romantic. Far and away from her realm's influence on the other side of the portal, her touch still made his guts clench.

"You have no more secrets to trade," she said.

"They won't let us in," said Johnathan. He knew it was a long shot. It wasn't like he and Vic had tried very hard. But he still hoped the fairies would be reasonable with a shared stake in the forest.

The Morrigan threw back her head and laughed, high and cruel, a visceral reminder of what stood before him. A chill slid in place of his disappointment. "No, beautiful one. They are terrified to open the portal to one such as you."

Sweat beaded on Johnathan's forehead. Heat continued to churn in the pit of his stomach, a veritable furnace. Did he still have a fever?

"One such as him? What does that mean?" Vic snarled.

The Morrigan didn't spare him a glance.

"I still don't like dead little boys," she said.

Johnathan could hear Vic grind his teeth.

"Well, I don't give a fig what you like, you overstuffed—"

Johnathan clapped a hand over Vic's mouth.

The Morrigan chuckled. "Finally, there's your true self."

She lifted her veil, the angles of her face no less severe than Johnathan's fractured memory of them. The Morrigan overwhelmed the senses, no matter what realm she occupied, but there was something in the symmetry of her horned crown and the horned skull entity that finally clicked into place.

"Are creatures from the Nether really demons?" he asked.

The Morrigan's smile was a blade's edge, twice as sharp. "You don't need to ask me questions anymore, beautiful one. The rules between us are different now."

Her words were a nightmare he couldn't wake from, but there were other lives at stake here. Johnathan sucked in a deep breath and reached up to clasp her wrists. "Then answer me."

"We are all echoes of one of another," said the Morrigan. "The Other, the Benign, and the Nether. We were here first, before humans began their ever-encroaching crawl, but we never truly belonged."

Johnathan rolled that over in his mind. Other, Benign, Nether—the Morrigan had mentioned these words during their first encounter, though he didn't understand them. "These names, are they different realms or the beings that reside there?"

"One in the same, sweet one, the ones who came before, pushed out by the metals and mettle of man." The Morrigan purred, swaying her weight from one leg to the other, her movements reminiscent of a viper's warning.

Johnathan swallowed at the mental comparison. "You're *all* fairies?"

Her lips twitched. "Is that what you call us? I'm afraid the answer is both no and yes. The Nether and the Benign would be the different faces of a coin. We, the Other, are the neutral hand that coin spins upon. But this is not the answer you need for your quest."

"Your lot come through as you please," said Vic, "but the Nether required a bargain to gain a foothold in our world. A bargain Mr. Fairchild made, with ill understanding of the consequences."

"To gain a foothold to this realm, the Nether need a bargain from a child of Adam, as the Benign require the permission of Eve's line," said the Morrigan, her fingers flicking in the air to the rhythm of her words. "Because they are not content to play. Their appetites demand more, and they can exude more influence once they find a way into your realm."

Johnathan frowned. "So the Nether seeks to tempt man, and the Benign needs a woman's permission to enter their realm?" If Nether were demons, what were the Benign? The Morrigan's description made it seem they were no more benevolent than the Nether.

The Morrigan yawned, showing off canines that framed the bottomless darkness of her throat. "How human to think in such terms. The line of Eve is steeped in secret shame. Eve's children crave redemption, forgiveness, the cleansing sear of the Benign. The ilk of Adam are tainted by pride, easily tempted, and malleable to the Nether's influence."

Realization clicked over. "The demon didn't choose them because they were women, it chose them because—"

"They were tainted and pure," said Vic. "But they were highly sheltered country girls."

"Temptation comes in many forms, little liar," the Morrigan purred. "Desire for flesh, for wealth, for life. A demon will seize on whatever it can manipulate under its influence."

"And the Other are content to tease both lines, as long as you follow certain rules." said Johnathan. "Does that make you the neutral of the three?"

The Morrigan bowed her head. "We adhere to our rules, but the demons of the Nether, they are...opportunistic."

"That foothold," Johnathan shifted with unease. "What is it exactly?"

The Morrigan leaned into him, the movement so abrupt he didn't have time to back away.

Her lips brushed against his ear as she wrapped her arms around his neck, their pose reminiscent of a lover's embrace. "Tell me, beautiful one, what did his blood taste like when it hit your tongue?"

In the soft lilt of her voice echoed the whistle of spears, the screams of a thousand dying animals, the low braying call of endless hounds, and the hunter's horn. Whatever the Morrigan said about the other fairies fearing him, she feared nothing. She was fear incarnate, the thrill and death of the hunt made flesh; what made the low creatures cower in their dens against the dark of night.

Flames flickered to life under Johnathan's skin. He tried to ignore the sensation, focusing on the proximity of the Morrigan.

Johnathan turned his head. "The sweetest wine."

He sought Vic's gaze, afraid what he would think of that admission, but there was a knowing look in those gray eyes.

A satisfied hum left the Morrigan's mouth, a purr against Johnathan's skin. She brushed her cheek against his before she pulled away. Something ancient and primal shifted under her pale, taut skin, and Johnathan wondered what lurked beneath that layer of pulp.

"There is a rift, a tear in your world, that bleeds the influence of the Nether. It is the anchor of Cernunnos, he who bargained, and serves as his foothold on this plane."

The name knocked around his skull, the shadow of the horned giant in the wood rising from the bracken, the etched coin dangling around its neck. Not a forest spirit at all, but the demon they sought. The demon had opened a rift between their realms. Did the rift act as a door? Was it already open, spilling more creatures from the Nether than any of them realized?

Recognition colored his errant encounter in a new light that shot icy fear through the heat in Johnathan's gut. He shivered. Had Cernunnos let Johnathan live because he'd scented his mark on him?

"Do you know what Cernunnos wants here?" Johnathan's voice was steady.

"Nether, Other, or Benign, we all crave the children of Adam and Eve, each for a different purpose. The Nether is hungry—it seeks to consume, to grow." The Morrigan's voice took on a decadent cadence, a dark song that swayed through her body. "They will consume the settlement of Cress Haven, then spread—rampant, unchecked, a festering wound to taint the cities of man."

He had one last question for the Morrigan, one he almost hoped she couldn't answer for the suspicions it would confirm. "Who told Fairchild how to bargain with the Nether?"

The stranger Mrs. Fairchild described may have told her husband he would summon a spirit of the wood, but that seed of knowledge had a malevolence Johnathan couldn't ignore, not if he was right.

The Morrigan's stare pierced him, pinioned on the edge of an abyss. "You know this answer in your heart, beautiful one, if only you have the courage to face it."

Vic's shoulders hunched beside him. "John?"

His jaw clenched, unable to answer, but the Morrigan took pity on him, patting his cheek hard enough to bruise. The gesture was almost affectionate. Johnathan inhaled for strength. "Dr. Evans. Alyse said he visited over a year ago, and...he matches Mrs. Fairchild's description of the informative stranger."

. . .

Vic swore, clearly connecting the dots. "I should have killed that man the first time he came to Cress Haven."

Johnathan's breath rushed out of him. The situation was as dire as he feared, worse, with Dr. Evans' involvement. "We'll deal with him after we close the rift."

"Excellent," snapped Vic. "Just how do you propose we do that? We don't even know where the damn thing is."

The Morrigan's bones rippled under her skin. Vic hadn't posed the question to the fairy, but she snapped forward, her expression a quicksilver flash of curiosity and cold rage as she snatched Johnathan's forearms.

Her claws sank deep into his skin. Johnathan yanked, but the Morrigan held fast, impossibly strong. Vic frantically grabbed at those deadly hands. The Morrigan didn't budge an inch.

"You're poisoning him!" cried Vic.

Johnathan could see it, a vile blackness that slithered through his veins on a deadly march toward his heart. Agony washed over him. The flickering fire in his gut roared to life.

"A kiss of nightshade, a dollop of arsenic, sharper than the serpent's tooth and stronger than dead man's blood," sang the Morrigan.

"You're killing him," Vic choked out.

"Such sentiments, little liar. Perhaps you care enough to save him." Though her claws were in Johnathan's arm, her gaze was on the vampire. "What would you risk to keep him? Could you forge a bond, stronger than the call of his realm? A tether intangible as flame, stronger than the call of gold." Her hypnotic voice carried Johnathan through a wave of pain before it became too much.

Johnathan screamed, a guttural slash of sound born in the heat that burgeoned up from the pit of his stomach and roared through his veins. The Morrigan hissed through a mouth of sharp white teeth and released him. The tips of her claws smoked, her fingers blackened to the first joint. Vic released her in shock.

He expected anger, hoped for fear, but the Morrigan's feral smile was the worst. "Do you see, beautiful boy, what a glorious beast you will make?"

Johnathan wanted to vomit. He'd hoped, despite evidence to the contrary, that he had somehow evaded the same fate as Lydia Fairchild, but at the Morrigan's words, he knew his fate, knew what he would become. The truth swirled inside his veins.

Blood still oozed from the puncture wounds left by the Morrigan's claws, a grisly gauntlet that circled his wrist. How could he be something so atrocious when he still felt so much himself? And why? Why him? Why had he been singled out? Was he human at all anymore?

Vic's stilted roar brought him back to the moment, fury lacing every word. "What did you do?" he snarled. "The old ways be damned, witch, I will rip you limb from limb."

The Morrigan smiled. "Little liar, I did not cause this. I merely revealed the creature that already lurks beneath that pretty face. Lay your anger at Cernunnos' cloven feet."

Johnathan buried the despair that threatened to break him. Jaw set, he forced himself to meet the Morrigan's gaze. "How do we close the rift?"

There would be time to mourn what he had lost later.

The ancient fairy tipped her head to the side and sighed. "Bargain made is bargain broken. The child of Adam demanded riches, and riches were given. Gold coins, cast in the Nether, cooled in virgin blood. Find the coins of Cernunnos, one or two will do, cast them into the rift and declare 'Our bargain is done.'"

"That seems too simple." Vic's voice was tight. *Now* he was rattled.

"We are simple creatures," said the Morrigan, a weight to her words. "A material bond is far weaker than one born of blood, little liar." Her gaze turned skyward as she pursed her lips. "Go. Your time grows short. The demon's servants will be strong enough by the next sunrise."

"Ah, see, there's the catch I was waiting for," grumbled Vic.

The Morrigan chuckled. "Perhaps I still find you amusing after all, little liar."

"Bully for me," said Vic.

The Morrigan's veil slipped over her face of its own accord but Johnathan knew her gaze was on him. It was a physical thing, keen as the caress of a knife. "Once the rift is sealed, the Nether will reclaim any unfettered ilk."

Johnathan watched her fade into the shadows. He knew when she was gone. It was easier to breathe.

Vic knelt in front of Johnathan and gently took up his hands. "Did you know?"

Johnathan shook his head. "Not really. I don't feel any different." He looked out into the woods. Did the Society agents manage to kill the beast that attacked him? "When Sykes came at me, he injected me with the Judas Choice, same as you. They must have thought you turned me to save my life."

Vic cleared his throat. "Similar reaction, I take it?"

"I didn't think about it at the time. We grappled. I got Sykes in a chokehold by some fluke."

"And snapped his neck," Vic finished. "I wondered how you managed that."

"I didn't mean to. I was trying to make him pass out," whispered Johnathan. "How long do you think I have before I become a servant of Cernunnos?"

Vic's grip tightened, his brow set in a hard line of determination. "I will help you figure this out, John. I swear it. We will seal this damn hell rift and we will fix this. Together."

"Right. First we have to find it." They had a Devil's bargain to undo, though Johnathan couldn't shake the sensation his time was now short as well.

CHAPTER TWENTY-SEVEN

WAS HE HUMAN ANYMORE? THAT WAS THE WORRY.

Johnathan didn't know if he could answer such a question yet. His thoughts were a mess, and he'd be damned if he could figure out how to trigger whatever otherworldly ability he had the two times he'd been poisoned. Twice in less than four hours—that had to be some sort of precedent.

Vic played sentinel beside him, clearly lost in the churn of his own thoughts while Johnathan contemplated the possible changes to his state of being. If he wasn't human anymore, *what* was he? He couldn't be the same creature as the unfortunate Lydia Fairchild, could he? Wouldn't he have already turned into the same wretched misshapen beast as she did? He wasn't a ruined ghost like Mary Elizabeth either. Least, he didn't think so. Surely, someone would have told him if he displayed specter-like qualities.

He didn't feel like a demonic creature was about to burst from his human skin. Actually, he had a hankering for a bowl of stew or a decent sandwich. He was fair famished. Food, sadly, did not appear to be in his immediate future.

Alyse waited for them at the edge of the wood, hunkered down in a copse, hidden from sight of the main road. Her perceptive gaze flitted between the two of them. "What happened in there?"

Johnathan squinted at her. "Does your father ever protest your gallivanting about with two unspoken-for gentlemen?"

She raised a brow. "I'm a spinster. Nobody cares a wink for spinsters." She turned to Vic with a head jerk in Johnathan's direction. "Where did the sudden lecture in social etiquette come from?"

"He's having an existential crisis," said Vic.

"God, you can't go telling everyone that," snapped Johnathan.

Vic pointed at his human accomplice. "I didn't tell everyone. I told Alyse. She's an oubliette of secrets."

She glanced between the two of them, her fine brows raised. "What sort of crisis?"

"Johnathan is now one of our mystery beasts," announced Vic. Johnathan groaned into his palm.

"Oh, does this mean he's a werewolf, like the Faoladh of Ireland? They don't follow the cycles of the moon, you know, not that we are close to a full moon. We're about to hit the new moon, full dark," said Alyse.

"No, I'm not a bloody werewolf—how do you even know the cycles of the moon?"

Alyse shrugged. "Seemed relevant to cover my bases when these murders took a turn to the preternatural. I read all the folk tales and legends I could find, everything from barrow wights, Hellhounds, pixies, and kelpies to find a supernatural cause. You don't have to be sensitive about it. I bet lycanthropy is perfectly manageable."

Johnathan heaved in exasperation. "For the last time—wait, why are you here now? Weren't you watching Evans and his men?"

She crossed her arms. "They're gone."

The two men stopped in their tracks. "Gone," Johnathan repeated, unable to recover his wits. "What do you mean they are *gone?*"

Alyse rolled her eyes. "That mad Dr. Evans and his men cleared out of the town while you were out here bickering with fairies. Left on this road barely an hour ago."

"But they can't just *leave,*" Johnathan sputtered. "The threat is still here!"

She made a face. "Well, looks like it's up to us, like it was before they showed up and tried to kill everyone. Learn anything useful this time?"

"We know how to stop it," said Vic. He relayed what the Morrigan told them without mention of the poison incident.

Alyse tugged on her bottom lip. "Seems awfully simple.'"

"Well, we do have to find Fairchild's bargained gold *and* the rift before sunrise, or the Nether will consume the town," said Vic.

Alyse cocked a brow. "There's always a catch."

"Maybe not as difficult as we think," said Johnathan. "I encountered the creature behind Fairchild's estate. The rift likely formed close to where the bargain was struck, one would think."

"A bit of luck then," said Vic. "Pray that it holds."

Alyse grinned. "Let's ransack a house, boys."

The Fairchild estate sat untouched, despite the demise of its occupants. The trio had to wait until dark to approach the property in order to avoid suspicion. Alyse spent their remaining daylight hours attempting to cajole and convince her father to take her siblings to visit her aunt two towns over. It wasn't until Vic finally stepped in and added a nudge of compulsion that the pastor agreed to take the Shaw household out of immediate danger. The harried Pastor Shaw loaded his brood into their cart and set out with the sun nipping at their heels. Alyse insisted it made her feel better to know her family would be momentarily safe if events took an ill turn. With their head start, the Shaws might be able to outrun whatever emerged from the Nether if she, Johnathan, and Vic failed to stop it, for a time. It was a healthy dose of pessimism, but it kept Johnathan from focusing on his own woes.

Cress Haven did not exist on the same crunch and grind of time as the city. Mr. Fairchild was dead more than a week, his death reported by none other than Vic, but since there was no body recovered, the service was brief and quiet in customary country fashion. Since Vic last saw Mrs. Fairchild wandering off into the woods, she was presumed missing, though Johnathan had a glimpse of her fate. No one truly mourned or questioned the death of the man and his wife, though whether that was due to Cernunnos' influence on Cress Haven or Mr. Fairchild's nature was unclear. Word had been sent to the next of kin, but it would be days before anyone arrived to handle the estate's affairs, which meant their luck held as they proceeded to burgle a dead man's house.

"If you were to store demonic coins in your house, where would you keep them?" Johnathan asked.

Alyse's resourcefulness came through. She produced a lantern from somewhere in the house. It emitted a mellow orange glow that scattered the shadows of the Fairchild residence like a dozen startled ghosts. Johnathan couldn't help but think of Mary Elizabeth's ghost, and a shudder chased down his spine.

"He was a businessman," said Vic. "We'll check his study first, then his rooms. John, care to scout the grounds?"

"I doubt he buried his gold in the backyard," said Johnathan.

"True, but the demon's servants might be close, and I don't think they'll attack...one of their kind," said Vic. He gave him an apologetic look. Even Alyse shot Johnathan a sympathetic glance.

"Oh. Right," he said. He supposed it made sense, though the realization left a bitter, ashen taste in his mouth.

The shadows of the house re-established themselves once Alyse's lantern vanished into the interior. Quiet as the grave, the sounds of Johnathan's companions were muted by the thick walls of Nathaniel Fairchild's home. He wondered what the man thought as he signed away his soul, if the gleam of gold blinded him to the nature of his bargain. What had Fairchild felt when the demon claimed his daughter as payment?

"How was Lydia Fairchild tainted and pure?" Johnathan mused aloud, a vain attempt to break the silence that lay over the house like a layer of grave dirt. What desire let Cernunnos twist his influence over her mind, body, and soul?

A ripple of movement tugged at the corner of his vision, something seen but not seen. So subtle that he wondered if his senses were haywire too. But he turned his head.

Mary Elizabeth shuffled across the room without a sound, clad in a translucent white shroud with a train dragging on the ground behind her like the Grim Reaper's bride. She paused at the mouth of a hallway opposite to the one Alyse and Vic took, which led to the family's living quarters, and turned to Johnathan.

A nonexistent wind caught and teased her dark curls, her face as lovely as he remembered. The front of her dress bore the stain of her death, a grisly mass across her abdomen. She held up an outstretched hand and curled her fingers in an unmistakable gesture.

Johnathan followed.

She didn't speak to him now. Maybe she couldn't. He didn't exactly know the rules for ghosts. They usually had something to say, and it was best to listen.

He was still surprised when she led him into Lydia's room. It was mostly unchanged from the day he dove through her window, but there were a few key differences. The mirror to the vanity was cracked, a shatter-star pattern, as if someone took their fist to it. The pretty dress that had been hanging from the back of the changing divider lay scattered in torn ribbons across the floor. Did Lydia enter the home and do this herself? The window to her room was still open, wide enough for a girl to climb in and rage against her lost humanity.

Johnathan touched his fingers to the cracked mirror, saddened for the child she'd been. What did it matter how she was tainted and pure? She was a girl, not yet a woman, lost to violence and the stupidity of a father who should have protected her.

The thought made him angry, so very angry. None of his "fathers" protected him either. Abandoned by the father of his flesh, bitter and afraid of the father he loved, and left to die by Evans, his mentor, his caregiver. The one who subsumed Sir Harry in his heart, though he didn't deserve it. His mind echoed the sentiments of that shattered mirror. He wanted to put his fist through the glass until he could no longer see his reflection in the shards.

Mary Elizabeth appeared behind him, sadness in her eyes, perhaps mourning the lost girl who once occupied this room, or the lost man who occupied it now.

Johnathan stared at her. "Why did you bring me here?"

She shook her head and pointed to Lydia's empty bed.

He frowned and turned away from the mirror. "What do you want me to see?"

The specter was gone.

Johnathan circled the room. The bed was untouched, the sheets stiff and tight, neatly made, only to gather dust. The porcelain doll sat propped up against the headboard, emotionless glass eyes reflecting the shattered mirror.

What did Mary Elizabeth want him to see?

He lifted one of the silk-covered pillows. The doll fell forward, synchronized with a peculiar pull in his gut. With two fingers, he plucked the back of her dress. A hum vibrated up his arm so hard that he nearly dropped the blasted thing.

Johnathan grabbed the doll with both hands and sucked in a breath. The coin's presence rolled through his bones, a thunderous chime that left a ringing echo in his head. A painful sensation, he wanted to clap his hands over his ears, but he knew the action was useless. The sound was internal, an unused sense he suspected was a result of his "altered state."

He tore open the back of that petite taffeta gown. There, where the porcelain neck attached to a cotton-stuffed body, tucked into the seam, was a crude cut gold coin. A symbol was stamped on it, the face half-hidden, but Johnathan knew what he would see when he pulled it free.

Some newfound instinct made him hesitate to grab it. He could hear the low, ugly song of the coin every time his fingers drew near.

The need was worth the consequence.

He braced himself and grasped the gold. Pain hissed through his teeth as if he'd plunged his hand into a bucket of molten lead. Pulling it free, the edges of the coin cut into his fingers, a payment of pain and blood. The same horned symbol was carved into its face, the same he'd seen repeatedly in bone, in ash, etched in wood, and branded into the palm of his hand.

"Cernunnos," he whispered.

The metal burned hotter. His vision cut out, shrouded in a thick gray fog. Johnathan threw back his head at the rush of wind that caressed his skin, the sensation of his body moving to a separate location while he remained stationary.

Faster, faster, the wind howled in his ears, echoed by the mournful cry of a lone beast. The hair on his arms rose as other beasts joined the howl. He picked out nearly a dozen voices. Their call itched at his skin, an instinctual prod at the heat nestled inside him. He resisted it, but he couldn't resist the other pull.

The call abruptly stopped, and his body rocked at the cessation, the world coming into focus in shocking clarity, tinted by shades of midnight.

The Nether rift stood before him, a gaping maw that bled nightmare creatures into this world who slipped and slithered off into the night. It undulated beneath his gaze, an exposed wound, and when he peered deep, he swore he could see the writhing mass of the Nether's inhabitants, gathered, waiting. The rift pulsed in time to his heartbeat.

Johnathan jerked his gaze away. His lungs couldn't get enough air. He panted, trying to observe as much as he could, to take advantage of whatever magic pulled him here, and bring the information back to Vic.

Two rough-cut stone braziers lit the scene. The flames blazed so hot that their hearts burned blue. There was a clearing of a sort, the brush and bracken tossed away, and lined with some sort of crude fence. He took a closer look. His stomach clenched. A barrier of discarded bones, cracked open, the marrow scraped clean.

Across from him, on the other side of the rift, the horned demon rose, the same creature he encountered in the woods, but changed, altered by its time and wielding influence on this plane. Cernunnos now appeared complete, limbs thick and strong, his primeval body fuller. That glowing red gaze bore into him. Johnathan wasn't afraid. He was excited.

"No!" The coin slid through his blood-slicked fingers. Johnathan found himself hurled back from that eerie in-between space so fast that he gagged and dropped to the floor. He vomited bile, strands of saliva clinging to his lips. Vic and Alyse rushed into the room while he fought not to heave up his guts.

"What happened to canvassing the perimeter?" Vic smoothed Johnathan's hair from his face. His cool hands were blissful against Johnathan's too-hot skin.

"Vic, look," Alyse whispered.

The damned coin lay between Johnathan's splayed hands. He could sense it, humming.

"You found one." Vic sounded worried. "We tore half the house apart. How did you even think to look here?"

"I can hear it," Johnathan rasped.

Vic moved in front of him and cupped Johnathan's face with his hands. He forced Johnathan to look into his calm gray eyes. "Still human, John."

The relief was palpable. How could Vic possibly have known Johnathan needed the assurance?

"There's someone outside," whispered Alyse. She dropped beside them, her hand on Johnathan's shoulder.

Anger flashed in Vic's eyes. "It's the Society. I can hear Evans ordering them about."

"What? But I saw them leave!" Alyse's hand rubbed circles on Johnathan's back. She scooped the coin off the ground and deposited it in one of the hidden pockets of her dress. "Can you move, boy?"

"Here I thought we were past you calling me boy," he said, his voice hoarse.

"I'll consider you a man when you have more than a hint of scruff on your chin and can remain upright for longer than a day," said Alyse. "Come on, up and at 'em."

Vic and Alyse seized Johnathan's arms and levered him to his feet to move away from the window.

"Do you think they heard me yell?" Johnathan asked.

Alyse raised a brow. "I'm certain half the town heard that bellow."

"I saw the rift," whispered Johnathan. "I know where it is."

"Excellent. Now we simply have to evade your Society friends," said Vic.

"Friends don't kill friends," said Johnathan.

Vic held a finger to Johnathan's lips. Understanding, he nodded, falling in behind Alyse. His legs grew heavier with every step, but he managed to keep up with Vic, who sidled along walls and peered around every corner. They were near the main section of the house when Vic pulled back with a hushed curse.

A crossbow bolt sprouted on the wall an inch from his head. He looked up and met Johnathan's gaze.

Dr. Evans was here.

The whine of a bowstring pulled tight creaked across the room. Their attacker reloaded another bolt while they stood gaping at each other.

"If you're still alive, I suspect my young protege is with you."

Johnathan jumped at the matter-of-fact tone.

Dr. Evans continued. "Tell me, fiend, did you break Sykes' neck or did Johnathan?"

"Don't say anything to him," Vic mouthed.

Johnathan swallowed. The muscles of his chest were too tight, pinched around the wounded beat of his heart.

"I wondered, but he was always a simpering sort. Weak, could never bring himself to do what needed to be done." The precise click of heels on the hardwood floor belied Evans' exact position in the room. His steps moved closer and closer, a purposeful taunt.

Heat flickered through Johnathan's veins. Could he duck around the corner and punch his mentor in the jaw?

Vic violently shook his head, reading the intent in Johnathan's face, and gestured back towards the open window in Lydia's room. The thought of running set Johnathan's teeth on edge.

"It's no surprise he betrayed his own kind for another blood drinker," Evans drawled. "He enjoyed being a pretty plaything far too much. Too in love with death, that one. Would have stayed with his master until the fiend drank him down. Couldn't even strike the killing blow. Pathetic little wretch."

Johnathan dug his nails into his palms until the sting of fresh cuts sliced through the roar in his ears. Vic went still, a predatory air stealing over his features. Alyse looked between them, wearing a mask of ill ease.

"I should have written him off then and there. It would have been a mercy to slide a blade through his heart—"

To Johnathan's great surprise, it was Vic who snapped. Snarling, he spun around the corner, but he didn't have the chance to attack.

Dr. Evans rammed into Vic and pinned him to the wall, a spear through his shoulder. They neither heard nor saw the man exchange his choice of weapons, catching them both off guard.

Alyse's shriek rose over Vic's scream. Johnathan yanked her back a second before Evans' second weapon—a blade—could slice her face. Droplets of black fluid slid off the blade in an arc.

Evans had coated his weapons in dead man's blood.

Johnathan shoved Alyse behind him. "She's human," he shouted.

Evans heard him. That didn't stop him.

The man grunted, pivoting to swing the blade in a downward arc. Sharp agony bloomed down Johnathan's chest where the knife caught him.

Alyse swore behind him. She didn't try to insert herself into the fight, quick to realize her vulnerability against someone of Evans' skill, but it was clear the Hunter wasn't trying to strike her. Evans watched him too closely, too expectant. Johnathan couldn't stop his body from purging the poison.

An unpleasant smile lit his mentor's face when the cut steamed, expelling the poison in the same peculiar fashion as when the Morrigan clawed him.

"You did kill Sykes, didn't you, boy?" said Evans.

"What does it matter?" Johnathan snapped. His gaze darted to Vic's pale face, who pulled the spear from his shoulder in a slow, painful slide. It was almost free, but the wound was full of dead man's blood. Johnathan wanted—needed—to tell Vic to flee, to drain the wound, but he didn't dare give away how close Vic was to unpinning himself.

"It matters, boy." Evans was close, too close. His dark eyes bore into Johnathan, a feral hunger that spooked him to his core. "I knew that day, when I brought your shuddering sobbing body to the barracks, you were exactly what I'd searched for all those years. I merely needed to shape you. Tainted and pure."

Johnathan stared at the man who'd mentored him for the past eight years. The truth of Evans' involvement with the Nether's presence in Cress Haven was something Johnathan had accepted the moment he sat across from him in the tavern. But to hear from the man's own mouth that he'd manipulated Johnathan so deeply since their first interaction, that the root of their entire relationship was a great lie, punched down in a way that rocked his foundations.

Evans had guided every aspect of his training. Gave Johnathan his first weapon. Showed pride in his pupil's accomplishments, and took time from his immense duties at every turn to lend an ear to Johnathan's fear and uncertainties. The relationship he thought existed between them was a greater myth than the many creatures he'd encountered since his arrival in Cress Haven.

"Do you know how difficult those conditions are to foster in a male child?" Evans spat on the ground at Johnathan's feet. "Two decades, three, I devoted my life to procuring the rarest of beasts for the Society's use. And now here you are, in the flesh, but not for long." He jerked his head to the side. "Take them."

Johnathan was too rattled to react, too slow to dodge the net that closed around him. The heavy net seared every inch of his skin that it touched.

Alyse screamed when Evans' men seized her from behind. They'd entered through Lydia Fairchild's bedroom window while Evans kept Johnathan and poor Alyse distracted. Johnathan fell to his knees, unable to think through the pain. His gaze slid to Vic.

The bloodied spear lay on the floor, the vampire nowhere to be seen.

CHAPTER TWENTY-EIGHT

THE WORLD CAME TO A FINE POINT OF PAIN UNTIL JOHNATHAN FOUND himself torn free of the infernal net. The first thing his conscious mind registered was the clang of metal when Evans' man shut the cage door.

A cage. They put him in a bloody cage!

Johnathan did a quick study of his prison. It was a cage alright, on wheels, akin to the sort used in carnivals for display. It had a barred, wooden door surrounded by iron slats wide enough to put his arm through, if he dared. Two horses were bridled and hitched to the wagon, surrounded by a mass of agents who traipsed through the Fairchild's back yard, ready for battle.

Evans watched Johnathan through the bars, close enough to grasp, but Johnathan hesitated. There was a chill in the air; it licked his skin and wafted off the metal, a whisper of promised pain if he touched. He settled back on his haunches and returned the stare.

Evans crossed his arms. "Excellent. Your instincts are working."

Johnathan's jaw flexed. "What, exactly, am I to you?"

His mentor took another step forward, daring Johnathan to reach through the bars and grab his sagging neck, pain be damned.

"What you've always been. A tool for the Society's use."

Johnathan's attention snagged on one of the Society's men, dragging Alyse from the house. She struggled at first, but once her gaze found Johnathan, she ceased, holding her head high as they led her to the cage.

The man opened the cage's door, roughly pitching her inside. Johnathan caught Alyse before she hit the floorboards.

He bent over her, but there was no sense of privacy under Evans' gaze. "Are you okay?"

She nodded. A bruise bloomed on her cheek, which made him furious, but Alyse shed no tears. Her expression was cold, clear-eyed fury, leveling a glare at Evans. "Vic got away."

Johnathan closed his eyes, lest his reaction give away even more under Evans' watchful gaze. *Good.* His heart ached that he was unable to see Vic one last time, to pursue all the things he wished to experience with the beautiful vampire, but ultimately, he was relieved that at least one of them would survive this.

Alyse jerked her chin forward. "Why is he watching us?"

"No doubt it's for something horrid and nefarious."

Johnathan didn't like the smirk that drew across Evans' mouth. The man slapped the frame of the cage. "Move out."

The floor lurched under them. The horses moved away from the Fairchild estate, into the old pine trees behind the house, following the path he took, chasing after the beast that was Lydia Fairchild. Johnathan had a sinking feeling that he knew where they were headed.

He inhaled the woody scent of the forest and attempted to distract himself with the construction of their cage. He'd been so sure the bars were iron, but now, with a closer look...

"Are you any good at recognizing metals?" he asked Alyse.

"They're silver," she said. "I heard the men talking."

"Silver? Why silver?"

Alyse's eyes went wide, and what color remained in her cheeks drained away. "My God. You really *are* a lycanthrope—"

The rap of wood on metal made them jump.

"Iron for the Other, silver for the Nether, gold for the Benign," said Evans. He fell in pace with the momentum of the cage, knocking his wooden cross against the bars. The dry pine needles crunched audibly beneath his heavy steps. "The gifts bequeathed to Adam and Eve to protect their mortal lineage from the taint of the realms."

"Never read that verse in scripture," said Alyse.

"Oh you wouldn't, my dear. Over the centuries, the Society made it their mission to remove all mention of these realms, to erase them from the minds of man. We've scrubbed every study, every account, even the scripture of the church until fairies became nothing more than children's stories, while demons and angels were moral tales for the wavering wills of adults," said Evans.

"Don't call me 'dear,'" Alyse snapped.

Johnathan glared at him. "Why?"

Evans shrugged. "Man is too corruptible. Better they dismiss such creatures as tall tales than seek them out."

"But they *do* seek them out. In ignorance, with no idea what dangers they are dealing with," said Johnathan. "The Society is supposed to protect humanity, not leave them to fumble blindly into a bargain with spirits they don't realize are demons."

That line was meant directly for Evans, a nod to his role in their situation— the stranger who slipped a suggestion in Mr. Fairchild's ear.

Evans took the jab in stride, his expression smug. "Words of naivete, boy," he countered. "The sacrifice of a few is worth the advancement of our goals. We've saved countless more by erasing the truth from collective memory, enough pieces and hearsay left intact for their own superstitions to protect them."

"Our mother used to pin iron horseshoes over our windows to protect us from the fairies," said Alyse, the words begrudging, as if she hated to contribute to the conversation but couldn't help herself.

"You see," said Evans, "there are always a few from the Nether who stray, no matter the precautions taken. We've dealt with each incident over the centuries, but it's left us at a deep disadvantage."

Alyse sneered. "You seem to be doing well enough for yourselves."

Evans waved his hand. "We keep the regular rabble in check with relative ease. The Other are troublesome but have low tolerance for the growth of industry. Too much iron in the air, you see. The Benign were always standoffish. They rarely bother in this age. The Nether, however, their hunger is ever reaching, and their bargains are disastrous."

"How disastrous?" Johnathan hated how the man's words hooked him, his reluctant need to know Evans' secrets.

Evans gave a casual shrug. "History is rife with their influence. The fall of Rome, the plagues, the great London fire, the disappearance of the colony at Roanoke, each born from the vicious greed of the Nether."

"Seems humans couldn't forget the Devil," said Johnathan.

"Indeed," said Evans. "We underestimated the influence of the Nether on man, the depth of their corruption. The Nether doesn't simply play or hunt humans, they taint them, change them into something else. They whisper and convince, their methods deceptive and secret until it is too late."

The grand-standing confession put Johnathan on edge. It was never a good thing when a man like Evans readily told their secrets. It usually happened when they knew, without a doubt, they had nothing to fear from revealing their truth.

They plunged beneath the shadowy canopy of the woods near the rift. Johnathan's unease grew the closer they drew to the inevitable showdown that waited.

Evans' voice continued to wash over him. "Massive casualties, loss of good agents, hours of manpower and effort to contain each incident, we were hard pressed to find an advantage."

A thread of pressure unwound around Johnathan's spine. He faced the man who'd made him. "What does this have to do with me?"

"Your existence was a boon, the answer to a long-sought question," said Evans.

Alyse had no compunction to grasping the bars, taking a swipe at Evans that he easily avoided. "More cryptic offal," she snarled. Her sensible wool skirts had been torn up to her knees when the Society agents dragged her from the Fairchild's house. There was little sense for propriety as she crouched back beside Johnathan, not quite touching him but not keeping her distance either. She spat her words at Evans. "Why hold back? Crow about your grand victory. You don't intend for me to survive this night."

Johnathan didn't bother to silence her. She was right.

She was in a cage with a beast for a reason.

Evans had the nerve to chuckle. "You will serve your purpose. You seem attached to the theory of lycanthropy. An intelligent deduction for a young woman such as yourself, but the hounds of the Nether follow far different rules, rules that can be manipulated."

"Hounds of the Nether..." Alyse mumbled the words, then shut her eyes, pressing her fingers to her temple, clearly searching her own thoughts. Suddenly, she gasped, grasping the bars of the cage, her expression incredulous. "You're trying...you're trying to catch a *Hellhound?*"

"Catch?" Evans laughed. "Caught."

Alyse glanced over her shoulder, wide-eyed, at Johnathan. The pit of his stomach writhed.

"You set me up for this," said Johnathan.

"The best method of tracking creatures of the Nether is to use one of their own, one we could control," said Evans. "I've spent the last eight years grooming you for this purpose, seeding suggestions in every fool's ear. When that idiot Fairchild finally made his bargain, we merely had to put the pieces into play, allow the lure of your tainted innocence to draw the demon to you. Let it turn you. Then you would be ours, a tool to fight the Nether, created within our halls."

"I will do nothing for you," snarled Johnathan.

"Once we bind you to this plane, you won't have a choice," said Evans. "The Hellhounds are servants, be they bound by a demon master or a human one. Your will shall be the will of the Society, our greatest weapon and most obedient soldier. No protest shall pass your lips. You shall carry out every task without question, without fail." There wasn't a hint of fondness or familiarity in his mentor's expression, his cold gaze watching Johnathan. "There will be nothing left of the feckless, fiend-sympathetic whelp you were."

Johnathan launched himself at the bars. Evans took a step back, laughing, while the scent of burnt flesh overwhelmed Johnathan's senses. The pain seared him, a lance to his rage. He collapsed back onto the floor of the cage with a gasp. Evans observed his reaction and he walked away to join the other agents. There were over thirty men with him, far more than Johnathan noticed skulking around Cress Haven, waiting in the wings. They walked around the cage in a loose formation, weaving between the bare-bone pine trunks, their packs heavy with silvered weapons and nets meant to trap more Hellhounds. Dread pooled in his gut. Johnathan knelt on the cage floor, trying to block out the clank of their metal-bound packs.

"I do not like that man," said Alyse. She settled in her skirts beside him and grasped his arm to assess the extent of the damage. "Good lord, silver does *this*?"

"Aren't you afraid of me?" Tears tracked across his temples. Eight years, he'd lived a lie. Sir Harry died for a lie. The Society didn't save him from a fiend, they merely killed off his surrogate father so they could use him. It would have been better to die by Sir Harry's hand. He would have died at the hand of someone he loved.

Alyse gently pulled his head onto her shoulder to stroke his hair. Her thumb swiped the side of his face. She winced.

"Your tears are scalding." She stopped him when he tried to turn away from her. "Of course, I don't fear you, idiot. You're still a silly man-child who can't grow a beard to save his life." Her fingers maneuvered around his tears, continuing her ministrations of comfort. "Are we headed where I think we are?"

Johnathan nodded. "He's bringing us to the rift."

"We can't let that bastard win." Alyse set her chin. "Do you know anything about how this binding works? This isn't servitude. He said he'd take your will. That's enslavement."

"I do not know." Johnathan was sick of figuring out riddles. He wasn't sure it mattered anyway. The point was that Evans intended to use him, a lure once again.

"I didn't know I was becoming a Hellhound until you put a name to it," said Johnathan. The question was, when would he change? Did it require a trigger? Or was there some sort of maturation process he wasn't aware of, a delay before he shed his human skin? He knew so little of the process or how Lydia changed back and forth from monster to girl. Cernunnos was the demon responsible for his condition, but it was Evans who raised him to be a target. The man had crafted this situation, planting the suggestion in a man willing to believe and greedy enough to take the risk. He'd plucked Johnathan from the streets, nurturing him along, unaware of his purpose, until his grand scheme came to fruition.

Johnathan didn't know who the greater monster was, the demon who sought to consume the town and beyond, or the fanatical zealot who decided a few human lives were worth the cost of procuring a Hellhound weapon for the Society.

The pine trees were thinning around them, the trunks of many blackened, as if they'd been licked by flame. A muted heat steadily grew the closer they drew to the rift. Grim determination settled on the agents, their steps slowing the closer they came. Johnathan watched them, torn, wondering how many knew the details of Evans' plan, men he once admired and emulated.

"I think they intend to seal the rift," he said. "The Morrigan said something about the Nether reclaiming any 'unfettered ilk' still on this plane."

Her fingers stilled. "That includes you now," she said.

"I think Evans has planned this long enough to account for that," said Johnathan.

Alyse grasped his hand. "Vic will come."

He sat up at that. "He better grab you and run like hell. Where's the coin?"

Alyse looked at him, knowing in her eyes. "You are *not* sacrificing yourself—"

Johnathan took her hand. "Alyse, I won't let them bind me. I won't."

Her lip quivered. "Just wait, John. Wait for Vic. We can still survive this."

"What if he doesn't make it in time?"

"He will," Alyse hissed.

The wagon rocked to a stop. Johnathan looked up at the gaping mouth of the rift, far larger than a simple tear in the air. It was a wound, twice as wide as he was tall. A thousand bloody shades writhed beneath the distended fleshy membrane, strained to the breaking point. Any moment the thin barrier would burst and unleash the incorporeal demons of the Nether. Free to construct grotesque bodies of bone, branch, and bracken, like the horned Cernunnos, who watched their approach on the grisly throne Johnathan glimpsed in his warped vision.

He sat beside the throbbing rift, a demonic usher, bathed in firelight. As if greeting them, the flames whipped to a frenzy in their braziers stationed around the rift, beacons to those within. They were out of time.

Johnathan didn't know what to expect. A bloody brawl between the horned Cernunnos and the Society agents? He doubted Evans would come unprepared for this encounter. Johnathan had barely begun to scratch the surface of this mystery, this realm, but those new inner instincts recognized Cernunnos, sensed the bond between them like an invisible chain around his neck. This was the being who orchestrated the bargain with Nathaniel Fairchild, Johnathan's anchor and current master on this plane.

"This is not good," he whispered. The Society agents crawled at the edge of the clearing, a hive of ants kicked into action. Johnathan watched, incredulous, while they broke out tripods, mounting crossbows and readying their horrid silver nets. Evans strolled through the line, his gaze fixed on the demon. They intended to shoot it? As if bolts would be anything but an annoyance to a being of that size?

Cernunnos growled, rising from his throne of cobbled bones beside the rift. Johnathan saw what he'd missed before, the pieces of the grisly centerpiece that were fresher than others, still encased in their mortal flesh. He recognized the rotting face of Mrs. Fairchild, the back of her skull cleaved off.

Alyse pressed against his side. "That's what Mr. Fairchild bargained with? What kind of idiot would do that?"

"A selfish one," said Johnathan.

The air rippled when Cernunnos moved toward them, heated by the horned entity's presence. His nostrils flared, venting clouds of white steam through the midnight-hued air. The ground blackened beneath his stumplike feet, each footstep marked by the orange glow of embers. Johnathan couldn't look away, mesmerized, tethered to the creature in every vein, every nerve, hooked to the bone.

"John, look at me," whispered Alyse. "Don't look at it."

How could he not? Cernunnos was glorious. Cernunnos was everything. He would kneel before the dark god in utter supplication. He would hunt for Cernunnos. He would kill for Cernunnos.

"Fire," said Dr. Evans.

The whistle of crossbow bolts sung through the air, snapping Johnathan from his reverie. He screamed as they sank into Cernunnos, the silver-tipped heads embedded deep with mortal-wound precision.

But Cernunnos was not mortal. He crashed to his knees, the ground vibrating from the impact, and he bellowed his rage at these fools. He would show them the power of the Nether, strip the flesh from their bones while they cried out their final agony. His intent, his very thoughts, pounded into Johnathan's mind.

Johnathan clutched the bars tight, mindless of the silver that burned his hands. He screamed for Cernunnos to come no closer. To flee.

The great beast shook his head, struggling to rise and meet his foes.

Dr. Evans stepped forward and leveled an odd-looking pistol Johnathan had never seen before at the center of Cernunnos' forehead. He pulled the trigger while Johnathan called to his master.

The flash and boom broke his senses. Johnathan reeled, a horrid ringing in his ears, the world a mass of blurred shapes that slowly dissolved to Alyse's frightened face. Her mouth moved, but he couldn't hear the words.

Johnathan shook his head hard. The world sharpened.

"He killed it," Alyse cried.

Johnathan stared in shock through the bars of the cage. Cernunnos lay slumped on the ground, its skull-mask shattered into a mass of dark bloody tissue and fragmented bone. His gaze locked on Cernunnos' chest, relieved by the subtle lift and fall.

"He lives," whispered Johnathan.

But not for long.

Dr. Evans planted one boot on Cernunnos' chest, that terrible weapon aimed at the Great One's throat. Every muscle in Jonathan's body tensed at the sight of his master in danger, until something inside him snapped.

A guttural rumble rolled up through Johnathan's chest.

"John?" Alyse thrust herself back against the bars of the cage.

Johnathan barely registered her presence. The pit of heat inside him ignited. His veins burned beneath the skin as fire crackled through his blood. The air in his lungs was a bellows to the great heat, fanning the flames until smoke streamed from his mouth.

"Prepare yourselves, gentlemen. The pack draws near." Evans observed Johnathan with rapt attention, fervor in his gaze. The moment swelled, the silence that fell after the sound of the battle horn.

Johnathan's skin was too tight. Cracks riddled the taut surface of his hands, his forearms, that pulsed with an orange glow.

"That's it, boy. Let it come."

"You heartless bastard!" Alyse's voice broke the silence. "He's one of your men. How could you do this to him?"

Johnathan turned towards her voice, pulled by the crumbling part of him that clung to humanity by the fingertips.

"I do what needs to be done," said Evans. "You're about to witness one of our greatest triumphs in the battle for mankind. Sadly, it shall be the last sight you see, but take heart that your death will gift our dear boy a human form once more."

"You self-important, pompous ass," Alyse shrieked at him.

"And the world will suffer one less sharp-tongued female," sneered Evans.

Their banter broke off at the first ragged howl echoing through the surrounding woods. Johnathan watched, detached, as Alyse cowered in the corner, a flicker of real fear on her face. That small struggling part of him wondered why her death would gift him humanity.

A frozen wedge drove through the fiery haze of his thoughts, cool clinical notes from the Prospective side of his mind. He hadn't transformed when he woke from the fever. He should have. All evidence pointed to the contrary, except they were attacked, and whether he intended or not, he took a human life in the form of Sykes. Murder was the key to staying human?

"What a bloody awful catch," he muttered.

Alyse gasped out a laugh, a sad broken sound that gave him a pang of guilt. He was the reason she was in this situation.

"There you are," she said.

He wasn't certain how long he could hold on like this. He prayed it would be long enough because he knew what was coming. "When I tell you to," he said, turning to the woman who had become a friend, "I want you to run."

"I'm not—I can't leave you like this, John."

"Yes, you will. Now, I *need* the coin. Give it to me."

"Dammit, no—"

"Please, Alyse." He dropped his head to whisper for her ears alone. "We both know it's up to me. They will shoot you down, even if I can manage to get you out."

"Vic. Will. Come." Tears glistened in her eyes.

His mouth worked, tasting the lie on his tongue, but he had little choice. "Vic isn't here, Alyse."

The truth was that he could smell Vic, stalking along the edge of the clearing, his scent a mix of spices, intoxicating even at this distance. It surprised him how easily he picked that scent from memory.

And Vic wasn't alone.

The pack circled the woods, a dozen Hellhounds summoned to protect their fallen master. The first sauntered through the tree line, a nightmare come to life, coal black fur over an asymmetrical frame. Her eyes burned with twin flames while her maw overflowed with too many teeth. Johnathan knew it was a female. They were all females.

This one paused in the shadows of the braziers with a soft whine. It hurt to look at her, the sacrificial lamb.

"Take it down," snapped Evans.

Bolts punched into her body, silencing her yelp. A keening sound rose up Johnathan's throat.

Alyse looked horrified. "They're going to kill them all?"

Johnathan's control hovered on a razor's edge.

"They'll keep one," he choked out.

Evans wanted to make the Hellhounds servants of the Society. He would ensure a legacy by keeping a breeding pair.

A familiar ugly hum vibrated up his arm as Alyse slid the coin into his palm. She leaned her head against his shoulder, a sweet familial gesture. "I'll hold his arms while you rip out his throat," she said.

He kissed her forehead. "Never change, Alyse."

"Right now," she whispered, "I just hope I live."

Cernunnos' hand lifted from the ground and fell with the finality of a judge's gavel. Johnathan turned Alyse's face into his shoulder when the second hound sailed out of the darkness and closed her jaws on an agent's face.

Evans barked orders to stand and fight, but the hounds had their orders. They sent their weakest to distract and to die while the others circled their targets, their attack precise and planned, with the addition of a last-minute ally—the enemy of their enemy.

Hounds and agents ignored Vic's sleek shadow slipping through the fighting pairs. Johnathan had to protect the only two people he cared for anymore.

It was now or never.

He sat Alyse aside and gripped the bars. The pain ate away his control in increments. His bellow held a feral edge, but the bars bent, just wide enough for a slip of girl and her voluminous skirts to escape through to freedom.

He reached for Alyse, alarmed by the blackened tips of his fingers. "Off you go," he rasped.

She looked stunned at first but moved once she saw that Vic was there to catch her. The vampire clutched Alyse to him, brushing his lips against the girl's temple in a gesture of personal reassurance.

Vic stared over Alyse's shoulder at Johnathan, his expression stark. He reached for Johnathan, silver gaze intent. Vic could spirit them both away, leaving the Hellhounds and Agents to their battle. Johnathan wanted to allow it, but then he would tear them apart with a Hellhound's teeth.

Johnathan wrenched the gap in the bars back together and collapsed, a mass of pain. "Go."

Vic clutching Alyse tight to his side and swore, staring at Johnathan with agonized longing. "John, no, please—"

"I can't stop it," Johnathan gasped out. He needed Vic to run, to know the one he'd come to love escaped Evans' grasp.

Alyse struggled to look at him, the realization of his trickery plain on her face.

"No, John, don't! Come with us! Vic, please!" she fought Vic's grasp, but he lifted her into his arms, and after one last glance over his shoulder, ran.

Johnathan watched them vanish into the darkness, his heart heavy. He knew, and Vic knew, they couldn't stop this transformation. Surrounded by the cacophony of battle and death, the final shreds of Johnathan's humanity evaporated like so much smoke.

Johnathan fell forward as his spine curved up and up, the angle so sharp it crunched his ribs and stole his ability to speak, to scream. The coin fell from his grasp and rolled straight through the bars. It continued to roll, a glint of gold in the carnage until it spun, a flicker and flash in the dark, and toppled into the pool of blood around the first Hellhound that died.

Tight, too tight, his skin crackled and curled away like burning parchment. He shook himself, the remains of his former shape rolling free in a rain of ash. The world was bathed in a blood-colored lens, marred by bright white flares, living heat. He prowled the length of his cage, a low growl in his throat. He was surrounded by poison.

Lydia Fairchild emerged from the shadows, her scent sweet as honey with a hint of delicious rot. His gaze swung to her, the instincts of his new flesh stirring at the sight of her. She was a promise whispered in the night, a packmate, made for him, another creation of the master's will. Her gaze sought him out while he watched her.

She moved on human feet, running toward him. He should want to reclaim a male's form for her, but the stirrings withered as quick as they formed. She was just a girl, an innocent, and she was not what he *wanted*.

The human who pinned their master to the ground stepped into her path. He called to a trio of men who threw a net of silver wire on the female. Johnathan barked a challenge. He would tear out the human's throat for the insult to one of his kind. Kill all who challenged his master! He would—

A vampire slammed against the bars. "Johnathan!"

He jumped back with a yip. His mind recoiled in confusion, the duality of his personality warring with itself until he inhaled spice and snow. The mating heat that had failed to ignite at the sight of a ready female blazed to life in the presence of the vampire. His desire for Vic doubled, tripled, to what he'd known before until he groaned. An instinct to claim and to serve throttled Johnathan, unable to reach the vampire through the barrier of silver. The female whined in pain, a piteous sound that pierced through his ramping desires.

Vic glanced over his shoulder and read the scene. "I'm going to gut that man."

Not if Johnathan got there first.

Vic turned back to him, calm as ever. "I'm going to let you out."

Johnathan's ears flattened against his skull, more of his humanity pushing through. It wasn't safe to do that. Johnathan wasn't safe. He dare not hurt his beautiful vampire.

He crouched down on all fours, head bowed.

Vic gaped at him. "Don't get cold feet on me now. Come on!"

Movement shifted over Vic's shoulder. Johnathan surged to his feet with a snap of teeth, but the warning wasn't enough. Evans drove a long blade through Vic's back, shoving the point hard and fast into the wooden corner post of Johnathan's cage.

"Pinned twice in one night," said Evans. "Your luck is shit, vampire."

Vic gasped through his teeth. This close, Johnathan could see how pale he was, how weakened the first fight had left him. He turned his face toward the cage.

That gray gaze held Johnathan's, and raw excitement shivered through him. The vampire grabbed the bottom frame of the cage with one hand and tore the wall of bars free. The show of strength surprised Evans, who took a single step back.

"Get him," said Vic.

Johnathan launched at his ex-mentor. This time, there was no barrier to stop him.

The coppery tang of blood gushed into his mouth, where his teeth sank into Evans' throat. He shook him like a terrier with a rat. Releasing the pulp and shredded flesh, he left Evans to choke on his own blood.

The transformation was immediate. Bones cracked and shifted. Fur shrank and smoothed away into human skin. The blood-red world faded to muted shades of gray while the fire inside Johnathan smoldered down to the coals. It left its mark on him in powder-burn traces along his more prominent veins.

Sucking in great gulps of air, Johnathan forced himself to stand, keenly aware he wore not a stitch. He yanked the blade from Vic's chest.

Vic grunted and rubbed at the wound, already closing but much slower than it should have. Johnathan forgot to cover himself, giving Vic more than an eyeful.

Despite their situation, Vic spared a moment to ogle Johnathan's bloodied, naked state. "Good heavens, you are an absolute delight." He peeled off his outer jacket and offered it. "You owe me a shirt *and* a coat, my love."

Johnathan pinched his lips together and gratefully tied the garment around his waist. A frontal flap was better than nothing.

"Uh, John," said Vic, his voice wary.

Johnathan glanced up to find the battle in full swing. While he'd carried out the dark deed of dispatching Evans, the hounds had rallied around their master, who'd recovered enough to join the fray. Cernunnos bellowed, the sound tugging at Johnathan's bowels. He almost ran headlong into the bloody conflict when Vic grabbed his hand.

"We have to get out of here."

Johnathan looked at him, willing to follow the vampire anywhere, but they couldn't leave yet. Vic knew this, despite his words. Together, they stood and watched, mere observers in a conflict that went beyond them. The hounds now attacked as a pack, giving an advantage to their lesser number. Three or four of them tore into a man at once, their bodies shifting back to feral females that seized whatever weapon they found on the ground, be it blade or branch. They cut down the shocked agents with vicious efficiency until the change twisted their bodies again. The far greater threat was Cernunnos himself. The demon boasted several grievous wounds, but his rage overwhelmed the remaining agents, tearing them apart in a spray of blood and innards with his clawed hands. Their sizable contingent of a few dozen men rapidly dwindled under the brutal assault. Vic and Johnathan stood hand in hand, an unwilling audience to the absolute carnage but removed from it.

The screams and wails of dying men eventually tapered off, the buzzing hum of the rift taking precedent. Cernunnos knelt on the ground, his rage spent, while his life blood continued to ebb from his wounds.

The victorious hounds circled their master, *his master*, watching Johnathan.

A blush crept up the back of Johnathan's neck. Several of the hounds had regained their human forms, not a scrap of clothing between them. Demon servants or not, it didn't seem proper to look at the naked young women. Never mind that the Society agents lay in pieces, scattered on the forest floor.

Unbelievably, Evans was still alive, though his death sounded in each gurgling breath. His defiant gaze met their approach.

"They'll...hunt...you...down."

The faint words bubbled up through the blood in his mouth, but Johnathan heard them well enough. He could sense the differences now, the gifts of the creature who slumbered beneath the faint veneer of human skin. He hated it.

"Yes," he said. "But they won't catch me."

"John, we have a problem." Vic sounded almost panicked.

Not that Johnathan could blame him. The sky was growing light with the approach of dawn. The rift bulged outward, the strained sac about to burst. The creatures of the Nether, sensing the nearby carnage, hungered to come through.

"Is Alyse safe?" He wanted to make sure she was far from the violence.

"Yes. I carried her into town before I rushed back here."

"I know what to do," said Johnathan.

The Morrigan's words filtered through his thoughts. The Nether would reclaim its ilk. As a Hellhound, that meant him too. There had been a lingering dread that he wouldn't survive this encounter, he just hadn't expected it to end like this.

He crossed the blood-drenched clearing, trying to settle his thoughts. He didn't dare look at Lydia Fairchild, still caught in Evans' silver net. What he had to do would doom them both, would condemn all the girls to the same fate.

He hated that he couldn't save them, but their humanity, like his own, was lost. He tried to shut out Lydia's whimpers, and knelt to retrieve the gold coin, coated in blood. Appropriate as it had brought so much death. He gripped it tight between his fingers and approached the writhing rift.

Vic blurred to a halt beside him. "You have the coin."

Johnathan's heart broke. Vic didn't realize it yet, what would happen when he sealed the rift. That was fine. It was better this way.

He leaned closer, nuzzling Vic's cheek, memorizing his scent to keep it with him wherever the rift took him. If only he'd taken more advantage of their time together, but there was no time to ponder regrets, or what could have been.

Johnathan tossed Fairchild's coin into the rift. "Our bargain is done."

CHAPTER TWENTY-NINE

CERNUNNOS WAS THE FIRST TO STIR. THE GREAT HORNED ONE TURNED his ruined face to Johnathan, an air of resignation in the sluggish movements. Steam streamed from his nostrils in a sigh. The battle won, but not the war.

It was a good fight.

The silent voice crackled against Johnathan's awareness. The bulging strain of the rift suddenly convulsed, the protuberance sucked inward. The barrier rippled with the faint screams of the denied demons as the Nether began to reclaim its ilk. The grisly throne rattled, bones new and old flaking to dust.

The first kiss of sunlight lined Cernunnos' prone figure, who turned to ash. The Hellhounds curled against one another in their human bodies. They held hands and shut their eyes against the glare of the morning sun, an odd sense of relief in their expressions while their bodies slowly crumbled away. Vic stared at the fading Hellhounds in stunned horror.

Johnathan braced himself. He didn't feel it yet, that coming apart. Maybe because he was the one to cast the coin. Maybe because he was the newest one. Too many variables to say for sure.

Lydia Fairchild's struggles stilled. He finally let himself look at her now that it was the end. The silver net marred her skin, but she was still beautiful. Her eyes glowed an unnatural orange, an internal flame trapped in her irises.

Johnathan brushed the corner of his eye. What did *his* eyes look like? Not that it mattered. He wouldn't be around to study his reflection.

"Thank you," said Lydia. She closed her eyes, a smile on her lips as she turned to ash with the rising sun.

Why would she thank him? He'd damned them all to the Nether. Or perhaps, only Cernunnos would be dragged back into the hell realm, and his creations were simply released from their wretched state. Johnathan could reconcile himself to death. It was a short life, so many opportunities wasted, so much heartache. Maybe it was time to rest.

He stiffened at the loss of feeling in his fingers, waiting for them to char and disintegrate.

"No," said Vic. "Oh no, no, no. Dammit, John!"

Vic snatched him up, rushing him beneath the shade of the nearest tree. The strategy appeared to work, the fade slowing, though Johnathan's skin continued to turn gray, the hue like a spreading stain.

Vic gripped his wrists tight, as if he could keep Johnathan from disappearing through sheer stubborn will. "Why didn't you tell me?"

"I had to stop it," said Johnathan.

The rift bulged out one last time, a final rage against the light, before it collapsed in on itself and sealed with a faint clap of thunder. The flames in their braziers shrank and sputtered, guttered as they burned through the final influence of the Nether realm.

It wouldn't be long now. Not even the shadows could keep him here, only delay the inevitable. At least he could enjoy Vic's company for a few more seconds, minutes, however long he had. Johnathan was grateful for that.

He brushed his lips over the back of Vic's hand. The vampire was having none of that, pulling Johnathan into a desperate embrace, cool lips eating at his own fever-hot mouth. If this was how he was to die, Johnathan decided it was a good end.

"No!" Vic broke away, pressing his forehead against Johnathan's. "I promised you we would figure this out." Tears streamed down his pale cheeks. "This isn't fair."

"It doesn't matter," said Johnathan.

It was far from fair.

"Of course it matters," said Vic, his voice fierce. "This isn't right. The Society still wins."

"Least Evans won't be around to see it," said Johnathan.

Vic shook his head. His thumbs smoothed down the side of Johnathan's face. The ashen hue crept higher. The surface of his skin began to stir, fine gray powder swirling as Johnathan began to disperse. The pressure of Vic's grip increased, but it was harder for Johnathan to feel it now.

"There has to be another way. There has to!" Vic gasped. "You don't deserve this end."

"Don't I?" He'd helped kill Sir Harry, someone he loved. He allowed himself to be manipulated for years by the Society. And now, he was a monster.

Vic smacked his forehead hard against Johnathan's. "Idiot."

"Ow," said Johnathan.

"Then don't talk about yourself like that."

Vic still hadn't let go of Johnathan's face. It didn't stop the process, but he wondered if the contact slowed it somehow. He was grateful for every moment he clung to with Vic.

"The Morrigan knew this would happen," said Vic.

A small smile played on Johnathan's lips. He didn't regret coming to Cress Haven. He was fortunate enough to meet Alyse and Vic, and he got to see something as fantastical as the Morrigan. For all their games and strangeness, the fairies gave him a grand gift.

A new bond to cherish.

"Forge a bond stronger than the call of his realm," whispered Vic. He shook Johnathan's arms. "Johnathan, help me save you. Help me keep you here! Tell me what to do!"

He stared at Vic, Evans' taunting words coming back to him. Deep down, in the wildest part of him, he knew the answer.

"A Hellhound is a servant," he whispered. "Be they bound to a demon master or a man."

Vic winced. "Are you certain?"

Johnathan looked away from him. The braziers were still lit, the fire no larger than a candle flame. "I don't know. I don't know the methods or the rules. He wanted to use me like a dog, to hunt his enemies. And Cernunnos' will superseded mine. I couldn't fight his influence. Hellhounds appear to be ready-made servants."

"I wouldn't know how to bind you like that," said Vic. "I *couldn't* bind you like that."

Johnathan snorted. "Can you think of any other way?"

Vic swallowed. "There is something we could try."

"What—" Johnathan gasped as the spread of ash accelerated.

"We don't have a lot of time," said Vic, his voice tight, but he maintained the facade of calm. "I won't force you John and I don't know if it will work. Do you want to try?"

He couldn't look at Vic, transfixed by the sight of his legs crumbling to ash beneath him. Could he even come back from this point? "I—I have to kill to become human again. Every time I shift. I can't live like that."

"Then we find another way," said Vic. "I have. It can be done."

Johnathan met Vic's gaze. There were deep shadows under his eyes, evidence of his blood loss and the strain of his healing abilities. Vic's skin was parchment pale, yet somehow he looked more human than Sir Harry ever had. Johnathan wished he'd found Vic first. He could imagine a very different life with a creature—with a *person*—like Vic.

Johnathan didn't want to die.

"Yes," he said, his voice barely a whisper.

Vic didn't hesitate. He kept a hand on Johnathan, as if afraid to let him go for a second and tore open his wrist with his teeth. "The Morrigan asked me what I was willing to risk to save you. How I could anchor you here." He sucked in a breath, offering his bleeding wrist to Johnathan. "Vampires don't follow rules as the fairies, but there is power in blood, power in the offering. It might be enough."

Johnathan's gaze searched Vic's, trying to stifle the surging urgency of his crumbling body. Doubts plagued his mind. The risk, the unknown, Vic's theory was a wild stab in the dark, and neither of them knew what could happen if it did work.

The vampire held his breath. A smile tugged at Johnathan's lips. The decision was well and truly his to take.

He bent his head and latched onto Vic's wrist. The vampire's blood was a jolt to the system, like lightning mixed with the sweet wine taste on Johnathan's tongue. The blood slid down his throat and dropped, a physical anchor in his stomach. Life flooded back into him, and he gasped at the painful tingling in his limbs.

"Ha!" shouted Vic. "It's working."

Johnathan's intestines boiled. He braced himself as his arms and legs began to reform.

He hadn't felt a blessed thing when his limbs began to crumble. Now, his veins humming with Vic's blood, he felt every second of it. He rode the sensation. He wanted to live, didn't he? What was life without a little pain?

A lot of pain.

The process finally rolled through him and left him a puddle of sweat and flesh curled up on the blood-saturated ground. There was a horrid sour aftertaste coating the inside of his mouth. He was fairly certain he was lying in the remains of a former Society agent.

"I feel like something crawled in my mouth and died three days ago," said Johnathan.

"You definitely need a bath," said Vic. He grinned at Johnathan, naked relief in his face.

"You say the sweetest things to me," said Johnathan.

The two of them looked at each other, surrounded by death and ashes. The realization simultaneously hit them both; they survived.

Vic hauled Johnathan up, clutching him close as he claimed his mouth, a frantic kiss Johnathan returned with equal enthusiasm. His hands roamed the vampire's body, worshipping the smooth skin of his back, the chiseled angles of his abdomen. Mindless of the filth that clung to them and the violence that surrounded them, they committed themselves to the moment, two beings who found one another despite the incredible obstacles in their way. Finally, they broke apart, leaning into each other for support. Vic's cool breath panted against Johnathan's neck, a glorious contrast to the warm sun that now kissed his naked back.

"What now?" Johnathan glanced at the surrounding carnage. "The Society will come to clean this mess up. I can't stay here."

Vic gripped his face, Johnathan's fear and hope reflected in his gaze. "*We* can't stay here," said Vic.

Johnathan breathed out a rush of relief, nipping at the vampire's neck in a way that made Vic shudder and groan. They were a team now.

Vic cleared his throat and gave a polite sniff. "First, we get you some clothes. And a bath. Then, we run."

"But Cress Haven is your home." said Johnathan. "What about Alyse?"

Vic's smile was bittersweet. "Home isn't a place, John. And don't you worry about Alyse. She is strong enough to survive without me. Now, if you'll excuse me, I need to write a goodbye letter."

Guilt tore into Johnathan at the weary slump of Vic's shoulders. "I could run on my own, Vic. Everyone who knows about you is dead. You're safer without me."

Vic waved him off. "Don't be an idiot. Do you even know how to purchase a train ticket on your own?"

"Of course I do," snapped Johnathan.

"With what money?"

He flinched at that. He didn't even have clothes on his back.

"But—why? Why stay with me?" He didn't understand how Vic could simply drop everything to run with him. Bond or no bond, being with Johnathan was a risk.

Vic gave him an odd look. "Do you really not know? After everything?"

Oblivious, Johnathan gaped at him, but as Vic neared, that cloudy gaze turning darker and darker, he finally understood.

Vic's kiss was almost punishing in its ferocity, bruising Johnathan's lips, marking him with a promise of other, deeper things.

Johnathan couldn't respond, too stunned to speak.

"I'm staying with you because I want to," said Vic. "Because I can't imagine my future without you in it." With that, the vampire turned and walked toward the tree line. He flashed a half-smile over his shoulder, one brow raised. "You coming?"

Johnathan smiled in return, the feeling so strange after so much

carnage and misery. But he couldn't look back. Something good—
something right—awaited him.

He broke into a jog, reaching Vic's side. The sun shone down through
the trees, bathing them in warm, pure light.

"Us against the world?" said Vic.

Johnathan slid his hand into Vic's grasp. "I'd have it no other way."

CHAPTER THIRTY

THE LATE AFTERNOON SUN HAD BEGUN TO DIP UNDER THE HORIZON when Alyse reached the clearing. The path was gone, swallowed up by the wood, even the tracks of the cage Evans used to bring them to the rift seemed to have vanished in the light of day.

She didn't dare tell anyone what happened. What would she say? They'd call her hysterical and lock her up, and that simply wouldn't do. Vic told her he'd be back by sunrise. He promised. Alyse was going to throttle the idiot when she found him. And Johnathan! Dammit, she hated how they made her worry.

Alyse bit her lip. Was Johnathan still alive? She couldn't avoid thinking of the worst outcome. That last sight of him...

She finally found the clearing by the smell. The stink of rot was so ripe it made her eyes water, but the stench and the buzz of flies led her to the site sure as Ariadne's string.

Saliva pooled in her mouth at the scene. Her mouth puckered against the reflex to vomit, but Alyse swallowed it down. She crossed the battlefield with short, shallow breaths, searching through the bodies. The society men were torn to pieces. Not a single one of them was intact. Was that bastard Evans among them? She hoped Johnathan ripped him to pieces.

She paused at a smear of bloodied grass, near the center of the clearing. The blood and viscera were all human. All evidence of the Nether, from the horrid throne to the Hellhounds, were gone. There were piles of ash in a circle close to the crude stone braziers, now cold and streaked with soot. Was Johnathan one of those piles? Her heart hurt at the thought.

Where were they?

Alyse stomped her foot in frustration and cringed when the movement sent little puffs of ash into the air. "Sorry," she whispered to the dead.

Confused, she searched the area. There wasn't a hint of Vic, or Johnathan, to be found.

Alyse held her grief close to her chest for the long trek home. The scavengers would come soon to pick at the remains of the Society men, and she would let them, let the forest claim them. Her thoughts wound themselves in circles, but an answer waited for her on the desk in her room, sealed with Vic's familiar wax crest.

"This had better be good," she muttered, breaking the seal on the note.

My heart,

We are safe. I'm afraid I must break my promise. Johnathan and I need to run before the Society regroups. I pray you find this note before you visit that dreadful scene, but I know you are too stubborn to stay away. It's what I love about you. I wanted to protect you from the more violent aspects of my existence, but now, in the hour of choice, I find I am desperate to keep you close. Selfish of me, I know. We are bound for the station in Hampshire. I will take Johnathan to New York. I would be honored if you would join us. You will always be the family of my heart. I would never have survived here without your guidance and generosity. No matter what you decide, remember to follow your heart, dear one, and never bury your true self.

Forever yours,

Victor

Alyse read the letter twice over before she carefully shredded it into strips. She would burn the paper in a moment. Her relief swamped her. Johnathan was alive. The day was won, and Vic wanted her at his side.

Her thoughts turned over. The Society would never leave them alone.

Evans spent three decades searching for a Hellhound. That sort of time investment wasn't the work of one man.

She paced, a plan formulating in her mind when her toe connected with something solid. Alyse glanced down at the mysterious gun Evans used to shoot the Nether creature. Vic must have left it for her, finally acknowledging her capability. Curious, she picked it up, surprised at how light it was for its size.

A weapon felt right in her hands. Her fingers closed around the metal, her mouth set in a grim determined line. She had a train to catch.

EPILOGUE

JOHNATHAN KEPT VIGIL BESIDE VIC AT THE BACK OF THE TRAIN. BOTH of them watched the station while the conductor called for final boarding.

"She'll be here," murmured Vic.

He hoped so, if only for Vic's sake.

"Why New York?" he asked as a distraction, though he was curious.

The proximity to Boston was near enough to make him nervous. He wished the solution was to put an ocean between him and his old home, but Johnathan knew there were chapters of the Society in other cities, across the known world. It was only a matter of time before word of Evans' death and failure spread. Would they accept the idea that Johnathan turned to ash like the other Hellhounds? *Unlikely.* The Society's methods were too thorough. They encompassed all realms of investigation, mystic and material, a combination of magic and science. They would know. Then they would hunt Johnathan. To kill or to capture, neither fate was a pleasant one. How long could he and Vic possibly outrun them?

"I have an acquaintance there who might help with our little Society problem," said Vic.

"Another vampire?"

"Sure," said Vic.

Johnathan did not like that answer.

He shifted in his suit. He didn't know where Vic found it. It fit him perfectly, but his skin itched beneath the material. The clothes were too thick, suffocating, and made him sweat profusely. It left him with an unpleasant swamp-like sensation, but it was a small price to pay for civility. The goggles would be the harder adjustment. They muted his vision to shades of dark gray and limited his field of vision, but they were a necessary evil due to the unfortunate state of his eyes.

The train lurched into motion. Vic bowed his head. Alyse hadn't come.

"Could she follow us to New York? Maybe something held her up," said Johnathan.

"Perhaps." Vic sucked in a breath. "Did I ever tell you about the time I hid from the law in a brothel for six months?"

"What? No!" Johnathan watched the landscape begin to scroll along, the train picking up speed. "Why were you running from the law?"

"A trifling matter, but let me tell you, those ladies were devastated to see me go," said Vic.

Johnathan laughed, even though Vic's words were surely exaggerated than true and brought a rush of heat to his cheeks. "I would be devastated to see you go as well."

Vic leaned closer and pinched Johnathan's chin. "Not a worry you have to face, John."

A smile tugged at his lips. Johnathan sighed, the sound of relief curling away into the air as the train sped them toward their new adventure.

───

From the shelter of the station, out of sight, Alyse watched the two figures standing at the back of the train until they were minuscule specks on the horizon.

She kissed her fingers and pressed a hand to her heart. "Until we meet again, my loves."

The train bound for Boston would depart in an hour.

Thank you for reading! Did you enjoy? Please add your review because nothing helps an author more and encourages readers to take a chance on a book than a review.

And don't miss book two in the Midnight Guardians series, A DRAUGHT OF ASH AND WINE, available now. Turn the page for a sneak peek!

You can also sign up for the City Owl Press newsletter to receive notice of all book releases!

SNEAK PEEK OF A DRAUGHT OF ASH AND WINE

Johnathan Newman was about to burst out of his skin.

This was a literal problem for him now. As he sat, muscles wound tighter than a coiled spring, he feared for the safety of the sleeping passengers around him. Heat surged through his veins, searching for release, for a hint of weakness. He grasped for a mental anchor, focusing on the uneven clank of the train over the tracks. The car swayed and bumped along, the regular irregularity of the movement lulling the exhausted passengers around him into a fitful slumber. The motion did little to quell the uneasiness knotted between Johnathan's shoulders, his forced calm fleeing from the internal reach of fire.

His knees jogged up in down in a rabbit rapid rhythm, matching the tap of his fingertips along the hard edges of his seat. Shallow breaths fanned the air, a shimmer of heat escaping from his parted lips that sent a jolt of alarm down his spine. Taking a deep breath would be worse, akin to an assault of his new sharper senses. He fought hard to ignore the varied scents clogging the air, vicious as a hornet swarm stinging his nose. Where the hell was Vic?

Had he really expected to get a handle on his new condition in a matter of days? Johnathan was a fool. The thought made him wince, fingers tightening briefly on the edge of his seat until the wood whined in his grip. 'Condition' made it sound far less life altering than the truth. He peered out the window, trying to evade the direction of his thoughts. Outside the half-shuttered window, the train slithered through the surrounding forest like some great metal serpent, drenched in the shades of night. The vibration of the tracks shivered up through the soles of his boots. Cress Haven and the possibility of his former life catching up to them were now separated by time and distance. Vic's boundless charm kept most unwanted attention off them, and when that failed, a touch of vampiric glamour made their departure far smoother than Johnathan could have hoped.

But being surrounded by a train full of people for hours pulled at him. A reaction, Johnathan was loathe to admit, that he should have expected from a lifetime of chasing monsters driven by innate appetites.

Though, if pressed, Johnathan wasn't sure what he hungered for. Flames were the crux of his waking thoughts, burning through his dreams. He didn't know why the fire licked at the underside of his skin with increasing urgency.

What he did know, with each slow, crawling mile, was he had left his humanity far behind.

The path of his thoughts wove inward, caving to his newest obsession: scrutinizing the differences. The gloves on his hands chafed against too sensitive skin, too hot and sweat slick, the press of his thicker, sharper nails strained against the leather at the tip of each finger. He couldn't call them claws, not yet. Giving voice to the term, even in the privacy of his mind, made it too real. If he stared at his gloved hands long enough, he suspected steam would escape through the seams.

Worse were the glasses, the heavy, wide frames butted against the bones of his eye socket, creating a tunneled view, while the lenses further muted colors. They didn't affect the clarity of his vision, but they obscured a discomfiting amount of his peripheral view. He didn't dare take them off.

His gaze flicked to the artificial darkness framing his world, worrying at it the same way his tongue touched the new fine edges of his teeth. Too many changes, too much sharpness and heat. A betrayal of his body that he dwelled on in those quiet moments when his only company was the tangled mess of his thoughts. A preoccupation that distracted from the knot of frustration, hurt, and rage of that night.

Stop. Johnathan inhaled a sharp breath through his nose before he could stop himself. The sharp tang of greasy hot metal surrounded him, threaded with sweat, body odor, stale syrupy sweet perfume, pungent tobacco smoke, hints of boiled mutton, meal flour, and a dozen other scraps he couldn't identify. A condensed wallop of scents, strong enough to make his head spin. The sense of smell was the biggest change, one he hadn't adjusted to in any capacity. There was no time to adjust. Johnathan didn't want to adjust. *He shouldn't be here. A wolf among sheep. A monster. He should have died.*

Johnathan fought to rein that thought in. He'd made his choice, limited as it was. Easier to ignore the unwelcome thoughts when he had a distraction. Unfortunately, his favorite distraction currently argued with the porter about their current accommodations.

Despite Johnathan's intention to avoid complications, Vic noticed his unease, suggesting they sequester themselves in one of the compartments of the sleeper car. An accommodation Johnathan stubbornly argued unnecessary, but Vic merely raised a brow until the back of Johnathan's neck grew hot. The private luxury of a sleeper compartment had been above his means in his former life, but that wasn't what sent a flush to the roots of his hair. He could practically hear Vic's smooth voice whispering in his ear. *Come now, Johnathan, we can think of something to occupy ourselves.* Their destination was hours away and while the idea of sharing a sleeper car with Vic was thrilling, it added another layer to his anxiety.

It wasn't that Johnathan didn't want to be alone with Vic in close quarters because he did, very much, but the heat clawing inside him soured the mood. He silently begged for Vic's return, clenching his jaw hard enough that his pulse throbbed inside his head. This went beyond his limited grasp of his new state, an intangible sense that had gained on him since Vic left him alone.

A feeling Johnathan couldn't voice, though it curdled in his stomach, akin to dread. It crawled between the knot in his shoulder blades, twining around that vise of nervous energy inside him, a constricting coil incensing his panic. Johnathan jerked around, staring into the faces of the sleeping passengers, searching for the source yet unable to pinpoint it. Frustration pricked at him.

The door to the passenger car slid open, and for a moment, at the sight of that smug, far too charming grin, the dread and anxiety vanished. Vic flowed down the aisle, moving across their shifting conveyance with a dancer's grace. Even through the dark lenses of Johnathan's glasses, Vic remained vibrant. The deep auburn red tint of his hair was threaded with moonlit bronze, loose from its usual queue to curl around his angular face. Mischief shone in his bright silver-grey eyes, snaring Johnathan's full attention. It wasn't until Vic's long fingers curled over the top of his seat that Johnathan remembered to breathe again. The now intrinsic scent of Vic washed over him, dominating the tangle of other scents surrounding him. A wild scent of deep dark woods, threaded with hints of citrus and gentle wildflowers that was a balm to Johnathan's taut nerves. The overwhelming desire to bury his face in the crook of Vic's neck and let the rest of the world melt away rocked him.

"I've emerged victorious," said Vic, tilting his head. "Of a sort. Come, let us celebrate the fruits of my labor."

"Of a sort? You were gone nearly an hour," said Johnathan, his tone piqued. Fifty-two minutes to be exact. Far longer than he'd expected. Johnathan raised his brows, refusing to let his companion see the depth of his relief. Vic's smile consistently threw him off balance. He didn't think he would ever regain his equilibrium around the other man.

"Took a fair bit more negotiating than anticipated, but I think it will be worth the effort," said Vic.

Johnathan's lips twitched. "Couldn't you compel your way in?"

"Johnathan, how scandalous." Vic pressed a hand to his chest in mock indignation. "It so happens the sleeping car is full up and rather than compel some unfortunate soul out of their well-earned rest, I sought out a suitable substitution." His leaned down, his spicy scent wrapping around Johnathan as Vic reached for his hands. "A little nook for just you and me."

Johnathan's pulse spiked and with Vic's fingers circling his wrists; it was clear by the man's knowing grin he noticed. The anxious heat, however, remained persistent, intruding on Johnathan's more amorous thoughts. Vic's good humor dimmed, a crease marring the smooth skin between his brows when he noticed Johnathan's demeanor.

"Come on, John, let's get you out of here." Vic's thumb smoothed over the back of his gloved hands, shifting his grip to lace their fingers together.

A tug got Johnathan up from his seat, his thoughts tumbling together where unease clashed with desire. There hadn't been time for privacy since their flight from Cress Haven, their train bound journey punctuated by absent touches and longing glances that made him equal parts flustered and nervous. Was it only two days ago he'd courted death and damnation? Barely confirmed his burgeoning feelings for Vic before his world shattered.

Johnathan still hadn't processed he was here, alive, and while he'd established a fair level of trust with Vic through their shared trials, he couldn't ignore the dismaying gaps in his knowledge regarding his companion. An unequal knowledge, where Vic possessed most of Johnathan's secrets after their encounter with the Morrigan. He hadn't lived long enough to accumulate many. Vic had lived through centuries.

At the rear of the car, the same niggling sensation distracted him. Johnathan stopped short and glanced over his shoulder. A final futile search, his senses clipped by the infernal goggles. He shook it off, letting Vic lead him into the gap between cars, the rushing wind a welcome relief on his heated face. Following Vic through another car half full of dozing passengers, the mire of Johnathan's thoughts continued to tangle in on itself. He was a ball of anxious energy by the time Vic guided him through the sleeper car to the far rear of the train, holding the door open for Johnathan with a flourish.

Their suitable substitution was the luggage car. The luggage was stacked in tall, tight columns against the walls to make room for a thin mattress, hopefully a spare from the sleeping car, covered in clean sheets.

"How quaint," said Johnathan, attempting to keep his tone neutral though a note of disappointment must have slipped through. He couldn't miss an experience he never had. The luggage car was probably a safer space for him to be if his tenuous control snapped.

"So quick to judge. Get a feel for it first," said Vic. Johnathan bit down on the grin that teased his mouth and ducked through the door.

The floor around the mattress was swept and laid with sprigs of fresh herbs. Johnathan took a cautious whiff, surprised by the earthy scent of fresh sage that overpowered everything else without blowing out his olfactory senses.

"Where did you get fresh sage?" Johnathan took a deep breath, relishing the herbaceous air. The constant press of fire beneath the skin slackened.

"A gentleman's agreement between myself and a compliant tradesman," said Vic with a secretive grin.

"How did you know it would help?" Johnathan turned to face him, unable to glance at him sideways due to the limiting goggles.

"You forget, my dear Johnathan, you aren't the only one with heightened senses," said Vic. He tugged Johnathan down onto the mattress. "Not as grand as a sleeping compartment, but I think we'll make do."

"More than adequate," said Johnathan, his throat gone dry. The mattress pad sank under his weight, betraying the hard wood beneath. Johnathan crawled across it and sat on the far side to remove his shoes, embarrassed he forgot to do so before clambering over the clean sheets. Immediately, he tugged his laces into a gordian knot. Johnathan clenched his teeth, resisting the urge to rip apart his only pair of boots. He reached deep into his exhausted well of patience to untangle them. Vic ceased his frantic hands with a touch, flicking the knots apart to slide off Johnathan's boots which he carelessly tossed to the end of the mattress.

"Now that we're alone, let's have these off," said Vic, his voice a touch deeper, roughened by his evident desire. A shiver of anticipation rolled through Johnathan's chest, shifting to confusion when Vic reached for his face. Vic gently tugged the glasses off, tucking them into Johnathan's coat pocket.

"There," Vic murmured. "Much better."

"Oh." Johnathan blushed. Color and light rushed back in, a physical release accumulating to exposure. The world was no longer shuttered, and it was filled with Vic. That knowledge crashed into Johnathan and he surged forward, his gloved hands threading through Vic's hair as he sought lips he knew were soft and full.

He could be bold when it came to kisses, confident he possessed enough skill to keep Vic on his toes. Johnathan swallowed Vic's surprise, tasting the seam of his mouth. Vic opened for him. Johnathan accepted the invitation, tentatively exploring until his tongue flicked one of Vic's fangs. A groan poured into his mouth. Vic wrested control, peeling off Johnathan's coat and pushing him down onto the mattress. Vic's long fingers stroked up Johnathan's side, sliding under his shirt to skim a cool touch over his overheated skin.

Johnathan sucked in a breath, his muscles flexing in anticipation. Were they doing this? They were really doing this. Was he ready for this?

What was *this?* "I've—I've never done this before." A flush flared up his neck, across his cheeks, rankled by his inexperience.

Vic's brow cocked up. "Done what exactly?" His fingers continued their upward path, lifting Johnathan's shirt. "Hmmmm?" He shifted, straddling Johnathan's legs. Bending down, Vic pressed his lips to Johnathan's throat while a free hand traced the muscles of his stomach in an agonizing downward progression.

"What—" Johnathan wheezed, cut off when Vic licked along his pulse point. "What I assume we are doing?" he managed, embarrassed by the high note in his voice. Vic's hand slid further down, its destination unmistakable. Johnathan didn't realize he held his breath until that hand paused at his waist, his breath leaving him in a rush when Vic's fingers splayed over his belly.

"Oh, what are we doing then?" Vic's tongue gave a lick up the side of his neck, a teasing lilt in his voice.

"This?" Johnathan bit back a noise when Vic deftly unfastened his pants. Another pause that made him want to yell.

"Say the words, John," said Vic. His hand crept lower.

"Intimate relations," Johnathan bit out, straining to keep still. Vic snorted, and dropped his head to Johnathan's shoulders, attempting to muffle his lost composure. His hand moved away to brace on the mattress as he threw back his head for a full-throated laugh.

"Damn cock-tease." Johnathan flopped back down with a huff, throwing an arm over his face to cover his pronounced blush. Vic pinched his chin.

"No, don't look away," said Vic. Johnathan peeked out from under his arm. Vic's merry grin eased some of his embarrassment. "I'm sorry, John. I didn't mean to laugh, but you are just—" He bit his lip, giving a glimpse of fang while his gaze slid over Johnathan like a physical caress. Not so long ago, the sight of teeth would have made him nervous, and they still did, for an entirely different reason. "We'll work on your pillow talk. Though that blush does terrible things to my self-control"

The words made him blush harder. He wasn't the former monk in this relationship, though he might as well be compared to Vic's history of conquests. Nor had his companion let the austerity of his surroundings deter him from relations while human. "I'm sorry."

"Don't you dare apologize," said Vic, sitting up, his hands on Johnathan's chest. His expression turned thoughtful. "I haven't enjoyed myself this much in ages."

Johnathan frowned at him. This sentiment he didn't understand. The man left behind his home and dearest friend for a bond newly formed and barely understood between them, one Johnathan clung to with disconcerting ferocity. "You're on the run because of me."

"That's half the fun." Vic's eyes were silvered in the dim space of the luggage car; the forest choked moonlight cast striated shadows across the ceiling. Johnathan stared up at him. This new form also still adjusted to Vic. Johnathan could see far better in the dark, akin to the night creatures he'd been trained to hunt. To his new vision, Vic's pale skin held a barely perceptible pearly luminescence, an otherworldly hue he never noticed while he still human. Tangled strands of auburn hair haloed Vic's face, evidence of Johnathan's touch. The sight sent heat pooling southward. Delighted wonder lit Vic's expression.

"Your eyes are glowing," said Vic.

The words were a bucket of icy water, dampening his ardor so fast Johnathan cringed away from him.

"John?" Vic grabbed his shoulders. "Oh god, John, what is it?"

Hide, that's what he wanted to do. He wanted to curl into a ball, bury his face in the bedding. The reminder of his inhumanity thrummed beneath his skin, the lick of flame that soured the pleasant sensations Vic caused only moments ago. The urge to hide was so strong he turned on his side, dislodging Vic from his position, but he didn't cover his face. He simply couldn't, torn between his desire and his shame to be seen, his expression stricken.

"John, please talk to me?" Vic pleaded. "You were right here with me. Where did you go?"

Johnathan swallowed hard, his clothes suddenly too tight, the fabric straining between his hunched shoulders. His hands closed into fists, the tips of his *claws* pricking through the leather. Unease flushed through him. "I'm sorry," he rasped, trying to give voice to his discomfort. "I just —I'm not—"

Not human anymore. The words stuck in his throat. How could he say something like to Vic, who hadn't been human in centuries? Except,

Johnathan's rather violent transition was fresh, one he'd far from acclimated to, or the grim bloody future it entailed. A future they hadn't discussed. Nor had they discussed the perils of their present, including the possibility of their pursuit. Johnathan had no idea how deep Dr. Evans' machinations within the Society ran. They might have avoided direct contact with his former comrades, but that didn't mean they weren't being hunted. It was a matter of not if but when the Society caught up to him.

The biggest unspoken question was *how* Johnathan remained on the earthen plane. There was now a creature lurking inside him, one that posed a growing threat he gauged by the heat raging inside him. His body may be human for now, but how long would that last? The demon who created him had returned to the Nether, possibly dead, though Johnathan very much doubted that was the case. If the creature broke free, there was only one method he knew to return to human form and the truth made his stomach roll.

"Johnathan, look at me."

He turned, need overshadowing his shame. Vic kneeled over him, far closer than he expected.

"You're still you," said Vic, cupping his jaw. He brushed his lips over Johnathan's brow.

"How can you be so sure?" Johnathan caught his wrist, craving the contact though his doubts continued to spiral. "We haven't known each other that long."

Vic pursed his lips. "Are you no longer Johnathan Newman, annoyingly stubborn Prospective of the Society?"

"Ex-Prospective," muttered Johnathan. "I'd doubt they'd take me back now."

Vic tugged out of his hold, dropping his hands to his thighs. "Would you want them to?" He stared at Johnathan with an unreadable expression.

"God, no," said Johnathan, with more vehemence than he intended. His final encounter with his former mentor churned a deep well of guilt and rage, not something he wanted to explore in current company. The Society would either kill him, or Dr. Evans' remaining subordinates would attempt to subdue him again, a shuddersome fate. He sat up with a sigh, scrubbing his face. "I've ruined your amorous intentions, haven't I?"

That distant expression disappeared in a leer. Vic leaned forward, a gleam in his eye. "You most certainly have not."

The train jolted, the squeal of metal sliding along metal a painful stab in Johnathan's sensitive ears. Gritting his teeth, he clasped the sides of his head. The violent rocking nearly toppled Vic, who braced himself on the floor, an incredulous look on his face when the train came to grinding stop.

"That might put a damper on my amorous intentions," said Vic.

Johnathan wanted to answer him, but the sense of dread he'd left behind in the passenger car smothered him. "Do you smell that?" A sharp, acrid scent swamped his senses. Johnathan sneezed, the scent coating the inside of his mouth until he gagged.

"Smell what?" Vic frowned, nostrils flaring as he sniffed the air. "I don't smell anything, aside from a few humans in desperate need of a bath."

Johnathan barely heard him, muscles pulled taut. The heat doubled in his chest, sizzling through his veins. He exhaled, a faint curl of smoke rising from his mouth. "Something's here."

Vic's jaw tightened. "Can you describe what you're sensing, John?"

The question grounded him, somewhat. Johnathan tried to internally map the terrible dread. "I don't know," he admitted, uncertain the sensation was quantifiable. He lifted his nose, forcing himself to reach through the pleasant cover of sage. Old sweat, cooling metal, coal smoke, perfume, tobacco smoke, a faint influx of smells the human Johnathan never picked up on. Trying to solve a puzzle with a tool he'd never used before, he plucked away the layers he recognized until one gave him pause. "I smell gun powder."

The perplexed expression on Vic's face now mirrored his own. "There are a lot of persons who carry a gun for many reasons." Vic rolled his lower lip, a telling fidget. "It would be best if you stay here. I'm going to scout the train." Vic rolled away from him, giving Johnathan a pointed look before he donned his shoes and left.

A simple request, to stay put, and one he loathed to follow. Johnathan's knees began to bounce once more, unable to keep still beneath his mounting worries and suspicions. Their train had stopped two or three times to onboard passengers, only one of those stops long enough and close enough to his former home base in Boston for possible pursuit.

The Society couldn't have caught their trail that fast. Could they? Dr. Evans' entire team was demolished in that clearing. Except...Johnathan knew how the Society operated, or at least he thought he did. Whatever plan his former mentor had in play, it wouldn't be confined to the unfortunate souls who accompanied him to Cress Haven. Not with that many Agents present. It would normally take weeks to mobilize a full response, but what if there were more waiting for action, in case things went wrong? What if his entire chapter house was aware of Dr. Evans' plan? Embittered by the idea, Johnathan stood up and paced the strip of cleared floor beside the mattress, pondering his life and the keen sense of isolation that remained. Aside from Dr. Evans, his ties to his fellow Prospectives were, generously said, superficial. His life in the Society hadn't been a pleasant one, but now Johnathan was adrift, a newborn monster without a purpose, with Vic providing his only tether to the world.

Vic hadn't ordered him to stay, yet Johnathan automatically listened. Vic wasn't a superior officer or an Agent who out ranked him. Johnathan sneered at himself, disgusted by his blind Prospective's obedience, and yanked open the door. He poked his head into the proceeding passenger car. There was no sign of Vic, the car eerily silent. Closing the door, he stifled the urge to continue pacing like a caged wolf since there was scant room for such an activity. He had to trust Vic, who was more than capable of looking after himself. Shutting his eyes, he sought to center himself.

Don't dwell on the fact his single tie to this Earthen plane was currently scouring the train for danger without back up. Johnathan swore, quickly yanked on his coat and shoving his boots on his feet. It was possible, he was now convinced, the Society followed Johnathan and Vic on the train from Boston, possibly even from Cress Haven. They might have waited until the train was isolated by the imposing wilderness, far from any farmland or town, before they struck. After Evans' manipulation of Cress Haven's unfortunate residents, he doubted a train full of sleeping, innocent passengers would give them pause to enact violence.

Johnathan stumbled into the attached passenger car, struggling to finish tying his laces. Vic's citrus and musk scent lingered, beckoning him to follow. At the last second, he remembered the glasses in his pocket. Muffling any of his senses at present seemed a poor choice, but the last thing he needed was some unsuspecting passenger panicking at his fiery gaze. He shoved them back on his face, concentrating on the pull of Vic's scent. The hint of gun powder was stronger now. Johnathan's pace sped up, his muscles going lax and loose with a hunter's intent, steps silent while his hands dangled free, ready for ambush.

His leather gloves creaked with each flex of his fingers. The sounds made him flinch, too loud, too close. Rolling his shoulders, he reached through the jittery bundle of nerves currently pulsing in his chest for the calm mind of his training. Why was it so difficult to summon that side of him now?

Johnathan stopped inside the sleeper car and leaned against the wall. He wouldn't be useful to Vic like this. Sorting his incensed thoughts, he tried to reclaim a rational foothold. *Could* Dr. Evans' men be responsible for this? Unlikely, the effort to organize pursuit so quickly after the devastating blow to their resources and manpower was further crippled by the power gap of Dr. Evans' death. This could be a large wild animal or a herd of stubborn deer clogging the tracks, something else equally ridiculous. And yet....

Dread continued to clench his nerves.

Foolish not to listen an insistent warning, no matter his mastery of the sense. Johnathan pushed off the wall, trying not to be obvious as he scented the air like an untrained bloodhound. No one poked their heads out of the sleeper cabins. He slid open the door between cars, met by the thick, sticky scent of pine and moldering vegetation. The train had stopped in a heavily forested area, the trees so close they reached out to grasp at the roof with green needle thin fingers. Out among the trunks, he caught shots of movement through his tunneled vision, nocturnal animals going about their business, ignoring the invasion of human progress in their realm. A heavy wind buffeted him. Johnathan braced himself against the handrails while it ruffled his hair, bearing another flood of scents. There it was again. Gun powder, and another acrid smell he couldn't place, strong enough to sting. Where was it coming from? Perhaps a marshal and company on board? It wasn't beyond the realm of possibility. What worried him was Vic's scent came from the same direction. He pushed his way into the next car. There were more passengers in this one but most of them ignored his entrance, stubbornly trying to reclaim their rest or grumbling about the sudden stop.

Stalking past them, his steps slowed the closer he came to the end of the car. That awful scent was overpowering, made his eyes water. *What was it?* Had something died? Death and decay were familiar smells, but perhaps they registered differently to his new senses. His hands shook when he reached to open the door to the next car. What was wrong with him?

A hand came down on his shoulder. Years of training kicked in before the rest of his mind caught up. Johnathan seized the wrist above that hand, shoving his hip back. The focal point of gravity shifted, pulling the figure over his shoulder in a throw he had practiced until his muscles ached. Vic hit the ground with a huff, a mix of irritation and bemusement on his face. Mortification froze him in place, the shocked murmurs of the other passengers ringing in his ears. They hadn't noticed Johnathan until now. Impossible to ignore an oaf tossing around his traveling companion.

"I believe I told you to stay put," said Vic, not even winded.

"It was more of a suggestion," said Johnathan, "which I determined to be a daft suggestion."

"That's fair," replied Vic. His voice remained even, his reaction skewing toward amusement when he nodded at Johnathan's fixed grip on his wrist. "Plan on letting me off the ground? Or do you prefer me in this position?"

Johnathan was certain the back of his neck would burst into flames. "Sorry," he muttered. He released Vic's wrist and stepped away, realized he left Vic sprawled on the floor without assistance, and stepped forward again to offer him a hand up.

"That's sweet, John, but you are standing on my coat, and I rather like this one." Vic's grin turned into a full leer. "Though I see you weren't very thorough in your dressing." His voice was murmur for Johnathan alone, his appraising gaze drifting upward. Johnathan glanced down to discover he'd forgotten Vic unfastening his pants earlier. His blush crested up through the back of his head, flushing through the curve of his ears while Johnathan attempted to subtly right his clothes.

"You can stop with that look now," Johnathan snapped.

"But I enjoy this side of you so very much," said Vic. "Not to mention the view—"

Dread slid an invisible blade against Johnathan's spine, stripping his civilized veneer. A snarl ripped from his throat, a sound so vicious and inhuman several of the passengers screamed and scrambled away from him. Johnathan ignored them, his entire focus on the dread, now a physical thing to his senses that moved toward him. Vic rolled to his feet in a seamless movement, crouching beside Johnathan without touching him.

"What is it?"

Johnathan couldn't answer at first, there were no words. He tracked the dread approaching them, unable to describe in his own thoughts how he did so. An instinct he couldn't ignore, though it baffled the remnants of his rational self. In his mind's eye, the dread was a shadow, threaded in gold, heralded by a soft chiming sound. His skin crawled at the innocuous sound, carrying the scent of gun powder and violence. Ill intent whispered in his thoughts, riling the creature inside him until Johnathan feared he would transform right then and there.

"I don't know," Johnathan bit out, his voice an octave lower than usual. The muscles of his jaw locked. A tight knot of heat thrummed in his gut. He tried to reign it in, wholly aware he had no idea how to do so. Fear bit down on him, winching his muscles in place. Not a fear of the unseen, unmeasurable dread, but of himself and what he would do to the innocents in the car should the beast break through his skin. "Get them out of here. Please." The words were ragged, reflecting his internal struggle.

Vic didn't stop to question him. He spun to the other passengers, and while Johnathan couldn't see his face, he could feel the soothing effect of Vic's voice, laced with a vampire's compulsion. "Everyone, out of concern for your safety, I must ask you to rise and file out in an orderly fashion to the next car."

If Johnathan wasn't concentrating so hard on keeping control, he wouldn't have been able to hide his shock. A vampire could compel so many humans at once? They *were* compelled, leaving the car in a parade of shuffling feet without question or protest, though he doubted any would fight the suggestion to get away from him. There would be time for marvel and wonder about Vic's vampiric abilities later. Survival came first.

A tinkling sound filled the air, the soft chime of silver bells vibrating through his bones. Johnathan's head snapped up. It was no longer in front of him, but behind them. Two people had appeared in the car, their entrance announced by the dread clouding around them in a palpable haze. Tension buzzed through Johnathan. One of the two strangers had masked their movements.

Masking ratcheted the element of danger. The Society coveted those techniques that bordered on magic, requiring extensive training of the mind and body for a student to master. When dealing with so many inhuman threats, one couldn't ignore such a useful tool. Those who managed to learn were swiftly promoted through the rank and file, sent on the deadliest of missions. Masking took years to master, and most hunters never achieved it. Johnathan stared at their foe, surprised by their youthful appearance. The man's clean shaven face maintained a hint of youthful softness, possibly younger than Johnathan, dressed more in line with a clerk than a Hunter. The only softness the stranger possessed. He was shorter than Vic's humble height by a few inches, but stocky. The Society uniform he wore hugged his muscular frame, neat and crisp without single wrinkle. Close cropped dark hair slicked back against his skull. A pair of spectacles framed dark, black eyes, lit from within by cold rage.

His female companion was a waif, her pale wispy hair drifting around her face in a cloud. An unfamiliar crimson uniform fitted snug against her tall, willowy physique. As Johnathan had never seen her apparel on a Society Agent, his unease escalated. His gaze flickered to the strange instrument strung between her hands, a series of strings and chimes rippling in her steady grip. The source of the chiming....and the dread. Johnathan couldn't look away.

"It seems our target is not alone, Sister Wilhem," said the man.

Sister Wilhem tilted her head, her features obscured by strands of ash blonde hair, except for her pale eyes, a clouded milk white. She regarded them, her expression serene. "A regrettable development."

"Shall I destroy this creature then?" The man stepped forward, cracking his knuckles. "Or take them both for study?"

Vic tensed beside him. Johnathan frowned at the two Agents. Their terminology bothered him, not for the obvious disdain in their tone, but their indeterminate target. The man didn't move, his hateful gaze snapped to Jonathan. Violence emanated from him, a throbbing pulse that baited reciprocation.

The instrument in Sister Wilhem's hands emitted a cascading chime. Hunger tightened her features. The sound scraped under his skin. Johnathan froze at the unsettling sensation racing through his system.

"No, Luthor. Don't kill him," she said. Her gaze remained fixed on them, pinning Johnathan in place when Luthor stepped forward. The sense of dread tipped over a ledge.

An animalistic sound rose from Johnathan's chest, one he thought impossible for a human throat. The threat was too much, too close, and Johnathan didn't know if he could protect Vic from the pair. He shifted forward a step, blatantly placing himself between Vic and the obvious threat.

"What are you doing?" Vic hissed behind him, grabbing his wrist. Johnathan didn't budge, his gaze fixed on the other male.

Luthor paused, regarding Johnathan with cold calculation.

Sister Wilhem hummed. "Interesting. Take them both down."

Vic tensed. "I believe that is our cue to depart," he drawled. "Good day, my lady, sir." He gave a hard tug on Johnathan's wrist, taking a step back toward the door. Luthor struck.

The Agent moved with a serpent's swiftness, whipping a blade in their direction so fast Johnathan couldn't guess its destination until Vic plucked it out of the air a few inches from his face.

"Young man, that was rather rude," he scolded, wagging the blade at Luthor. "You should really...watch..." Vic's gaze widened, his words trailing off. His hand shook. The blade dropped from his slack grip.

Johnathan wrapped an arm around Vic's waist and kicked the door open behind them. He tossed Vic over his shoulder, turning away from the pair to make their escape. A trio of blades buried themselves in his exposed back. Johnathan grunted, vaulting over the rail to hit the ground running. Luthor tracked their progress. Another blade whizzed by, burying itself in a tree trunk. Johnathan dove into the arms of the surrounding forest, but the Agent didn't press the attack.

Soon, the presence of the Agents and the dread they carried waned to nothing. Johnathan knew, sure as the sun rose, the hunt had just begun.

———————

Don't stop now. Keep reading with your copy of A DRAUGHT OF ASH AND WINE available now.

And find more from Kristin Jacques at
www.kristinjacques.com

Don't miss book two of the Midnight Guardians series, A DRAUGHT OF ASH AND WINE, available now and find more from Kristin Jacques at www.kristinjacques.com

---

Johnathan Newman is a changed man, and he has the claws to prove it.

Following their bloody confrontation in Cress Haven, Vic and Johnathan flee the town in search of answers. Johnathan's human life has ended, but his journey has just begun. Grappling with violent instincts and a supernatural bond to the vampire he's falling for is complicated enough, but a dangerous new enemy is hot on their heels.

The machinations of the Society reach farther than either of them realized. Their foe's dogged pursuit forces the pair to seek sanctuary. Vic brings Johnathan to the Estate, a haven for creatures nestled in the wilderness of upstate New York. Taken in by the Estate's unusual proprietors, Johnathan soon learns not even sanctuary is safe for one of his ilk. This haven provides the pair an opportunity to explore their burgeoning relationship, and Johnathan a chance to learn control- A skill he is desperate to master, no matter the cost.

Because time is not on their side. The Society's Agents are catching up to them, armed with a weapon straight from the Heavens. With their enemy's plans creeping toward fruition, humans won't be the only ones they have to worry about.

All reviews are **welcome** and **appreciated**. Please consider leaving one on your favorite social media and book buying sites.

Escape Your World. Get Lost in Ours! City Owl Press at www. cityowlpress.com.

ACKNOWLEDGMENTS

Every book I write is a voyage, fraught with wonders and perils. And like every voyage, I couldn't have reached the final destination without an amazing crew.

Thank you to my fabulous editor, Charissa, for her advice, her patience, and being a champion of this story. Thank you to the crew at City Owl for believing in my cinnamon roll vampire hunter.

Thank you to my Wattchicks for continuing to share your joys and worries and all the little things that have kept our bond strong over four countries and two continents. Thank you Lucy & Nicole for being the listening ear and pillar of support during those many, many moments of existential crisis. Thank you to the Saltmates, MB, Laynie, Candace, Amber, and Sarah, for the laughs and the rants.

And lastly, thank you to my partner, who reminds me not to worry about things beyond my control, and who keeps me grounded even when the ground feels like it is falling out from under us.

ABOUT THE AUTHOR

KRISTIN JACQUES is an award-winning author of speculative fiction for teens and adults. She currently lives in small town Connecticut with her partner, sons, and two gremlins who think they are cats. When not writing, she's usually chasing her boys around or catching some excellent b-horror movies. She is currently working on projects full of magic, mystery, and delight.

www.kristinjacques.com

facebook.com/krazydiamondwrites
twitter.com/Krazydiamond07
instagram.com/krazydiamond_writes
bookbub.com/profile/kristin-jacques

ABOUT THE PUBLISHER

City Owl Press is a cutting edge indie publishing company, bringing the world of romance and speculative fiction to discerning readers.

Escape Your World. Get Lost in Ours!

www.cityowlpress.com

facebook.com/YourCityOwlPress
twitter.com/cityowlpress
instagram.com/cityowlbooks
pinterest.com/cityowlpress